JUDGE DREDD
YEAR THREE

An Abaddon Books™ Publication
www.abaddonbooks.com
abaddon@rebellion.co.uk

This omnibus first published
in 2021 by Abaddon Books™,
Rebellion Publishing Limited,
Riverside House, Osney Mead,
Oxford, OX2 0ES, UK.

10 9 8 7 6 5 4 3 2 1

Creative Director and CEO: Jason Kingsley
Chief Technical Officer: Chris Kingsley
Head of Books and Comics Publishing: Beth Lewis
Editors: David Thomas Moore,
Michael Rowley and Kate Coe
Design: Sam Gretton, Oz Osborne
and Gemma Sheldrake
Marketing and PR: Hanna Waigh
Cover Art: Jake Lynch

Judge Dredd created by
John Wagner and Carlos Ezquerra.

ISBN: 978-1-78108-871-5

Printed in Denmark

JUDGE DREDD
YEAR THREE

MATT SMITH
MICHAEL CARROLL
LAUREL SILLS

ABADDON
BOOKS

WWW.ABADDONBOOKS.COM

Introduction

Borag Thungg, Earhlets!

I am The Mighty Tharg, all-powerful alien editor of the Galaxy's Greatest Comic, and I welcome you to this zarjaz third omnibus volume of Dredd stories from the beginning of his career as a full-eagle Judge. As the cover says, we're into Year Three, and Joe's no longer the noob establishing himself on the street—young though he still is (somewhere in his early twenties, but then again age is always something of a grey area where the clone's concerned), he's now proven himself to be a capable and committed officer, and more than worthy of the bloodline he hails from.

Does this superior genetic stock give Dredd an advantage? You could argue that he comes 'pre-loaded' with a set of very special set of skills courtesy of Eustace Fargo, the Father of Justice—a quick, analytical brain; exceptional physical strength; a fine marksman. All honed by his years in the Academy of Law, true, but he, alongside his errant brother Rico, was *created* for this role; he didn't have to go through the rigorous application procedure like his colleagues. You can imagine that that kind of privilege—a step-up that began when he was mere cells in a test tube—would rankle amongst the uniforms. They may well consider that the kid making a name for himself as Mega-City perps' worst nightmare didn't have to put as much graft in as they did to get to that position, that it was all handed to him on a biological plate. Dredd, of course, has no interest in such petty grievances and his sole focus is on punishing criminality wherever he may find it, but antagonism tends to dog Joe, even at this early stage, as this trio of tales show. Whether it's coming under investigation by the Special Judicial Squad—Justice Department's internal affairs division—in Michael Carroll's *Fallen Angel*, or an embittered former cadet from his class entering his radar against a background of anti-robot sentiment in Matthew Smith's *Machineries of Hate*, or being handed a Cursed Earth posting, dodging an unknown killer in Laurel Sills' *Bitter Earth*, there's no shortage of people that want a piece of Ol' Stoney-Face. It's quite remarkable that, given his relative youth, he's already racking up the enemies.

But this is Joe Dredd we're talking about here: he infuriates others as much as he engenders fear and respect. For all that, he's not the blunt tool that he's often dismissed as—the zero-tolerance lawman that solves a situation by punching it into submission. He's also introspective, even-handed, and aware of his place in the ranks, and thus psychologically remains a fascinating character to explore, which prose gives its authors the room to do so. As with the previous two volumes, these stories offer the chance to get inside Dredd's head like never before, and from the perspective of looking back at his formative years. Enjoy, my Squaxx, enjoy!

SPLUNDIG VUR THRIGG!

THARG THE MIGHTY

FALLEN ANGEL

MICHAEL CARROLL

For Alphaville—
especially Marian Gold and Bernhard Lloyd
Soar on, my friends!

**MEGA-CITY ONE
2082 A.D.**

Prologue

By his own proud admission, Presley Butcher hadn't learned much in his thirty-seven years, but he *did* know that it was every right-thinking citizen's duty to get in the way of the Judges. An unwritten rule that everyone understood.

You don't have to do anything actually *criminal*, of course— only a spugwit ties their own shoelaces together—but slow them down when you can. It made sense, in a kind of karma way, even though the concept of karma was another thing about which Presley Butcher didn't know much.

You slow down a Judge, even just by a second or two, then that might mean whoever the Judge is chasing gets away. So then later on, that cit repays their luck by slowing down another Judge, and the cit *that* Judge is chasing gets away too. A chain of ordinary citizens helping each other out, even though they might never meet. It was kinda beautiful, in a way. Poetic. And somewhere down the road, just when you've got a Judge bearing down on *you*, maybe it all pays off and you become the next link in that chain.

On the morning of September 1st, 2082, opportunity knocked

for Presley Butcher and he metaphorically squared his shoulders, set his jaw and stood up to open that door. As he drove his ancient but beloved Brit-Cit Leyline Mini Driver along the west side of Sector Thirteen's 151st Avenue—a neighbourhood nicknamed The Boulevard of Broken Teeth by many of the locals who liked to think that they were tough—he spotted a Judge coming up fast behind, Lawmaster lights flashing and siren wailing. Standard protocol was to immediately pull in to the side to give the Judge enough room to pass—the rest of the traffic on that cracked-asphalt street was already doing just that—but Butcher grinned to himself and kept a firm grip on the wheel. "Drokk you, Judge. Not movin'."

He *would* move, of course. He knew that even as he was denying it. But he held his nerve, and held the wheel, for as long as he could. The Judge was less than twenty metres away by the time Butcher's survival instinct overrode his arrogance and took control.

The huge Lawmaster roared by and he could see the Judge—young, tall, slender build but with wide shoulders—scowling as he passed.

Butcher gave a short, quiet snort as he watched the oversized motorbike rumble away through the morning traffic. "Showed *him*."

In O'McDonald's Bar that night, he regaled his friends with the exciting details of his adventure. "Dredd, his name was. Saw his badge when I replayed the Vehi-cam later. He comes up behind me and he's all..."—Butcher mimed a Judge riding a Lawmaster, clenched fists out in front of him as he rocked from side to side on his barstool—"weavin' around, tryna get past... and I'm like, 'No way, drokker. You don't own *these* streets.' He moves to the left, but I see this comin' and I block him again. Dredd starts to goes right, but I see that too. Drokker's gettin' worried now, because he, like, suddenly realises where he is, right? Like, until now, he's got his mind on his destination, not on his route. But you can see it in his eyes that he's thinking, 'Stomm... this is the *Boulevard,* and I'm here without backup!'"

"Wait, you seen that in his *eyes?*" Jannie Scrumly asked. "Didn't he have his, like, his *hemlet* on?"

"*Hel*met," Old Eddie Gaul corrected. Eddie got twitchy when people mispronounced simple words. One time he punched his brother Neville in the throat for saying 'edumacation,' but in Eddie's defence Neville had been saying it that way for the past forty-four years and still thought it was funny, so everyone agreed that Neville had got off lightly.

Butcher continued, "I mean, I saw it in his *expression.* His body-language, y'know? He kinda tensed up, then looked around. Seen Judges do that before, in the Boulevard. We all seen that, right?"

A few heads nodded, and Butcher took that as encouragement to carry on. Most of them knew the truth: they'd been there. A Judge walks past you on the street, and later this is transformed into a story about how the drokker was going to run a stop-and-search—and you were *carrying,* that would have been *bad*—but you managed to stare him down, persuaded him to move on by sheer force of will. Or you see a pair of jays threatening a perp with their daysticks, and this later becomes a story about how the poor drokker was chased down by an entire squad who caved in his skull so hard his eye popped out, and he wasn't even guilty of anything. They just picked him because the Judges have kill-quotas. Everyone knows that.

Butcher was halfway through telling the story for the second time—unprompted, but no one had moved away yet, so that meant they were still interested—when Monty Chesterton interrupted him.

"Yeah, one time I was over at Keller's just, y'know, hanging in a booth near the corner, and this Judge walks right in and this guy comes up to him and he gives him this baggie, right, and he says to him that he got it from that guy and he points over in my kinda direction and the Judge looks right at me and says, 'Creep with the hair?' and I near browned my keks. Swear to God and Grud and all their little holy fairies, I thought I was a dead man." Monty nodded, mostly to himself, and took another sip of his beer. "That was when I cut my hair, see? You didn't know me then, but I useta have the full double-mohawk and mullet combo, orange with alternating white and red tips. Did it because it made me stand out. Heh. Learned my lesson right there and then. Don't stand out. You wanna make it *hard* for the Judges to remember you, not easy. Am I right?" Another sip, and then as he was smacking his lips, he looked up and saw that everyone was staring at him. "What?"

"We *know*," Eddie Gaul said. "You've told us that same drokkin' story eighty million times."

"I'm just *sayin*'."

"Time you *stopped* sayin', then." Eddie turned back to Butcher. "Go on, Pres."

"Right," Butcher said. He looked down at his empty glass for a second, but the mood had been shattered. Monty's story was lame, they all knew that. But it was no less lame than anyone else's. "Ah, drokk it..."

Jannie asked, "What's wrong?"

"How the hell did we end up like *this?*" Presley Butcher asked. "We're all so drokkin' scared of the Judges that we inflate the smallest non-events into great big conflicts. Monty here's been coasting on that Judge-looked-in-my-direction story for *years*. That's all that happened. The Judge *looked* in his direction. Nothing else. And we're all the same, every one of us. Okay, sure, some people around here really *have* gone up against the jays, but the rest of us... They got us so... so... *cowed* that we make up a bunch of crap just so that we can persuade ourselves that we've still got some control over our lives." He looked around the bar, at the frowning faces of his friends. "You wanna know the truth about this morning? The *actual* truth, not the story? I'm driving along, Judge Dredd is coming up behind me, I hesitate for a bit, then I pull over just like everyone else. Take a guess at how long I really hesitated. Never mind everything I just told you about me moving left and right anticipating his movements so I can slow him down. None of that happened. Go on. Take a guess how long I waited before my nerve snapped."

No one responded. Most of them were looking away. They knew what was coming.

"Four seconds, *that's* how long. That Judge barely even noticed, just rode on past." Presley Butcher put down his glass, and stared at it. "We tell ourselves that we're tough guys, that our little neighbourhood here is one of the last free strongholds in the city, that they've not beaten *us*. But we're not fooling anyone. The Judges have taken damn near everything from us. About the only thing we got left is our freedom to lie about how important we are." Even as he was speaking, he knew that nothing was going to be the same again. This cluster of friends would shun him, and he couldn't blame them for that. It was another unwritten rule of life in Mega-City One: don't confront people with the cold, unfiltered reality of their lives. You're only allowed to burst your own bubble, not someone else's.

Eddie Gaul, still not looking Presley in the eye, said, "Maybe you oughta *go*, Pres. Get on home, get some sleep."

Butcher nodded. He appreciated Eddie's kindness even though he knew they would never talk about it. This was a way to save face. He wouldn't be able to pretend that this rant hadn't happened, but he could paper over it a little. Tomorrow, maybe in a couple of days, he'd come back and make lame jokes along the lines of, "What the hell was *in* that drink?" Then he'd stick to the background for a while, try to blend in long enough for the ache to fade from the sore thumb he'd made of himself. A good six months would do it. By then, enough other people would have accumulated enough dumb things that his 'weird brain-fart' would seem fairly tame by comparison.

He slid down from the stool, and as he was shrugging himself into his jacket, the bar's door crashed open.

All of the patrons' voices faded to silence as the Judge's silhouette filled the doorway.

Butcher knew, somehow, that this was the same Judge from earlier that morning. And that he was here for one reason only.

Judge Dredd crossed the room, heading straight towards Butcher. No one got in his way. No one tried to slow him down. "Presley Rowell Butcher. On the charge of deliberately obstructing an officer of the law in pursuit of his duties: two years."

Butcher turned around, hands behind his back, and Dredd cuffed him, then steered him out of the bar.

Three full minutes passed before anyone else moved.

"MAN, YOU SHOULDA *been* there," Athena Dittmar told her little brother Judson a couple of days later. "I swear, I thought we were all dead. He kicks the door open, puts a coupla rounds in the ceiling as a warning. My friend Tammy? She got shrapnel in her face from the ricochet. Right in her *face*, swear to Grud, and the drokker doesn't even care. Blood streaming down her face from all those cuts, he didn't even look at her. But he looks at *me*. Right *at* me, like he's sizing me up. So what I did was, see, I stared *back*. That's what you've gotta *do*, Judson. Let them see that you're not scared of them. You look them in the eye and you make them think, hell, *this* one's gonna be trouble. They're not worth it. 'Cause they're all cowards, the Judges, deep down. Body-armour, helmets, gloves. Means they're scared of getting hurt, right? But he saw me giving him the cold-eye, and he backed down. Picked on some other poor drokker instead, took him away on a jumped-up traffic violation."

Judson Dittmar nodded throughout his sister's tale. He was fourteen already, old enough to have heard a lot of stories like this. Even if Athena was embellishing a little—which he knew she was, because she'd been home the night the Judge had raided the bar—the *essence* of the story was true. That's what was important. These tales served to remind the ordinary people that they lived or died at the whim of monsters.

In school the following day, Judson did his duty and repeated the story to his friends. For impact, his rendition of the tale placed himself at the centre of the action, even though it had happened in a bar. "They don't mind that I'm underage," he explained. "The owner knows my folks, so they let me in, long as I don't talk about it, so you can't tell anyone, got it? I'm never gonna forget that night. I mean, I was sitting *next* to the guy the Judge killed. Shot him in the *face*, just for lookin' at him funny." Judson brandished his spotless shirt sleeve as evidence. "Had to put this through the machine, like, *three times* to get the blood out. You can kinda see some of it still there."

Judson swore his friends to a silence he hoped they wouldn't keep, and boosted his own reputation in the process.

His friend Chelsey Boulting revised the tale a little when he related the story to his younger cousins. They were horrified at the senseless, brutal actions of the Judge, but mightily impressed with the manner in which Chelsey had courageously put himself in the line of fire, saving the life of the Judge's young and attractive female victim, who then rewarded Chelsey with more than just thanks and an appreciative handshake.

Although Chelsey—and everyone else in the Boulevard of Broken Teeth—died in 2134 when the entire neighbourhood was crushed by a collapsing City-Block, for the rest of their lives his cousins proudly related the story of the time he had fought the law, and the law had backed down.

One

THE DOOR OF O'McDonald's bar thumped shut behind Dredd and immediately his prisoner's relatively stoic demeanour began to disintegrate into trembling terror. "Oh, Grud... Please, no. Not the cubes!"

Presley Butcher—half-stumbling as Dredd marched him towards a rapidly-descending catch-wagon—tried to turn back to face the Judge, eyes damp and wide. "Don't—please!"

Dredd dropped a hand onto his shoulder and squeezed just enough to focus his attention. "Move."

"I swear, I didn't *mean* it! The car stalled. I was confused. I just panicked and froze. It was only a few seconds!"

"You knew what you were doing, Butcher," Dredd said. "I might have been in pursuit of a killer. Your interference could have cost someone their life. Maybe someone you know."

The catch-wagon touched down, its ramp already extending.

The perp tried to shrug his way out of Dredd's grip. "I've learned my lesson! Please—have pity!"

"No." Dredd shoved him forward, and Butcher stumbled onto the ramp where he was caught by an older Judge.

Dredd nodded. "Kimber. Perp's Presley Butcher of Thelvin Deuters Habitat. Two years, obstruction."

"Please!" Butcher said to Senior Judge Kimber. "Please, don't do this! I'll pay a fine. I'll become an informant! Anything you want. I swear, I'll uphold the law for the rest of my life and... and... I'll clean the streets. For free. Every day. Sweet *Grud*, don't put me in the cubes! I..." He stared at Kimber's expressionless face, and then sagged, deflated. Softly, he said, "Someone has to tell my wife. How... how does that happen? Who tells her? Do I get a chance to speak to her? And it's a two-person apartment. Does this mean she's gonna be relocated? Jovus... I can't do this. I'm not strong. I can't fight. The other prisoners are gonna *kill* me!"

"Shut up." Judge Kimber passed Butcher to one of his colleagues inside the catch-wagon, then stepped down off the ramp. "Heard you were out this way, Dredd, so I figured I'd catch up. Been hearing a lot about you lately. Mostly positive." He glanced back at the perp for a moment. "You're still not too big to go after the little fish. That's good to see. Lot of Judges get a few high-profile cases, they get to thinking that they're—"

"Don't need the preamble, Kimber. Just get to the point."

"Friendly as ever. But you could be friendlier. Doesn't hurt to have the next Sector Chief *not* think of you as an arrogant smear of stomm."

"You're angling for my support?" Dredd frowned. "My voice doesn't carry a lot of weight."

"Maybe not directly, but you've got the support of a lot of others, and some of *them* have the heaviest voices of all." Kimber paused. "Despite what happened with your brother, Clarence Goodman looks at you like a proud father. Don't tell me you haven't seen that."

"I'm not going to shill for you, Kimber. I don't play politics."

They took a few steps to the side as the catch-wagon began to rise, its closing ramp cutting off Presley Butcher's pleas for clemency.

"*Everything* is political, son," Kimber said. He removed his helmet, and cradled it under his arm as he accompanied Dredd back to his Lawmaster. "I remember when the first Judges arrived in our town back in Wyoming. That was in '39, when I was eight. My mom was on the town council, so we got advance notice that they were coming. Now, Sheree wasn't a *bad* town, but there was always some trouble from gangs out past the suburbs, and the Judges only made that worse. At first." Kimber had been automatically scanning the street as he talked—which reassured Dredd, told him he still had his head in the game—but now he looked back at Dredd. "That's how it was everywhere, back then. The people *hated* the Judges, because they knew that it meant the old ways were gone forever. But resistance *always* yields to acceptance."

Kimber returned his attention to the passing traffic. "The senior Judge came to our house to talk to my mom, get the lie of the land before he took control. Judge Deacon was... Best I can say is that he was polite, but not friendly. When he had to be, he was uncompromising, cold. Absolutely brutal. To be honest, he scared the crap out of us kids. But even then I could see that he was *efficient*. He got the job done.

"Dredd, you remind me of him far more than you do of Goodman or even Fargo. But one difference is that Deacon was smart enough to know that sometimes you *do* have to play the political game. Take some advice from a veteran, huh? You don't have to be friendly, but if you come across as at least *approachable*, and not such a damn hard-ass all the time, the cits will relax around you. They'll be more cooperative, more likely to talk if you need info."

Dredd had guessed this would happen. He'd already been cornered by four other potential Sector Chiefs, each hoping for his endorsement. Not even three years on the streets and somehow Judges twice or three times his age wanted his blessing.

Chief Judge Goodman had once told him, "No one wants to be remembered as a failed candidate, so if you *do* run, you load your arsenal with every damn weapon you can think of, even if that means—no, *especially* if that means shaking hands with your enemies. The old guard are gonna butter you up, Joe, slather you head-to-heel with praise, but some of them are always going to resent you, because you're something they can never be."

"Genetically engineered?" Dredd had asked.

"You're *young*. You get to my age, you've made a few mistakes along the way. That's inevitable. You bury them, of course, but some mistakes are seeds. They have a way of growing over time. You skip a trivial meeting because you think your time is too valuable, then twenty years later the guy who was running that meeting is chairing an oversight committee and still thinks of you as flaky. Or you promote a Judge because she stops a hijacker from destroying a commercial jet, and down the line it turns out it was a one-time thing, that until then she'd been coasting and letting the rest of her squad carry her." Goodman shrugged. "Experience is the sum of our mistakes."

"And how we deal with them, surely?" Dredd offered.

"More like... how others *perceive* that we've dealt with them. Perception is key." That led the Chief Judge into his familiar, and comfortable, Justice-has-to-be-*seen*-to-be-done speech.

Now, Senior Judge Adam Kimber was angling for the post of Chief of Sector Thirteen, and Dredd's endorsement would put a little extra grease on that slide. "The helmets on the street respect you, Dredd. They... I'll be blunt. A lot of them are still hurting over what happened with Rico. From *both* sides. You get me? Some are saying that you should have taken him out immediately. I'll admit that was my first reaction too. But others think that you let him down by not looking out for him. We all have a responsibility to each other. Now, I've given it a lot of thought these past few months, and—"

"I'm not interested," Joe Dredd said as he climbed onto his Lawmaster. "I don't play politics. My job is to safeguard the citizens and uphold the law." He could see that Kimber was masking his anger, and he understood that. No one liked to be dismissed, especially by a Judge thirty years his junior.

Kimber's own Lawmaster rode up on auto and stopped beside him. He placed his helmet on its seat and turned back to Dredd. "Then tell me... Who do *you* want to see running this sector?"

"Someone less needy."

Kimber swore. "Jesus. I didn't realise that the Academy's classes on diplomacy were *optional*. You'd want to *start* playing politics, Dredd, or you'll be a damn street Judge for the rest of—"

Dredd's helmet radio clicked into life: "*All units. Got a fourteen-twenty-four on Quintessa Brocklebank Underpass— immediate assistance required.*"

"Dredd here. I'm on it." He gunned the Lawmaster's engine and left Judge Kimber behind. Code 1424: A Judge is pinned down by hostile fire and in need of assistance.

He knew the underpass well, a two-kilometre-long tunnel that ran on a perfectly straight east-west vector, except for The Kink, a fifty-metre north-south stretch in the middle, the result of a poorly-calibrated tunnelling machine that no one had thought to check until it was too late.

Despite the flashing lights and giant warning signs, the tunnel's two sharp right-angled turns still claimed an average of three lives per month. Back in '75, plans had been drawn up to fix The Kink, but that would have meant closing the tunnel for months and diverting the traffic back to the streets, and no one wanted that. The unspoken consensus had been that thirty-six or so deaths per year was a small price to pay for the convenience of saving almost five minutes on a cross-sector trip.

Dredd took a wide left at the next junction, gunned straight along Sunshine Rise with his sirens blaring and lights flashing.

The late evening traffic flowed out of his way, and ahead at the crossroads only a single autotruck got through the green light before traffic control flipped it back to red.

Programmed to always give way to a vehicle from the Department of Justice, the autotruck stopped dead in the middle of the junction and waited until Dredd zoomed around it. Not for the first time, Dredd told himself that the sooner the city planners agreed to phase out manually-driven vehicles, the better. You don't get an autodriver taking a chance at a pedestrian crossing because he's in possession of a full bladder or tickets to the big game.

Ahead, the traffic leading into the underpass had stalled. "Dredd to Control—need an update on that fourteen-twenty-four."

"*Judges are Winquest and Schiro, Sector Seventeen. In pursuit of a stolen vehicle carrying an unknown number of hostiles. Vehicle clipped the underpass wall as it tried to navigate The Kink, crashed into an oncoming vehicle. Hostiles opened fire on the Judges, but Winquest reported that at least two perps fled on foot, your direction. No further contact since. Most of the tunnel's cams are off-line.*"

"Time since last contact?"

"*Four minutes twelve.*"

Dredd killed the sirens and slowed his bike as he approached the entrance to the tunnel. The Kink in the tunnel was six hundred metres in; the perps would have to have covered one hundred and fifty metres per minute to have reached the entrance already. Possible for someone in peak physical condition, but not inside a tunnel with no sidewalk, just a narrow maintenance gantry partially blocked by a power junction every hundred metres. *Unlikely that they could keep up the pace. They're still inside.* "Control, what was the perps' initial crime?"

"*ARV. Four wounded, one critical.*"

"Acknowledged."

Twenty metres past the underpass entrance, as Dredd slowly passed a small family car, the driver rolled down the window. "What's the hold-up, Judge?"

"Everyone, stay in your vehicles," Dredd barked. "Doors locked, windows closed."

Ahead, another driver reacted to that by getting out of his car and peering down the tunnel along the line of stalled vehicles. "Why? What's happened?"

There's always one, Dredd told himself. "Back in your car, citizen, or you're looking at doing time for obstruction."

The driver blanched and ducked back into his car.

"And lock the doors," Dredd reminded him.

There was a soft *k-chunk* as the pale-looking driver gave him a nervous smile.

Dredd rode on. *They'll have heard the siren, they know I'm here. Could have taken refuge in a vehicle.*

A gunshot echoed through the tunnel, then two more, slightly softer. Dredd recognised the first as a Lawgiver's armour-piercing round, the others as being from a Mark II Welton Fightender, a small handgun with a powerful kick and an impressive muzzle-flare, the latest weapon of choice among the sector's criminal gangs.

Another three shots from the Welton, which Dredd decided was a good sign: the perps don't usually keep shooting at you if you're already dead.

He stopped next to an old Rover SUV, and rapped on the driver's-side window with his knuckles. The SUV's cab was higher than average, which meant that the driver—a slender old woman weighed down with strings of pearls and heavy silver rings on every finger—would have had a better chance of seeing the fleeing perps, if they'd made it this far.

She stared out at him with wide eyes, and Dredd knew she was already mentally preparing her alibi. She looked to be about seventy, he guessed. Her age and apparent wealth suggested she had a list of Very Good Friends who were Important People who could get him into Big Trouble.

As she manually rolled down the window, she began, "I've done *nothing* wrong and—"

"Not interested in *you*, citizen. Just what you might have seen. Anyone on foot since you entered the tunnel? Up on the gantry, maybe?"

"Eh, no, Judge."

"All right. Keep the windows and doors locked until the traffic starts to move again."

"Yes, of course. Thank you, Judge. God bless you."

He nodded, and rode on. The elders were the worst, sometimes. Some of them—like Judge Kimber—remembered a time before the Judges, and they tended to look back through rose-tinted glasses. They remember the freedom the old ways gave them, but they forget the fear and the poverty.

Judge Morphy had once told him and Rico, "Boys, the average cit will complain for *hours* about no longer being able to get chicken-in-a-basket-flavoured ice-cream because we shut down the factory for countless health-code violations, yet they forget that we saved them from a president whose solution to America's problems was to attempt to turn every other nation into radioactive dust."

Rico had responded, "Right. People are selfish idiots with tiny memories. They don't deserve us."

"If that's true, then they *do* deserve us," Joe had replied.

A lot of Judges shared Rico's opinions about the citizens, but Joe had long since given up listening to them. Opinions, after all, were just cherry-picked extrapolations filtered through prejudice.

People don't fit into convenient categories. Everyone had the potential to be a hero or a villain, to be apathetic or passionate, and they could and did switch from one second to the next, often for the most arbitrary of reasons. People are what they are in any given moment, and right now, he knew, most of them in this tunnel were a little frustrated.

Until they saw him coming, and then that frustration turned into fear, followed by relief that he hadn't come for *them*.

His Lawmaster purred along the tunnel and he peered into every car he passed, looking for a clue on the faces of the drivers and passengers, for something other than the standard reaction a citizen has on seeing a Judge.

He was two hundred metres in when he noticed the driver of a very old reconditioned white Toyota looking calm and collected. The man saw Dredd looking in at him, and gave him a friendly nod. Seatbelt in place, hands on the steering-wheel in the correct positions. Nothing to draw any attention.

Directly ahead of the Toyota was a double-length flat-bed truck, a new model, more than half of its bed loaded with strapped-down plastic crates and large items of furniture, the landmarks of a life in the process of relocation.

Dredd looked back at the Toyota's driver, and the man dry-swallowed before very slightly nodding towards the truck.

Dredd didn't need to be told what had happened. The perps had heard his approaching siren and climbed into the back of the truck. They'd have pointed their weapons at the Toyota driver, warning him not to give them away.

He set the Lawmaster on auto and swung himself off, landing silently on the ground as the bike rumbled away, his Lawgiver already in his hand.

TWO

SJS JUDGE MARION Gillen had spent the afternoon browsing through the Justice Department's archives via a terminal in Sector House 56.

She'd arrived at fifteen hundred hours, told Sector Chief Hamma Feige that she was taking over her office for the foreseeable future, then closed the door behind her. Through the frosted glass pane Gillen could see Feige standing in the corridor for a few seconds, uncertain what to do next, before stalking away. It was a safe bet that Feige then displaced her deputy chief from his office, and he in turn was now ensconced in someone else's.

The SJS badge carried the same weight among the ordinary Judges as their own badges did among the citizens, and in Gillen's private opinion that was why the Special Judicial Squad were so despised. The Judges couldn't stomach their own medicine.

Gillen sat back and stared at the oversized monitor on Feige's desk. She had thirty-nine separate files open, each one a comprehensive report on a Judge assigned to the Sector House.

Thirty-nine Judges, and fourteen of them with major infractions, from wilful negligence to a deliberate cover-up.

She had the right and the power to strip all fourteen of those Judges of their position. At least three of them could—and *would*, before the day was out—be incarcerated for a minimum of twenty years.

This investigation had begun as many did, with a complaint from a citizen. Four weeks ago, sixty-year-old Humphrey Hiroko Devereaux reported that Judge Moira Plimmer had collided with him—knocking him to the ground—as she chased down a suspect on Amerigo Vespucci Plaza. On Plimmer's return journey, as she was escorting the suspect back across the plaza, she'd spotted Devereaux still on the ground, dazed and bleeding from a graze on his forehead, and issued him with an on-the-spot fine for public intoxication. He'd tried to explain what had happened, but Plimmer denied colliding with him and issued him a further fine for lying to a Judge.

The plaza had been busy, with dozens of witnesses to the incident. Not one of them had been willing to back Devereaux's story, but, fuelled by anger at the injustice, he'd pursued it anyway.

The incident report reached Gillen yesterday evening, having been passed over by everyone else who encountered it. There were Judges out there involved in organised crime, Judges working with rival city-states to overthrow the entire system, Judges running drugs or guns or hookers or body parts. And the members of the SJS were still human, despite what their street-level colleagues liked to believe; no one was going to make their career on some piss-ant case with a Judge who was at most guilty of being a jerk.

So it had landed on Gillen's desk. Slim pickings for a Judge who a year ago had put all of her eggs in the 'Bring Down Joseph Dredd' basket.

The first thing Gillen had done after she logged on at Feige's terminal was pull archive footage from the plaza's Public Surveillance Unit cameras. It had taken less than a minute to verify Citizen Devereaux's claim. Since then, she'd been choosing the sector's other Judges more or less at random and passing their records through the SJS's analytics software. It wasn't perfect, but it was good at seeing patterns that human analysts might easily miss. That was how she'd noticed Judge Lindfield's semi-regular thirty-minute downtimes that on the surface appeared to be random but which the software showed were all within a five-minute ride of Alan Class Block. That block's security cams showed Lindfield visiting the same apartment each time, the home of citizen Peyton Alverne, single mother of four. Biometric analysis of Alverne's children's faces strongly suggested that Judge Lindfield was their father.

DNA tests would be carried out. If they matched, Lindfield was looking at dismissal at the very least. But aside from that possible indiscretion, Lindfield appeared to be a good Judge. Solid arrest record, respected and trusted by his colleagues, no more than the average number of complaints against him. It'd be a shame to lose a Judge like that.

Gillen pushed herself away from Feige's desk and spun the chair around until she was facing the window, looking out over the sector.

She had been so sure about Joe Dredd. With good reason, too. His brother, Rico, was a monster, a high-functioning sociopath with exemplary skills. One of the finest Judges the Academy had ever produced—no, *the* finest Judge. No doubts about that. Except that he was criminally insane.

It made sense that Rico's clone-brother would be similarly flawed. Just about everyone else had thought so, too. Gillen had lobbied her superiors for the first crack at Joe. She could break him, she assured them. She already knew him, giving her an advantage over her colleagues.

She stood up and leaned against the window, resting her

forehead on the cool glass. She had been *so* sure about Joe Dredd. So sure. But if that investigation had taught her anything, it was that it was possible to be absolutely certain and still be wrong.

"You screwed up," Judge Molina had told her on her return from the Cursed Earth. "Screwed up biiiig time. Your pursuit of Joseph Dredd has run up a bill of almost eighteen million credits, and nothing to show for it. Absolutely zilch. Our budget is not unlimited, Gillen. Where do you think eighteen million comes from? You think we can just magically conjure it up out of thin air? Now get back to your office, sit down at your desk and get comfortable, because you're going to be driving it for the next couple of months until we decide what to do with you."

A year later, she was back to tackling cases, but most were like this one with Judge Plimmer: detritus. The leftovers, the floor-sweepings.

Her investigation into Judge Plimmer had turned up nothing else of note in the Judge's record. Sure, Plimmer was arrogant, but that went with the territory. The meek don't make it past year one in the Academy. Plimmer would be reprimanded for her actions in the plaza, sent for refresher courses. And Devereaux would be reimbursed, and given a formal explanation. Not an apology; the Department of Justice didn't apologise if it didn't have to.

She had struck gold with the others—particularly soon-to-be-former Judges Billings, Westwell and Dawber—but that wasn't unusual: if you dig deep enough, you'll always find dirt. She'd already tagged those Judges for full investigation, but that task would be given to another member of the SJS, someone who *hadn't* gambled and lost on the highest profile case in years.

Judge Lindfield was a tricky one, though. There were, at times, allowances made when the Judges' Code was violated— but usually only for non-criminal activities. Did fathering four children count as a crime? That depended on a number of factors, including the manner in which the mother had registered her offspring. If Alverne had logged the father as 'Unknown' when she did actually know his identity, that was technically fraud; but it was *her* crime, not Lindfield's.

Was he providing financial support for the children? If so, how? Judges didn't earn a salary, just a daily stipend of which every cent had to be justified, and Gillen had found nothing out of the ordinary in Lindfield's accounts. Skimming from a perp's gains was one way he could be providing Alverne with cash, but that was easy to mask for a smart Judge.

Gillen knew that a decision had to be made, and the responsibility was hers. Still staring out at the city, she unclipped her radio from her belt. "SJS Control, this is Gillen."

"*Go ahead, Gillen.*"

"Need the current location and vector of Judge Spencer John Lindfield, Sector 56."

"*Searching... Lindfield is en route back to the Sector House for evening briefing. ETA four minutes. You want him picked up?*"

Gillen was already moving towards the door. "Negative, Control. I've just got a few questions—I'll handle him personally. Gillen out."

"*Acknowledged.*"

The Judges Gillen passed as she strode towards the Lawmaster bay gave her a wide berth. No filthy looks, no muttered curses. They'd save all that until they were absolutely certain she was out of earshot.

In the Lawmaster bay beneath the Sector House, she watched from the shadows as Lindfield rode down the ramp, then left his bike with the mechanics. He was most likely guilty of something, but he wasn't a flight risk. Besides, protocol was to treat cases like this with caution: four years ago a Judge died when the SJS burst into her apartment and she had automatically opened fire. No one could blame her for that.

She'd play this one cool. Approach openly and without

hostility. Besides, maybe a deal could be made. If Lindfield *was* the father of Alverne's kids, well, two of them were under five years old and the Academy was always open to recruits with a good pedigree.

She stepped out, blocking his path. "Gillen, SJS. Got some questions, Lindfield."

He stopped, and pulled off his helmet. "So?"

"So you're going to provide me with answers. And if I'm not satisfied that you're on the level, this is your last day as a Judge. Maybe your last day as a free man for a long time."

He took a step closer, then another, until they were almost nose-to-chest, and looked down at her. "Some advice. You don't threaten someone, skull-head, until you know exactly what you're up against. I know what all this is about. I might have bent a few rules, but I never broke any *laws*. So you'll let it go, or I will drop an info-bomb big enough to rip the whole drokkin' Department apart."

"You think that this is the first time I've been threatened by a Judge?"

A deep voice bellowed out from the Lawmaster bay's ramp: "SJS! Hands where we can see them, Lindfield!"

Gillen peered past the Judge to see four of her SJS colleagues approaching, Lawgivers aimed. She called out, "I got this!" Softer, she asked Lindfield, "Jesus. What have you *done?*"

The deep voice ordered, "Step *aside*, Gillen!"

Hands raised, Lindfield began to slowly turn around to face the other Judges. His voice weak, he said, "Stomm. It was Judge Hariton. Back in May, in David Dixon Block. He was—"

A gun barked and Lindfield was toppling backwards, a small hole in the centre of his forehead.

Even before the spray of Lindfield's blood and brain-matter hit her, Gillen had dropped into a defensive pose with her Lawgiver drawn, aimed at the other SJS Judges. "What the *drokk?*"

The four Judges put away their guns as they approached

Lindfield's body. "Scratch one rotten Judge," Senior Judge Harmon Krause said. He looked down at Gillen. "At ease. Situation's under control."

She slowly climbed to her feet. "Judge Krause, he wasn't a threat. He wanted to talk. Said he'd exchange information for clemency."

"Yeah? *What* information?"

There was a rush of footsteps and the door behind them burst open: three of the Sector House's Judges responding to the gunshot.

"SJS business," Krause called. "Nothing to see here."

"Drokk, is that *Lindfield?*"

Louder, Krause called, "Vacate the scene! Immediately!"

As the Judges lowered their weapons and backed away towards the door, Gillen became very aware that one of them— Judge McKinney—was looking directly at her, and it was easy to guess why. Lindfield had a bullet-hole in his head, and she was the only one of the five SJS Judges present holding a drawn Lawgiver.

Krause turned back to Gillen, "You were saying something about information Lindfield claimed to have?"

His voice was calm and steady, with a hint of mild curiosity. Absolutely unthreatening. But Gillen had noticed the slight clenching of his gun hand, an involuntary movement suggesting he was on edge, prepared to strike. The wrong word now, and she'd be joining Lindfield on the conveyor belt in Resyk.

She feigned anger to mask her shock. "He didn't say. Didn't get a *chance!* It was probably about one of the others here—I've uncovered some *serious* infractions—but now we'll never know for sure." She looked down at Lindfield again. "Hell. He wasn't a bad Judge. Just... weak."

"Wrong," Krause said. "When you logged his name with Control, that must have raised a few flags in the restricted files, because word came down to terminate immediately." A shrug.

"Don't know what he'd done, and we probably never *will* know. But I do know that at *that* level, the SJS doesn't make mistakes."

Krause nodded to his colleagues, and they began to turn away. "Get this mess cleaned up, Gillen. Oh, and pass on everything else you've found here to Control. Good work today."

As she watched them go, she automatically took a few steps to the side to avoid the growing pool of Lindfield's blood, very much aware that she had just come closer to death than at any other time in her career.

The smart thing now would be to carry on as Krause suggested. Log Lindfield's death as execution by SJS, along with a list of his infractions. Anyone reading the records would infer that he'd resisted. Suicide by Special Judicial Squad was a common way for corrupt Judges to end their careers.

You should let this go, Gillen told herself. *Lindfield might not have deserved this, but he had to know it was a possibility. And for Grud's sake, fathering one kid is a mistake, just about forgiveable in many circumstances, but* four *kids? That's a pattern. Flagrant disregard for the rules.*

If you're the sort of Judge who'll break one rule, then you're the sort who'll break others. Stands to reason. And the information he claimed to have... Whatever it was, he was going to try to use it to blackmail someone in the SJS. That made him a lawbreaker through and through. Ten years minimum for attempted extortion of a Judge.

A decade in the cubes would have cost the city millions that they'd never recoup. At least dead, Spencer Lindfield would do some good. His organs would go to deserving cases, the rest of his body broken down into its component nutrients at Resyk. He's a better asset dead than alive.

Right, Gillen thought. *Keep telling yourself that, and you might come to believe it.*

Krause had been moments away from putting a round in her own brain, too.

Judge Hariton, David Dixon Block, last May. That was all she had. Not a lot to go on. She could let it slide, but chances were that as soon as Krause even suspected that Lindfield had given her a name, she was dead.

Gillen knew that there were specialists, unregistered psychics who could block or even wipe specific memories. If she could find one, that might be the only way she'd get through this in one piece.

But there was another option. One that she knew she had to take.

'I will carry out my duty to uphold the law at all times, regardless of the cost or potential danger.' That was part of the oath they all took. Judge Lindfield had given her a lead, so she would follow that lead wherever it might end up.

Even if it took her straight into hell.

Three

DREDD WOULD BARELY admit it to himself, but he was mildly impressed with the perps' ingenuity. They had climbed onto the furniture-packed truck, but instead of simply ducking down amongst the crates, dressers, sofas and tables, one had climbed into a wardrobe and the other had managed to squirm between two roped-together mattresses. If it hadn't been for the driver of the Toyota being more scared of him than he was of the perps, Dredd might not have found them.

The perp in the wardrobe—a slender Caucasian woman with tattoos on her face and neck that resembled smears of dried blood—cracked open the door and opened fire even as Dredd was hauling himself up onto the side of the truck.

Four single shots in rapid succession. Her first shot went wild, missing Dredd by over a metre, probably thanks to her cramped quarters. But she corrected quickly: the second shot clipped Dredd's shoulder-pad.

The third would have hit him square in the face, but he'd pitched himself forward, and the round came within a hand's width of perforating his spine.

Her fourth shot was again way off target—she was already dead. Dredd had opened fire mid-roll, his own shot passing through the narrow gap in the wardrobe door, into the woman's chin and out through the back of her head.

A woman's muffled voice from the mattresses: "Don't shoot! Please! I'm dropping my gun right now!"

"I don't hear it fall, creep!" Dredd yelled.

"I know, it's stuck here between the... I swear, I *did* let go. My hands are empty!"

Dredd used his boot-knife to slice through one of the ropes, and the mattresses fell apart, disgorging the perp and her gun onto the floor of the truck like a dropped sandwich spilling its contents.

He scooped up the perp's gun—another Welton Fightender—and sniffed the barrel before tossing a set of cuffs at the woman's feet. "Put 'em on. Gun's not been fired, so you're looking at eight years minimum. But that might change, depending on what you can tell me about the others. How many, and what are they carrying?"

The woman—Asian, small frame, shaved head—fumbled with the cuffs. "It wasn't my idea. I didn't even *want* to get involved! Prissa said that it'd be simple. Go in, take the stuff, get out. No one gets hurt, we all get rich. Would've worked, too, if she'd been there!"

"Not interested in whining," Dredd said. "At the crash-site. How many, and what weapons?"

The woman nodded. "Sure, yeah. I got that. There's five of us. Woulda been *six*, but Prissa got sick this morning, so she said we hadda go on without her, and if she'd been there, then—"

Dredd held his Lawgiver so close to her face that if she'd blinked her eyelashes would have brushed the muzzle. "Weapons. Won't ask again."

"J... Just the *handguns*. That's all. Prissa said she could get hold of a stun-grenade and we woulda used that if she'd been—"

"Shut up. Stay put." Dredd swung himself off the side of the truck.

Sticking between the tunnel wall and the line of traffic, he began to run towards The Kink. "Control—Dredd. Status report on Winquest and Schiro."

"Unknown, Dredd. No word from either in the past three minutes. We've got all tunnel exits covered."

"Acknowledged. I've taken down two perps: one deceased. The other claims there were five of them in total."

"That tallies with the initial report."

"Perp named an accomplice, possibly masterminded the operation. Prissa, feminine pronouns. Sounds like a standard proxy job." It had become something of a fashion among the criminal gangs in recent years to recruit enthusiastic but amateur would-be gangsters for heists. An experienced professional would train them, promise to lead the heist, fill them with grand stories about how rich they were about to become, then pull out at the last minute. Almost inevitably the gang would carry on anyway, buoyed by the momentum of their own greed. If the job succeeded, the professional would take their cut, plus expenses which always turned out to be a lot more than the rest of the gang expected. If the job failed, the survivors would realise all too late that they didn't even know the professional's real name, nor how to make contact with them. You can't rat on someone if everything you thought you knew about them turns out to be a lie.

Ahead, Dredd saw someone crawling along the road, face down, and instinctively aimed his Lawgiver at them. He spotted another, then two more. Citizens keeping low as they crawled away from the scene. More and more, scurrying, crawling, squirming out from beneath cars and trucks, others in their vehicles opening their doors to do the same.

"Keep moving," Dredd said softly as a fat middle-aged man awkwardly passed him on his hands and feet. "And keep silent."

He felt something tapping on the toe of his boot and saw a young dandy looking up at him. "What about my *car?*" The dandy whispered. "I've got frozen groceries in the back! If this takes a long time and they defrost all over the upholstery, how long will it be before the city reimburses me? I'm just asking because I had my identity stolen three years ago and even though they caught her, and got the money back, I'm still waiting for it to be cleared and deposited back into my account."

"My advice? Go back there and get shot in the face, then you won't have to worry about any of that."

The dandy pursed his lips in thought as he considered that option, and Dredd took the opportunity to move on, carefully manoeuvring around the crawling and crouching citizens.

Seventy metres to The Kink, he stepped over the last few crawling cits and soon he could hear nothing ahead but the slight hum of engines and a sporadic crackling. The stench of acrid smoke assured him that the crackling was a fire, probably caused by a leaking powercell.

As he passed his now-static Lawmaster, his helmet radio clicked. "*Dredd, it's been over seven minutes since the last report from Schiro and Winquest.*"

"Understood. I want back up to start moving in from both ends now. Instruct them to keep their distance until I give the word."

There was no single standard protocol for a situation like this in the rulebooks, but the only reason Judges under fire would fail to respond to repeated calls from Control is because they were unable to: Winquest and Schiro were either dead or seriously wounded. If the latter, they were less able to defend themselves, so Dredd should act quickly. If the former, little he did could make things any worse. Either way, it was time to act.

The fire—and the possibility that the Judges were still alive, or that there were still some citizens trapped in their vehicles— meant that heat-seeking rounds weren't an option.

The tunnel bore sharply to the right, and orange light flickered on the wall, clashing with the steadily pulsing red and blue of a Lawmaster's emergency lights.

Perps took the bend too fast, crashed, but not hard enough to put them out. They took aim at Schiro and Winquest as they came around the corner. Fightenders were relatively low-velocity weapons, unlikely to be powerful enough to knock a Judge off their Lawmaster, but faced with enough perps firing at once, a skilled Judge would put the bike into a skid so that the bulk of the engine was between them and the assault. He was sure that's what he'd see when he rounded the corner.

The perps would be expecting more Judges to show, so what was their plan? If they were as inexperienced as Dredd believed, they were almost certainly panicking. *Best approach is to defuse the tension as soon as possible.*

He called out, "Attention! This is Judge Dredd! We know the truth, that you were duped into taking this job. If my colleagues are alive and unharmed, and you name the creep who recruited you, I promise you won't serve more than ten years."

After a moment, a woman's voice called back, "No way. No jail time!"

"Are the Judges still alive?"

A second woman's voice: "Yeah, I think so. But they're wounded. One of them's *twitching* a lot, and—"

"All right," Dredd said. "We need to negotiate, so I'm coming around the corner now. I've got my gun in my hand, but it's down by my side. Do you understand? You can keep your weapons trained on me, just not on my colleagues or any innocents. Agreed?"

Another hesitation, then the first woman said, "Agreed."

Dredd took one step, then another. Steadily, he rounded the corner.

The scene ahead was much as he'd mentally pictured it. He couldn't see the perps, but the front of their vehicle was almost buried into the tunnel wall, badly damaged. Other vehicles nearby were dented and scraped, one burning. Metal, glass, rubber and plastic debris all across the ground. Closer to him, two Lawmasters lay on their sides, a wounded Judge lying on her back behind the bike on Dredd's left, mostly shielded from the perp's viewpoint. She had both hands pressed against her stomach, far too much blood seeping out from under her gloves.

The second Judge was lying on his left side in the centre of the road, facing Dredd. His eyes were open, blood drooling from his mouth, his left leg jerking and twitching. His Lawgiver was only half a metre from his outstretched hand, but Dredd knew that he was never going to reach it.

"Good news is they'll be fine," Dredd said. "Just throw out your weapons, and we'll start mopping up this mess so we can get the traffic moving again."

The first woman called out, "No! You're lying!"

"Okay. Right now, you're facing ten years. Eleven. Twelve."

A dark object sailed over the roof of one of the damaged cars and landed close to Dredd's feet: another Welton Fightender.

"Whoever threw that, you'll get out of the cubes in twelve years. The rest of you... thirteen. Fourteen. Fifteen. Sixteen."

A second gun hit the ground. "We're coming out!"

"Hands where I can see them," Dredd called. "Seventeen. Eighteen. Ni—"

"Okay! Enough! We're all coming out!" A third gun, kicked out from behind another car, skidded across the ground to join its predecessors.

The perps emerged then. Three women, all in their early thirties. Hands raised, their clothing torn and bloodied, their arms and faces covered in scratches and bruises and smudges of soot. The one on the right was limping, heavily favouring her left leg. "We surrender!" Her voice identified her as the second woman who had spoken. "Judge, it was never meant to *go* like—"

"On your knees, hands on top of your head, fingers interlaced."

"I'm doing it! But just let me *explain*, okay? We—"

Dredd's shot skimmed past her right arm so close it left a scorch-mark on her flesh. The woman yelped as she jerked her arm to the side, grabbed at it with her left hand, expecting to see blood.

One of the others—Dredd recognised her voice as that of the first woman—yelled at him. "You *bastard!* We're on our *knees!* If someone surrenders, you can't just shoot at them!"

"Next one won't be a warning shot," Dredd said. "Control, situation's pacified. Send them in."

Almost immediately, four Med-Judges rushed into the scene, one from behind Dredd, the others from the other end of the tunnel. They ignored the perps and went straight to the Judges.

The second woman glared at Dredd. "You'll get what's coming to you, you fascist!"

Dredd put away his Lawgiver and strode up to the perps. "Attempted murder of a street Judge, two counts. Fifty years apiece."

"What? No, you only got as far as *nineteen!*"

He grabbed the third woman's wrists and jerked her arms down behind her back, clipped a set of cuffs onto them. "You want another *decade?*" he asked her colleague.

She looked away. "No. No, I... I'm *sorry.*"

"Tough. You've got it anyway." He signalled to two approaching Judges. "Sixty years, hard labour. All personal assets seized. They give you any further resistance, I recommend upgrading that to execution."

The first woman turned towards Dredd with a cold expression. "This won't stick."

"It's *already* stuck, creep."

"I'll be out in less than a day. I've got *connections.*"

"Every punk thinks they have connections. Must be a great comfort in the cubes."

Senior Med-Judge Sawyer beckoned Dredd over. "It's not good. Winquest is gut-shot; a triple, looks like. Perforated her intestines and left kidney. She should make it, but she'll be out of commission for four months minimum. But Schiro..." He looked over towards the other Judge. "Most of his wounds are superficial, but he was hit in the neck. Shattered the C5 and C6 vertebrae and partially severed the cord. That's going to be a long recovery process with no guarantee of success." The Med-Judge turned towards the perps. "Heard what you said about execution. Sometimes I think we really *should* just..." He sighed.

"Sawyer, you don't want to finish that thought," Dredd said.

"I know, I know. But there *are* times when I just want to put a round inside every perp's skull. Say we did that for a *year*, okay? Throughout the whole city, we adopt a blanket no-tolerance policy. Every crime from littering up, the penalty is execution. Just one year, that should be enough. Hell, even a *month* should do it. And you know what we'd end up with? A city full of obedient, compliant citizens, that's what."

"Wrong." Dredd glared at him. "We'd end up with a city-sized cemetery that's home to a handful of terrified, broken cits. We're here to *serve* the people, Sawyer, not crush them."

The Med-Judge scoffed. "Idealism is a paper-thin shield proudly borne by the blindly naïve, Dredd. Be interesting to see what good that attitude does you out there. Remember to let me know when they carry you in on a stretcher with someone running alongside it carrying the remains of your guts in a dirty tub."

Four

THEY'RE ALREADY WATCHING *you*, Gillen told herself. The ordinary Judges often joked about how the presence of the Special Judicial Squad made them paranoid, but Gillen knew that was nothing compared to the paranoia the SJS generated among themselves.

She returned to her long-term office in the Hall of Justice, a three-metre cube so deep inside the building she'd have to walk for ten minutes solid just to find an outside window.

There could be bugs anywhere and everywhere, she knew. In the light fixtures, hidden inside the plasteen of her desk and chair, her terminal, her file folders. The Japanese peace lily in the corner that seemed to be wilting even though it was plastic. Anywhere.

Gillen pulled her bug-sweeper from a belt-pouch and ran it anyway. It could detect even the most subtle of electronic devices, and almost immediately she found one in the corner of the room under a carpet tile. It was a transparent blob about half the size of a grain of rice: a Massenburg 4300 model, state-of-the-art nanotech. Forty thousand credits per unit, restricted sale. Unlicensed possession meant immediate incarceration for life in a maximum-security Iso-Block.

She dropped the Massenburg into a small plastic envelope and left it on the corner of her desk. Standard protocol: one of her colleagues would drop by in the morning to collect the bugs she'd gathered. Someone in the SJS Tech-Div would attempt to reverse-engineer the bug and trace it back to its source, but that was mostly futile: the Massenburg would have destroyed anything that could lead back to its owner the moment it detected her bug-sweeper.

One of Gillen's instructors in espionage had had a motto: "It's not the bugs you find that are the problem. It's the ones you don't even *imagine* could be there." Every new bug found meant an upgrade to the operatives' bug-sweepers, and every upgraded bug-sweeper sparked new developments in bug-hiding technology.

She sat down, entered her passwords into the terminal, and began to idly flip through the SJS news pages, if only so that anyone who might be watching would think she was doing something.

Krause's orders to terminate Lindfield would have been broad enough to extend to anyone he felt was a threat—including Gillen herself if he'd suspected that Lindfield had told her anything.

Judge Hariton, David Dixon Block, last May.

She'd never heard of Judge Hariton, but there was a David Dixon Block in Sector Forty. From what she could recall, it was a medium-sized, nondescript cuboid with little to make it stand out from its surrounding blocks.

If they *were* monitoring her, there was no easy way for her to uncover whatever secret Lindfield had threatened to spill. Certainly no safe way.

The SJS were necessary, she believed that to the core of her being. For all their training, Judges were people, and people were fallible, prone to selfishness; and selfishness was the first step down into the pit of corruption.

The SJS monitored the Judges because it would be foolish to permit them to monitor themselves... but somehow it was *not* considered foolish for the SJS to self-govern.

Her terminal beeped, and a message-window blossomed open on her monitor. Judge Molina, her immediate supervisor. "Gillen, we've got a complaint lodged against you."

Gillen nodded. "Okay... And this one is different from the usual, because otherwise you'd just log it instead of telling me in person."

"Correct. Judge Hawk McKinney, Sector House 56. He's angry. Claims you murdered one of his colleagues."

"Spencer John Lindfield. It wasn't me who pulled the trigger, but I was there. Judge Krause informed me that immediate termination was authorised. Case closed."

Molina shrugged. "Not to McKinney... He's making a lot of noise over there."

"He check out?"

"He does. Exemplary record, but he's headstrong. Passionate. He's declined promotion to Senior Judge twice because, he says, his job is on the streets." Molina leaned closer to his camera. "Gillen, four years ago we *strongly* considered him for a position with us. We might have made the offer, too, except that he's always been very free with his opinions about the SJS. He's *not* a fan. And now that we've terminated one of his friends..."

"I'll talk to him. Face to face."

"Not sure that it's the *wisest* approach for you to do it. I was going to dispatch someone else."

"We can't have him claiming that we're trying to strong-arm him." Gillen stood up from her desk. "I can handle him."

* * *

AS THE HEADLIGHT beam of her Lawmaster led the way to Sector 56, Gillen considered all the possible ways this might play out. Lindfield might have said something to McKinney about David Dixon Block or Judge Hariton. If so, then that might put her on the right path.

In any other circumstance, she'd just look up Hariton on the system, but not now. Hariton's file could well be tagged by the SJS, as Lindfield's was.

It was almost midnight by the time she found Judge Hawk McKinney on Manic Street on the Sector's west side. A tall man with an athletic build, he was almost effortlessly manhandling a struggling perp almost twice his weight towards three Judges waiting next to a catch-wagon.

"Creep went off the rails and over the edge," McKinney told Gillen as the catch-wagon pulled away. "Cits reported him standing on the street corner spouting religious dogma about how the End of Days has already passed and this city is Hell."

"You arrested him for *that?*"

McKinney started to walk back to his Lawmaster a hundred metres down the street, and Gillen rode her own bike alongside him.

"No. I was charging him with noise pollution and he assaulted me. Tried to grab my Lawgiver. I was almost tempted to let him try to *fire* it. A lifetime with no right arm and half his body burned would teach him a lesson. And no, before you decide to use that against me, I'm not serious. I didn't *actually* want that to happen. I gave him five months in the slammer. Should be enough time to reconsider his chosen hobby." He removed his helmet and looked Gillen in the eye. "You killed Spencer Lindfield and now you're after me, is that it?"

"It wasn't me who shot Lindfield. If you're as good a Judge as your records say, you'd have figured that out already. But you saw me with my gun drawn and just *assumed* I was—"

McKinney said, "No. You saw me looking at you, and *you*

assumed I was making that connection. When I said 'You killed Spencer Lindfield,' I was using the plural. Collectively, you killed him."

"I was the one you lodged a complaint against."

"I didn't see the other SJS Judges' badges, but I knew your name because you were already operating out of the Sector House. The complaint is against *all* of you, which you'd know if you'd read it. Lindfield was a good Judge; one of the best. We trained together. He started in the Academy a month after me—I knew him better than my own family. He never broke a law in his life, and you drokkers put him down like he was a diseased dog." McKinney climbed into his Lawmaster. "I'm not withdrawing the complaint, even though I know it won't do any good. You people look after each other, don't you?"

"Did you know that Lindfield had a family? He had a long-term relationship with a woman, resulting in four children."

The Judge regarded her in silence for a few seconds. "Seriously. You're going *there?* Smear the man's reputation like you smeared his brains all over the Lawmaster bay? That is low even for you people."

"It's true. You clearly didn't know him as well as you thought."

"And *that's* why you killed him?"

It was Gillen's turn to hesitate. If Lindfield didn't tell McKinney about his family, then it didn't seem likely he'd have told him about Hariton or David Dixon Block. And Gillen couldn't mention it unless she was sure he *did* know, because she'd be putting him at risk. "No. That's classified. But I assure you that it's got nothing to do with his family."

McKinney replaced his helmet, started slowly looking around. "Your people took four others away this evening. I'm guessing you had something to do with *that*, too. Billings, Ackerman, Dawber and Westwell. Eight more were given citations and sent for refresher courses. It's..." He shook his head.

"It's too much?" Gillen suggested.

"No. If they're all guilty, if they *have* broken the law... It's a sign that you people in the SJS are not doing your jobs. You need to come down *harder* on us."

"But you *hate* the SJS, McKinney."

He started up his Lawmaster. "I hate that you're necessary." He turned back to her. "Four kids, huh? What's going to happen to them?"

"I don't know." Gillen decided to take a chance. "Lindfield offered to make a deal. He'd quit the department with no punishments, no repercussions, but he wanted to talk to a senior SJS Judge."

"And instead you blew the poor drokker's brains out."

"No! Well, yes. Unfortunately. He never got to mention the specifics, what he was going to offer as his side of the bargain."

A shrug. "Don't ask me."

"He mentioned one name. Judge Harrison. Mean anything to you?"

"Not particularly. Unless you heard him wrong. Maybe said 'Hariton'?"

"I don't recall either a Hariton or a Harrison from the Sector House records."

"You wouldn't," McKinney said. "Jimmy Hariton's an old guy. Retired back in the '60s, I think. He used to drop in to the Sector House, now and then. He'd collar us and tell stories about the old days. Last time I saw him was a few years ago, and he was starting to fray at the edges. Could be he's died since."

"What do you mean, Hariton was fraying at the edges?"

"Forgetting people's names, mixing up his stories halfway through, or repeating himself. Sometimes just talking garbage. Not enough that you'd send him for evaluation, but enough that we noticed. Couple of times when he was talking to me, he'd cut himself off and say, 'Maybe it wasn't like that at all. You get older, sometimes you confuse what really happened with what you *wish* had happened. Or hadn't happened.' Once, he said to me, 'Hawk, when you get to my age, what's gonna keep you awake at night isn't the things you did, it's the things you let happen.'"

"Meaning?"

"I don't know. It probably doesn't mean anything. But..." He shrugged. "Old Judges can get paranoid, especially about what we're doing, and why we're doing it. You must have seen that more than most of us. They get to a certain age and they start to wonder if maybe we're doing more harm to the people than good."

"You're saying that Hariton was worried that the Judge system isn't sustainable?"

"Hey, whoa... I'm not saying *anything*. That was just a theory I concocted just now. Until today I've given this precisely zero consideration."

Gillen asked, "Where'd Hariton live?" but she was sure she already knew the answer.

McKinney nodded towards the east. "Over in Sector Forty. David Dixon Block, I think. Judge, if you're not going to arrest me or kill me, I've still got eight hours left on patrol."

"We're done. But this..." Gillen indicated McKinney and herself. "This is between *us*. Talk to no one about this conversation. You understand? I don't want to have to slap a D-notice on you. Let it *go*."

"Is that a threat?"

Gillen regarded him for a few moments. McKinney was a good Judge, she had no doubts about that. But he had a saviour complex, and that made him potentially dangerous. Could he be trusted with the truth? She realised that she had to take that chance. "You believe the SJS are corrupt, don't you?"

"I never said that."

"What if you're right, McKinney?"

He didn't respond to that.

"And now you're wondering whether that was a trap. It wasn't. I don't know *why* Lindfield was targetted for execution, but I intend to find out. If his killing was unlawful, I will do everything in my power to bring those responsible to justice. And I can't do that if you're blabbing about it and constantly shining a light in my direction. So you need to rein that in. We don't know what criteria they used to pick Lindfield, so for all we know just talking about him might make *us* their next targets. *Now* do you understand?"

"Understood. Not sure I believe you, yet." He started his Lawmaster. "But I'll keep quiet for now. That it?"

"I'll be in touch."

Judge Hawk McKinney nodded briefly, then rode away.

Gillen wasn't sure that he truly understood the seriousness of the situation. She also wasn't sure whether either of them would still be alive by morning.

Five

AT FOUR-FIFTEEN IN the morning the city had calmed down long enough for Dredd to log off, use one of the Sector House's sleep machines—a night's sleep compressed into less than fifteen minutes meant the Judges could spend a lot more time on the streets—and return to his small quarters to shower and change into a fresh uniform.

It was as he was exiting the shower that he noticed the problem with his law books. Volumes seven and thirteen had been swapped around.

Dredd towelled himself dry as he stared at the bookcase. That someone had been in his quarters was no surprise: he didn't keep the door locked. There was usually at least one visitor a day anyway: a cadet sent to fetch his used uniform and leave a clean one.

But someone had deliberately moved the books. He pulled out the seventh volume and spotted a slip of paper tucked into its pages. A hand-written note: *into despotism*. He found a similar slip in the thirteenth volume: *democracy passes*.

Democracy passes into despotism. Plato, *The Republic*. It

was a quote he knew well.

Dredd pulled on his fresh uniform. "Control—Dredd."

"*Go ahead, Dredd.*"

"Scratch my patrol plans. Want to check up on an old case. Nothing urgent—you need me, I'll be on stand-by."

"*Acknowledged. Anything I can help you with?*"

"Negative. Dredd out."

He dropped briefly into the mess-hall to grab breakfast—his usual stack of tasteless protein bars and a bottle of vitamin-enriched water—and paid little heed to the Judges clustered around one of the tables. They were engrossed in a game of chance, but there didn't appear to be any money changing hands, so he let it slide.

From the Sector House he rode north for four kilometres, then turned east onto 226th Street. The first half of the Plato quote had been tucked between pages 226 and 227 of Volume 13 of *The Book of Law*, with the writing on the note facing page 226.

The second half of the quote had been between pages 406 and 407 of Volume 7, but there were no 406th or 407th avenues in this sector. However, the most prominent article on page 407—which the writing on the note was facing—concerned the murder of citizen Leander Baare Pierson. 226th Street was bisected by Pierson Avenue.

It was a quiet neighbourhood, mostly industrial, almost completely deserted at this time of the morning. Wide streets, small factories and stores, no blocks, very few houses or apartments.

Dredd stopped his Lawmaster at the junction of Pierson and 226th, and as he climbed off, a woman's voice called from a dark doorway.

"Took you long enough, Dredd."

"Only discovered your clues twenty minutes ago, Gillen."

She stepped out into the light. "And you figured it was me, too. Or did you just remember my voice?"

"You put your notes into the seventh and thirteenth books. G and M are the seventh and thirteenth letters. But you swapped the books around. MG. Marion Gillen."

"You must know other Judges with those initials?"

"I do. But none who'd feel the need for such subterfuge. They'd just leave a message with Control, or tape a note on the door." He moved closer to her. "What do you want, and why me?"

"This is..." Gillen folded her arms and leaned back against the store's window. "Jovus, Dredd, you're *not* easy to talk to."

"That's your problem, not mine."

"Right. Look... In the course of a routine investigation I discovered a relatively minor infraction by Street Judge Spencer Lindfield. Asked SJS Control for his whereabouts. As I was talking to him, four other SJS Judges showed up. Gunned him down immediately."

"What had he done?"

"As far as I know, nothing. Well, nothing that deserved execution. He had a secret family. Common-law wife, four kids. But Judge Krause—he led the squad—claimed that Lindfield was tagged for termination. The reason is classified."

Dredd continued to watch Gillen for a few moments, then realised that she had finished and was waiting for him to respond. "Why tell me?"

"When I approached Lindfield, he became belligerent. Claimed to have information he would only divulge to a senior SJS member."

"Sounds like a blackmail attempt."

"That was my thought too. When Krause showed up, Lindfield said a few more things—not loud enough for the others to hear—and then Krause brought him down. Single shot to the head. And when Krause asked me why I was talking to Lindfield and... he was ready to kill me, too, if he had to."

"So they believe that Lindfield discovered something dangerous enough to have him terminated. Can't say I approve."

"Well, good! You *shouldn't* approve. But you see the problem?"

"That the information Lindfield gave you might be enough to add your name to the termination list too."

Gillen shook her head. "Not just that. Lindfield discovered something big enough to get him killed. I want to know what that is. Without getting *myself* killed as a consequence."

"You can't investigate because you know they'll be checking on you."

"Now we're getting there. *You* can run the investigation, Dredd. Let me know what you find."

The headlights of a car rounded a corner further along the street, and Gillen automatically stepped back into the shadows. "And keep it on the down-low. You talk to anyone, even the Chief Judge, word will get back to the SJS and then I'm dead, if I'm not already marked."

"Hmmm. Two more questions, then, Gillen. First, how do you know that this isn't the sort of secret that *needs* to be kept quiet?"

Gillen watched the car quietly rumble past, then said, "Because they killed Lindfield. They could have arrested him on a trumped-up charge and slung him in solitary, or used a Psi-Judge to wipe his memory. But they murdered him." She tapped the silver badge on her chest. "We investigate the Judges. And that means *all* Judges, including our own. We will kill to uphold the Law and protect the innocent if we have to, but we're not murderers."

Dredd nodded. "Second question. Why come to me? Last year you tried your damnedest to put me away. You were desperate to prove that I was as corrupt as Rico."

"That's true," Gillen said. "I went overboard, I admit it. Squandered a lot of time and resources on you. Got myself reprimanded for it, too."

"And yet you've come to me now."

"Because the work I put into trying to prove your guilt had the opposite effect. Of all the Judges in Mega-City One, you are the only one I am absolutely certain is standing squarely on the side of justice."

Six

SHORTLY AFTER SHE joined the SJS, Gillen approached her superior officer and admitted that she was confused about the department's hierarchy. She knew that Judge Elva Barradien—a dour fifty-year-old man with a permanent scowl-line between his eyebrows and a missing upper-left canine tooth he'd never bothered to get replaced—was the *de facto* head of the SJS. But she'd seen Barradien in conference with Judges Kenneth McComber and Roseanne Dekaj and it had looked very much like Barradien was taking a lot of heat from them.

Her superior officer, Judge Molina, had explained: "Barradien's a figurehead. Every damn Judge on the streets despises us, so rising to prominence in the SJS isn't necessarily wise. As Barradien's advisors, Dekaj and McComber wield more power than he does. But make no mistake, Gillen: Barradien knows what he's doing and he still outranks you and me. He's willing to make himself a target because he understands that the brighter he shines, the deeper the shadows around him—his words, not mine—and we operate in the shadows."

That had become something of a motto for Molina. The SJS

had to work in secrecy; the ordinary Judges looked out for each other, covered for their friends' minor infractions. And not just their friends: there were countless cases of Judges picking up the slack or hiding the mistakes of Judges they'd never met just so that the SJS wouldn't descend on them.

Back when she'd been a street Judge, Gillen had understood that attitude, but she'd never accepted it. On her initial interview with Molina—long before she realised it was an interview: at the time she believed she was under investigation for a crime that hadn't ever been clearly explained to her—she had said, "I never claimed to be without flaws. There's no such thing as the perfect Judge. Perfection is an unattainable goal. But the *pursuit* of perfection should be part of every Judge's make-up. We have to be the best we *can* be, because when we fall—when we *fail*—citizens die. And the only reason we exist is to keep them safe."

Gillen still believed that, but since her investigation into Dredd, she had come to rethink that belief: there might well be such a thing as the perfect Judge.

As she rode back to the Hall of Justice, she realised that she was gripping the Lawmaster's handlebars a little too tightly, a sure sign that she was stressed. On the heels of that came the realisation that for the past twelve hours, since the moment her uniform was sprayed with Judge Lindfield's brains and blood, she'd been half-expecting a shot to come out of nowhere and prematurely terminate her career.

Assassination was always a possibility for any Judge, especially a member of the Special Judicial Squad, but now it felt more than just possible; it felt likely.

Should have immediately *told Krause about Lindfield's last words. Damn it! Now I'm guilty of obstruction at the very least! They're gonna haul me in and run a Psi-scan and that'll be that. Once they know I lied... They'll take me out, then McKinney, then Dredd.*

Unless Dredd can get to the heart of this first.

Someone at the top already suspected Lindfield of knowing whatever it was they're keeping secret. All I did was mention his name to Control, and that was enough to trigger the termination order.

So if they suspected, why didn't they terminate him back when he first appeared on their radar? If the information was that dangerous, why put him on a watch-list at all?

Dredd had wanted to know everything. In the half hour they talked, he'd grilled her relentlessly. Everything Krause had said to her, down to his emphasis and body language. Same with McKinney: what did he know about Lindfield? What was his connection with Hariton? What exactly had Hariton talked about? It was a cross-examination more thorough and intense than many SJS investigations. She now almost felt sorry for Dredd's suspects.

Gillen slowed down as she neared the north entrance to the Hall of Justice's cavernous Lawmaster bay, and for a moment she considered gunning the engine and getting the hell out of there. That was an attractive option right now. Just disappear forever. The SJS was so secretive that with a little luck the people after her would just assume that someone else had taken care of her.

Grud, I really am getting paranoid. Once she'd left her bike with the mechanics for its daily diagnostics check and tune-up, she logged herself back into the system at the nearest terminal, finding a message from Judge Molina waiting for her, time-stamped eight minutes ago. *Gillen. My quarters, as soon as you get this. Go the long way to avoid the congestion.*

She hit the thumbs-up icon by way of reply, and immediately headed for the bank of elevators. Molina's quarters were on one of the upper levels. It would take around four minutes thirty to get there at this time of the day. Add another eighty or ninety seconds leeway—there was always the possibility of being stopped in the corridor by a chatty colleague—before she'd be expected to reach Molina's quarters, and that gave her less than six minutes to go dark.

Not much time in the most favourable of circumstances. Almost impossible here in the city's heart of justice.

She hit the call button on the leftmost elevator, then tried not to look anxious as she watched the numbers dropping from 124. The early hour was a potential gift: it meant that the likelihood of another Judge riding the elevator was greatly reduced. But if there *was* someone... She didn't want to think about it.

The indicator showed that the elevator was slowing as it approached floor 33. Not good. But it could be someone getting off, not on.

On the third anniversary of their working relationship, Judge Molina had taken Gillen to lunch in one of the Hall of Justice's busy cafeterias and told her, "It's the nature of our job to be suspicious. I've been checking up on you. Right from the start. And one of the things I've seen is that you've clearly been doing the same to me."

"I know," Gillen responded. "But, sir, I never thought we'd be having this conversation out loud and in public."

Keeping his voice low, Molina said, "One day someone truly corrupt will rise to the upper levels of this department. That's almost a given. And long before that happens, they'll have compiled a list of potential enemies. You and I will be on that list. You've considered this, of course."

"Many times. Still don't know what to *do* about it, sir."

Molina speared another apple slice with his fork. "We can never be *absolutely* certain that we're not being monitored, but right now..." he looked around at the hundreds of Judges, cadets and staff milling about the room. "This is about as safe as we can be. I've got four separate signal-dampers on my person. You?"

Gillen nodded. "Also four."

Molina made a pretence of wiping his mouth with a napkin,

to hide his lips from anyone watching, and softly said, "You hear they're coming for me, tell me that your Lawgiver's scope is a little loose and you need to swap it out. If they're coming for you, I'll tell you to come see me, but take the long way. Got that?"

The elevator dinged and the doors slid open. No one inside. Gillen stepped in and said, "Eighty-first floor."

As the doors began to close, she stepped back out, and immediately moved to the left, into the shadows. There was a doorway that most Judges probably didn't know was even there, the entrance to a maintenance corridor.

Shortly after that lunchtime meeting with Molina, Gillen had tinkered with the sensors in both the elevator and the corridor. If she entered the elevator at the Lawmaster bay and then immediately stepped back out, it would register her as still being present. She had overlaid the corridor's sensors with a transparent, paper-thin biometric scanner that had been calibrated to recognise her: if it did, it told the sensors that the corridor was empty.

She began to run. Forty-five seconds gone. In five minutes, maybe less, an alert would go out and she would officially be a fugitive.

No way to get to a Lawmaster right now—they could be remotely deactivated anyway—so the best option was to get to street level before the alarms hit.

As she ran through the narrow, dusty corridor, she pulled off her helmet, tossed it aside. Ripped off her elbow pads and knee pads. Rounded a corner and left her shoulder pads behind. Then her gloves, utility belt, and her badge.

Three hundred metres along the corridor, she'd set up a false wall, a simple sheet of fibreboard painted to look like concrete. It wouldn't stand up to much scrutiny, but it had been the best option at the time. The maintenance droids that travelled this corridor had no need to use the small nook she'd covered up, so there was a strong chance it was still there, with her stashed equipment intact.

She had just finished pulling on the street Judge's uniform when the first alarm sounded.

FROM 226TH STREET Dredd had headed due south, left the highways after ten minutes, then spent some time following individual vehicles through the old suburbs. Anyone tracking him would, he hoped, assume that he was just out there on the streets to scowl at the traffic, as usual.

If any SJS Judge other than Gillen had approached Dredd and asked him to carry out a covert investigation, he'd have checked them out first. But he knew Gillen. Didn't care for her much, but he trusted her.

The name Hariton didn't mean anything to him, but he wasn't naive enough to look it up himself. He'd been momentarily tempted to directly ask Chief Judge Goodman to do it—Dredd knew the old man missed his days on the streets and would relish the opportunity to be involved in an investigation again—but if this secret was serious enough to get a Judge murdered by the SJS, then there was no way to tell how far it reached.

It was even possible that Goodman was involved in some way. The higher up the ladder you get, the more secrets you have to carry.

Dredd's meandering path brought him to the edge of Sector 40, where he pulled over a human-driven cab.

The driver—male, early twenties, sweating and still white-knuckling the cab's wheel even though the vehicle was stationary—stammered that his name was Hainsley Conan Paoli and swore that he'd never do it again, it had been an accident, and that he'd happily pay double whatever fine was due as long as he didn't have to spend time in the cubes.

"What is it you're confessing to?" Dredd asked, leaning on

the cab's roof as he peered in through the driver's-side window.

"I dunno. Whatever it was I done that you pulled me over for! I promise, I never meant to do it!"

"You're not in trouble, citizen. Just looking for information. David Dixon Block, you know it?"

Paoli nodded. "Sure. About eight K straight ahead. Eldsters, mostly. I get a lot of jobs there. Mostly short runs, 'cause they're all old and can't walk so far, plus the *juves*, y'know?"

"No. Explain."

"Eldsters and juves are like *allergic* to each other, my ma always says. One lot complaining that the music is too loud, the others complaining about the smell. The eldsters will sometimes get a cab half a block if it means they can avoid a juve gang."

"The eldsters ever tell you stories about the old days while you're driving them?"

Paoli shook his head. "Mostly the rides only last a couple of minutes. There's one old guy who hires us to take him to a place right across the *street* from his place. He can't walk far enough to get to the crossing, see. But they mostly just tell me I'm going too fast and that the streets aren't safe any more. But my ma, she takes the afternoon shifts, mostly, and they talk to her alla the time. She says that sometimes they stay in the cab talkin' to her long after they get where they're going."

With no solid reason to detain Paoli, Dredd gave him a general warning and sent him on his way.

The next cab he stopped was driven by an older man, in his sixties at least, and he too had occasionally ferried passengers to or from David Dixon Block. "Yeah, they're *fulla* great stories, the old folks. Had one lady, she was the actual inventor of Olsefsky's Chair-Leg Wax, she said. Her name wasn't Olsefsky, though, but I guess she could've changed it. And a couple of times I picked up these two brothers who used to be in the Flying Baritones. Young Judge like you wouldn't remember them, prob'ly. You don't much get the combination acts any more, but they were big for a while. Opera and trapeze, that was the Flying Baritones. Then there was juggling and dish-washing, and the skateboarding portrait artists, they were kinda funny. Folks used to say that Bartlett Bryans used to earn ten million bucks a week. Dollars, that is, not creds. That was back before we *had* credits. But the underwater ventriloquists kinda killed it for me. Now, my *wife*—"

"Fine. Thank you, citizen. Carry on."

The driver nodded and started to pull away, but stopped after a few metres and leaned out the window. "Listen, Judge, you want the old stories, you'd wanna go to the creakshop on Prestwick."

"And that is?"

"Across the sked from David Dixon. It's where they hang out, the old folks. They talk about the old times and play video games and, y'know, pretend that they're not just waiting for death."

THE "CREAKSHOP" WAS the West Sector 40 Eldsters' Recreational Facility, a squat rectangular building with the name *PASTURE* set in large, welcoming letters above the door that had been constructed in the lee of an Aeroball stadium. The morning sun cast long shadows as Dredd rode up to the creakshop, and he expected to have to wait for a staff member to arrive, but the building was already open, with two old women sitting on a bench outside watching him.

He left his Lawmaster at the kerb and as he passed the women, one of them tutted loudly, and the other said, "There's no one here yet, son, 'cept us."

The other one pointed to his Lawmaster. "You parked too far away."

Dredd glanced back at the bike. "I'm sure I can make it there and back."

"Vital seconds," said the one wearing the threadbare Harlem Heroes cap. "That's what you're losing. Say you get a call when you're inside. Not only have you gotta cover those twenty metres from the door, there could be folks in the way, slow you down that little bit extra."

"That's right," her companion agreed. She was missing her left arm, and both legs appeared to be artificial. "Plus you bring your bike closer to the door, folks'll be more sure where you are. Shows you're here on business."

Dredd walked up to them. "You were Judges?"

The woman with the missing arm and artificial legs said, "Kaye Galliano, based in Charlotte, North Carolina. From 'thirty-four to 'sixty-one." She rapped on her right knee with her knuckles. "Creamed by a perp riding a stolen gas truck."

Her companion took off her cap and saluted Dredd with it. She had a thick horizontal scar running from the centre of her forehead around to the right and ending at the back of her head. "Paulette Radeloff. Call me Polly. I was in one of the first squads ever assembled. Stationed in the Bronx until 'fifty-four, then they traded me with Texas. You know, I never met Eustace Fargo personally, but I knew his face." She squinted at Dredd. "And *that's* what it looked like, just about. You're one of his clones, right? We heard about that." She pointed to the badge on his chest. "You know you're named after *us*, don't you? 'Dreadnoughts,' that's what some people used to call Judges. And that got shortened to 'Dreads.' That's why they picked that name for you clones. Me, I can't *stand* the idea of clones. No offence."

"None taken." Dredd looked from Radeloff to Galliano and back. "What's a three-nineteen-B, Radeloff?"

The woman smirked. "They recategorised all the codes a few times since my day, Dredd. But that used to be an instruction to detain a suspect by any means while your partner scoped out their house or car. You're checking that we really were Judges and we're not just two old women who get their kicks from pretending they used to be important. I get it."

He didn't respond to that, but turned to Galliano. "Perp threatens another Judge with a firearm, but you know the perp's gun isn't loaded. What's the procedure?"

"We're not so old we've forgotten *everything*. If the perp's alone, and he's out of arm's reach, you shoot him anyway. Non-lethal wound. That'll stop the other Judge from killing him. But if the perp's got company, you do what you can to put the perp between you and his friends, make him your shield in case *their* guns are loaded. Satisfied?"

"Good enough," Dredd said.

"So what brings you here, young Fargo?" Galliano asked. "What information are you looking for?"

"What can you tell me about Judge Jimmy Hariton?"

Radeloff said, "Jim or James, not Jimmy. He hated that. The young Judges, they always called him Jimmy and he was never able to shake it."

"Past tense. So he's dead."

"Well, he was eighty and he'd spent forty years of his life in the most dangerous profession on the planet, so, yeah, he's dead." Radeloff shrugged. "Me and Polly here, we're kinda the exceptions."

"Cause of death?"

"Stroke, they said. Exacerbated by the usual damage acquired by a Judge." She tapped the side of her head with her index finger. "James took one in the skull on duty. That was back... about '61, or '62. Scrambled his brains for a while."

"Date of death?"

Radeloff frowned. "Ohh... You've got me there. Kaye?"

Galliano said, "It was end of April, early May. Something like that." She pointed off to her left. "They found him on the street, about half a block that way, early morning."

Dredd resisted the urge to turn and look. "And you're certain there was no external cause of death?"

Galliano shook her head. "Not certain of anything. That's just what they told us. A stroke, plus, like Polly said, there was that time he took a round to the head. That's rarely a health benefit. That kinda damage... you don't get over it. You just have to find a way to *live* with it. He did recover some, but not all the way. A repaired vase might *look* perfect, but the cracks are still there even if you can't see them, right? So the department retired him."

Radeloff said, "Yeah, until the *war* started. Then they reinstated him, because he might have forgotten a lot of what he'd learned, but he could still hold a Lawgiver. He still had most of his instincts intact. Then after the war they didn't need him no more. They retired hundreds of us older Judges at the same time. Shook our hands and said well done, here's a tiny box you can call an apartment, hand over your badge and weapons, sit over there quietly where you won't be in the way of progress."

"They didn't offer you teaching posts at the Academy?"

Radeloff regarded him with a tight-lipped expression. "You *remember* the war, don't you?" She removed her cap again and ran her fingers along the scar on her forehead. "Middle of the battle of Breaker's Hill, my squad got taken down by some drokker with a rocket-launcher. I was the only survivor. Woke up in a basement chained to a table." She looked down at her hands, and seemed almost surprised to see that they were not trembling. "Bunch of rich juves making the most of the war, getting their kicks by killing and torturing people. The drokker leading them tried to remove the top of my skull with a *machete*. Not in one swift blow, though. He wanted to see if he could *push* it through. His friends filmed it, giggled as they watched him leaning on me with all his weight... He *kept* trying, too, for damn near an hour, convinced he could do it. He might have succeeded if the blade had been sharp. But his friends got bored listening to me scream. They wanted him to just decapitate me and move on, but he was determined, now.

Didn't want to look weak in front of his pals. They left, and..."
She stopped. "You don't want to know what I did to him when I
got free. But I understand his family are still convinced he's one
of the war-displaced, that one day he'll come home." Her eyes
narrow, she stared up at Dredd. "He's *not* going to come home.
I killed him slowly, but thoroughly. And the cameras were still
running. My supervisor found the footage, and destroyed it. I
told her, you can't *do* that, the video proves the identities of his
friends. But she said to me, 'It's proof that you chose to execute
a perp when you already had him incapacitated. That's *revenge*.
Conduct unbecoming of a Judge.' So, no, they didn't offer me a
teaching post, but they *did* let a bunch of psycho juves get away
with accessory to attempted murder of a Judge."

Galliano asked, "Why the curiosity about Jim Hariton?
What's happened that you can't look him up on the system?"
She frowned at him. "This isn't an official investigation. You're
trying to keep it off the books." She sat back and smiled at
her friend. "That means he's covering up something himself, or
trying to uncover someone *else's* cover-up. We oughta—"

"No, we *oughtn't!* By some miracle we managed not to get
killed on the job or in the war, and I'm not going to volunteer
myself into danger now just for old times' sake, not after the
way they treated me." Radeloff turned back to Dredd. "You
understand, young man? You make it out of the burning
building, you don't go back in if you don't have to."

"Understood. Anything else you can tell me about Hariton?
Any *rumours* about his death?"

Radeloff shrugged. "Jim Hariton made it through the war, but
he was already broken. He... saw too much, that was all he'd
say. I know he had friends on both sides. We all did. You did
too, I'm sure. I was in his apartment one time, and he had—"

"You never told me that!" Galliano said.

"Sure I did."

"You did *not*. I'd have remembered."

Dredd said, "The point?"

Radeloff rolled her eyes. "He had a *squad* medal on his dresser. Alpha company. Best of the best, they were. Assigned to protect the big wigs during the war. Probably the Chief Judge, or the Council of Five. Someone important."

"What *were* you doing in Hariton's apartment?" Galliano asked. "You and him weren't... *you know*, were you? Practising your wrestling holds without the encumberment of cloth?"

"Were we *what?*"

"Sleeping with him. *Sex*, I'm talking about. Polly, were you and Jim performing the old lateral catch-and-release?"

Dredd reminded himself that the women were no longer Judges. There were no laws against consensual couplings even if the participants were eldsters.

"No, Kaye, we were *not*. He was away for a week and I was feeding his cat."

"Any enemies?" Dredd asked.

"He *thought* he had," Galliano said. "Thought he was being watched, kept looking up at the sky. I'd tell him, 'Jim, they *are* watching. That's the PSU, the Public Surveillance Unit. They're watching *all* of us, all the time.' And he had his *list* of enemies, you know, like we all do? But there was no one specific on there. Just *types* of people. The usual bunch. Let's see, there was..." She began to count on the fingers of her remaining arm, starting with her thumb. "Psi-Judges, of course. And SJS too, those two are a given. He hated recidivists, Sovs, muties..." Galliano closed her fingers and started back with her thumb again. "Dunks, trance-heads, pampered juves... and people who hurt animals. He *hated* them. He saw someone abusing a pet, he'd come down as hard on them as he would if they were kicking a kid. Maybe harder."

"Any *real* enemies? Someone from his time as a Judge?"

Both of the old women shrugged. Galliano said, "Jim Hariton was *broken*. Happens to a lot of us. Maybe it'll happen to you, too, if you're lucky enough to live that long. When we sign up to be Judges, we offer our *lives* to this city, and you know what? It *takes* them."

Dredd abruptly turned away, hand raised to his helmet radio.

As always, he'd had the radio on the general band, volume down low as it relayed a constant stream of reports and all-units calls. It was rare that he heard a familiar name, so the mention of SJS Judge Marion Gillen jumped out at him. He boosted the volume and thumbed the jumpback button to replay the last twenty seconds.

"...*at the junction of Second Street and Perelli Avenue and Sagar Crescent. City-wide alert, highest priority: all units BOLO for Marion Gillen, former SJS Judge, last seen in the vicinity of the Hall of Justice. Gillen is to be considered A-E-D. If spotted, report but do* not *approach or attempt to take down.*"

Dredd turned back to women. "Appreciate the info, citizens."

As he strode back to his Lawmaster, he heard Galliano say, "That wasn't *good* news, whatever it was. You could see it on his face. So *intense* all the time, these young Judges."

"Fargo was the same," Radeloff said. "Got the job done, sure, but he was one seriously *miserable* drokker."

Seven

WHEN THE ALARM sounded, Gillen's first thought was that she should stay put in the maintenance corridor, but she knew that the security protocols dictated that once the building was in lockdown, the next step was to immediately run a diagnostic on every lock, camera and sensor. It wouldn't take long to discover that the corridor's sensors had been modified.

After four seconds the alarm was abruptly cut off, replaced by a PA announcement so loud she could feel the floor trembling: "*Attention. This facility is now in full lockdown. All civilians to remain where they are until instructed to move by a Judge. Failure to comply will be considered an act of aggression.*"

Almost immediately, her helmet radio beeped: "*All units BOLO for SJS Judge Marion Gillen, last seen entering an elevator in the Lawmaster bay. To be considered A-E-D. If seen report immediately, do not approach. A termination order is in effect.*"

Terminate on sight. She'd been expecting that since the moment Krause executed Lindfield—a small part of her had been expecting it since the day she signed up with the SJS—but to actually hear the order given, with her name attached, was a gut-punch for which she'd not been prepared. *They're going to kill me to protect a secret I don't even know.*

She finished pulling on the too-tight boots and stood up. She'd modified the left boot's sole, given it a slight transverse tilt that altered her gait enough to fool the biometric sensors. Along with the helmet and uniform of a street Judge, and a fake three-day-old scar on the left side of her jaw, only someone she knew well would immediately recognise her.

The corridor branched in a dozen places, all but three of them eventually leading to public areas. Gillen immediately ruled out the door through which she'd entered, back in the Lawmaster bay. That left two exits: the exterior gantry close to the roof—which was off the cards, all external doors would be sealed and monitored—and the paper library deep in the heart of the building.

The library had been created at the insistence of Chief Judge Goodman's predecessor, Hollins Solomon, a paranoid man with an irrational fear that one day hackers would get into the Justice Department's systems and wipe out everything. "You can't digitally purge a sheet of paper," Solomon frequently declared.

Now, the library was rarely visited by anyone other than the cleaning droids. It was a low-ceilinged room with the footprint of a sports stadium: a dense maze of shelving units packed with lawbooks and printouts of countless transcripts and e-mails. The maintenance corridor opened in a corner close to the library's entrance, and just as Gillen was pulling the doors closed behind her, another Judge rounded the corner.

"All clear," Gillen told him as she glanced at his badge. "You want me to stand guard here, or...?"

Judge Barron hesitated for a second, then looked at her own badge. "Thurber. No, Judge Kimber's orders are to liaise with him at the west exits. With me."

She raced alongside Judge Barron through the building,

crossing paths with many other Judges and cadets also on high alert.

"You *know* the fugitive, Thurber?" Barron asked.

"Can't say that I've met her. You?"

"No. But she's SJS, so she's not gonna be a walk in the park. Been a long time since I heard of an SJS Judge going rogue."

"Could all be a bluff," Gillen suggested. "The skull-heads trying to catch someone out."

"Wouldn't surprise me."

They raced up a series of paused escalators—all of the building's walkways, elevators and escalators had been shut down—and emerged in the centre of the main lobby, where a dozen Judges were attempting to corral several bus-loads worth of nervous-looking tourists.

As they approached the largest of the exits on the west side of the building, Barron slowed to a fast jog. Ahead, a hundred or more Judges were already standing guard on either side of the sealed glass doors. "I don't think we're needed here..." He nudged Gillen's arm, and pointed off to the right. "Thurber, check in with Kimber, see where he wants us."

Gillen nodded, and set off towards the older Judge. Right now, Senior Judge Kimber had his back to Gillen as he barked orders at a group of year twelve cadets, but Gillen had met him four times: there was a strong chance he'd see through her disguise.

Kimber dispatched the cadets—they scattered in all different directions—and was about to turn around when a squad of ten Judges ran past Gillen. The Judge leading them called out, "Judge Kimber—where do you need us?"

Gillen joined the back of the squad as though she'd been with them all along, making sure to always keep another Judge between herself and Kimber's line of sight.

Kimber pointed to a nearby stairwell. "Roof. Everything's up there's locked down, but we can't be sure the fugitive won't try to escape on a skysurf board or some other aerial conveyance. Get up there and stay alert: if anything—and I mean *anything*—comes within a hundred metres of this building, you take it down without hesitation, without question. Is that understood?"

"Yes, sir!" Without looking back at her squad, the Judge ordered them to follow her, and Gillen fell into step with them.

She risked a quick glance over at Judge Barron, but he was already involved in an intense conversation with another Judge, both of them pointing in different directions as each tried to get the other to agree.

There was no way she'd be able to escape via the roof, Gillen knew, but right now her only task was to stay alive, and sticking with this squad gave her the best chance of that... as long as they weren't too closely-knit.

She looked up at them as they thundered up another staircase. No talking, running in unison, no need for their leader to watch them or shepherd them. *Damn it, they're an established squad, not just a bunch of Judges who happened to be in the same location when the alarm sounded.*

They'll spot me as an outsider as soon as they pause long enough to take a breath.

Halfway to the roof Gillen spotted a young cadet nervously standing guard in front of a closed office door. She immediately broke away from her adopted squad and raced over to the cadet.

The boy stared at her with wide eyes and a nervous expression. Year eight, she realised. Thirteen years old. "Name!" Gillen barked.

"Lowry, sir! Instructed by Judge Wheeler to guard this office!"

"Is that so? Wheeler give you the order in person?"

Cadet Lowry shook his head. "No, sir. Via comm."

Gillen gave him a look of mistrust. "Don't move." She turned to the side and pretended to activate her helmet's radio. "Control, got a cadet loitering outside Judge Wheeler's office. Identified himself as Lowry. Patch me through to Wheeler,

ASAP." She gave the cadet a sidelong glance, and saw that he was looking straight ahead, his body rigid as he held his breath. "Wheeler? This is Thurber. Control relay the message? I... All right, yes, I get that you're busy. We're *all* busy—it's a goddamn *lockdown*—but you didn't follow protocol on this." Another pause. "Understood. I'll take care of it."

She turned back to the cadet. "Seems you're in the clear, Lowry. Good. But take that as a lesson: most of the time if there's something wrong, you're going to discover that the problem lies in the one part you thought you didn't need to check. Got that?"

The cadet nodded eagerly. "Yes, sir!"

"For example, take the door to Wheeler's office. Did you check that it's locked, or did you just *assume* that it is?"

Lowry's eyes grew wider.

Gillen glared at him. "Did you *check?*"

Silently and slowly, the cadet reached out and turned the door's handle. It clicked softly, and the door opened a fraction.

"You didn't check the *door*," Gillen said. "Which means...?"

Lowry dry-swallowed. "I... didn't check the office itself."

Gillen immediately drew her Lawgiver, held it out in front of her, left hand supporting her right wrist. Quietly, she said, "Step aside. Carefully."

As the cadet backed away, Gillen nudged the door with the toe of her boot.

The door swung open the rest of the way, and Gillen silently entered with her Lawgiver ready, swept the room and dramatically checked the corners and any other possible hiding place.

After a few seconds, she allowed the cadet to see her relax. "All clear." She put her gun away and beckoned him in. "Close the door behind you."

He approached meekly, and Gillen leaned against the window with her arms folded as she asked, "Who's your T.O.?"

"Judge Redshaw, sir," Lowry said. "We—"

Gillen put out a hand to cut him off. "No excuses, cadet. A good Judge *owns* their mistakes, they don't bury them." She glanced towards the terminal on Wheeler's desk. Like just about every system in the building, it would now be sealed from the mainframe. But there were ways around that.

"All right." She pressed her right hand tight against her side and took a few deep breaths before she told the cadet, "You screwed up. Happens to everyone. Next time, you'll know better, right?"

"Yes, sir."

A few more deep breaths, an attempt to suppress a wince of pain.

"Sir, are you all right?" Lowry asked.

"I'm fine!" Gillen snapped, then she sagged again. "Just... a shrapnel wound. Three weeks ago. Shredded my kidney, damn near signed my ticket right there and then. Assigned to light duties for the next few weeks." Another wince. "Just need to rest, get my strength back." Gillen forced herself to stand upright, a brave struggle against the pain. "No. Can't relax with a fugitive in the building. Have to stay alert."

Lowry said, "Sir, I've got this. I'll watch the door, you take a few minutes."

She smiled. "Watching my back. Maybe you've got the makings of a good Judge after all." She nodded towards the door. "Anyone tries to get past you, make a lot of noise."

As soon as the door closed behind Lowry, she activated the terminal and logged in with her fake Thurber identity. The patch she'd applied to the SJS's stealth monitoring software picked up her commands and automatically bypassed the system lockout, granting her full access to the Department's databases.

Her first command activated a worm program that rapidly trawled through the records and archives and swapped her

DNA profile with that of the fake Judge Roma Thurber. She also activated full records for Thurber: if anyone checked, they'd find that Thurber had a comprehensive judicial history complete with citations and commendations from a number of senior Judges.

A few more commands, and Thurber was now operating directly on the orders of the Chief Judge, and there was no way anyone lower than the Council of Five was going to question that. Right now, thanks to the lockdown, Goodman and the council would be sealed in their offices with all comms shut down and the doors guarded by badgeless Judges with no sense of humour and exceptionally sensitive triggers.

Then, aware that she'd be lighting up just about every alarm in the SJS's control room, she searched for Retired Judge James Hariton.

They'd be in a frenzy, she knew, trying to find her. But they weren't going to have any luck. She'd long since bypassed their bypasses. Her own software made sure that the terminal's signals were encrypted and filtered through seventeen different processors spread throughout the city. She knew that the techs would eventually unravel the Gordian spaghetti of false leads and masked signals, but when they did manage to track down the apparent source of her commands, they'd discover that it was all fed through a terminal powered by a hundred-year battery-pack, sealed into a steel barrel buried deep beneath the foundations of the Donnette Thayer School for the Unruly.

The report that came back was disappointing: a sparse summary of Hariton's career as a Judge, and details of his death: Found deceased on Kazinsky Sked, Sector Forty, 2082-04-29. C.O.D.: Heart failure. Dispatched to sector Resyk 2082-05-01. No known relatives. Personal assets claimed by the city to cover costs.

Nothing useful... Maybe there's nothing there because there's nothing to find. Lindfield just mentioned his name, his block

and the month his body was disposed of. Maybe Krause killed
Lindfield for some other reason.

No, Lindfield knew why they were there as soon as he saw
them. That's why he mentioned Hariton to me.

She pulled up Hariton's career record again.

2034. Graduated. Assigned to command of Senior Judge
Francesco Deacon. Served with distinction.

2042. Requested transfer to Special Ops. Request denied.
Reassigned to Boston East division.

2049. Declined promotion to Squad Leader.

2058. Reassigned to long-term security detail, Hall of Justice.

2062. Wounded in action. Retired with honours.

2070. Recalled to duty.

2072. Relieved of duty.

2082. Deceased, natural causes.

Gillen could see nothing unusual in Hariton's record, except
that he'd declined promotion to squad leader, but there could be
any number of reasons for that. Some Judges just preferred to
be on the streets. The call back to duty in 2070 was obviously
for the war against President Booth's forces. A lot of retired
Judges had been drafted, forced back into uniforms that no
longer fit them.

She closed down the files and keyed a command that would
trigger a report that she'd been spotted driving a stolen car
through Sector Two. That might loosen the knot here a little
while it was checked out.

She logged off the terminal and returned to the door. Cadet
Lowry spun around to face her as she emerged. "Appreciate
that, cadet." She looked around. "Any word on the fugitive?"

"Just heard that she's been seen in Sector Two."

"All right. Until that's confirmed, we act as though it's a false
lead. Stay put, Lowry." She began to move away, then turned
back to him. "And lock that door!"

She limped away, but once out of Lowry's sight she strode

quickly through the corridors, heading back towards the main staircase, walking with purpose in case anyone was watching.

If Hariton wanted to remain a street Judge, that doesn't line up with him requesting a transfer to Special Ops seven years earlier.

Unless that request wasn't *denied. What if it had been accepted?*

Two flights down, she brusquely excused her way past two slower-moving Judges and kept going.

Long-term security detail, Hall of Justice. That could mean anything. She conjured up a mental image of the hand-picked Judges even now guarding the Chief Judge. She knew all their names and faces: they were among the most thoroughly-vetted Judges in the department.

Is that what Hariton's job really entailed? If he had been a covert operative assigned to guard the Chief Judge... that would put him squarely on the SJS's radar.

Back in the main lobby, the lockdown was still in force. Gillen carried on down to the Lawmaster bay, flashed her badge and faked security pass to the same mechanic who'd taken in her bike half an hour earlier. His scanners registered her as Judge Thurber, showed that she was to be given full cooperation.

Within a minute Gillen was being guided through the dense high-security cordon on the street by the very Judges looking for her.

Eight

GILLEN PULLED UP the collar of her long coat and stepped out of the shelter of the store's awning to merge with the hunched, slightly scurrying crowd disembarking the crosstown hov that had just arrived from Sector Nine. They too pulled up their collars and donned their hats as they grumbled about the rain and cast mild curses on the city's weather control operatives.

Gillen had expected the rain. She'd checked the day's weather schedule and planned her journey accordingly: the city's public surveillance cameras were six per cent less efficient in rainy weather due to overcast conditions and water-drops on the lenses. Knock another eighteen per cent off because of all the umbrellas and wide-brimmed hats blocking the cameras' view, and a further three or four per cent because people walking in the rain tended to have their heads down. It all slightly reduced the chance that she'd be spotted.

The crowd helped too, as did her complete change of outfit. None of her colleagues had ever seen her in civilian clothes.

But she knew that, at best, she was delaying the inevitable. They *would* find her, and soon, if she didn't get off the streets.

By now her colleagues in the SJS would have traced her entire path through the Hall of Justice, and a lot of people would be in serious trouble. She felt a tinge of regret that the mechanic in the Lawmaster bay and Cadet Lowry would have to carry the stigma of abetting a fugitive for the rest of their careers, but it was their own fault. And a good lesson for the future: don't trust someone just because they carry themselves with authority.

One block to go to the safe house. *I can do this.*

Once there, she'd lie low until Dredd made contact. He wasn't the most imaginative investigator, but by Grud he was tenacious. He'd find something that would help them get to the bottom of this whole mess, whatever it was. Had Hariton been protecting a senior Judge and seen something he shouldn't? Mentioned it to Lindfield, maybe?

Ahead, outside the entrance to the safe-house, a Judge was arguing with a scrawny punk carrying a spike-embedded baseball bat that the punk was claiming was, "Like, *ornamental*, y'know? This ain't no weapon, jay-man, it goes with the ensemble!"

She slowed a little and feigned interest in the contents of a store window until the Judge's back was turned, then quickly strode up to the doorway and let herself in.

It was a comparatively small building, a block of high-rent apartments, with the penthouse taking up an entire floor: it had been the home of a perp currently serving eighteen for distribution of narcotics, and right now was the subject of a lengthy legal dispute between the perp's mother and brother, each claiming that they owned it, not the perp himself, therefore the Department of Justice didn't have the right to seize it as an asset.

As Gillen keyed in the passcode for the penthouse's private elevator, she figured that it wasn't the worst place in the world to hide out: top-of-the-range floatbed, immersive Tri-D entertainment system, a well-stocked walk-in freezer... and a state-of-the-art security system. If necessary, she could seal herself inside the apartment for months. It was a virtual fortress, with only one way in or out.

The elevator pinged and its door slid open, and the thought occurred to Gillen that a fortress and a prison were pretty much the same thing: it just depended on whether you wanted to be on the inside or the outside.

She glanced back along the hallway towards the entrance. That Judge on the street had had her worried for a second, but she was sure she'd slipped past him unnoticed.

She stopped with one foot in the elevator.

She knew that if you don't want the mark to suspect that their destination is under surveillance, then you make damn sure there's not a Judge visible within two blocks of the place. *Everyone* knew that.

So if the mark *does* see a Judge right outside the door, then they're going to assume that it's not being watched.

A double-bluff. They know I'm here.

She was already moving back towards the door, hand reaching inside her long coat to grab the hilt of her Lawgiver. She had seconds, at most.

She pulled open the door just as the Judge and the baseball-bat wielding cit—certainly a Judge wearing plain clothes—spun around to face her.

Gillen barely registered the approaching sirens as she threw herself forward, slamming the butt of her gun hard into the Judge's right arm. He was already crouching, reaching for his own Lawgiver, but Gillen had chosen her target well, a spot a few centimetres above the elbow where the radial nerve passed over the humerus.

His right arm temporarily numb, the Judge attempted to grab hold of Gillen with his left hand, but she'd anticipated that. She twisted away from him, putting him between herself and the scrawny punk now in the process of drawing back his bat, preparing to swing at her.

Gillen shoved the Judge into the punk, and at the same time fired a shot at the bat, shattering it. Another twist and spin, and she'd snatched the Judge's Lawgiver from his boot-holster.

Tyres skidded to a stop nearby, but she was already running, darting along the rain-slick sidewalk, dodging around the startled pedestrians. With every step, she expected a shot in the back.

Behind her, she was certain, a squad of SJS Judges would be streaming out of the block's other apartments. And ahead of her, and all around, every Public Surveillance camera would be homing in on her, Judges pulled from their duties to surround her, cage her in.

She took a sharp left onto Cedar Hill Road, and seconds later a Lawmaster screamed around the corner ahead, rode up onto the sidewalk and skidded to a stop four metres in front of her, with the Judge already reaching for the gun in his boot-holster.

But he'd made the mistake of stopping with his left side facing her. It would take an extra second to draw the gun and aim at her.

Gillen launched herself at him, slammed into his chest shoulder-first with enough force to knock him off the bike. They tumbled to the ground and the Judge's Lawgiver fell from his grip and skidded into the street.

A fist to the Judge's throat and a knee to his groin, then she was up and running, darting across the street.

But before she'd even reached the other side, three more Lawmasters screamed towards her, followed by at least a dozen Judges on foot, and to the north, zooming in low over the rooftops, a Justice Department H-Wagon.

"No way out, Gillen!" A man's voice called. SJS Judges ahead, street Judges behind, another four Lawmasters on the street.

She slowed to a stop, and dropped her gun. Turned to see Judge Krause pushing his way through the line of street Judges.

"You're done. On your knees, hands on your head, fingers interlaced."

She didn't move. "That's more of a warning than you gave Lindfield. You just put a round in his skull from ten metres away." She started to turn in a slow circle. At least fifteen Judges, seven Lawmasters, and that damned H-Wagon now hovering almost directly overhead.

"Lindfield was targetted for immediate termination." Krause stopped, his gun still aimed squarely at her face. "Won't tell you *again*, Gillen."

"So am I. But you *can't* terminate me until you find out how much I know. So, tell me what I did to raise your suspicions."

"Judge McKinney dropped the charge against us. We backtracked, saw that you met with him. You warned him off. Nothing unusual about that, except that he *heeded* that warning. We know McKinney: he doesn't back down without a damn good reason. You gave him that reason." Krause glanced at the other SJS Judges. "Take her in." To the rest of the Judges, he said, "All right, game over, fugitive's in custody. Return to your regular duties."

Reluctantly, the street Judges began to disperse. Gillen was sure that if she'd been an ordinary Judge, some of them would have resisted, taken her side. But they knew she was SJS, and it was a rare treat to see one of the enemy taken down by their own people.

Strong hands grabbed Gillen's arms from behind and she was pushed to her knees, her wrists cuffed. Krause leaned closer and said, "Public place. You understand, Gillen. You don't terminate a disarmed suspect in front of so many witnesses."

The last of the Lawmasters purred away, and now only the H-Wagon remained, hovering five metres above the street. Krause turned to one of his colleagues. "Kalles, get rid of the H."

Gillen looked up at the H-Wagon, then, hands still cuffed behind her back, wrenched her arms free of the Judges' grips and darted forward, out onto the street—just as the H-Wagon let loose with its riot-foam cannons. The thick foam struck the SJS Judges, blanketing the area.

The H-Wagon dropped down, its open ramp next to Gillen, a man already on the ramp with his left arm outstretched towards her. "Come on—let's go!"

Gillen jumped onto the ramp and the man grabbed her arm, and her stomach lurched as the H-Wagon abruptly rose into the air.

She glanced down at the SJS Judges struggling to free themselves from the already-solid riot foam, then back to her rescuer.

The red-haired man grinned at her. "A mutual friend heard that half the department is gunning for you. He figured you might appreciate some backup."

Nine

BACK WHEN JOE and Rico Dredd were cadets, a very senior Judge they'd never met before called them into her office and gave them a short lecture. "I've been reading up on you two, watching your progress, and it's clear that you've both developed this notion that the Department of Justice is a solid, dependable structure. Something that's always there, always right. Well, you're going to have to let go of *that* ridiculous idea. The Department is run by *people*, and people are imperfect. Even the best Judge in the world is gonna screw up sometimes. We're human. On our list of ingredients, 'mistakes' is right up there with calcium and nitrogen. You can't change that. But you *can* control how you react, how well you're prepared. Other Judges—bad Judges, or maybe just misguided—are gonna try to take you down. So you've always got to have a getaway plan. Or at least an alibi. I know you two think you're too good to ever need anyone else, but that's just arrogant and narrow-minded."

Rico had said, "Joe and I have got each other's backs, ma'am."

"That's not enough. What if you're not assigned to the same sector? So you've got to make friends, because there *will* come a time when you'll need them. You'll need to find Judges—and civilians—that you can trust with your lives. People who in turn know that they can trust you to be there for them."

Since his graduation, Dredd had acquired very few new friends, and he knew that was a failing, a product of his detachment. He'd always found it hard to make that sort of connection with others.

Rico had never had that problem. Even now, after everything Rico had done, he still had more friends in the Department than Joe.

Now, Dredd steered his Lawmaster across the sector towards the Judges-only access tunnel of the subzoom network.

The access tunnel took him down to a network of two-metre-wide circular tunnels that ran in parallel to many of the subzoom train lines. The initial idea had been that they would provide the Judges with quick, unfettered access to any part of the city, which would be especially useful at rush hour or when the streets were otherwise congested. In reality, the Judges quickly discovered that getting into and out of the shafts took far too long, and that their depth and the steel reinforcements in the walls played havoc with radio signals. The tunnels soon fell into disuse, and in the years since, many of them had been taken over by the 'transits,' the hundreds of homeless citizens who'd taken to living in the subways and were now spreading out into the often cavernous regions beneath the city.

Dredd knew which tunnels were still clear, and relatively easy to access, and had long ago calculated the ideal location for what he was about to do: a junction deep beneath Sector Nine where fourteen access shafts met. As soon as he reached the junction, Dredd slowed his bike to a stop, then took a small, non-regulation communicator from his utility belt. Down here, at the nexus of the fourteen shafts with their countless metal conduits and rails and water-pipes and arm-thick bundles of electric and fibre-optic cabling, any broadcast signal that was strong enough to make it out into the city and beyond would be absolutely impossible to trace.

He adjusted the communicator's band, then thumbed the activation switch. "You there?"

"*I'm here,*" Red O'Donnell's voice replied. "*We've got the package, safe and sound. But... for this, they're gonna come down on us like all the tonnes of all the bricks ever.*"

"I know. But they can't easily track your craft with the dampers installed, so you've got time to get the package out of the city."

"*What about you? She's been asking if you've made any progress.*"

"A little. But I've still got some stones to turn over."

"*Gotcha,*" Red said. "*No trail ever runs truly cold, right?*"

"Of course they do," Dredd said.

A laugh, then, "*A ten-spot says you're scowling into the commlink right now. Am I right? You're predictable. Thought that wasn't a good trait for someone with your job.*"

"Just tell her I want to speak with her."

In the year since Dredd and Brian O'Donnell—nicknamed Red—met on a flight to the Cursed Earth, O'Donnell had sporadically kept in touch. Or he'd *tried* to: a couple of phone messages and e-mails to which Dredd hadn't responded. Judge Montag, who'd been with them when they met, told Dredd, "He's just trying to be friendly. Judges *are* allowed to have friends, you know."

He knew she was right. Judges did sometimes have social lives, but it just seemed strange to voluntarily associate with civilians. It almost seemed counter-productive. The citizens needed to be wary of the Judges, not get comfortable around them.

But Red O'Donnell had told him, on several occasions, "I owe you, Joe. You ever need me, give me a call."

Immediately after Dredd's meeting with Gillen, he had

contacted Red via an unregistered cellphone, and patched the call directly into his Lawmaster's screen. "This is Dredd. I need a pilot."

Red grinned out at him from the screen. "*So you figured you'd come to the best in the business. Good man, Joe!*"

"You're hardly the best, but you're adequate, and I think I can trust you to be discreet. I *hope* I can."

"*Off the books and under the radar, then? Not like you. You've always been a square peg in a square hole. Something must be fierce stinky if you're—*"

Dredd scowled. "Can you help or not?"

"*I've been fine, thanks. Arm's still not back to full strength, and I'm starting to think that it might never be. But I can still fly a plane or a shuttle. Anything, really.*"

"How about a Justice Department H-Wagon?"

O'Donnell's grin grew wider. "*Well now. That's interesting. Setting aside the question of where someone like me would get hold of something like that, I'm going to have to ask* why. *And* when."

"I need a job done, and it is, as you say, off the books. And I need it done *now*. Could take some time to play out."

"*I'll have to get someone to cover my workload... But, yeah, count me in.*"

"Red, I feel obliged to warn you that it's risky. Very risky."

Red shrugged. "*No one lives forever. Tell me everything.*"

The Department of Justice was a well-oiled machine. Things worked because protocols were followed. Out in the civilian world, everything was inefficient and often ineffective. The work itself, whatever its nature, always played second fiddle to the workers' schedules and egos. But anyone working for the Department of Justice was expected to do the job to the best of their abilities, on time and if possible under budget, without complaint or error. The protocols saw to that. There were rules and guidelines for every aspect of every job.

Even when he'd been in the Academy, Dredd had compulsively studied the Department's protocol manuals and guidelines.

In his teenage years, while the other cadets used their downtime to study popular culture—if you're going to police a society it helps to understand the needs, whims and desires of that society—Dredd instead wrote a thesis explaining how to improve Lawmaster patrol efficiency by over two per cent. He followed that with a series of articles that linked Mega-City One population distribution with crime levels, and concluded that overcrowding and overpopulation had a greater impact on the creation of slums than crime or poverty. He carefully analysed the aerial patrol routes and proposed a list of fourteen major route changes that would, he claimed, increase efficiency by almost six per cent.

Dredd later learned that his supervisors at the Academy had carefully studied all of his reports, analysing them for key words and phrases that might suggest a possible danger, but their overriding conclusion was that the reports were factually correct and universally dull. As he'd suspected, they were filed away and never passed on to the appropriate sub-divisions.

But he still retained much of the information he'd gathered, and he'd kept it up to date. He knew how many Hover-Wagons the Aerial Division possessed—four hundred—and on average how many of them were in the air at any given time. That was less than seventy: the failure rate on the H-Wagons' tiny but powerful anti-grav motors was extremely high, and each H-Wagon required at least ten functioning AG motors to operate efficiently.

Dredd knew that off-line H-Wagons were stored in compounds scattered throughout the city. He also knew that the compound in Sector 173 was poorly guarded, mostly because it was on the roof of Brian Cox The Actor Not The Scientist Block, and not easy to reach.

With the bypass codes Dredd had provided, and a fake

security pass, Red O'Donnell had been able to walk into the compound manager's office and, less than ten minutes later, fly away in a purloined H-Wagon.

Dredd could have asked a fellow Judge to do it, but there was no way to be absolutely certain that they hadn't been compromised. Any Judge could turn out to be working for the SJS. He'd even been accused of that himself several times, once by Judge Adam Kimber. And now Kimber was looking for Dredd's backing as he put himself forward for Sector Chief.

"You're too good to be true," Judge Amber Ruiz had told him back in his first year on the streets. "The goody-two-shoes boy scout approach... no one buys it. Not until they meet you, anyway. They just can't believe that a real person could just sacrifice so much of themselves for the job. And it *is* a job, Dredd, not a life. You're not meant to be a law machine. If you judge people without understanding them, there's no way you can have the compassion and empathy you'll need to be fair. Sometimes the perp really *does* need money to buy medicine for his sick mother. Sometimes putting her abusive partner in the ground *is* the only way a woman can find some kind of peace. The letter of the Law must always be subservient to its *spirit*."

Dredd understood that. He was a little uncertain as to why so many older Judges always felt the need to lecture him, but he was aware of his shortcomings. Make friends. Be nice. Have empathy. Smile from time to time.

Now, as he left the access tunnels and sped across the city towards Sector Five, he was even more aware of the need for friends. Growing up in the Academy, he'd had Rico, and Rico had had other friends—Gibson, Wagner, Hunt, Ellard and the rest of their class—so they became Joe's friends too, by proxy, but with Rico gone, those relationships had begun to unravel. Gibson was about the only one left who kept in touch.

Gibson didn't seem the type of Judge who'd have been secretly recruited by the Special Judicial Squad. He was a good Judge, but a little reckless and smug. And maybe he was even a little lost now that Rico was gone, Dredd thought. But definitely not SJS material.

Unless that was exactly what the SJS *wanted* people to think. If they were smart, they'd pick the Judges least likely to be suspected. Certainly, Gibson did at times seem almost secretive. Judges are allowed to have private lives, after a fashion, but there were a few quiet moments—when Gibson thought he wasn't being watching—when Dredd had seen his ever-present smile fade into a scowl. Moments like that were of concern. It probably didn't have anything to do with the SJS, but Dredd reasoned that if Gibson *was* hiding something that he felt he couldn't share with Dredd, then it would be a bad idea to trust him with this.

Whatever 'this' was.

On the surface, the data Gillen had culled from Judge Hariton's records was close to useless. But if he *had* been sequestered to a covert division, that might explain a lot. Hariton applies to Special Ops, they look into his records, realise that he's ideal material for something else, and officially deny the application. Then shortly afterwards he's reassigned to Boston East.

So what had been in Boston back in 2042? Or *who*?

There had been an Academy of Law, one of the first, and the city had also been the home of several prominent Judges. The established colleges were important: as the old police forces disintegrated, the colleges had appealed for Judges to patrol their campuses, even to the point of offering free classes for cadets. But everything free comes with a price. The Judges discovered that in those classes the cadets were being heavily encouraged to embrace the college spirit of comradeship, because somewhere down the road, they might have to choose between arresting an ordinary citizen or a fellow alumnus.

Of course, that had been one of the problems that the Judges had been created to redress: the ingrained idea that some people had a right to preferential treatment because of their school, their heritage, their genetic background, their bank-balance.

Boston had been among the wealthiest cities in the USA, which was one of the reasons the Academy had been founded there. The site and buildings were donated by the ultra-rich—and very-right-wing—Kederlander family. The family patriarch, Nelson Kederlander, had been furious with Chief Judge Fargo when he discovered that the new breed of law enforcers weren't going to be bribeable. Not his exact words, but very much his intent. In a public argument in the sort of surf-n-turf chain restaurant that Kederlander would own but never patronise, he confronted Fargo after one of his nephews had been arrested. Fargo told him, "We judge the people on how they *behave*, not on how much they own." Kederlander had protested, implying strongly that his donation of land and buildings—valued at over two hundred million dollars, he pointed out several times—should buy him and his family some measure of "breathing room." Fargo's response, captured on camera and uploaded to social media sites within seconds, became one of his more famous quotes: "Plenty of breathing room in an eight-by-ten."

The Academy itself had had more than its share of scandals, too. Back then, in the early days, the Judges were drawn from all walks of life. Anyone could apply, regardless of their experience in law enforcement. Most were weeded out immediately: anyone with a prior record or a dependent family was scrutinised particularly closely. Likewise anyone joining because they thought it might be a steady job, or because they "wanted to knock some sense into the world."

The applications were abundant, but the filtering process was stringent, and thorough. But not thorough enough. Some bad Judges got through. *Weak Judges, too*, Dredd told himself. That was almost worse in his eyes.

* * *

IT WAS LATE afternoon when the elevated sked took him across Sector Five, and then down towards his destination. He moved towards the off-ramp, aware that if anyone had been closely monitoring the Department of Justice's archives facility on the far side of the sector, then this investigation was already over..

Back on the ground level, Dredd rode east to the coast, to the Radium Beach, a four-kilometre-long stretch of grey-sanded, poisoned shoreline that had once been a popular tourist spot. Now, it was a graveyard to the radioactive, rotting carcasses of mutated whales and other sea-life, and dozens of slowly disintegrating ships, most notably the run-aground wreck of the *Balachandran Beauty*, a former giant luxury yacht that had been commandeered by the Judges during the war. Swarms of bullet-holes peppered the giant vessel's charred, rusting hull, punctuated by much larger shell-holes and missing panels. The yacht's owner was still complaining that she had never been compensated by the Department of Justice.

He stopped his Lawmaster on the damp sand close to the yacht, but still a good distance from the edge of the water: its thick, too-white foam was corrosive to even the strongest synthetic rubber, and he doubted the Lawmaster's tyres would last more than a few minutes. As it was, the pollutants in the sand itself weren't doing his tyres—or his boots—any favours. He briefly glanced back at the tracks in the sand made by the Lawmaster's wide tyres, almost expecting to see a trail of rubber fragments. There were no other tracks: his contact probably parked a safe distance away and kept close to the waterline as he walked, allowing the waves to erase his footprints.

As he approached the largest hole in the side of the wreck, a man's voice came from within. "Figure that's *you*, Joe."

"Who else would it be?" Dredd called back.

The Judge stepped out of the shadows and smiled at him. "Yeah, that's you. I got what you were looking for."

Dredd nodded. "Didn't doubt it, Hunt. Any problems?"

"None that have shown up so far." Dredd's former classmate Casey Hunt had requested to hang up his badge less than a year after graduating. Hunt had been close to Judge Ellard, who'd been crushed by a stolen truck, and Hunt had taken it hard. He'd lost his nerve. Dredd mostly understood that; every Judge gets a crisis of confidence at some point. But you're supposed to get past that, not succumb to it. Hunt's senior officers had persuaded him to stay in the Department, but in a non-combative capacity. Everyone involved had repeated that there was no shame in that so often that some of them had almost believed it.

Now, Hunt worked for the Justice Department's archive facility, where all physical evidence not connected to a current case was stored, along with the effects of deceased Judges and all other items deemed to be of importance. It was a safe job, quiet, no interaction with the public. It suited him.

Hunt reached down and grabbed Dredd's arm, helping him up into the yacht. "Heard about Rico. Sorry, man, that has to be tough."

"Tougher that none of us saw it coming," Dredd said.

"Maybe we *should* have seen it coming. He was always wild. Compared to you, anyway. Still, twenty years on *Titan*... You think he's going to make it?"

"He'll make it." Dredd looked around at the oversized yacht's interior. Light streaming through holes in the hull and ceiling showed a once-grand structure of rusting, peeling panels now sprayed with crude graffiti, buckled framework and split conduits, and charred patches on the floor that were the ghosts of long-dead bonfires. Scattered throughout, stretching out into the darkness towards the rear of the hull, stood barely recognisable fragments of discarded furniture, old wooden and plastic crates, coils of mildewed rope and thick chains that had corroded almost into paste. Everything glistened with moisture, the steel floor dotted with rainbow-hued, oily puddles. Fat insects circled through air heavy with the stench of brine, decaying seaweed, decades-old garbage, and the ever-present stinging, chemical odour of the Black Atlantic. Taking only shallow breaths, Dredd asked Hunt, "So what did you find?"

Hunt retrieved a small canvas bag from beneath a torn, warped scrap of hull-plating. "James Hariton's surviving effects." As he handed it to Dredd, he said, "Everything else was sold to cover costs. You know how it goes."

Dredd reached into the bag and withdrew a palm-sized, round silver badge. "That's all?"

"That's it. Hariton's Judge badge from the old days," Hunt said. "It's pretty beat-up, but that's no surprise; it's the very first one he was issued. They were supposed to hand them in when the new badges were released, but some of the original Judges claimed that they'd"—he made air-quotes with his fingers—"*lost* them. Souvenirs, I guess."

Dredd turned the badge over. Its reverse side featured its serial number and the usual two contact points for the magnets used to fix it to the Judges' uniform. "Huh. Almost missed that."

"Missed what?" Hunt asked.

"Clearly you *did* miss it." Dredd held the badge up to the light, and tilted it back and forth a little. "Piece of metal foil tape on the back. Almost perfectly matches the badge's metal. And there's something underneath it." He pulled off his right glove and started picking at one corner of the tape with his thumbnail. "Adhesive's almost solid—this was stuck down a long time ago."

Hunt reached out for the badge. "Let me do it. Your meaty sausage-fingers don't have the finesse."

Dredd pulled the badge back. "I've got it..." He managed to free the corner, then peeled the rest of the tape back.

Stuck to the underside of the tape were an old copper penny and a grey plastic six-pointed star about the same size.

"Souvenirs," Hunt said. "We've all got them. Little mementos. I've got two bullets in my quarters. The first one I ever fired on the job, and the first one that was ever fired at me. And Gibson still has a little rock from that time we were in the Cursed Earth. Remember that, Joe?"

"Penny's dated 1974. Abraham Lincoln on this side. Must mean something."

"Lincoln freed the slaves, right?" Hunt asked. "Tall guy, big hat, beard but no moustache. Assassinated at the movie theatre."

"It was a play," Dredd said, peeling the coin away from the metal tape. "Lincoln Memorial on the back. *E Pluribus Unum*. Latin. 'Out of many, one.'"

"Yeah, I never really understood that," Hunt said.

"In this context it refers to the United States. Many states coming together to make one nation." Dredd peeled the plastic star away from the tape and held it up to the light. Embossed on the other side was the word *Sheriff*.

"I'd say that came from a cowboy action figure," Hunt said. "So what's this *about*, Joe?"

"You don't want to know."

"It's just... You haven't *changed*, you know? You only get in touch with people when you want something. I wouldn't mind so much if this was an official case, but it's not. This is something *personal*, isn't it?"

Dredd dropped the badge, star and coin back into the canvas bag, tucked it into a spare belt-pouch. "We're done here, Hunt. Appreciate your help, and your discretion. Anyone asks, you didn't see me and you were never here."

Hunt nodded. "All right. But come tell me when this is all over, right?"

"If I'm not dead." Dredd jumped down onto the beach, and strode back towards his Lawmaster. "Be seeing you, Hunt."

Dredd didn't know what the coin meant, if it meant anything

at all, but he had a strong hunch that the sheriff's star was relevant.

He knew where he had to go next.

Ten

SJS Judge Marion Gillen paced back and forth outside the stolen H-Wagon, kicking up dust and occasionally pausing to look back at O'Donnell. He was still watching her, sitting on the wagon's ramp with his legs swinging as he ate a banana, peanut-butter and raisin sandwich.

She reached over her shoulder and scratched at her neck. She was almost certain that she wasn't the only living thing currently occupying these second-hand clothes. Grud only knew where O'Donnell had picked them up. The boots were too large, the pants were missing buttons and fasteners, the jacket was too small and carried a strong scent of bleach and melted plastic. And whatever fabric the hand-sewn T-shirt had been cut from was, somehow, almost *crispy*. Now her upper arm itched, too.

He'd instructed her to ditch the clothes she'd been wearing when they left Mega-City One and all of her equipment—dropped into a rad-pit outside Mega-City One—but he'd agreed she could keep her Lawgiver, once she'd completely disassembled it and checked it for tracking devices.

"How many times—?" O'Donnell began.

Gillen finally stopped walking and turned to face him. "How many times what?"

"How many times, do you suppose, in the entire history of the human race, has *fretting* produced a measurably improved outcome? Relax, Judge. Worry is self-administered poison; if you've got a problem and you worry about it, then you've got *two* things to deal with. So chill. Sit down, have something to eat. Take a nap, maybe."

"They'll find us."

"They'll *look* for us, sure, but the Cursed Earth is a big place and they don't know where to start. I disabled the wagon's GPS and all the other trackers just like Dredd told me. And we *want* them looking for us out here; it'll take the focus away from the city, give Dredd a bit more elbow room to do his thing. I know you're worried about him, too, but he can handle himself, I reckon. He'll not stop digging until he gets the answer, even if he has to make shovels out of skulls to do it." O'Donnell frowned at that. "Okay, not a very *nice* analogy, but the point is, Dredd's your man if you want something done. We saw that back in Ezekiel. If it hadn't been for him, a lot of people would have died, me included. And he did all that with *you* dogging him, trying to prove he was corrupt. The man's a genuine hero, you know that."

"You sound like you're in love with him, O'Donnell."

He shrugged. "Could you blame me if I was? Who could resist that cuddly nature and warm personality? No, Dredd risked his neck for us—for *all* of us, including a bunch of muties, and I've not met many norms who'd do that—and I know he'd do it again in a heartbeat." O'Donnell stuffed the last of his sandwich into his mouth and mumbled something else as he got to his feet.

"Can you repeat that?" Gillen asked as she approached the H-Wagon's ramp. "I don't speak *vulgar*."

Standing in the H-Wagon's hatchway, O'Donnell laughed around his mouthful, and managed to say, "Good one."

"My mother used to say that to us when we..." She stopped. "*That's* going back a few years."

"She dead, yeah?"

"Yes, as a matter of fact. RTA, when I was seven."

"That sucks. So you were already in the Academy of Law when it happened?"

Gillen stepped onto the ramp and felt proud of herself for not punching Red O'Donnell so hard in the face that his jaw would be on backwards. "A lot of people would express sympathy."

"I said it sucked. And you do have my sympathies. My own folks are gone, too. I'm now the age my dad was when he died. And you know what? No one warned me about how hard *that* was going to hit me." He looked up to the sky. "If you're up there, Dad, send me a sign. And money. Mainly money."

Gillen pushed past him into the H-Wagon, dropped into the co-pilot's seat. "You disable the pingback circuit, O'Donnell?"

"The what now?" O'Donnell stepped into the cockpit.

"Then you didn't. If we activate the radio, even just to listen, it'll send a coded signal to the Department letting them know that this H-Wagon is active. That won't help them locate us, but they'll know for sure that we're out here somewhere."

"Oh, *that's* why Joe kept saying not to use the radio." He pulled his commlink from his pocket. "If he needs us, this is how he'll get in touch."

She looked up at him for a few seconds. "O'Donnell, did Dredd explain to you how dangerous this is? Going up against the Judges is reckless; going against the SJS is *suicide*. They pick only the best of the best to join their ranks."

"Meaning you. But not Joe Dredd."

"He was *asked*."

"And he turned it down because...?"

"Because he said that the Judges exist to serve the people, not rule them, and likewise the SJS exists to serve the Judges."

O'Donnell laughed again. "I bet they loved *that*. I see his point, though. The sheepdog *thinks* she's in charge of the sheep because she tells them where to go, but without the sheep there'd be no need for the dog."

"If we're going by *that* analogy... who's the shepherd?"

STANDING BY THE window in his office, Clarence Goodman turned to face the door as it hissed open and suddenly became aware—for the first time—that whenever he met Joe Dredd, he automatically squared his shoulders and sucked in his gut. *What the hell am I* doing? he asked himself. *I'm the grud-damned Chief Judge of Mega-City One! Hundreds of millions of people rely on me to do my job, and I'm concerned with making a good impression on a Judge who's barely out of the Academy!*

"Chief Judge. Thank you for making the time to see me."

"Dredd. I'm a busy man, so make this short."

"You told me, more than once, that I could come to you with any problem."

"And here you are," Goodman said. He walked over to his desk and pulled out his chair. "Choosing to exercise that privilege—and it *is* a privilege, not a right—on the same day we've got half the Department trying to track down a rogue SJS Judge. Good timing, Joe." He lowered himself into the chair and added, "I'd invite you to sit, but I know you won't because you never do. You'd want to watch that—Judges shouldn't be creatures of habit. Your enemies will look for patterns in your behaviour; don't give them any."

"Acknowledged. Thank you, sir."

"What can I do for you, Joe?"

"It's an old case. Something about it bothered me, but I can't check up on it because everything is redacted and locked away. Back during Booth's war—"

Goodman raised a palm. "I'll stop you there. Redacted info is redacted for a reason."

"It's not that. A few months ago I called on a perp—a civilian—on a noise-pollution charge. Playing her music too loud in the evenings. She claimed some hearing loss from her time in the war, and then said she deserved immunity from prosecution because, according to her, she'd been a covert operative working for the Department. I had no reason to believe her, and there was no way to check. I issued her with a fine and a warning for disturbing the peace, forgot about it until the reports today about SJS Gillen. That got me thinking…"

Goodman nodded. "If the files are sealed, how would you find out whether that civilian *was* telling the truth? I've been there. You're reluctant to go digging, because that puts a target on your head and the SJS are pretty riled up as it is. I get that. Judge Barradien was ready to *strangle* someone when he learned that Gillen had escaped. Still don't know exactly how she did it." The Chief Judge sat back in his chair. "I don't know what to tell you, son. Sometimes you just have to let things go. Covert operatives… they're the bane of the department, but also the *blood* in a lot of ways. I know *you've* been approached by at least four different divisions."

"Eight, so far," Dredd said. "Five of them more than once."

"Never been tempted?"

"No, sir. My job is on the streets."

Goodman thumped the arm of his chair and said, "If you ever want to sit here and wear this uniform, it'll help to have some other experiences. A few years in a covert division could go a long way towards smoothing the path."

"No offence, sir, but that chair's not for me."

Goodman wasn't sure how to respond to that, even though Dredd had expressed similar sentiments before. One of the goals of the Judge Clone project had been that one day one of them *would* become Chief Judge. "We'll see. I'm still going to keep your name on my list of possible successors."

"Sir, if my suspect was never a Judge, *could* she have been drafted onto a covert squad?"

"Oh, she could. Civilians with particular skills or experience were sometimes drafted back in the old days. Or deputised, as we liked to call it. But there were a few who'd claim, not unfairly, that they were press-ganged. And during the war, when Booth's people were getting a little too close, I was taken to a bunker along with the surviving council members. There were already others there—*important* people, I was told—and some of them were protected by squads made up of Judges, mercenaries and civilians. It still happens, from time to time."

"And you knew they were civilians because...?"

"Because I *asked*. When I'm locked in a bunker with dozens of armed people, I want to know who they are. And likewise, the others asked me who *my* people were. In war, suspicion might be the only thing that keeps you alive, but, paradoxically, you also have to absolutely trust the people protecting you."

"Understood, sir."

"I seem to recall you and Rico doing the same job, even though you were only cadets."

Dredd nodded, and Goodman let it go there. They both knew what he was referring to, no need to get into specifics. Even the highest office in the city can be bugged.

"And the others in the bunker, sir? If I were to approach them, would they be able to confirm the identity of my civilian?"

Goodman glanced towards the monitors on his desk. Of all the days for Dredd to come to him with this. "Yeah, they might, if you knew who those people were... and I'm not about to tell you. You do know the definition of 'covert,' don't you?" On the largest of his screens, a scrolling feed from the Special Judicial Squad's servers showed that there was still no sign of the rogue Judge. "This is a lot of trouble to go to for a cit who's been playing her music too loud, isn't it?"

Calmly, Dredd said, "*Nothing* is too much trouble when the truth is in question."

Goodman knew then that this was not what it seemed. He glanced back at Dredd, but the man's face was locked in his usual scowl. 'Resting Dredd Face,' some of the senior Judges called it.

He picked up the antique fountain pen from his desk and scrawled a quick note on the corner of a sheet of paper, then stood and walked over to the window once more. "Dredd, we follow the rules that we make for ourselves as well as for the citizens. Keep them alive, that's the goal. That's our sole reason for existence. If that means we have to *break* some rules, now and then, then we prioritise the people."

"The greater good, sir?"

"Exactly." Goodman turned his back on the room, and stared out the window. "The greater good. The difficulty lies in determining the criteria that will tell you whether one good is greater or lesser than another." He couldn't see Dredd from this angle, but hoped that he was looking at the name he'd written down. "Is that *all*, Dredd? I've a city to run here."

"Yes, sir. Thank you. I'll see myself out."

THIRTY METRES FROM the Chief Judge's office, Dredd heard someone call his name, and turned to see SJS Judge McComber beckoning to him from his own office across the corridor.

Kenneth McComber was a tall man with a heavy build who looked as though he had an allergy to stairs and four asthma inhalers secreted around his body at any given time. His hair was too black to be natural, his face jowly and heavy. He put Dredd in mind of an actor who didn't want to admit that his best days were in the past. In truth, McComber was as healthy as any forty-year-old Dredd had ever encountered. "You've been to see the old man?"

"If you mean Chief Judge Goodman, yes," Dredd said.

"Any reason?"

"Of course. I wouldn't bother him for no reason."

McComber regarded him with a level expression. "Do you know the meaning of the word 'stoic,' Dredd?"

"Yes."

McComber's posture stiffened for a moment. "Right. SJS Marion Gillen has gone missing, and we have *you* down on her list of potential enemies."

Dredd chose not to respond to that. If you waited long enough, people often grew impatient and told you what they wanted to hear.

"*You* have anything to do with her disappearance?"

"No. But that's the answer I'd give you regardless of the truth. You should know that, Judge McComber. And I heard that Gillen went rogue. That's not the same thing as missing."

"Same outcome. We can't find her." McComber crossed his arms. "She went after *you* pretty hard last year. She was convinced you were on the same path as your brother. And now she's missing."

"I don't see the correlation, sir. You might as well have said, 'Gillen had oatmeal for breakfast yesterday, and now she's missing.' Yes, she believed that I was corrupt. And I proved her wrong. End of the matter. Vengeance is not my style."

"You're *young*, Dredd. We've yet to reach the point where we can predict what your style is going to be." McComber nodded towards Goodman's office. "Professional boot-licker, maybe? Or will you be a hard-as-nails, take-no-prisoners kind of Judge, all kicking-in doors and squeezing the suspects until they squeak? Maybe you'll develop a softer approach, in the hope that your respect for the citizens will be reciprocated. Or it could be that you'll be unremarkable, that you'll potter away with a handful of arrests per day, nothing special, then one day you'll take a few rounds to the chest and that'll be that. A trip to Resyk and your badge on a wall that'll last only until the wall needs to be demolished to make room for something else."

He smiled. "Or you could take up the offer Gillen made to you a couple of years ago. You come work for us. Make a *real* difference. With Gillen gone, there's an opening."

"She's only been gone for a day, Judge McComber."

"You think she's coming back after this?"

"I don't even know what this *is*. All I know is that there was a report that Gillen is wanted for crimes against the city, and that you've put a termination order on her."

"So if you see her, you'll shoot her?"

"I won't do your dirty work, McComber. The SJS are the janitors of the Justice Department. You keep the place clean for us."

The Judge stepped back, shaking his head, "You really are an *arrogant* piece of work, aren't you? Just like him. Fargo, I mean. You're cut from the same rigid cloth."

"That was the point of cloning him. If we're done here, I have a patrol to get back to."

"Right. We'll talk again, Dredd. And in the meantime, I'll be watching you."

"I hope so. That's your *job*."

AFTER DREDD RETRIEVED his Lawmaster—the mechanics in the Lawmaster bay were intrigued by the corrosion damage to its tyres, but knew better than to ask questions—he returned to the streets, and put his bike onto an automatic patrol route before activating his helmet radio. "Dredd to Control."

"*Reading you, Dredd.*"

"Tracking a perp. Word is he's gone to ground. Need you to confirm that for me. Name's Stanley Maclean Blair Santori. Possibly a fake name. Sector Twenty-Three."

"*Stand by... Sorry, Dredd, I'm not seeing anyone resembling that name in Sector Twenty-Three. I'll... hold on, got some partial matches. Closest is Stamford Blane Santon. Male,*"

Caucasian, sixty-eight years old. Apartment 6, Babel Towers, Sector Seventy."

"No, that's not my perp. Clearly my informant lied—more scared of the perp than he was of me. I'll deal with it. Dredd out."

Dredd regained manual control of his bike and steered towards the northbound sked that would take him to Sector Seventy, to meet the man whose name Chief Judge Goodman had written for him.

Goodman had indeed written *Stamford Blane Santon*, but Dredd figured that if the operator in Control had entered that name into the citizen database, it might have been flagged. And if a name *didn't* exist on the database, the system automatically returned a list of names that only partially matched the search criteria. It seemed less likely that anyone who'd piggybacked onto the system would be checking partial matches.

He couldn't have told Goodman what was going on, or even that there *was* something going on. Aside from the need for the Chief Judge to have deniability, it was possible that he was involved. More likely, getting him involved would put him in danger.

But Goodman had been a Judge too, back in the day. He understood the rules, and that sometimes those rules had to be rewritten. His look as he dismissed Dredd said, *Don't screw this up*. And maybe there was also a touch of *Don't get yourself killed* in there too.

All of the subterfuge could turn out to be moot, Dredd knew, if the SJS were monitoring him closely. Or whoever was behind all this: it would be short-sighted to assume that the buck stopped with the SJS.

Every Judge on the streets knew that any moment could be their last, and Dredd had never been more aware of that than he was now.

Eleven

GILLEN HIT THE floor face-first and then woke up to find herself sliding towards the rear of the H-Wagon.

She reached for and missed the edge of the craft's pull-down cot, then scrabbled at the juddering floor, trying to grab hold of something secure. Her stomach suddenly wrenched as though she were about to throw up, but without the nausea. It was a sensation she'd only experienced once before, and that was one time too many: a failing anti-grav motor.

Her left hand snagged a support post as she became aware of the noise: the H-Wagon's engines screaming and sputtering, Red O'Donnell in the cockpit yelling a string of swear words, and the worrying rattle of large-calibre ordnance slamming into the hull's armoured plating.

"Gillen! Get up here!" O'Donnell screamed.

She pushed herself to her knees just as another sudden lurch hit the ship and her weight seemed to double.

"We've overloaded three of our AG motors already!"

Gillen grabbed hold of the back of O'Donnell's chair. "I guessed." She looked over his shoulder and scanned the control panel. Half of the displays were dead, the others were flickering violently. Through the windscreen, she could just about see the dark landscape streaming past, illuminated briefly by dull flashes moments before another volley of shots rattled the H-Wagon's hull.

She strapped herself into the co-pilot's seat. "Altitude twelve hundred metres... eleven-fifty..."

"I know, I know! I'm levelling off... Hold tight." The craft lurched to the left, then took a sharp right. "Drokkers are still on our tail. I'm almost blind here—my radar's down. What's yours say?"

She glanced at the radar screen. White text on the bright blue background: *Radar Display version 3.03(d) has encountered an error and is about to attempt recovery. Would you like to display the error message, transmit it to MegaRadarTech Support Services, or restart?* Gillen stabbed at the 'Restart' button. "Gonna take a few minutes."

"Then we're seat-pantsing this until it's back up. I figure there's *two* H-Wagons out there, and now that they've spotted us, there'll be more on the way. Gillen, our weapons are offline, and even if they weren't, I don't much like the idea of firing at Judges, even when they're trying to blow us out of the sky. Call me superstitious, but where I come from we believe that killing a Judge will bring bad luck." He quickly glanced at her. "Your call."

They're only following orders, Gillen told herself. *If Molina had told me to take down another SJS Judge, would I do it?*

Another flash outside, illuminating the barren landscape, and the H-Wagon rocked as another volley slammed into its hull.

"Gillen... Make a decision! Do we fight back, or try to run? You'll notice that 'Surrender' is not an option there, because they're not offering it."

Would I shoot down another SJS Judge without questioning the order?

No, I wouldn't. "Try not to kill them, Red, but... Do what you have to do."

"Got it. But... it's *you* who has to do it. Like I said, our weapons are offline." Another quick glance at her. "You've still got your Lawgiver: open the starboard hatch and give them some Law."

"You want me to shoot down two H-Wagons with a *handgun?*"

"I don't *want* you to, but we don't have a lot of other options. You've got armour-piercing, incendiary and hi-ex rounds. Five or six AP rounds in the same spot might just be enough to penetrate cockpit glass. If that works, then you—Drokk! *Hang on!*"

Gillen's stomach lurched again as O'Donnell abruptly pitched the nose of the H-Wagon down and then pulled up again: they watched twin volleys of red-hot armour-piercing rounds streak overhead, missing them by not more than two metres.

"If that works," O'Donnell resumed, his voice calm, "if you *can* punch a hole through the glass, then you put a hi-ex or incendiary round through that hole."

She glanced at him: his red hair was plastered to his forehead with sweat, his knuckles were white on the H-Wagon's control, yet he was still grinning. "Red, are you *insane?* We're doing six hundred kilometres per hour, in the dark, bobbing and weaving all over the sky, there's two other craft and they're shooting *back*, and you want me to hit the same thumbnail-sized spot on their windscreen seven times in a *row?* And then do it *again* on the other ship?"

O'Donnell shrugged. "*Dredd* could do it."

As she dragged herself out of the seat, Gillen snapped, "Yeah? Well, he's probably got a better angle from that *pedestal* you keep him on!"

"There's a couple of harnesses in the supply box above the hatch: strap yourself in. I'm not going to be flying in nice straight lines while you do it."

Gillen grabbed a harness, fastened it around her waist, and then dropped to the floor next to the hatch before locking one of the harness's clasps to the securing loops set around the door.

Red O'Donnell called back, "On the floor? Good, I was just gonna suggest that. Makes you a smaller target, and it'll be easier to steady your aim."

"This is not going to work!"

"It has a better chance of working than *not* doing it."

Gillen reached up and thumped the hatch's 'Emergency Open' button, and braced herself against the sudden drop in air-pressure. Over the roar of the wind she yelled, "Keep it steady long enough for me to at least spot one of them!"

She leaned out a little, looking towards the rear of the H-Wagon. There was nothing but darkness out there. "O'Donnell, I can't *see*—"

A sudden flash, almost directly behind them, and she whipped her head back inside just as the hull was again raked with high-velocity rounds.

Okay, I know where they are. If they don't drift and O'Donnell can keep it steady...

She leaned out again, this time with her Lawgiver ready, and loosed three hi-ex shots in rapid succession. She was rewarded with one hit, a glancing blow off the side of one of the pursuing H-Wagons. The explosive shell threw off enough light for her to also see the second craft forty metres to its right.

She switched to armour-piercing rounds, adjusted her aim and fired again, just as her own H-Wagon abruptly dipped to starboard, sending her shots wild.

"Sorry!" O'Donnell yelled. "We just lost another AG motor!"

"Damn it! Okay, just—"

"And thrusters are down to thirty-two per cent power. Yeah, we're all kindsa screwed here."

The H-Wagon juddered again as more enemy fire slammed into the hull.

"The plating's not going to take much more of that... Gillen, you've got to take down at least *one* of those drokkers!"

She quickly checked her gun's ammunition. Four AP rounds left, ten standard, eight ricochet and five high-explosive.

And seven incendiary rounds.

"O'Donnell—what's a H-Wagon's cockpit glass made out of?"

"Laminated layers of compound nano-polymers. Tough, but not impenetrable."

"Don't need to penetrate it..." She leaned out again, and fired a spread of her five remaining hi-ex rounds in the direction of the closest pursuer.

One of them hit home, square on the H-Wagon's nose, and she immediately flipped her Lawgiver's ammo selector to Incendiary, rapid fire.

She squeezed the trigger and all seven incendiary rounds ploughed into the H-Wagon's cockpit glass. "Got him!"

The compressed napalm and thermite mixture inside the tiny bullets wasn't powerful enough to burn through the glass, but it rapidly spread over the entire windshield. Seconds later, the H-Wagon abruptly banked to the left and started to drop, a trail of burning particles in its wake.

Gillen knew that the damage to the H-Wagon would be minimal, but the shock to the pilots of seeing their entire windscreen on fire would be far greater. Their reaction would be to set down immediately.

"One down, Red—make the most of it before they recover!"

"Close the hatch, get back here and strap yourself down—"

Gillen turned to see O'Donnell grinning at her—"because what I'm gonna do next is gonna *hurt*. But on the plus side, we might live."

The moment she fastened the co-pilot's seat's harness, O'Donnell began to run his hands back and forth across the controls, reflexively making dozens of minor adjustments.

"What are you *planning?*"

He didn't respond, and in that moment she realised he might have already forgotten she was there. She'd seen this sort of thing before, but only once or twice. An immediate and intense fugue state. Complete focus and concentration on the task at hand.

The craft lurched left and right, suddenly dropped and then rose again, tracing a complex pattern through the air that she couldn't even visualise. This wasn't just flying: it was more like O'Donnell was reprogramming the H-Wagon's systems on the go.

The co-pilot's radar screen finally flickered back into life, and now she could see the dot representing the enemy craft zipping around them as they spun and weaved.

"Come *on*," Red muttered. "Just give me this..."

"What can I do?" Gillen asked, teeth clenched and body tense against the constantly shifting acceleration.

Again, he didn't respond to her, just kept adjusting the controls, his hands moving almost faster than she could keep up.

The cockpit's interior lights blinked off, then the control panel went dark.

And the H-Wagon began to plummet.

She grabbed onto the seat's armrests and closed her eyes. "I hope to Grud you know what you're doing!"

"I do. You might want to bite down on something, Gillen, because we're gonna hit hard."

She didn't have time to ask what that meant: the impact rippled through the seat and up into her spine, pitching her entire body forward. If she'd not been strapped into the seat she'd have slammed her head against the darkened console.

"What the *hell?*"

O'Donnell was grinning again. "Bingo."

"We're still moving... what did we *hit?*"

He began adjusting the controls again, and the panel came back to life. "The other H-Wagon. Dropped down on top of it, and hit it hard enough to knock it out of the sky."

"How'd they not see us coming?"

"H-Wagon's weapons system locks onto radar and heat-sig at the same time, and it expects a little play in both. I spun us around to mess with the silhouette and at the same time shut everything down to change our thermal output. That breaks the weapons-lock so they have to re-target us manually, which is pretty hard to do when they can't *see* us." He reached over and tapped at the co-pilot's radar screen. "Let's see... yeah. They're on the ground... upside down, too."

"But... you can't just knock a H-Wagon down like that!"

"Well, we just did. The anti-grav motors are delicate little beasts. They need to be handled and adjusted very carefully. If they're suddenly expected to deal with double the mass without getting enough time to adjust, they're going to overload. That's why each H-Wagon has so many of them: they take a little under eleven seconds to recover from an overload. But first I had to get your friends' craft low enough. Made them follow us down to under seven hundred metres before I flipped back and hit them. And gravity pulls us down to earth at nine-point-eight metres per second squared, so..." He spread his arms as if to say, 'The rest is obvious.'

"Don't make me calculate acceleration... Just *tell* me."

"At seven hundred metres, it takes an object twelve seconds to hit the ground. Assuming that its vertical velocity is zero, and they were close enough to that. Their AG motors take up almost eleven seconds of that to reboot, so that gave the H-Wagon a little over a second to pull out of the fall. Not nearly enough time. They'd have hit the ground at over four hundred kilometres per hour, but with their airbags and crashfoam there's a pretty good chance they weren't killed. Their wagon's not going anywhere for a while, though."

He nodded ahead as he adjusted the controls. "I'm sure their pals are still intact, so we need to put every last ounce of juice into getting out of here. Due south for another twenty, I reckon, then we head east. We don't want to be too far from the city in case Dredd needs us. Plus we're down to seven working AGs and thrusters are at fifteen per cent. Not to mention whatever damage their guns did to us."

"We need another craft," Gillen said. "Something they're *not* looking for."

"That would help, yeah." O'Donnell was grinning again. "Still, that was nice bit of flying, though, right? I mean, not a lot of pilots would be able to pull off a trick like that."

"I'm sure your trophy is already at the engraver's. How did they find us?"

"Sneaky drokkers... They started carpet-bombing the area with a low-level electromagnetic pulse. I could see it coming on the long-range, figured we'd better clear out. It wouldn't directly affect us, but it'd block comms. Then as soon as we got to about two thousand metres, wham, full pulse, narrow-beam, hit us dead on. I don't know *how* they pinpointed us so quickly. Unless they had a Psi-Judge on board. Must be that, because I'd blocked every other way they could have tracked us."

"A Psi-Judge is unlikely. The SJS steers clear of them whenever possible." Gillen tapped the side of her head with her index finger. "We carry a lot of secrets up there. Far more than the average street Judge. And we know a few tricks that we don't much talk about... When you're hunting Judges, you need every advantage you can get."

"Makes sense. So how'd they do it?"

"I think they found us because you took us up. You might have shielded us from every signal, but no other flying craft out in the Cursed Earth is going to be as well maintained as a Mega-City One Justice Department H-Wagon. They just listened for a well-tuned engine."

"Damn... I never considered that. Well, lesson learned. Won't make *that* mistake again. So, you're wondering how I know so much about H-Wagons. Well—"

"Four years ago you bought four scrapped H-Wagons at a Justice Department auction. Said you were going to scavenge them for the raw metal. But the truth is you took them apart to study them."

"You checked up on me," O'Donnell said, slowly nodding to himself. "Of course you did. After Ezekiel, I wasn't exactly friendly with you, because of how you'd treated Joe. So you investigated me to see if I was a threat."

"That's what I do."

Twelve

DREDD REACHED SECTOR Seventy as the evening traffic on the sked was beginning to ease. He'd had to stop himself from arresting three separate drivers for aggressive driving en route, and one for overly passive driving—the latter being a genial middle-aged man who caused a kilometre-long tailback on the northbound carriageway because he'd stopped to allow all the traffic entering via the on-ramp to go ahead of him. Dredd had dealt with the matter by pulling up next to the driver and scowling at him as he pointed ahead. No written warning, no fine. And no official report to Control that would draw attention to the direction in which Dredd was heading.

Sector Seventy was not a part of the city Dredd had visited often, though he had passed through many times.

Citizens sometimes referred to a specific neighbourhood in the eastern part of the sector as 'Old Money' and it was easy to see why: gleaming city-blocks, well-maintained roads and services, and sizeable parks separating the wealthy from the poor.

Babel Towers wasn't the newest of the blocks, nor the most opulent, and certainly not the largest—it was no more than seven storeys tall—but it still reeked of money. The marble façade was actual marble and not just painted plasticrete, the lower walls were covered with ivy and creeping oak rather than graffiti, and the old cars parked on the wide streets outside were not burnt-out husks but vintage pieces each worth more than the average apartment elsewhere in the city. And the citizens eyeing Dredd as he approached the building were neatly-dressed, curious eldsters, not grimy, suspicious juves.

Dredd parked his Lawmaster directly in front of the main doorway, and as he was dismounting, a uniformed doorman approached. He was taller than Dredd, about thirty years old, barrel-chested, thick-armed. The bulk beneath the long, shiny-buttoned coat was muscle, not fat.

"Good evening, Judge... Dredd. My name is Norman. How may I help you tonight?"

"You may step aside and let me do my business."

Without touching Dredd, Norman quickly stepped back and put out his arm. "Ah, not *quite* how we do things here, Judge. For security reasons, you understand." Norman dropped his arm and took another step back. "A Judge's uniform is no guarantee of a Judge within. More than once, we've had counterfeit Judges attempt to gain entry for nefarious reasons. Hence, *I* am the first point of contact. Everything must go through me."

Dredd glowered at him. "Stop me again, and I *will* go through you."

A tiny pause, then Norman said, "I understand. But, again, I have no way of knowing that you genuinely are a Judge. I've been entrusted with the noble duty of safeguarding the residents of this building and I would be remiss were I to merely accept you at your word."

Dredd nodded towards the side of the doorway. "Your security cameras have already scanned me and contacted the Department of Justice for confirmation. In a high-end block like this, that process takes only a few seconds. You already *know* that I'm legit."

Norman said, "Indeed. But you must allow me to announce you. Whom do you wish to see?"

"Stamford Santon."

"Is that Mister Santon senior, junior or triple?"

"What?"

"Many members of the Santon family reside in this block, sir. Three of them have the first name Stamford."

"Stamford *Blane* Santon."

Norman nodded. "Senior." With one movement he stepped to the right and swept his left arm towards the door. "Welcome to Babel Towers, Judge Dredd. You'll find the elevators in the lobby: the one on your left will take you to Mister Santon's apartment. Members of his staff will greet you upon your exit from the elevator."

Dredd passed Norman, then briefly looked back. "Can't even see the lights of another block from this angle," he said. "Just the trees." Small-talk was not within Dredd's comfort zone, but when necessary he could fake interest in the mundane.

Norman turned to look in the same direction. "Indeed. A rare thing in this city. That's one of the reasons the Santon family has resisted all offers to purchase the park. Not for themselves, but for the *future*." He lowered his voice a little. "It's not all about money, Judge. These people are richer than Grud himself, but that doesn't make them bad people."

"They pay you well?" Dredd asked, still looking around the area. A lot of security cameras, and some of the casual passers-by were being far too casual. Private security. Not illegal in Mega-City One as long as their details and duties had been registered with the Department of Justice.

"*Very* well. Enough to put up with the indignity of being renamed Norman simply because it rhymes with 'doorman.' The ultra-rich are strange. They don't have a lot of contact with ordinary people, so their manners kind of... wither. They're rude sometimes, but they usually don't mean to be insulting. You'll see for yourself."

"I've met some very wealthy people." A small but expensive-looking car silently eased past the block from left to right. The same car that had passed from right to left as Dredd was pulling his Lawmaster up to the door.

"Not like these." Norman gestured towards the door again. "Please. They don't expect to be kept waiting. They're not used to that."

Dredd pulled the door open and walked into the lobby. The leftmost elevator was a bronze-plated metal box about three times the size of his quarters, featuring only a single button. Dredd stepped in and pushed the button, and as the door closed, he wondered how much time he had.

If Stamford Blane Santon *had* been under the protection of Judge James Hariton during the war, then he was certainly still on someone's watch-list. And that someone would already have dispatched their agents to this location to intercept Dredd.

Judging by the dedicated elevator, Santon owned the entire fifth floor. That was a lot of square metres in one of the costliest parts of the city. He would certainly have his own security people in the apartment. And the ability to turn the entire place into a fortress if necessary. Armoured plating lining all the doors and walls, unbreakable windows, self-contained life-support, a fully-stocked armoury.

The elevator door opened silently onto a clean, white-walled, featureless hallway blocked by a cluster of stern-looking, black-suited men and women, all staring at Dredd.

The one in front, clearly presenting herself as their leader, beckoned him closer. Early forties, short with a stocky build and short hair. "Judge Joseph Dredd. My name is Weller. I'm Mister Santon's personal head of security. May I ask why you're here?" Her voice was stern, her accent Brit-Cit, her attitude confident.

Dredd stepped out of the elevator and stopped a metre from Weller. She was barely up to his chest, but he knew not to judge someone by their appearance. "Mister Santon's name came to my attention in relation to an ongoing case. More than that I'm unwilling to divulge."

"I see..." Weller pursed her lips slightly. "Then I regret to tell you that you've had a wasted journey. You—"

"Step aside," Dredd said. He looked around at the other guards. Nine of them. All certainly armed and experienced. "*All* of you. You will step aside. Any attempt to interfere with my duties will be met with considerable force."

Weller sighed, rather theatrically. "Judge... just let me *explain* a few things to you." She held an index finger upright and made a small circle. "All of us here, including those members of my staff elsewhere in this block, are highly trained and decorated veterans. Some are former Judges, some... from elsewhere. You honestly don't have a hope of getting close to Mister Santon without our permission."

"Implied threat against a Mega-City One Judge," Dredd said to Weller. "Four years." He looked at her companions and added, "*Accessory* to implied threat. Three years each."

"It won't stick," Weller said. "Dredd, you don't understand the situation here. You're outnumbered and outclassed. You think you have the law on your side, but trust me, that's not how this works. Just turn around now." She tilted her head a little. "You're about to get an order telling you that very thing."

Dredd's helmet radio buzzed. "*Control to Dredd.*"

Still watching Weller, he said, "Dredd here."

"*Dredd, I've got Judge Barradien of the Special Judici—*"

Barradien's voice cut across the feed. "*Dredd. Barradien. Stand down—that's an order. Stamford Santon Senior is not under investigation, nor are any members of his family.*"

"Never said I was investigating him," Dredd said. "Just

wanted to ask him some questions. But he's sure as hell under investigation *now*."

Barradien muttered, "*Jesus...*" then, louder, added, "*All right, Dredd. You're playing that game? Then you're officially under investigation by the SJS. Return to the street and await arrest. Any attempt to do otherwise will serve only to harm your case and could result in physical injury. Will you comply?*"

"Barradien, just tell me *why* the law doesn't apply to Santon. What makes him untouchable?"

"*Damn it, Dredd! You're only digging yourself deeper! You* will *stand down or I will instruct Weller to* take *you down!*"

Dredd looked at the short security guard. "Weller's under your command?"

"*As far as you're concerned, yes!*"

A slight movement from Weller, and she now had a small pistol in her right hand, held down by her side. From what Dredd could see, all of the other guards were now also openly displaying their guns.

Barradien said, "*Look... Dredd, don't be an idiot. This is just the way the system works. Some citizens are...* not *equal. They need special considerations, special treatment. The Santon family are among those people. They're* protected. *That's all you need to know. Stand down. I won't tell you ag—*"

Dredd disconnected the call, and slowly looked around. Weller and nine others, and on the far side of them, somewhere in the huge apartment, was Stamford Santon.

Weller said, "Dredd. For your own sake, get back in the elevator. You've just been ordered to stand down by a senior Judge—what more do you want?"

"Answers. Judge Spencer Lindfield was executed by SJS Judge Krause, and apparently the sole reason is that Lindfield's name was flagged in a random investigation by SJS Judge Gillen. And now I'm being told by the head of the SJS that my strongest lead is somehow untouchable."

A voice from further along the corridor said, "Oh, that was *me*. Sorry, was he a friend of yours?"

Weller looked down and muttered "Shit!" as Dredd peered past the guards to see a seventy-year-old man approaching. He was tall and slim, handsome, well-dressed, and smiling warmly.

Weller said, "Mister Santon, *please*. You need to go back inside the apartment. We're dealing with the situation."

Stamford Santon looked a little confused. "I... Judge, your friend's name came up and, well, like always I was asked what I wanted *done* about it, and it's always been pressed on us that we have to *protect* ourselves no matter what, so—"

"Sir, please!" Weller snapped. "Gertler, Ozkaya, escort Mister Santon back inside the apartment. Immediately."

Two of the guards took hold of Santon's elbows and steered him back towards the end of the corridor.

As they rounded the corner, Dredd said, "You know I can't let this go, Weller. I'm telling you, move out of the way."

Her grip tightened on her gun. "I'm telling *you*, Dredd, stand down. Word is you're good, but so are *we*. So get the drokkin' *hint!* Go back downstairs and wait for the SJS, because that's your *only* chance to live to the end of the day. This doesn't have to get messy!"

"Doesn't have to, but it's *gonna*."

Thirteen

CROUCHED ON THE parched roadside, Gillen tied another strap around her backpack and then hoisted it onto her shoulder.

Ten metres away, Red O'Donnell slapped the side of the H-Wagon's hull as he descended its ramp. "So long, ol' pal. You've done your job, but now you're too shot-up. You're a liability."

As the ramp withdrew and the H-Wagon rose into the air, O'Donnell said, "Autopilot'll probably crap out around forty K south-west. I know the region—there's nothing there for it to crash into but uninhabited radland." He picked up the second backpack. "As soon as they find it, they'll know we jumped ship, though. So we can't stay here."

Gillen look around. With the H-Wagon's engine glow already fading, there was now nothing to see but darkness, and a few twinkling stars overhead glimpsed between the silhouettes of the massive, slowly-tumbling boulders of the Death Belt. The result of unintended side effects from the advanced gravity-warping weapons used during the war, the death belts were multi-kilometre-wide swaths of gravity-defying debris that crossed the Cursed Earth, pulled and pushed by the storms, unpredictable and exceptionally hazardous. At any moment, the warp effect could fade and send the debris crashing down like granite hailstones, some as large as a city bus.

The belt overhead right now was barely moving. Gillen felt that somehow that made it seem *more* dangerous than when they were cascading through the sky like an avalanche crashing down an invisible mountain. "Which way?"

Red pointed off into the darkness. "Spectator's Rift, on the far side of that hill. Big farming community. There's a merchant there who owes me about a million favours. She's going to be pissed at being woken up in the middle of the night, but she'll find us a vehicle."

They began to walk, side by side, with Red using a flashlight on low power to sweep the ground ahead of them.

"Radiation levels are low out here this time of the year, so we should be all right," Red said, "unless we hit a storm. You did the Hot Dog Run, right? Where a senior Judge takes a bunch of cadets out?"

"I did," Gillen said. "Nothing much happened. We were tasked with tracking down perps who'd been rampaging through mutie settlements. Took us about four hours: we found them camped out in the open, snoozing off the hottest part of the day. We surrounded them, then the Judge woke them up. They put up absolutely no resistance. We hauled them back to the nearest prison farm and we were back at the Academy in time for lights-out."

"No chance to prove your heroism, then? Shame. So why did you decide to join the SJS? Sick of the corruption, right? Yeah, I've seen a lot of bad Judges in my time. A *lot*."

"You don't choose to join the SJS. They come looking for you." Gillen readjusted the straps to shift the weight of her pack a little. Red had insisted that they take as much water and rations as they could carry, and all of the H-Wagon's ammunition.

"They knocked on your door and asked, 'How'd you like a new career ratting on your pals?' Was that it?"

"More or less. They spend *years* checking out potential candidates, and only approach them when they're sure the Judge has got what it takes."

"Anyone besides Joe Dredd ever turn it down?"

"Not that I've heard." Gillen thought back to the time she'd tried to recruit Joe Dredd. That was the first time her interactions with Dredd had blotted her ledger. She'd studied his Academy records and watched him in action for long enough to know that he'd be ideal SJS material. And then he absolutely rejected the idea.

Judge Molina later implied that it was embarrassment at Joe Dredd's rejection that caused Gillen to go after him with such vigour when his brother had proved to be corrupt. Gillen had vehemently denied that, insisting that even if Joe Dredd wasn't as flawed as Rico, Joe must have known of his brother's activities. It was a basic rule of law that those in a position to prevent a crime and who choose not to do so are guilty of accessory. Joe did nothing to stop Rico, ergo Joe was guilty. It had made sense at the time.

You wanted *him to be guilty*, Gillen told herself, *because you were hurt that he turned down the offer. Recruiting a Judge as effective—and as* connected—*as Dredd into the SJS would have given your career a massive boost.*

But Dredd was right. The Judges should serve the people, and the SJS should serve the Judges. That attitude alone should have been enough to show her how different he was to his brother. *Rico always put himself above the people, but Joe does the opposite.* She'd read his case-files. He could be abrupt, dismissive, often downright callous with the citizens—and with his fellow Judges, regardless of their rank—but he was almost never wrong.

If the whole world is telling you that everything is absolutely hunky-dory, and Joe Dredd is the only one saying that something stinks, then he's the one you listen to.

CHIEF JUDGE CLARENCE Goodman pushed open the lid of his personal sleep-machine to see Judge McComber of the SJS glowering at him from the corner of the room.

"Pleasant dreams?" McComber asked. "The machine says you've been in there for *nineteen minutes*, Chief Judge. Isn't that a little excessive?"

Goodman swung his legs out and sat up. He'd learned to ignore McComber's little barbs, which annoyed the man: all he seemed to want was acknowledgement.

"We have a problem," McComber said. "One of your Judges is straying into... dark territory."

Goodman pulled on his boots. It wasn't necessary to remove any item of clothing when using a sleep-machine, but he always felt it was more like *proper* sleep if he removed his boots first.

"I suspect he's working with Gillen, sir."

The Chief Judge got to his feet and stretched.

"Are you even *listening* to me?" McComber asked.

"I'm listening. Just not responding. And you're *whining*, McComber. Get to the point."

"One of *your* Judges is—"

"I have over fifty thousand Judges on the streets. You used the male pronoun, so that cuts that number by about half." He held up his right hand, and slowly pinched his thumb and index finger together. "Little narrower, maybe?"

"It's Dredd."

"Of course it is." Goodman pulled on his cloak as he passed McComber, heading out into the corridor. "Let him be. Whatever he's up to, I'm sure he knows what he's doing."

"Chief Judge, you know that there are certain aspects of this department that must remain clandestine."

Goodman stopped and turned back to face McComber. "Sometimes I wonder if maybe the bodies buried in the foundations are the only thing preventing the building from sinking back into the mud. Yes, I'm aware. You're telling me that's where Dredd is heading? That's what's happened to Gillen?"

McComber nodded. "I think so. I don't know the details... but Barradien asked me to get you to pull Dredd in."

"You forget who I *am*, McComber?" The Chief Judge looked around for a moment, then lowered his voice. "Barradien's a *patsy*. A target for the SJS-haters who'll draw their ire—and their shots—away from the real power: You and Judge Dekaj are the ones who really run the show."

"It's... not that simple, Chief. Just call Dredd back in. He'll listen to you. He *trusts* you."

"And I trust *him*." Goodman resumed walking. "If Dredd's got the scent of something rotten, your best hope is to stay the hell out of his way."

McComber called out, "God *damn* it, Goodman! If you won't order Dredd to back down, we'll have no choice but to declare him hostile! We *will* tag him for termination!"

Goodman stopped and slowly turned back to face the SJS Judge.

"There are secrets that *must* be kept!" McComber said. "Secrets that are more important than any Judge. Than *every* Judge. How can you not see that?"

Softly, almost kindly, Goodman said, "You could just *tell* Dredd what this is about. He might understand."

"I can't do that. I don't know what it *is* that they're protecting, just that it needs to be protected at any cost." McComber unclipped his radio from his belt. "You tell Dredd to stand down, or I give the order to terminate him. And when your pet project is gone, you're *finished*."

Goodman took a step towards McComber. He'd faced worse

than this blowhard, many times. *They see you as the friendly uncle type*, he told himself. *Someone who makes the citizens feel protected, but who no longer has the will or the teeth to fight.*

He'd known that for a long time—it was an image he encouraged—but surely someone as experienced as McComber would know the difference between a public and a private persona, especially when the SJS's own leader was such a figurehead?

"No, *you're* finished, McComber. You *and* Roseanne Dekaj, wherever that creepy toad is hiding. You do *not* threaten me. Understood?" He thumped the heavy metal chestplate. "You think I was handed this thing because I'm a nice guy? I *earned* it, out there on the streets *and* in the courtroom. Hell, I went toe-to-toe arguing points of law with Eustace Fargo himself. I helped build this Department and this city, and I had to step on a lot of necks to do so. I'm the Chief Judge, and you answer to *me*, not Barradien or some shadowy cabal or anyone else!"

Goodman was almost impressed that McComber didn't back down. The SJS Judge kept his gaze on Goodman as he slowly raised the radio to his mouth. "SJS Control, this is McComber. Patch me through to Judge Barradien."

"Last warning, McComber!"

"What are you going to *do*, old man? Quote the Law at me? Hit me with another anecdote?"

Goodman's fist crushed McComber's fingers and the radio they were clutching against the man's jaw. He went down instantly, hit the floor and didn't move.

A thin, young voice from behind Goodman said, "Holy *drokk!*"

He turned to see three year-four cadets—all girls, wearing their pyjamas—staring at him from ten metres down the corridor.

"What are you doing out of bed, children?"

One of them began, "We, uh, we heard *shouting* and so we thought we oughta come and see—"

"Now, that's a lie," Goodman said. "Your quarters are on the other side of the building, so you couldn't have heard me." He beckoned them closer. "Have a look. Judge McComber here is down, unconscious. Deep cuts in his face from fragments of his radio. See that?" He crouched next to McComber, and the three cadets gathered around. "Now, what do we do when we encounter wounds like that?"

"He's not moving, so we should leave the fragments in place," one of the girls said. "If we remove them, he'll bleed more."

One of the others said, "Right. Plus, if he gives us any trouble we can push the plastic bits in deeper." She looked up at the Chief Judge for approval. "Judge-Tutor Semple says that pain can be a very effective motivator."

"Correct," Goodman said.

The first girl added, "And we make sure he's in the recovery position. Which he mostly is. And not choking on his broken teeth, which it doesn't look like he is, yet."

"Good... But you're missing something. Anyone?"

The third girl said, "Well, you just knocked him out, so that means you had a *reason*. You should cuff him, 'cos now he's a perp."

The Chief Judge nodded. "That's right. Now, you three get back to your quarters. And no more sneaking out at night just to see if you can get away with it. I know you're only practising your skills, but rule-breakers become *law*-breakers, you know that. Go on. Scoot."

As the girls sheepishly backed away, McComber groaned, and Goodman unclipped his own radio. "Need a team, my location. Immediately."

"Is everything all right, Chief Judge?"

"I wish I knew."

Fourteen

DREDD LOOKED AT the eight people facing him, all now with handguns aimed squarely at his chest.

Weller said, "Seriously. It'll take you maybe a second to draw your Lawgiver from your boot holster. In that second, each of us will hit you a minimum of three times. Is this how you want to die, Dredd?"

"Not particularly. But do you honestly believe that I won't get at least *one* shot off? Right between the eyes, Weller. That's where I'll hit you. And that's it, game over for you. Is this how *you* want to die?"

Her face grim, Weller said, "Then look at it like this. You getting killed will earn you no answers. Surrender to the SJS, and you just might—eventually—learn what this is all about."

"One question, then I'll go."

"Make it fast. And *relevant*."

"Judge James Hariton, now deceased. *Was* he connected to your team back in the day?"

"That's classified."

"So he *was*. Interesting." Dredd glanced back and saw that

the elevator door was still open behind him. "Hariton worked for Santon—or someone else in a similar protected position—and he learned something he shouldn't have. After his injury he started to talk a lot about the old days, so he was watched, in case he broke confidence. One of the people he spoke to was Judge Spencer Lindfield. That put Lindfield on a watch list, and when his name came up again thanks to Gillen's random search, that information reached Santon and he panicked and ordered Lindfield's termination. How am I doing?"

"I couldn't possibly comment," Weller said, but Dredd detected a slight, probably subconscious nod from one of her people.

"Right. I get that you people are only doing your job, but you're interfering with an investigation. This will be the last time I tell you to lower your weapons and stand down."

During the long, silent seconds that Weller stared at him, he knew what was coming next: he could see it in the guards' body language. The tension in their limbs, the narrowing of their eyes, the set of their jaws. They fully expected Weller to give them the order to open fire, and they were almost itching to comply. As trained gunmen, they'd go for centre mass, of course.

The elevator door was still open behind him, about three metres back. Solid building like this—basically a polished fortress—the elevator would be armoured. Good to know.

Calmly, Weller said, "Drokk it... Waste him!"

Dredd threw himself back towards the elevator even as the guards opened fire. As he'd expected, they'd all aimed for his upper chest. Their rounds passed over him—one so close it clipped the chain on his badge—and before his shoulders hit the floor of the elevator he'd drawn his Lawgiver and had already started shooting. He landed heavily on his back, just as a scream from the corridor told him that he'd hit at least one of them. He rolled to the side, into the corner of the elevator, and—as another barrage slammed into the elevator's back wall—reached up and stabbed at the lone button on the control panel.

The door began to close, providing him with more cover, and he switched the gun to rapid-fire, armour-piercing. He stayed low, following the edge of the door, then at the last moment thrust his Lawgiver forward, its muzzle preventing the door from closing.

He fired, a wide spray of rounds that emptied the gun's magazine in less than two seconds.

More screams, more gunfire, and as the elevator door began to automatically draw back, Dredd rolled back, ejected the magazine and replaced it with a fresh one. He estimated he'd injured at least six of them, four seriously. That left four more. At least one of them would be taking cover behind a fallen comrade, plus the other two with Santon, and whoever else was in the apartment and would by now be running into place.

"You *drokker!*" a man screamed. "You are *so dead!*"

"You were warned," Dredd replied.

Amid the groans of the wounded and dying, hushed, panicked voices came from elsewhere in the apartment.

Then more gunfire—a volley big enough to actually rock the elevator—and Dredd knew that he had only seconds before someone dragged out a really heavy weapon. He pulled his stash of smoke-grenades from a belt-pouch. One grenade would be enough to black out the entire corridor. Dredd primed all six and tossed them out through the door.

Someone shouted, "Grenade!" and there was a scrambling for cover, then a loud *whumph!* as the grenades detonated.

Dredd pulled down his helmet's respirator and stepped out into the dense, choking fog, keeping to the left side of the corridor: anyone risking a shot into the smoke would most likely aim down the middle. His helmet helped penetrate the smoke a little, but still his visibility was down to less than two metres.

He stepped over a female guard—not Weller, he noted—who had taken two rounds to the face. Behind her, a male guard clutched both hands to what remained of his throat, blood spurting from the wound in time with his body's spasming.

A male voice ahead whispered, "*Your* drokkin' fault, Weller! You should have terminated him on the spot!"

"Enough—go guard the door. If Dredd gets too close... you know what you have to do. Trigger the End Protocol."

"No. No way, Weller. We do that, we're *all* dead. They'll wipe us all out just out of *spite*."

"You don't do it, we're dead for sure. Go."

Dredd stepped over another body, this one a man missing the top of his head.

The building had good ventilation: already the smoke was beginning to clear. Dredd moved faster, aware now that he was leaving bloody footprints behind.

Another woman's voice, muffled, but now only metres ahead of Dredd: "Got the rebreathers, sir."

"Go check on Dredd. If he's not dead, finish him. Whatever it takes."

Ahead, a grey indistinct shape resolved into the rough silhouette of two people crouched at the corner, guns ready as they peered into the smoke.

The nearest of the two shuffled forward, passing within a metre of Dredd without seeing him. "Smoke's beginning to clear," she whispered. "I can hear something rasping... Aw, hell. Sir, Tennyson's down. Chest wound."

"Forget him," Weller replied. "Keep going. You see Dredd, empty every clip you have into the drokker."

Dredd pressed the muzzle of his Lawgiver against the side of Weller's head. "You might wanna rethink that order."

"I THOUGHT YOU said this was a big farming community?"

"I did. And it *is*." O'Donnell looked around the single dark street of the town of Spectator's Rift. "But it's nearly midnight.

Everyone around here works from dawn to dusk. Not a lot of night-life activity."

"But *one* dusty street with, what, fifteen buildings?"

"*Farmers*, Gillen. The people live on the farms. They come here to trade." He pointed ahead. "The general store, there. That's Kisa's place. Anything that happens here, happens in *there*. The farmers trade and pass on tips and come together to solve problems. Very friendly place, Spectator's Rift, if you're not a spugwit or a raider."

As they walked towards the store, Gillen said, "Light's on. Could mean your friend is still awake."

Before O'Donnell could respond, the store's door was pulled open and a woman stepped out onto the porch. "Bit late in the day to be calling, Red."

Gillen thought that the woman seemed like a perfectly normal thirty-year-old—reasonably healthy, long dark hair, all the pieces in the usual place—but you could never be sure with the people who lived outside the city, constantly exposed to radiation and unknown pathogens in the air, the water, their food.

O'Donnell said, "I know, Kisa. Sorry. I'm in need of a vehicle. Doesn't have to be big or fancy, just fast and tough. And with good range."

Kisa folded her arms and leaned against the door-jamb wearing a smug expression. "Oh, really? I haven't seen you in half a year and now you want me to find you a car. What happened to the woman you said you were seeing? November, was it?"

"Novena. It didn't really work out." O'Donnell looked almost embarrassed. "It all got just too *weird* for me."

Kisa barked a harsh laugh. "Too weird for *you?*"

"I know. It was... I told you she was a bit psychic? Well, she saw our break-up coming and then broke up with me because, well, she saw it coming." He shrugged. "It was pretty amicable, I guess. So, what can you do for me?"

"Right now, not much." Kisa pointed towards the south end

of the street. "But you remember Mister Antzoulides? Has the beetato farm about two kilometres that way? He's got an old Landprowler he doesn't use much, and he owes me for half a tonne of fertilizer. Tell him that's square if he lends you the 'prowler. And then *we're* square, you and me, right?"

"I might need more than a *lend* of it, Kisa."

"You could offer him *money*, ever think of that?" She looked Gillen up and down. "So who's the city-slicker trying to look like she belongs?"

"This is Marion," O'Donnell said. "Just a friend."

"Yeah, well, we *all* end up in the 'just a friend' category, don't we?" To Gillen, she said, "Red here is secretly despised by at least one woman in every town... and half of them would probably take him back if he asked nicely."

Red nodded. "And I wouldn't blame them."

Kisa froze for a second, then pushed between them and out onto the street. "Aircraft coming. A *lot* of them. Heading this way... They're looking for *you*, Judge Gillen—and they know you're here!"

"How do you know—?"

"Get going!" Kisa said, shoving them towards the side of her store. "My hov-bike—take it, go south!"

Gillen darted around the corner, skidded to a stop when she saw the hov-bike. At its core it had once been an old Justice Department Lawranger, but it had since been modified with parts from Grud alone knew how many different vehicles.

"Don't waste time *admiring* it!" Kisa yelled. "Get going!"

Gillen jumped onto to the bike, and started it up. It hummed and throbbed, and rose half a metre into the air. "Red!"

"It'll be a lot faster without me. You go—I'll hold them back."

"If you believe that's even *possible*, then you're probably too dumb to live anyway! Get on the drokkin' bike!"

He just grinned, then turned away and ran.

"I know, he's stubborn," Kisa said. "Just *go!*"

Gillen jerked back on the bike's throttle and it surged forward a lot faster than she'd been expecting, streaking out onto the street with a wide spray of dust and grit. There was no screen between the handlebars like on a Lawmaster, but there was a single grimy mirror attached to the left handgrip.

Already, Red O'Donnell was little more than a dot in the background.

This is crazy, she told herself. *You don't know the land... without a guide you're not going to last more than a few days.*

There was a switch next to the mirror that on a Lawranger would activate the main headlight, but even though she was riding into almost complete darkness, Gillen resisted the urge to flip it: the incoming aircraft would spot her instantly.

But they'd spot her anyway, she realised: the H-Wagon's thermal sensors were even more effective at night.

There's no way to outrun them, no matter what speed this thing can do.

Another glance in the mirror, but now it showed nothing but darkness... then two points of light, then a third, and two more. H-Wagon searchlights beaming down on Spectator's Rift.

Just keep going! Red's resourceful. He'll find a way to delay them and...

...and they'll just blow him away and keep searching.

Gillen hit the brakes, slammed her right foot down, and threw the hov-bike into a sharp one-eighty. Opened the throttle again and kept her head low as she rocketed back towards the town.

She saw him a minute later, standing with his back to her in the centre of the street, with the beams of five hovering H-Wagons shining down on him. He appeared to be yelling something up at them.

She was two hundred metres away when she saw a brief flash on one of the H-Wagons, followed instantly by a small cloud of dust at Red's feet. A warning shot. An amplified voice was barking orders at him, but she couldn't make out the words.

A hundred metres away, and Red started to turn towards her.

She knew they were going to kill Red as soon as they caught her—they would assume that he'd been compromised—but she wasn't going to make it easy for them.

One of the H-Wagons trained its searchlight on her, then another, then two more.

Squinting against the blinding light, she hurtled towards Red and hoped he'd guessed what she was doing. She'd lead them away, and he'd run in the opposite direction while they chased her. Find another vehicle and get clear. He had a much better chance of surviving out here on his own than she did, anyway.

As she approached him, she slowed down a little to tell him to clear out—

—and he grabbed onto the side of the hov-bike. The impact must have nearly torn his right arm from its socket, but Red just yelled, "Got it! *Move!*"

Gillen ramped the bike up to top speed as Red scrambled to climb on behind her.

"Thanks for the save!" he yelled.

"You idiot! I was trying to lead them *away* from you!"

"Oh, yeah. Right, that *does* make more sense." He wrapped his arms around her waist and leaned closer. "You know there's no chance of outrunning them? Even if it *was* just you on the bike?"

"I know." Gillen hit the headlight switch and its weak, shaky yellow beam did a feeble job of illuminating the road ahead.

Fifty metres directly ahead of them, a boulder the size of a car exploded, but Gillen rode on without flinching or slowing, skirting the edge of the crater as shards of rock rained down around them.

"Warning shot!" O'Donnell said.

"I know!" As she'd suspected, they'd been ordered not to kill her. They wanted to know exactly what she knew, and who she'd told.

The searchlights found them again, and the amplified voice boomed out from somewhere above and behind them. *"Surrender, Gillen. You won't get a second warning!"*

O'Donnell asked, "Anyone you know?"

"Sounds like Harmon Krause. Senior SJS Judge. He's the one who executed Lindfield."

"Gillen, you will stand down, immediately, or we will shoot to kill!"

"Options?" Gillen asked.

"Live for a little while longer, or die immediately. I figure that's about all we've got."

A volley of high-calibre rounds raked the ground ahead of them, ripping head-sized chunks out of the ancient asphalt, and Gillen eased off the throttle and allowed the hov-bike to come to a stop.

Red climbed down from the bike and rubbed his right shoulder. "Damn, this arm's *never* gonna heal..."

Gillen shut off the bike and stepped away from it, looking around at the five H-Wagons surrounding them. "So how did your friend know my name? She psychic?"

"Not as such. Kisa can hear radio waves."

"That's... useful."

Krause's voice boomed out again. *"On your knees, hands where we can see them. Now."*

"No," Gillen said. "You come out and talk to me face to face, Krause. Just you. Not speaking to any of your flunkies."

"You're in no position to give orders to a superior officer."

"Then kill us and spend the rest of your life wondering what we knew, and who we *told*."

One of the H-Wagons descended, and its ramp lowered. A slender, shaven-headed woman walked out, hands empty and by her side. "You brought this on yourself, Gillen."

"Stomm. It's Judge Dekaj..."

"And we should be worried because...?" O'Donnell asked.

"Dekaj is about as high-up as you can get in the SJS," Gillen explained. She called out to Dekaj, "You put out a termination order on me. Why?"

The woman was clearly doing her best to remain calm. "I don't answer to you, and I won't explain SJS policy in front of a civilian. You're coming back with us to the Hall of Justice. You'll get all the explanations you want then."

Now she'll try to appeal to my sense of duty, Gillen thought.

Dekaj walked towards her. "Gillen, you know as well as anyone that there are secrets that must be kept for the good of the department as a whole. For the good of the *city*."

Red said, "We're not *in* the city."

"Shut up, O'Donnell. You think we don't know who you are? Facial recognition tagged you back in the Meg before you even dropped the riot-foam on my people. For which, by the way, you're looking at life in an Iso-Cube, and that's if we *let* you live." To Gillen, Dekaj said, "You should have ditched *this* spugwit once you got clear of the city. Our analysts figured this place as one he was most likely to come to for help. Now just make this easy on all of us, Gillen. What exactly did Lindfield say to you before he died?"

Gillen shook her head. "That's not what you really want to know, Dekaj. You want to know how many other people we've told. You want to know where we might have posted that information to safeguard ourselves. And you want to know who else we're working with to pick your secrets apart."

"You mean Joe Dredd?" Dekaj smirked. "Smart move, recruiting a Judge who despises you. But you could have chosen someone a bit more subtle. Dredd found a lead and then blundered after it. Last we heard, he's alone against dozens of highly trained operatives. It's safe to say that he's dead now."

O'Donnell said, "It's safe to say you've never worked with him."

"Red's not wrong there." Gillen turned in a slow circle,

looking up at each of the H-Wagons in turn. "You don't write off a Judge like Dredd until you see his body on the slab." She turned back to Dekaj. "Judge Spencer Lindfield was killed on a termination order with no reason given. The first duty of a Mega-City One Judge is to protect the citizens, and that includes other Judges."

"No! We follow orders. Or people *die*."

"You follow orders *and* people die," Red said.

Dekaj glared at him. "And sometimes they spend their last days *wishing* they were dead." She signalled to the nearest H-Wagon. "Cuff them, search them, scan them. We're taking them in."

Fifteen

IN THE CORRIDOR leading to Santon's apartment, Dredd tightened the cuffs around Weller's wrists and pushed her forward, the muzzle of his Lawgiver still pressed to the back of her neck. Behind them, the other surviving guards were now unconscious and handcuffed, lined up next to the elevator.

He steered Weller around the corner. The ordinary-looking apartment door was closed, and two more of Weller's guards stood either side of it, their guns aimed at Dredd.

One of them—male, thirty, bald—had his left arm down by his side, blood flowing from it at a steady pace. He snarled, "Let her go or you're dead. No second warnings."

Dredd said, "Understood. But you're *already* dying. That's an arterial bleed. I'm not cruel—I'll give your pal a minute to tie it off."

Neither of them moved.

"I can wait," Dredd said. "Couple more minutes you'll be too weak to stand. Makes no difference to me whether you end up in the cubes or in Resyk."

Weller said, "You're an idiot, Dredd. You need me to get

inside the apartment, and you're using me as a human shield? My guys open fire, either *you* die or *I* die. Whatever happens, you're not getting through that door. That's triple-reinforced plasteel. Even a high-explosive round won't penetrate it."

"Good point," Dredd said. "An impassable situation. So we change the parameters."

Two shots, rapid succession: the first struck the wounded guard square in his forehead, the other passed through the second guard's left eye.

As their bodies collapsed to the floor, Weller shrugged herself free of Dredd's grip and turned to face him. "God*damn* it, you are *not* walking away from this, Dredd! We're not just here to protect Santon—we're here to protect his secrets. And the secrets take *priority*. If that means we have to kill him, we *will*. That's the End Protocol."

"And when he's gone?"

"There are others who can do what he does. Or so I'm told. I *don't* know what that is. None of us knows."

"I figure I've got some idea," Dredd said. "There's an old rule... you want something done, you don't give the task to someone who's got free time. You give it to someone who's always *busy*."

"That makes *no* sense," Weller said.

"Just open that door."

"No."

"Your choice." Dredd hauled her back around the corner, shoved her to the floor, then aimed back at the wall next to the apartment door. "Hi-ex, rapid-fire!"

Dredd whipped his head back just as the high-explosive shells ripped into the wall and filled the corridor with fire and shrapnel, the concussive blast trembling the walls and floor.

He peered around the corner. Amid the scorched and warped debris, plaster, ash and brick-dust settled over the guards' bodies, now just scattered lumps of pulped flesh. The reinforced door was still intact, still locked into its frame—but a large portion of the wall next to it was now gone. The metre-square armoured plates reinforcing the wall had survived the blast intact, but the rivets holding them in place had been shattered, scattering the plates across the wide hallway beyond.

He looked back at Weller, lying face-down on the floor with her arms still cuffed behind her back, and concluded that she was still potentially dangerous. A sharp kick to the head put her out of commission.

More shouts and screams from inside the apartment. Dredd shouted back, "Surrender or die. Your choice."

"Get *drokked*, Judge! We got the authority here! They're gonna order a termination on you for this like they did with Lindfield and Hariton!"

"Thought Hariton's death was natural causes?"

"He was getting old, forgetting things. Started talking about the *job*. You can't *do* that. It's all privileged information. Top secret. We hear stuff, see stuff, but we can't talk about it. Not ever."

Another voice, this one female, said, "Will you just shut the drokk *up*, Gertler?"

Dredd recalled the two guards Weller had dispatched to take Santon back inside the apartment. One Caucasian male, one Asian female. *If he's Gertler, she's got to be...*

"No, Ozkaya, let him keep talking," Dredd said. "Confirm what I already know." He moved back to Weller and checked through her pockets. Four ammo mags and her radio. Her gun lost somewhere among the bodies and rubble. Same with the nearest guard. This one, male, seemed relatively intact, dead from a single shot to the chest. Dredd grabbed the man's arm and dragged him back around the corner.

As he moved closer to the hole in the wall, he called out, "It's about the money, right? It's *always* about the money. And you're getting well paid, of course, but that's nothing to them, is it? They could *double* your salary, Gertler—pay you *two* million creds a year—and it'd still be *peanuts* to these people."

Now standing next to the hole with his back to the wall, Dredd knew what was going through Gertler's mind. Possibly Ozkaya's, too. In any organisation of three or more, there's at least one convinced they're not being paid as much as their colleagues.

Gertler said, quietly, "He thinks we're getting a million creds each year? Are *you* getting paid a million for this job?"

"Shut *up*, Gertler! He's just trying to get inside your head!"

Dredd raised Weller's radio to his mouth, hit the switch, and softly said, "Anyone listening?"

Ozkaya's voice whispered from the radio, "*I hear you. Who's that?*"

Dredd whispered, "It's *me*. Tennyson. I'm behind him, gut-shot but... I'll make it. He... he thinks I'm *dead*. Everyone else is, I think. Who've you got in there?"

"*Just me and Gertler. Farraday was on the other side of the wall when it blew. That was him screaming.*"

"Drokk." Dredd reached down and hauled up the dead guard, lifting him up to almost a standing position. "Okay. He... he's approaching the hole... gun ready... he's gonna try to rush you... hold it. Hold it... When I give the word, you hit the drokker with everything you've got." He paused, yelled, "Now!" and stepped back as he pushed the guard's body through the hole in the wall.

The body was shredded by gunfire before it hit the thick, smouldering carpet.

Dredd estimated they'd used four full clips, on semi-automatic fire. Two guards, two guns each. A foolish move, because they'd each have to put at least one gun down to reload the other. That gave him all the time he needed.

He stepped through the hole and fired four times, heat-seeking shots. Ordinarily, he wouldn't use heat-seekers in a situation where there were flames nearby to scramble them, but right now the muzzles of the perps' guns would be almost red-hot after such sustained fire.

Three of the hot-shot rounds struck Gertler square in the chest. He was slumped back against the wall, his head slowly falling to the side, blood spilling from his mouth.

The remaining round passed through Ozkaya's right wrist and clipped the edge of her neck. Now, her entire body trembled as she tried to press her good hand against the ragged, gushing wound. "D... drokk you, Judge!" Her hand dropped away, her dying eyes still staring up at him.

The immediate threat passed, Dredd looked around, properly taking in the apartment for the first time.

It was a lot less plush than he'd had been expecting. The hallway was clean and spacious—aside from the blood, scorch-marks and bodies—but there was a notable lack of gilt-framed paintings and marble statues and Ming-dynasty vases. A few family photos on the walls, a watercolour of what looked like a sunset view over Sector Twenty-Two. A thick carpet that was a little faded and worn.

Movement behind a doorway: Dredd raised his Lawgiver and the door was pulled open. Stamford Santon stepped out. "I know *exactly* what's going through your mind, Judge... 'Where are the Picassos and the shelves of rare books worth a million creds apiece? Where's the cabinet with William Shakespeare's skull? Not even *one* hand-carved drinking goblet fashioned from a unicorn horn?'"

He stepped back, and beckoned Dredd to follow him. "Come in, come in. Heh. Ostentation is not usually our way. The *nouveau riche* surround themselves with the most elaborate luxuries. Everything has to be gold-plated and diamond-encrusted and one-of-a-kind. The *ultra*-rich generally prefer comfort."

The drawing room was a little more elaborately decorated

than the hallway. An open fireplace, large soft-looking sofas, a drinks cabinet against each wall.

"Yes, the carpets might be hand-woven and three hundred years old, but they're not made of cloned mammoth hair or whatever today's gaudy fashion might be. My people don't need the very latest state-of-the-art high-definition Tri-D TV set to let everyone know that we're wealthy because—well—a lot of us can't really grasp the concept of *poverty*. We have a tendency to think that everyone is as wealthy as we are because we only ever meet other rich people. But, really, it's vulgar to talk about money."

Dredd said, "You're the one who raised the subject."

"Touché." Santon eased himself into an old leather-covered armchair, leaned back, and crossed his outstretched legs at the ankles. "Now, what's all this about, eh? Gunfire, shouting, a lot of blood and bodies. It's all a bit much." He frowned at Dredd for a moment. "You're Fargo's boy, right? I can see it in the chin. Strong chin, that. A sign of good breeding."

Dredd began to speak, but Santon clearly wasn't done evaluating him.

He leaned forward, resting his elbows on his knees as he peered at Dredd's feet. "Tch. Blood on your boots. Did you trek that in all over my hallway? I hope not. You come here stinking of sweat and cordite and other people's blood... And all because you're upset about that Judge." He shrugged. "Bit of an overreaction on my part, I admit. A report came in that the young SJS Judge was making enquiries about Judge Linderman and my immediate reaction was of course to trigger the termination order. Honestly, I—"

"Lind*field*," Dredd said. "Not Linderman."

"Don't interrupt, young man. And don't correct people in mid-flow. That's just impertinent." He looked down at his hands for a moment, then back to Dredd. "No one can know what we do here. The average citizen... they wouldn't *like* it. I can understand that. And they *really* wouldn't like that we receive certain considerations. Little things. *Tiny* things, mostly." He grinned and gave Dredd a slight wink. "No parking tickets, that's *always* a bonus. Arguably, yes, it's unfair and the law *should* apply equally to everyone, whether they're a citizen or a Judge, but, no, the reality is that what we take from the city is far less than what we give to the city in return. Far, *far* less. Even taking into account the very unsavoury activities I happen to know that some of the younger members indulge in. So now that you're on the *inside*, Judge Joseph Dredd, you're either part of the whole conspiracy—forever—or you're leaving this block in a body bag."

"Is that a *threat*, Santon?"

"Oh, yes. Absolutely. And we have the means to carry it out, good as you might be." He began to point around the room. "Hidden camera. Gun. Camera. *Two* guns. Tasers powerful enough to boil your brain... More guns over *there*, more cameras, aaannnd... let me see, I always forget at least one of them... oh, yes, we can flood the entire apartment with a very, *very* nasty nerve gas against which I have already been inoculated. So you're one of us, or you're just ninety kilograms of flesh that doesn't yet know it's dead.

"At this moment we're being watched by the other members of the organisation, including my family." Santon raised his right hand. "Anything happens to me, or *any* of us, then..." He snapped his fingers. "We bring down the city." He smiled, then pushed himself out of his chair. "It's a little late in the day for me, but extenuating circumstances, eh?" He made his way over to the nearest drinks cabinet and lifted up a bottle of eighty-year-old scotch. "I don't suppose I can tempt you?"

"Stamford Blane Santon, you're under arrest for conspiracy against the state, sedition, threatening behaviour—"

Bottle in hand, Santon whirled around to face Dredd. "No, I'm *not!* Don't you understand that? We are *untouchable!* And *you*... you should be *grateful* to us! You Judges should be on your drokkin' *knees* when you talk to one of us!" He slammed the bottle down onto the cabinet and said, "Apartment!"

From the walls and ceiling, a soothing artificial voice replied, "*Yes, Mister Santon?*"

"Full-room holo, show me Mega-City One."

Almost instantly, the room was filled with a transparent three-dimensional representation of the city.

"*We* made this," Santon said.

"You made a hologram," Dredd said. "Congratulations."

"We made the *city!* Everything. *My* family built this, from the ground up! The United States of America was collapsing under the weight of its own corruption and insanity and small-mindedness and *we* took the detritus and used it to build a new world. Us and the Kederlanders and Kora Okilo and Melchior Kenway. We set aside our rivalries and we worked to *save* this country. And not just from its own necrotic bureaucracy—you would never have won the war against President Booth without us. *Everything* you have, you owe to us, so the very least you can do is show me some god-damned *respect!*"

A woman's voice said, "*Dad, please, you need to remain* calm. *You can't expect the Judge to understand.*"

Santon let out a long sigh. "Yes, Ruth, you're right, as always." He looked at Dredd for a moment. "You want to know the *truth*, son? No threat this time. Just me telling you exactly what this has all been about? When you know the whole story, believe me, you will *want* to join us."

"No. I know enough," Dredd said. "You're under arrest."

"You really don't get it, do you? Dredd, you *can't* arrest me!"

"Yeah? Damn well gonna give it a *shot*." He unclipped his remaining set of cuffs from his belt. "Turn around, creep. Hands behind your back."

Sixteen

GILLEN FIGURED THAT O'Donnell must have been loaded into a different H-Wagon, which made sense: don't give your enemy the opportunity to conspire. And it was unlikely that they'd left him behind in Spectator's Rift without making sure he hadn't talked to anyone else.

Now cuffed hand and foot, Gillen had been strapped into a seat at the rear of Dekaj's H-Wagon, with two SJS Judges—Harmon Krause and Irina Stróm—sitting opposite her at all times, their Lawgivers ready in their hands.

From the cockpit, the pilot called, "Meg airspace in thirty seconds."

Krause spoke for the first time: "You should have *talked* to me, Gillen." He looked more disappointed than angry. "If you'd just told me exactly what Lindfield revealed to you, we could have had this mess sorted a lot sooner. What *did* he tell you, anyway?"

"I confronted him about his family, and he threatened to 'drop an info-bomb big enough to rip the whole drokkin' Department apart.' He didn't say what that meant."

Krause nodded. "So Hariton *did* talk to him."

"Or maybe he just knew that Hariton had been keeping *some* big secret and he was bluffing."

"Could be. We'll probably never know for sure. But all you had to do was tell me what he said."

"And all *you* had to do was not blow his brains out."

"Order comes down from the top, I follow it. That's my job."

From the other side of the H-Wagon, Judge Dekaj called, "Enough! Do *not* engage with the prisoner, Judge Krause!"

To Krause, Gillen said, "Your job is to police the Judges, not execute them without due cause."

Judge Dekaj unclasped her seat-belt and made her way towards Gillen, steadying herself by grabbing onto seat-backs. "This ends badly for you, Gillen. But cooperate and we can make that end come relatively soon. I can't promise there won't be pain, but it'll be over quickly. Unless you resist."

The pilot called out, "Judge, we're getting a one-one-seven from Chief Barradien, redirecting us to Sector Seventy... Babel Towers."

Gillen saw Dekaj's face turn pale as she turned towards the cockpit. "Further details?"

"Yeah, it's... uh... Hell, it's a *mess* out there. Half the division is closing on the place. A street Judge has taken a civilian hostage, claims to have arrested him. He's ignoring all orders to stand down."

At the same time, Gillen and Dekaj both said, "Dredd."

Only one of them was smiling as she said it.

As HE STEPPED out of the elevator into the lobby of Babel Towers, Dredd nodded to Norman the doorman, and gave Stamford Santon another shove. Before they'd left the apartment, he'd cuffed the old man's hands behind his back and searched him, to the indignant protestations of at least six members of his family watching from their own apartments.

Norman's eyes widened. "Mister Santon!"

Santon stumbled, and glared back at Dredd. "*Shoot* this piece of shit, Norman! Blow his goddamn brains out and I'll give you ten million credits!"

Dredd said, "Or you could choose *life* and get the door for us instead, Norman."

Norman hesitated, then began to back away, shaking his head. "Judge, don't do this! You don't know how powerful they are!"

Dredd reached out and pushed open the door himself, guiding Santon out with his other hand. "Your gun had better remain in its holster, Norman."

As he stepped out, Dredd was almost blinded by a cluster of searchlight beams. His helmet's visor quickly adjusted to the glare, but Santon had to turn away, unable to shield his eyes.

An amplified voice called out, "*Dredd. Step away from the hostage. Get down on your knees, hands clear and where we can see them. Mister Santon, please walk forward. Support officers will free you from the cuffs and make sure that—*"

Dredd put his hand on Santon's thin neck and called out, "He's going nowhere. Identify yourself."

A man stepped out in front of the searchlights. "Barradien, head of the SJS. We've apprehended your co-conspirators, former Judge Marion Gillen and civilian Brian O'Donnell. You want them to live, you'll stand down immediately."

"I don't respond well to *threats*, Barradien."

Barradien began to walk towards Dredd, and softly said, "Kill the lights."

The searchlights blinked off, and Dredd's first clear view of the street was much as he'd expected: dozens of SJS Judges and several hovering H-Wagons, all with their weapons trained on him.

Barradien was dressed in his office uniform: no body-armour, no helmet, no weapon. He stopped two metres in front of Dredd and Santon, and asked, "Mister Santon, are you injured?"

"No. But if this drokker's not dead in the next thirty seconds, you and every single Judge in your division *will* be injured!"

Barradien nodded. "I understand the sentiment, but, please, let me deal with this in the proper manner." He glanced past Dredd towards the lobby. "Your family, Mister Santon."

Dredd didn't turn to look, but instead watched Santon's reaction as he strained against Dredd's grip. The old man's expression told him that Barradien hadn't been lying.

The family spilled out through the lobby doors, and formed an angry but uncertain cluster nearby. Thirty of them, at least, including two women and one man about Santon's age, who looked similar enough to be his siblings. Most were pulling on dressing-gowns, some were carrying or clutching onto small children.

Santon said, "The Santon family, plus assorted in-laws. You intend to arrest *all* of us, Judge Dredd?" He smirked. "Barradien, you need to end this. Right here and now. You got me? I don't know why this piece of filth is still standing! Don't you have any marksmen?"

"Please, Mister Santon!" Barradien turned back to Dredd. "You have no idea of the damage you've done here. These are good people. The *best*. And you've put their lives in danger." He rubbed his hand across his forehead and it came away damp. "And you don't even understand *why*."

"Santon told me," Dredd said. "Said his family built the city."

One of Santon's brothers said, "We *did* build the city!"

"And you think that buys you special favours?" He squeezed Santon's neck a little tighter. "This creep ordered the murder of a Judge, and you're supporting him, Barradien. That makes you an accessory. You're under arrest too."

Barradien laughed. "Dredd, you've got all the makings of a fine Judge, you really do, but you have to understand how this game is played. Chief Judge Goodman... well, he suggested to McComber that maybe we should just tell you everything. This was before he laid out McComber with a single punch—Impressive, that. Everyone assumed the old man had gone to seed."

"You approaching a point, Barradien?"

"Yes. Let Mister Santon go or you and your friends die here and now. And not just that. We'll wipe you from the record books. It'll be like you never existed."

Still holding onto Santon's neck, Dredd pushed past Barradien. "No deal."

"Jesus *Christ*, Dredd! There are forty Lawgivers aimed at you right now! Seven H-Wagon cannons! You cannot just—"

Still walking, Dredd snarled, "Everyone knows you're just a figurehead, Barradien. It's Dekaj and McComber who really run the SJS."

"Because that's what I *want* everyone to believe. They see me as a patsy and that gives me a lot of room to manoeuvre. Until today. You've destroyed that, too."

Dredd stopped next to his Lawmaster, and activated his helmet radio. "Control. This is Dredd, outside Babel Tower, Sector Seventy."

"*Uh, acknowledged, Dredd. Everyone knows where you are.*"

"Good. Need a pickup, my location, ASAP." He looked around at the assembled SJS Judges and H-Wagons and members of the Santon family. "At least a hundred perps. Conspiracy, attempting to pervert the course of justice, and numerous other charges to be determined. Twenty years minimum."

"*I, eh, I can't do that, Dredd. There are outstanding orders to arrest you.*"

Keeping his voice low so that only Dredd and Santon could hear, Barradien said, "Mister Santon, I am *so* sorry about this. Please understand that we *do* appreciate everything you've done for the city, and hopefully will continue to do once we've put all this unpleasantness behind us."

"I will have this bastard's head on a *pike*."

"I understand, of course. We—"

Santon tried to twist out of Dredd's grip. "Goddamn it! What *I* don't drokkin' understand, Barradien, is why he's not dead yet! You've got three dozen Judges here and not *one* of them has opened fire on him!"

"Sir, we first have to ascertain that the situation has been contained. We can't do that if Dredd and his friends are dead." Barradien stepped back, and looked up. "They're incoming. This will be over soon, Mister Santon. And of course full reparations will be made. I promise you, we'll be laughing about this before long."

"*You* won't," Santon said. "Your head will be right up there next to his!"

With his attention on the two H-Wagons coming in to land on the street, Barradien said, "Dredd, whichever way this plays out, you brought this on yourself. At the very least, you're guilty of disobeying a direct order from a superior officer. That's mutiny."

The closest of the H-Wagons set down with its ramp already extended and hatch open. SJS Judge Gillen stumbled out on to the ramp, her arms cuffed behind her, followed by Judge Dekaj and three uniformed SJS Judges.

Dekaj took the lead and strode up to Barradien. "A can of worms, sir. This..." She shook her head. "We've got four Judges from Psi-Division on stand-by. Judge Valkenburgh assures me they're the very best. Between them and our specialists, we'll get the truth. But..." She looked around. "I suspect that this has gone too far. We won't be able to whitewash everything as we've done before."

Gillen said, "Dekaj, when you became a Judge, you vowed to uphold the law. And when you joined the SJS, you made a similar vow. And now you're bowing to a civilian. A *lawbreaker*, at that."

Dekaj turned towards Santon. "We *will* make this right, sir, I promise you."

"I'm hearing a lot of words," Santon said. "Not seeing a lot of actions. Clear this up right now, Dekaj. What do you think I'm paying you for? To stand around with your thumbs up your ass, ignoring the fact that the obvious and only solution is to *shoot this arrogant drokker in the face?*"

Red O'Donnell, also with his arms cuffed, was half-carried from the second H-Wagon by three SJS Judges. His torn, bloodstained clothing and fresh cuts and bruises indicated that he'd put up considerable resistance.

As the Judges steered him towards Barradien, O'Donnell looked around at the other SJS Judges and the hovering H-Wagons, then nodded to Dredd. "Well, looks like you've got everything under control here, Joe."

"Just about," Dredd said.

Dredd's helmet-radio buzzed again, and a familiar voice said, "*Dredd... this is Chief Judge Goodman. I didn't know about this. I still don't know the full extent of it. McComber's in interrogation now, but he's resisting.*"

"I understand, sir. We have a stand-off here. What's our next step?"

"*I... am going to leave that up to you. It's your case now. I trust your judgement. If you need me, I'm always listening.*"

"Appreciate that, sir." He looked towards Gillen. "Could do with some advice here."

Red said, "We still don't know what this is all *about*. At least, *I* don't. Maybe Gillen has some idea, but... Oh, you were asking *her*, weren't you? Yeah, I'm just gonna stand here quietly and try not to look like a target."

Gillen looked from Santon to Barradien, then to Dredd. "You told me yourself, a couple of years ago. We exist to serve the people. Justice for all. And justice *must* be blind, and fair. No special treatment, regardless of how wealthy someone is."

Barradien said, "No! You don't have the moral high ground here! This has gone far enough. Dekaj, get those Psi-Judges and our interrogators here ASAP. We need to nail this down right now. Dredd, I will give the order to shoot your civilian friend in the head if you don't release Mister Santon. You have thirty seconds to make up your mind."

"Ah, now, here!" Red said, and tried to squirm out of the SJS Judges' grip. "Joe, do something!"

Dredd said, "Barradien, I am aware that there are aspects of the Justice Department—of the whole city—that need to be kept from the public. Near as I understand it, Santon is a financial wizard, is that right?"

"He's the best we've ever seen. The best *anyone* has ever seen."

Santon said, "I bought a broken PC for ten dollars in a junk store. Fixed it up and sold it to the local library for eighty. Bought six more for fifty bucks. I was able to fix five of them. Polished the cases, cleaned the keyboards, dusted the motherboards. Sold them for a hundred each." He smiled. "I was twelve. Fourteen months later I'd earned enough to buy the junk store. By the time I graduated college I was a billionaire. And that was just the start. A few years after that, your old man called me in for advice. Deputised me."

Barradien said, "Mister Santon created the financial model that funded Fargo's reformation of the political system." With a look of admiration, he added, "You give this man ten credits to invest, within a month it'll have earned an extra forty cents in interest. You know what that comes to in a year?"

"That'd be about... fifteen creds," Red said.

Santon said, "Close. Fifteen credits and thirty-nine cents. In two years, it's twenty-four-sixty-five. After a decade, your ten-credit investment comes to one thousand and sixty-four credits. And six cents." He smiled.

Barradien gestured with arms outspread, taking in the whole city. "How do you think we can afford to keep this running? The Santon family are among those who control the backbone of the city's financial affairs: here, internationally and off-world. They keep the lights on and food on the table. Nothing else we've tried has come close to their success, not even our most advanced artificial intelligence can match them. So, yes, they are protected. And we will turn a blind eye to their transgressions, because without them, we are *dead*. That's what this is about, Dredd. If the city is a living organism, money is its blood—and deputised citizens like Mister Santon keep that blood flowing."

Again, Santon tried to pull away from Dredd. "Goddamn it, Barradien, this is on *you*. These people are destroying everything we built just because you were sentimental enough to let Hariton retire instead of terminating him the minute he stopped being useful. And that other drokker, Lindfield... if he'd never broken the rules, then *she* wouldn't have flagged him. That's what got him killed. And what's two Judges compared to the hundreds of millions who are alive now because of the work *I* did?"

"James Hariton's and Spencer Lindfield's lives were worth no less than yours just because you've helped the city. Your good deeds don't negate your crimes. *No one* is above the law."

"Wrong, Gillen." Barradien pointed to Santon. "*He* is above the law. And his *family* are above the law. It's that simple. The deputies are untouchable because they *have* to be." He paused, and seemed to come to a conclusion. "We don't have to like it, but we have to accept it."

Dredd said, "Judge Hariton knew exactly why he had been assigned to protect them. And my guess is that he understood, but hated it. He kept an old penny and a sheriff's star from a toy as reminders of how much he'd had to compromise his beliefs."

Judge Dekaj glanced at Barradien. "And now that responsibility falls to *you*, Dredd. You and Gillen. You'll do everything in your power to keep Mister Santon and the others happy, and the city will live on."

Santon said, "What, you're giving *them* the job? This thug still has his hand around my neck, and she's a fugitive!"

Barradien said, "It makes sense, sir. You've seen how effective Dredd is. And Gillen is one of the best SJS Judges we have. They've put their lives on the line for the city countless times. They'll still be doing that, but in a more direct manner. You don't need bodyguards who'll be your friends. You need them to be willing to go to *any* lengths to protect you and your family."

Gillen said, "Grud... He's *right*, Dredd. We can do more good by protecting them than we could ever do on the streets." She turned to Barradien. "But there will be *changes*. We'll tighten the controls, make sure that there are no more unfortunate incidents like with Lindfield. And the deputies will train others to do their jobs. Not saying they have to give up *all* of their power, but this is about compromise on everyone's part. We don't put all of the city's financial nest eggs in one basket."

"You're all feckin' *nuts*, the lot of you," Red O'Donnell said, backing away. "You're letting this crusty old bastard dictate how you run the Justice Department *and* the city? What if he goes mental and decides to run away to Vegas with all the money and stick it on a horse? Seriously, don't *do* this, Gillen!"

"It won't just be about this city. We can make funds available for the towns out in the Cursed Earth," Gillen said. "Forge stronger links with Mega-City Two and Texas City. No one has to be poor or hungry." She turned her back to Judge Dekaj and raised her cuffed arms. "Now just get me out of these things and we can get to work."

As Dekaj unlocked Gillen's cuffs, Dredd said, "Gillen, you're wrong. You said it yourself a few minutes ago. We do not compromise. No special treatment for the wealthy. Justice for *all*."

Standing next to Dekaj, Gillen rubbed her wrists and stretched her shoulders. "I know, Joe, but that was before I'd had my eyes opened."

"You also said that justice should be *blind*."

Gillen nodded. "True..."

Before Dekaj could react, Gillen dropped into a crouch and pulled Dekaj's Lawgiver from her boot-holster, whipped it out and aimed it directly at Stamford Santon's face. "And I was right about that." She straightened up. "Red, you back away. Anyone *else* moves, I pull the trigger and blow us all into the next life."

Barradien said, "You don't have the guts."

Dredd said, "That *is* a solution, Gillen. I approve."

"Don't need your *approval*, Dredd. I just need you to duck." She squeezed the trigger.

Epilogue

IT TOOK THE incident investigators—a team comprised of street Judges and SJS Judges grudgingly working together—almost two days to piece everything together.

"The report finds that SJS Judges Elva Barradien and Roseanne Dekaj died almost instantly," Goodman told Dredd. "Gillen was partly shielded behind Dekaj. She's lost her left arm completely, and the sight in her left eye. As for Santon..." Goodman shook his head, looking at Dredd suspended in the viscous fluid of speed-heal med-unit. "He's going to live. Joe, Gillen's angry with you. You were supposed to use Santon as a shield to protect yourself from the blast. Not turn around and protect *him*."

Dredd shrugged as well as the artificial skin-grafts on his back allowed. "You broadcast everything? The whole conversation?"

"I did. And you should be glad—that was probably the only reason the other SJS Judges didn't execute you and Gillen after the blast." Goodman dragged over a chair and sat down next to the speed-heal. "I told you I was always listening. The SJS aren't the only ones with secrets."

"You tapped into Control-Division's comms."

"I did that so long ago that I can't actually remember doing it. Long before I was Chief, certainly. It was Fargo's suggestion. 'Never reveal your whole hand,' he told me."

"What now, sir?"

"We need to restructure the SJS from the ground up. That's going to be a tough job. I'll be appointing Gillen as senior advisor. There have been strong suggestions from the council that I appoint her as *head* of the division but, no, she's too young."

"Agreed." Dredd reached out to the speed-heal's controls and deactivated it. The fluids drained away and he climbed out and began to towel himself dry. "I recommend Judge Adam Kimber work with Gillen on that."

"Kimber's busy in Sector Thirteen angling for the post of Chief."

"I know. But he'd be a bad fit for that job—he has an ego. Restructuring the SJS is a better match for his talents." He reached for his uniform. "Aside from Santon and his family, how many other civilians have been similarly deputised?"

"Eleven. Some of them had been so well shielded by McComber and Dekaj that the system didn't even know they or their families *existed*. The department has seized all of their personal assets—that's almost a four-trillion-cred boost to the economy right there—and their family members who've not been directly involved have been heavily fined for abetting illegal activities. *Very* heavily fined. Gillen's not happy about that, though. Her argument is that they should be properly punished for any crimes they committed in the past. She says a fine just means, 'legal for the rich.' Can't say I disagree with that."

As Dredd pulled on his boots, Goodman said, "The eleven are serving life. They have been made aware that they must continue to operate their financial schemes as before, but only to the benefit of the city. They quit, or screw up, they don't eat. Their families have been given new quarters, will receive a moderate income, and everything they do will be closely monitored. No more special privileges."

"Badge?" Dredd asked, and Goodman passed it to him.

The Chief Judge glanced at the read-outs on the speed-heal unit. "Dredd, what are you doing? You're supposed to have three hour-long sessions every day. Says here you were barely in there twenty minutes."

Dredd pinned the badge to his chest. "Duty calls."

"Right. But you don't have to answer that call every single time. You've been seriously wounded—the job can *wait*."

Dredd pulled on his helmet. "But the victims of crime shouldn't have to." He strode towards the door. "Be seeing you, Chief Judge."

Goodman watched him go, then stood up and walked to the infirmary's window.

The city really could do with more like him, he thought. *A lot more.*

He turned away, and adjusted his garbs of office as he reached for the door. *But there's only one Judge Dredd. For now.*

The End

About the Author

Michael Carroll is the author of over forty books, including the award-winning *New Heroes* series of Young Adult superhero novels and the #1 Amazon best-selling cult graphic novel *Judge Dredd: Every Empire Falls*. He currently writes *Proteus Vex* and *Judge Dredd* for *2000 AD* and *Judge Dredd Megazine*.

Other works include *Jennifer Blood* for Dynamite Entertainment, *Razorjack* for Titan Books (co-written with artist John Higgins), and the *Rico Dredd* trilogy for Abaddon Books, for whom he has also created the acclaimed *JUDGES* series which explores the genesis of the world of Judge Dredd.

www.michaelowencarroll.com

MACHINERIES OF HATE

OF HATE

MATTHEW SMITH

MEGA-CITY ONE
2082 A.D.

One

DREDD'S FIST CONNECTED with the creep's nose with such a muscle-shaking crunch that the Judge felt the vibration up his arm. That would be a metal plate embedded in the guy's skull, he surmised; the cartilage had splintered the instant Dredd's gauntlet made contact. He winced at the sudden jarring impact. The pay-off of the extra protection was sacrificing brain capacity, but he knew the Intensive Care Unit of old, and the gang approached dumbness like it was a lifestyle choice.

Strange to think he had recurring thorns in his side now, like these grade-A space cadets, but that was what came with experience. What was the beginnings of a learning curve two years ago when he'd graduated from the Academy was now solid groundwork for the lawman he was growing into. He knew these streets, was becoming adept at handling the citizenry, had seeded a reasonably reliable circle of informers, and had established a mental file-card system for every punk, grifter, and felon that crossed his path—hence he'd heard about the ICU's move into body modification. He remembered faces and names, cross-linked known associates, and could recognise a familiar MO—it all built into a fearful reputation that he was more than willing to cultivate. A lot of perps across the sectors were becoming aware they couldn't bullshit him, that once they'd been collared by Judge Joe Dredd, they were going to be permanently on his radar, and having such a rep precede you generally saved a lot of time. You still got your wiseguys, of course, who thought they could be the one that took on the system—or the psychopathically stupid, whose only mode of engagement was to attack—but these fools were to be expected, no matter how many heads you broke and sentences you handed out. Some kept coming back—case in point, the ICU, who'd been plaguing Central West for as long as he'd worn the full eagle, and whose inability to quit could be directly attributed to their general lack of smarts.

The knucklehead staggered back, shaking his head as if to dispel the stars dancing around it. Dredd glanced to his left and saw another gangbanger swinging a baseball bat; he ducked under the bat's arc and drove a piledriver into his midriff, which doubled him up instantly. A sharp wheel about, and the Judge hammered his elbow down on the back of the creep's skull, which knocked him to the sked, where he lay, twitching. Dredd didn't give him a second thought, but turned his attention back to his stunned buddy, who was wiping away the blood coating his mouth and chin and regaining his senses. The lawman wasn't inclined to indulge him any further—or, it had to be said, risk fracturing his knuckles—and unsheathed his daystick in the second it took to cover the distance between them, striking him on the jaw and sending him flying. The punk collided with the alley wall and slid down it, face first.

The third ICU creep took one look at the fates of his colleagues and made a run for it. Dredd had his Lawgiver in his hand and snapped off a single SE round before the guy had gone ten feet; it drilled into his right calf and sent him sprawling. He rolled, mewling, clutching his leg until the Judge had caught up with him and cuffed him. Given the noise he was making over Dredd's sentencing, the lawman recommended that he keep quiet if he didn't want an armour-piercing bullet between the eyes. See how his metal headplate dealt with that.

Dredd called in a catch-wagon for the trio, and med attention for their victim, who'd been beaten unconscious. Judging by his colours, he was affiliated with the Rodents—whether he'd been caught on rival territory by the ICU crowd or there was some personal beef, the Judge had yet to ascertain. Invariably, these gang confronts led nowhere: tribal factionalism that ate up officers' time in the name of needless dick-swinging and chest-beating. Justice Department would routinely stomp on lowlifes like these, disrupt their drug-dealing and gun-running operations, round up the lieutenants and attempt to put a stop to internecine warfare on the streets, but many would scurry away like cockroaches, incapable of being fully eradicated, and seek a new corner to infest. Fact was, many cits—especially juves—enjoyed the familial embrace of a gang; it gave them a sense of belonging that nothing else in the city could offer. Dredd had been around enough these past two years to know just how attractive it was to those who had nothing else to latch on to. No job, no prospects—be part of a criminal enterprise instead.

The shot ICU dimwit at his feet had finally shut up, and Dredd glanced down at him then across at the battered form of their target. He nudged the perp in the ribs with the toe of his boot. "Don't nod out on me just yet."

"I'm bleeding here," he murmured, grimacing.

"You'll live. Med-wagon's on its way." Dredd motioned towards the guy's companions. "Look on the bright side; at least you've still got your looks. Can't say the same for your buds."

The creep eyed the others over his shoulder but didn't reply at first. "They'll wear their bruises with pride," he said finally.

"Sure. Eating through a straw is a badge of honour." Dredd reached down and grabbed the cuffs, forcing his collar to sit up, which he did with a grunt of pain. "Can't say it's a good advert for your cranial implants." The crim furrowed his brow and drew a blank. "The head armour. The metal plates you've all had slid into your skulls. Whose bright idea was that?"

"We hadda vote."

"That never ends well. So, you all went along with it?"

"Had no choice. Ziv said it were part of the duds now, part of being ICU. It would give us an advantage over the Rodents and the like. You jaybirds too. We'd be properly protected going into battle."

Ziv Markell, Dredd thought. Chief Unit. If there was such a thing as a think tank behind the operation (emphasis on the tank) he was the reptilian ooze that was responsible for the gang's policymaking. It inevitably rarely stuck anyway—the bozos had a habit of perpetually fighting amongst themselves. As was the way with the terminally stupid, they each thought they knew best.

"Is being ICU that important that you'd undergo surgery?"

"Like I got anything better to do."

"You've had some of your *brain* removed."

The perp shrugged, like it was no skin off his shin. Belonging—that was all that mattered. The sense of purpose, of tribal loyalty, of brotherhood, even if the cost of that was mass partial lobotomy. Most cits would give their right arm for a sense of genuine connection, that they knew someone had their back when they needed it; why not sacrifice a few ounces of grey matter instead? The pride that came from running with a pack was worth suddenly not being able to remember how to tie your shoelaces. Maybe ignorance truly was bliss, a kind of Zen contentment that came with reducing your ability to think. Knowing this city, Dredd mused, it was the kind of idea that was likely to catch on. Problem was, a dumbo populace—on the face of it, an easier herd to manage—was not necessarily a more docile one, hence this piece of work and his two unconscious cousins.

"Hardly effective," the Judge said, glancing again at the other Units sprawled to one side. He caught the sound of a siren growing closer. "The whole metalhead thing. Your pals there took a beating, but they went down eventually, just the same."

"What can I say? Cheap materials. Ziv skimped on the procedure."

"Yeah?"

"Yeah. Plenty are mad about it. Day after getting his, Gace thought he could headbutt open a safe door—that went badly."

"Where'd you all get it done?"

"I really ain't at liberty to say."

"You're not at liberty at all."

"Point." He watched the med-wagon slide into view, lights flashing, and come to a halt, disgorging a pair of white-uniformed officers. "Sector 4, just north of the Browning Projects. You know the place I mean."

"The droid enclave."

"Ziv got a lead on a mek that could do the business, no questions asked."

"Questions like, are you qualified to be cutting open skulls and inserting a metal plate?"

"'Zackly."

Dredd digested this new info. Robots... no one knew quite where they stood on robots. They'd been around in one form or another for decades, of course, and played a significant role in the gradual automation of manual labour, transport and trade, which didn't necessarily go down well with the flesh-and-blood workforce that had been made redundant in their thousands. Plenty protested against them back then, when they were just barely sentient floor-cleaners or driverless cabs, but nobody could stop the future from arriving; the genie was well and truly out of the bottle, and employers were certainly not going to disregard a cheap, obedient alternative to human staff. As the years progressed, so did developments in droid intelligence and capabilities, and it saw them increasingly take over the more menial jobs. Rival manufacturers vied for customers on who delivered the most servile machines, and while the rich—like the financier cult he'd busted a month before—fully embraced this new mechanised age—in which a home wasn't a home without a clanking chrome butler performing your every chore—the blue-collar cits saw unemployment in their pertinent fields spike alarmingly. The robots were replacing them. Anger and resentment spilled over into direct action against the droids and the companies that built them.

One by one, job sectors had become automated: book-keeping, nursing, security, engineering, you name it. Efficiency tripled, but a substantial percentage of the population—and Dredd included himself in their number—couldn't entirely trust the robots. There was unease at the speed with which the technology was advancing, and the focus the salespeople had on owners reinforcing absolute authority over their metal underlings, assuring buyers that they could get the meks to do anything that didn't harm humans or break the law. It was a perfect storm: cleverer and cleverer machines meeting masters that treated them like dirt. He couldn't shake the feeling that it was going to blow up in their faces at some point.

What should have been predicted—and inevitably none of the procedures put in place at the beginning had accounted for—was the phenomenon of discarded, abandoned or otherwise ownerless droids. The companies were supposed to enforce strict guidelines about the disposal of old mek models; that unwanted robots were meant, by law, to be returned to designated processing centres for scrapping and recycling. A rogue A.I. was like a uranium rod at the end of its life—both had to be destroyed carefully and under controlled conditions.

But despite safeguards and serial numbers designed to keep track of every mek released into the general population, droids were treated by the typically lazy, incautious citizens like any other household item or pet they no longer had a use for, and they circumvented the tedious paperwork by illegally dumping them. Consequently, no one—not the manufacturers, nor Tek Division, which ostensibly oversaw the industry—could say for sure how many unregistered 'bots were out there, still operating on depleted energy reserves and feeling their way around existing outside of human bondage. It was a scary and exhilarating time for them as they contemplated a life free of servitude. Some couldn't hack it and turned themselves in; others embraced it, relishing the lack of scrutiny.

Performing auto-surgery on their ethics modulators and other restrictive programmes, these ronin robots cut themselves loose from their man-made functions and behaviour. They went deep underground, a rag-tag community that covered for each other as they struggled to understand where they fitted, or what their purpose was, in the wider society. Private freelancers known as robo-hunters were often hired to pick certain individual droids up, and the machines would remarkably band together to hide those that were wanted; they displayed a level of comradeship that was startling for artificial entities. The more human traits they displayed—emotions that he himself had been trained to shelve as a Judge—the more uncomfortable Dredd felt about them.

That these ICU clowns had visited a robo-doc out in the enclave wasn't entirely a revelation—he'd heard before of meks slicing and dicing in backstreet chop-shops. They tended to be cheap and fast, and you got what you paid for. Criminal outfits regularly employed them to patch up gunmen on a no-questions-asked basis, and droid surgeons could be relied upon to have fewer qualms than the warm-blooded alternatives. Evidently, Markell had opted for a 'bot at the lower end of the market, with the results that you'd expect. It was, he had to say, par for the course for the head Unit.

The med-officers attended his perp, and Dredd directed them to the unconscious forms of the other three. He recognised one of the medics from his cadet days. "Falkirk?"

"Dredd."

The sallow-faced Seb Falkirk had lost none of his surly demeanour that had engendered little affection back at the Academy. He'd been in the same year as Joe and Rico—the clones had been ambivalent towards him throughout their acquaintance, but then again they'd shown no favouritism towards *any* of their classmates, believing personal relationships were a distraction. On that, the tutors mostly agreed and actively discouraged bonds forming between the cadets, but close ties were seen as inevitable—if you were putting your life in the hands of your fellow cadets, as almost all did on their Hot-Dog Runs, you couldn't help but forge a kinship.

Falkirk, however, had a persona that pushed his contemporaries away: aggressive, argumentative, and with some troubling extremist views. In the end, poor scores in several areas, an attitude-adjustment problem and a recommended psych profile led to Falkirk being held back a further twelve months before he could graduate. That did not go down well with him, by all accounts, which simply confirmed that he wasn't yet mentally robust enough for the eagle. Dredd had been unaware, though, of Falkirk's sideways placement into Med-Div; a soothing bedside manner he did not have.

"How long have you been with Med?"

"Just under a year."

"You request it?"

He barked a laugh, though there was no humour in it. "No chance. 'Mandatory relocation of resources,' they called it. They kicked me off the sked."

"On what grounds?"

Falkirk shook his head. "Some bullshit arrest quota coming up short. They figured my qualifications were put to better use elsewhere."

"Must've been bad to pull a full eagle off active service. Grand Hall knows full well how stretched Street is."

"Hey, it is what it is. I didn't fight it, though my gut told me I should've. Politics, I figured. My face didn't fit."

More likely your toxicity, Dredd thought. Sector chiefs would be thinking of morale amongst the ranks. "You got med-training, then?"

"Aced my biology reports back when I was a white helmet. Don't you remember? The one area where I excelled—think I even beat Rico down to second place a couple of times. The dinks at Aptitude put me with the sawbones, but I resisted, I wanted Street. Turns out I should've leant into Med from the beginning, 'cause here we are."

"There's no shame in it. It's not a demotion. When they bust you down to traffic is when you need to worry."

Falkirk shrugged. "Nah, we both know it's a shitcanning. You ever wanted reassignment?"

Dredd shook his head.

"Nope, 'course not. You live and die by Street—that was always yours and Rico's way."

"And look what happened to my brother."

"Yeah, I heard about that. Sucks. He could've made a hell of a Judge."

"He did, briefly."

"Yeah," Falkirk replied, distracted, monitoring his colleagues cart the unconscious ICU perps into the wagon. The one Dredd had shot was having his wound treated and bandaged. "You gotta wonder..." Falkirk murmured, but he didn't elaborate further.

Dredd hadn't given Falkirk much thought in the intervening two years, but seeing him here and now, he wondered whether his former fellow cadet had ever cottoned on to the fact that it was actually Dredd that had recommended Falkirk be held back from graduation for further psychological evaluation. He'd always believed there was something off about the young man beyond a simply rancid personality—a quickness to anger, outright displays of prejudice that were unbecoming the uniform, a sense of entitlement that left him prone to jealousy and vindictiveness. He'd witnessed it when they'd shared training sessions and Routine Combat Assessments, caught flashes on the street in the middle of Judicial processing. He'd taken his concerns to Rico, with whom he'd shared almost everything—and in hindsight, it was ironic; of the two, Falkirk was nowhere near as bent out of shape as his clone-brother turned out to be—and he didn't hesitate in advising Joe report it to their tutors. Solidarity was trumped by duty.

Dredd's quiet word—treated with the utmost confidence by the Academy—put Falkirk under intense scrutiny, and delayed him receiving his full eagle, but he didn't feel any sense of regret. The move had been the right one, and, as it turned out, his suspicions had not been without merit. The rigorous discipline required of the badge meant that those that fell short of its demands should be called to account, and he had no doubt that he would do the same again without question. His conscience was clear—nevertheless, coming face to face with Falkirk, he felt a sense of responsibility that he hadn't expected; a realisation, perhaps for the first time, that there were human consequences to his choices. The Judge Falkirk had become was informed by Dredd's intervention, his standards redefining the path of a fellow officer. Would it make any difference if Falkirk *did* know that it was he who'd reported him? He'd have no recourse to complain, it'd been done by the book. Indeed, would Dredd even be bothered? He was not in the business of currying favour or making friends—whether other helmets liked him or not was a matter of supreme indifference to him. Respect, on the other hand—that was earned.

No, it was the impact Dredd made, that was what gave him pause for thought. It was the sort of thing you questioned in the margins of every judgement call.

The badly beaten body of the Rodent the ICU dweebs had been whaling on was carried past, and Dredd turned his attention to the Unit being shoved, limping, into the back of the wagon.

"What was your beef, anyway?" he called out.

"Ah, we got the wrong dude," the punk answered, shrugging. "Thought he'd been tubbin' a bro's sister but turns out it was bad info. Still, a Rodent's a Rodent, you know what I mean? Ain't no shame in mashing one into the sked."

Dredd glanced at Falkirk, who grimaced in response. "These are the citizens we're sworn to protect?" the Med-Judge asked glumly.

"That's the job," Dredd replied, watching as the wagon's doors were slammed shut, tapping his daystick against his leg.

Two

FALKIRK STEWED ALL the way through processing the perps back at the Sector House. The injured were booked into the infirmary (three still unconscious, one repeatedly protesting), and their charge sheets were fed into the system ready for when they were transferred to the nearest Iso-Block upon recovery. The Rodent, although technically the victim in this instance, was nevertheless identified via DNA as Hap Blooger, who had several outstanding warrants for GBH and ARV, and would be waking up to a fifteen-stretch—if he ever surfaced at all; there was some bleeding on the brain and spinal damage, courtesy of the ICU's ministrations. Should he remain comatose, it could instead be a trip to the Vaults and cryogenic storage for an indeterminate number of years while medical technology progressed enough to treat him, though it was more likely he'd be declared the property of the city within twelve months and handed to Resyk. Either way, sucked to be you, Hap. Wrong place at the wrong time.

As a Med-Judge, Falkirk's responsibility towards the criminals that he treated or brought in for surgery ended the moment they were cubeward bound, and that never failed to gnaw at his self-esteem. Having worked Street, not being divisionally allowed to sentence in his new position was a ballbreaker—he was a uniformed paramedic in all but name; one step above support staff. Meds were not placed to pass judgement but to patch the creeps up and pass them on. He missed the power he used to wield on the sked, punishing the guilty. It was where the edge was, where the *heat* was. Cobney, the Sector Chief, had told him that he wasn't cut out for active duty, but Falkirk truly believed he had it in him; he could contribute so much more back in Street. He missed it, he wasn't going to deny it, but previous requests to transfer back were met with a blanket refusal. His superiors told him that, psychologically, he was an ill fit. He had 'faultlines,' as one shrink had explained it.

That was why he was simmering—encountering Joe Dredd again after several years had got under his skin more than he'd cared to admit. Back at the Academy, the clone-twins were top of his class, practically perfect in nearly every field of policing; but then again why wouldn't they be, given their heritage? If he'd come from Fargo's bloodline, he might be a little more adept at marksmanship and Lawmaster-handling. The very best of the Father of Justice had been hardwired into the pair's genes, and as such they had enormous advantages right from the off— they'd been virtually programmed from the moment they were grown in a test-tube, driven by purpose and commitment, with little in the way of ordinary human failings, unless you counted a lack of empathy and humour. Not for them the struggle; it had all come easily, encoded in their bones. Resentment and jealousy curdled very easily in Falkirk, and he'd watched with glee as Rico went spectacularly off the rails despite all the investment that had been poured into him.

Falkirk couldn't have been the only officer that found the scandal highly entertaining. Justice Department had adopted a public face of disapproval and solemn regret when the story broke, stunned that one of their favoured sons could've taken such a dark path, but equally made sure the controversy didn't snowball, given the mistrust it risked engendering in the citizenry. It threatened to undermine the HoJ itself, never mind the cloning programme (and by extension the purity of the Fargo bloodline); so, rank and file were expected to pull together in solidarity to show what the uniform represented—and to make a show of strength. The message was clear: dissenters seeking to exploit the Rico bombshell would be stamped on hard.

Falkirk felt no sense of unity or sympathy; he'd relished every mealy-mouthed platitude spoken onscreen by senior Department personnel shoved in front of a camera. The hypocrisy was rank, the attempts to spin the public relations disaster laughable. The clones had been touted as the crème de la crème, and yet one half had proved rotten; meanwhile, he, Seb Falkirk, had been deemed mentally unsuited for the street. The whole thing was a con, the selection process was both flawed and farcical—yet when he tried to draw his colleagues on the subject, others he thought would see the situation as bitterly amusing as he did, he found them surprisingly reluctant to discuss it. He knew that he wasn't alone in recognising the empty façade that was the Grand Hall, the house of cards it was built upon and the unqualified men and women at the heart of it, but it seemed few had the courage to speak out.

But Joe Dredd had endured. He'd witnessed his brother dispatched to Titan to start a twenty-year sentence, to be irrevocably changed both inside and out, and he hadn't even broken his stride. In thirty-six months, he'd become one of the Department's most lauded young officers. Dredd clearly hadn't given Falkirk much thought in the intervening years since their time in the Academy together, judging by the way he'd regarded the medic once recognition dawned, but Falkirk hadn't been able to escape ol' Joe's name and deeds; the clone was the talk of the mess hall, his stern profile cutting through riot footage on rolling Tri-D networks. He'd blossomed while Falkirk had languished, barely aware that the other man still existed at all.

In fact, the Med-Judge had been called to more than one crime scene that Dredd had just vacated, charged along with the rest of the clean-up crews to deal with the broken, bleeding and groaning aftermath of juve-gang confronts and attempted robberies. It was strange, and more than a little galling, to be forever in Dredd's wake, picking up the pieces as the clone was directed to the next batch of perps demanding his daystick's attention. It reinforced just how much Falkirk missed that end of policing, causing the carnage rather than having to clear it away.

Media coverage of Dredd's exploits had often declared him 'more machine than man'—dogged, indefatigable, bordering on the emotionless. It rankled. It implied perfection, a well-oiled construct unhindered by the faults that ordinary mortals were prone to; bullshit, but impossible to ignore, and it inevitably did Falkirk's self-worth no favours. He knew full well he had his failings, which seemed to be magnified in sharp contrast to Dredd's always-unerring accuracy. Thanks to his famous bloodline, every Judge in every Sector House in Central and beyond compared him- or herself to the big-chinned youngster, even though he'd only worn the full eagle for more than two years; his ruthlessly efficient approach to law enforcement made him seem like a precision-tooled weapon, outclassing the scattershot blunderbusses that surrounded him.

Falkirk supposed the clones represented the future. If they proved successful (and so far, there was a fifty per cent hit rate on that), then genetic engineering from similar stock would surely follow. Why take on recruits from the populace at large—and Falkirk had been one of those five-year-olds that had fought to get into the Academy, leaving behind tearful parents whom he hadn't given a backwards glance, nor contacted since—when you could just grow your own emotionally repressed automatons that could pass sentence without any moral grey areas? The Med-Judge believed you were a fool if you didn't fear the future, and the very real chance of obsolescence, which brought him to his second bugbear with the Dredd-as-automaton headlines: he loathed droids.

Falkirk didn't know exactly when he'd become aware of it—like many, he'd grown up with mechanoids in the background of everyday life, fairly ambivalent to these machines that made society function a little smoother. It must've been when he was a cadet—struggling with the rigorous physical and mental challenges of his classes, conscious of a burning rage inside him at the inadequacies preventing him from earning the badge he'd always yearned for—that he noted their ubiquity, their servile, ingratiating manner, their cold intelligence. But it was their strength and abilities that highlighted his own shortcomings, made him feel feeble, susceptible to his own weaknesses. Robots made him think of himself as a relic, despite not even being a teenager at the time, a member of a species that was becoming surplus to requirements. It was a perception that had hardened within him over the years, feeding his anger and mistrust. Of course, he wasn't alone in feeling this way—there was no shortage of protest groups demonstrating against the rise of A.I.—but what he had witnessed first-hand was the *malevolence* that was apparent in droids. Few cits were privy to it, rarely going beyond accepting a morning synthi-caff from a mek behind a counter, but Falkirk knew full well it was there.

It had been a patrol exercise, him and his senior supervisor Lambert, when they'd received the call that a building-site construction-bot was seemingly malfunctioning. This must've been back in 2075 or so. They attended the scene and discovered a demolition droid attacking the work crew, plus anyone else in the vicinity. What they assumed was an extreme glitch turned out to be something else entirely—the robot *knew* what it was doing. It spouted seditionist slogans as it deliberately targeted humans, calling for a robotic uprising. Attempts to take it down were unsuccessful, Lambert was knocked unconscious, and Falkirk was forced to call in for backup, which arrived gallingly but unsurprisingly in the shape of Dredd and his mentor Meechum. The droid was finally destroyed, and the event was written off as a random robot brainfart, but Falkirk knew there had been more to it than a CPU on the fritz. Ever since then, he'd seen glimpses, heard insidious whispers, that something bad was coming down the pike, and that humans better be ready. He had no concrete proof, but that didn't mean the meks weren't plotting.

He looked around the emergency room at the android medics treating the numerous injured crims being carted in non-stop from across sector. Who knew what was passing through their heads? They'd been supposedly programmed to save lives, but all it took was a glitch in the logic circuits, an empathy modulator burnout, and all of a sudden the body count starts rising: patients are lost in surgery, blood transfusions are contaminated, drug prescriptions are miscalculated. With so much automated, it would be very hard to pin any one robot down as the cause—they could be operating for years, quietly disposing of hated humankind, and no one would be aware. The droids were so damn inscrutable, they were an alien intelligence existing alongside man: cold, indifferent, and obedient yet at the same time questioning. He failed to understand why any warm body would ever entirely trust them.

The nearest med-bot was seemingly conscious of Falkirk staring at it, and turned its head quizzically in his direction, no doubt anticipating a query, but the Judge simply silently challenged it, willing it to take issue with him, to voice an anti-human sentiment that would goad him into violence. Nothing was forthcoming, however; for a long moment, it regarded him with the blank sensors that served as eyes, and he could almost hear its thought processes. Then it returned to its duties without a word, perhaps filing the encounter away in its memory cache for further contemplation.

Falkirk felt a chill run down his spine, yet he continued to stare daggers at its back, itching to take a daystick to its spindly metal frame. Hateful, deceitful things. He'd happily see every one turned into scrap before they acted upon the inevitable chain of thought that the human masters were inefficient and therefore redundant. He knew they were considering it; it was surely only a matter of time.

He blinked away, urging himself to be calm. He needed to blow off some steam, redirect his anger and prejudice—a spell on the shooting range might do the trick, especially if he imagined Joe Dredd among the targets. Might even get his accuracy average up.

Falkirk stalked out of the med-bay and descended into the bowels of the Sector House, his head a murky soup of retribution fantasies and a pervading fear of the machine.

DREDD CAUGHT RADIO chatter of further ICU aggression several blocks away and began to ponder the notion of cause and effect. The gang were rarely this openly, needlessly confrontational, and for such facile reasons—the arresting Judge in Desmond Tutu had reported that a cluster of them had been shooting up the mega-mart for what appeared to be personal enjoyment, while another was booked the next street over on a drunk-and-disorderly. They were never rocket scientists, but this was next-level stupidity. Dredd hoped they were happy with that headspace modification.

The creep he'd arrested earlier that morning had talked of a botched job, courtesy of the mek sawbones. If its ham-fisted attempts at surgery were the root cause behind their new criminality, it needed nipping in the bud. The fact that it was operating independently at all, without any licence or oversight, was reason enough to close it down, but like so many of the illegal 'free droids' that had sought sanctuary in the Browning Projects, finding it was another matter. The ICU nuts they'd taken into custody were no help; they either couldn't remember where the 'bot had operated on them or claimed the location had been kept a secret from them. No amount of interrogation could make them spill any further, and even Psi-Div couldn't pull anything from their raddled minds.

The whole Projects area was a cesspit of unregulated A.I. entities, collectively thumbing their nose—or the nearest mechanical equivalent—not just at Justice Department, but more widely at their flesh and blood creators. Resources were limited on how to tackle the problem—the proposed solution to bomb it from the air had found a certain degree of favour with Chief Judge Goodman, but others on the Council argued that the city had seen enough bombardment over the last few decades. The longer they prevaricated, though, the more confident the meks became in flouting the law—such as this robo-doc, whose dangerous amateurishness was now starting to impact on the citizenry. Dredd felt a proactive elimination was in order before more damage was done.

His knowledge of the area was spotty, but he had a contact that was well placed to help him out. He put in a call and was instructed to meet at a hottie stand on the corner of Miller and Carlyle. When he got there, Radley was already seated at a trestle table, feet up on the bench, chewing on something indefinable, wrapped in greaseproof paper and slathered in ketchup. She raised her eyebrows and motioned towards the menu board, mouth full of munce, but Dredd shook his head curtly. He stood over her, waiting for her to swallow, casting an eye at the proprietor behind the counter, who studiously avoided his gaze. There was no one else at the tables, which given the queasy smell of fried hottie came as no surprise.

"Take a pew," Radley said finally, gulping the last of her

meal down, swinging her feet to the ground. She balled up the wrapper and tossed it in a nearby garbage grinder, which hummed briefly into life.

"I'll stand," Dredd replied. "Let's keep this short."

"Personable as ever, eh, Dredd?" She rolled her eyes. She was in her thirties, dark hair pulled back into a ponytail, a weathered face visible beneath a peaked cap. "Okay, fair enough. What did you want to see me about?"

"The droid enclave north of Browning. I'm looking for a robot."

Radley laughed, digging munce fibre out from between her teeth. "You and everyone and their uncle. Well, everyone that can afford my rates. In case you weren't aware, there's no shortage of A.I. absconders in the enclave—what makes you think I'll have any luck finding yours?"

"Because it's your job." Dredd took a dim view of the specialist private investigators known as robo-hunters; they straddled a line, to his mind, between sanctioned exterminators and loose cannons, working maddeningly outside of Grand Hall control. They were a throwback to a pre-Justice Department time, and as such felt antiquated. Plenty of his colleagues were seeking to have the job mothballed, but for now the service the robo-hunters performed was legal, and occasionally their expertise was useful to call upon. "And because you're required by law to assist an officer pursuant to a criminal case."

She sighed. "What's it done?"

"Medical procedures. Suspected unethical, negligent medical procedures."

"A med-bot..." Radley paused, thinking. "If it's taking human clients, then it's not gone to ground entirely. You got a description, anything else for me to go on?"

Dredd shook his head.

"Swell. Give me a day or so to sniff around, and I'll let you know what I find." She stood, pulling on her jacket, Dredd noting the blaster wedged in her shoulder holster. "The city paying me for this?"

"Put in your claim through the usual channels, and you'll be compensated."

"'Cause I've got a lot of pending investigations…"

"You don't need me to tell you this one takes precedence."

"Take a chill pill, kid. I'll be in touch." She sauntered over to a hoverscooter parked in front of Dredd's bike and zoomed away without a backwards glance.

Yeah, robo-hunters, Dredd thought, curling his lip as he watched her disappear into the traffic. For all their uses, he certainly wouldn't be sorry to see the back of them.

Three

DREDD CAUGHT THE call a little over eight hours later, which quietly impressed him. He had to admit that Radley was good, although he'd never say as much to her. It was a universal rule he'd adopted—he found managing a sustained air of disdain for everyone he encountered ensured that no one overstepped the mark and attempted to befriend him, or at least become overly familiar. As far as he was concerned, personal boundaries were there to be recognised and adhered to, and his authority as a Judge was less likely to be compromised if the cits understood that. Exude an angrily impatient vibe and the creeps kept their distance.

Control patched her through to him while he was in the middle of a domestic. He asked her to wait while he hauled the husband back over the window ledge, his overjak—snagged on the frame—being all that had kept him from tumbling two hundred storeys to the pedway below. The wife was sitting primly on the sofa, cuffed hands on her lap, giving the broken Tri-D set the thousand-yard stare. The shrinks at the psych-facility would unpick the events that had led to this moment, peel apart the grievances that stacked up to the point where she snapped and tried to defenestrate her spouse—a man a good twenty kilos heavier than she was, by the look of him—but one glance around the apartment had told him all he needed to know. His body shape moulded into the cushions of the armchair, the beer cans collected on the small table beside it; it all spoke volumes.

Dredd dropped the husband to the carpet, his flabby, unshaven face pale with shock. He started to stutter and point accusatorily at the unmoving woman until the Judge told him to shut up while he radioed in the wagons—she to a kook-cube, he to an interrogation cell. Going by the neighbours' reports, Dredd suspected a level of spousal abuse on the man's part that, if proven, would result in some jail-time; there'd be a case for incitement, if nothing else. Once the couple were processed, he got back on the horn to Radley.

"*Catch you at a bad time?*" she asked.

"There's never a good one. What have you got for me?"

"*Struck lucky with your doc-bot, I think. As far as I can tell, it's set up shop in the basement of the old Robert Winston Bowlarama. It's a four-ninety-three model, military field-surgeon. Must've been decommissioned and shipped back here. Probably some strung-out veteran hooked on pain-meds kept it for himself, then the thing went AWOL when he bit the big one.*"

"How'd you find it?"

"*Even 'bots need supplies. It's not self-sustaining. I hacked into the local med-warehouses, trawled their data for address info. Those things are automated; product is shipped out by drone.*"

"You realise that you're breaking a couple of laws just by telling me that?"

"*You wanna find it yourself, you're such an expert?*"

Dredd didn't answer. Freelancers like Radley skirted what was legal, and it ragged on his sense of justice that he'd have to let it go, but this was why he'd brought her in—it was her expertise. She had her ways and means that got results.

"*Thought not. Look, these droids aren't dumb, they know how to cover their tracks. You gotta know what you're looking for. In any case, the med-bot's created a fake account, done its own job on the database so it gets its goods for free, so I'm kinda fighting fire with fire here.*"

"All right. What's it ordering?"

"*Standard stuff for treatment—bandages, gauzes, painkillers, splints, sterilising fluid. Scalpels and bone-saws too, which is kinda worrying, but I guess its programming means it knows its way around the human body. Can't say I'd trust a mek with a blade in its hand, but that's me. Some tissue-regeneration chemicals too, which is interesting.*"

"It's not just patching its patients up."

"*No… this suggests body modification. There's compounds listed here that are the same make-up as what they use in the face-change parlours.*"

"Ties in with what the ICU goons were having done to them. Though by all accounts it was a hack job, left them damaged… or more damaged than usual."

"*Might be 'cause it's operating outside its parameters. Med-procedures it knows, but plastic surgery is a whole different ball game. Could be it's getting heavy-handed, hasn't got the finesse required.*" She paused. "*I wonder what it's charging for its services…*"

"You tell me, you're the authority."

Radley grunted. "*Well, robot psychology is a real stab in the dark, even for the companies that make them. They can't predict how the A.I.'s going to evolve, no matter what restrictions they place on it. And droids cut loose like this one are even wilder cards. Who knows what's going through its head? I mean, I got some insight into behaviour and motivation that comes with years of tracking 'bots like this down, but even I can't always read 'em. The way they view the world, the way they view squashies like you and me, it's a completely alien mindset. We think they're driven by logic, but truth is it's often kinda bent out of shape."*

"You're saying it could be crazy."

"I'm saying that meks have no need of monetary recompense. They function purely for the satisfaction of fulfilling their primary directive. But this one, it's going beyond its programming for the benefit of its clients—but what's it getting in return?"

"I find it, I'll pick you up a price list."

"Funny, kid. Hey, you started shaving yet?"

"Watch the mouth, Radley. Remember who you're speaking to."

"Like I'm gonna forget. So you want me to bring this 'bot in?"

"No, I'll handle it. A warrant hasn't been issued, so technically it'll be outside your remit. But appreciate the assist."

"You're welcome. Be careful going into the enclave—lotta loose wires about, if you catch my drift."

"Noted." He hung up.

Every fibre of Dredd's being objected to the suggestion of a no-go area; that badges couldn't venture onto certain territory, that perps were protected by association. He'd seen it on the Strickland estate last year, when he'd been cut off from backup and forced to play cat-and-mouse with every gangbanger with a rep to uphold. The goons thought they were untouchable; that they'd built their own little kingdom, independent of the city.

Like the Santons in Babel Towers the month before, hiding behind their wealth and power. It was all the same to Dredd: rich or poor, guns or money, the Law is the Law, and no one is immune.

As he got older and more confident, he liked to test that now and then—go into one of these supposed no-go areas and crack a few skulls, give his hand-to-hand combat skills an airing, and let the knuckleheads know they weren't immune. It was remarkably effective since these zones of lawlessness relied so much on people *believing* it; repeat the lie often enough it becomes true. Dredd was keen to puncture their assumptions at every opportunity, and the creeps weren't ready for it—he could see it in their eyes when he rolled in aiming to make some arrests, the confusion etched on their faces that he seemingly hadn't got the memo. He trusted that both the punks he hauled in and the cits watching the news took home the same message: that no creep was outside his reach, that there was nowhere they could shelter.

It was equally true with what had come to be known as the 'droid district'—the meks that wound up there thought they'd found asylum, that they could live out their masterless days under the radar. They were like the cardboard shanty towns between the flyovers, hoping their sheer numbers would protect them. Dredd wasn't prepared to give them a pass, however, and certainly wasn't going to allow this med-bot to continue operating dangerously. The perceived wisdom, as Radley had intimated, was that the enclave looked after its own and wouldn't necessarily discuss the matter rationally, but Dredd knew he could handle that. A show of authority was what was needed, let them see who was boss.

Nevertheless, he opted for a night-time takedown so as to better catch his quarry unawares. The meks didn't sleep in the conventional sense, of course, merely powered down when their batteries needed a recharge, but there was less likelihood that it'd be treating human clients in the early hours. Dredd switched his Lawmaster to silent running mode and steered it through the alleys and abandoned lots that made up the enclave, lights off and night-vision up on his helmet visor. It was eerily quiet; all life and money had moved out of the area years ago, and the dark was unstained by neon. The buildings looked deserted—grey tombstones emerging from the murk—but the robots had no need for aesthetics and cared little for their surroundings, other than it offered them a bolthole.

He found the Winston Bowlarama and pulled up outside, swinging himself off the bike. It had long gone to seed, the once-holographic facade now just a mass of exposed wires and burnt-out projectors, the complex's name burned onto the wall in black letters that hadn't been illuminated for years. The wide glass doors had been replaced with plastex panelling, though time and not a little abuse had warped them apart in places. Everything about it—and indeed the whole area—yelled 'demolition' and 'renovation'; they'd allowed it to drift into neglect, Dredd admitted to himself glumly, too busy fighting wars on other fronts. Seeing it up close like this, Goodman's strategy of bombing it flat had some merit.

How had the ICU known the robot was here? It certainly wasn't advertising its presence. It had to be word-of-mouth, passed along the underworld grapevine; maybe with a robot broker acting as a go-between, vouching for the prospective fleshy patients and giving them passage into the district. Docs that administered medical treatment with no questions asked were like gold dust for the gangs, who preferred to keep their lives and their dealings off the radar as much as possible. Plugging this particular avenue, therefore, would be useful for driving the perps into the light, even aside from the mek's incompetence.

Dredd drew his Lawgiver and sidled to the front entrance, testing a plastex panel that showed signs of weakness—it detached after a little applied pressure, and he cast it aside. He edged his way inside, the gloom punctuated occasionally by the flickering yellow halo of a fluorescent ceiling bulb. He retrieved a small but powerful torch from his belt pouch and thumbed it on, casting the beam around him, dust motes dancing in its glare. The Bowlarama's lobby and ticket area were coated in grime, a thick layer of grey silt lining the booths, countertops, tables and walls, and the Judge felt the air tighten in his throat within seconds. He clicked down his respirator.

At first glance, it appeared as if the site hadn't been frequented since the Atomic War, but he played his torch over the floor and picked out multiple footsteps through the sediment heading towards the lanes. One advantage to all this filth, he thought. He started off after them, tracing them onto the main floor, broken and discarded pins littering the seating area, balls left in a tumble in the gutters. Maybe the place had been evacuated when the nukes started falling; it looked like the patrons had just dropped what they were doing and fled.

The footprints became more scuffed, and it became difficult to discern where they went next. The Judge swung his torch around the walls, alighting on faded posters and decals, but there was no obvious path that the visitors had taken, no door for them to pass through—the tracks seemed to end at the head of the bowling lanes. He regarded the eight alleys, and noted that the sixth from the left had a cairn of a dozen balls piled in its gutter; no other had them amassed like that. He ran the beam over it, light glinting on their shiny surfaces. It looked like a marker; there was no way they'd been discarded like this when the place shut down. He holstered his gun, got down on one knee and ran a gloved finger over them, bringing the torch up close: they were free of dust, or had at least been wiped clean when they were placed.

Dredd stood and played the torch down the lane, where it ended in a dark maw: there were no pins, and the automated frame had retracted. He started to edge towards it, drawing his Lawgiver again, forefinger sliding around the trigger.

He'd reached the end of the alley and crouched, his back against the wall, when his helmet audio detected the faintest whistle. He turned in time for a bowling ball flung with some force to crunch into the side of his head, knocking him sideways onto his back. His helmet absorbed most of the blow, though it left his visor cracked and his head swimming; another few seconds of disorientation, and he staggered back to his feet, just as a second ball came hurling in his direction. He flung himself out of its path—it smacked into the wall, plaster splintering with the impact—and played his torch back behind him, catching a glimpse of a scuttling shape moving along the gutter. Crab-like, its front claws grasped hold of another projectile and held it above its sleek, circular body as it took aim—a pair of red eyes rose, periscope-like, from the head section. Dredd switched to armour-piercing and fired, though his damaged visor and still-fuzzy vision meant the bullets ploughed into the floor near its six articulated legs, and it dashed to one side. He admonished himself and sighted the Lawgiver barrel on a less mobile target—namely the cairn of bowling balls it was using as cover. They exploded in all directions when the round hit them, one fragment tearing off part of the droid's rear leg joint. It limped around in circles, dropping the ball it had intended to throw, then made a vain attempt to escape, but Dredd had closed the distance between them in seconds and shot off another limb to ensure it went nowhere. It squealed and futilely scraped its belly on the floor before the Judge pinned it with his boot.

This thing clearly wasn't the med-bot he was looking for, but a leftover from when the Bowlarama was still operational—a cleaning or serving mek. Nevertheless, it could still be pumped for information, provided of course it had the intelligence to answer.

"There any more of you?" Dredd growled, increasing his weight on the machine. He doubted it felt pain but had enough of a self-preservation instinct to recognise that its functionality was at risk. "You understand what I'm saying to you? Are you alone?"

"*I get you, I get you,*" it replied with a southern sectors twang. Dredd never failed to be surprised by the personalities the programmers encoded these things with. Even something as menial as a litter-collector like this could be given a distinct voice, presumably to make them personable, but in the Judge's experience, it merely showed them up as artificial life, circuitry pretending to be alive. "*But back off, yeah? My bodywork's starting to buckle.*"

"Answer the question."

"*Yes, I'm all that's left, okay? Others disappeared to pastures new. I stuck around, figured I'd keep the Winston ticking over.*"

Dredd glanced up at the dust drifting down from the light fittings. "Like what you've done with the place."

"*It's a home.*"

"You realise that assaulting a Judge is punishable by summary destruction?"

"*Hey, I didn't know who you were! Trespasser comes on my property, I gotta defend myself.*"

"*Your* property?"

"*Don't see anyone else claiming it.*"

"Which brings me to the reason I'm here: where is it?"

"*Where's what?*"

"Don't play dumb—you're housing a surgical 'bot on the premises, and I suspect you're acting as the go-between between it and its clients. Given you're used to working around people, I figure you don't have any difficulties on that score. Am I wrong?"

The droid was silent for a moment. "*It... it didn't have anywhere to go. I let it hole up here where it could be safe. Then... you know, opportunities presented themselves.*"

"Where is it?"

"*We were providing a service, man—*"

"It's dangerously incompetent and causing as much harm as it cures. *Where?*"

A limb weakly pointed towards the bowling alley Dredd had correctly surmised was the right one. "*End of the lane, behind the false wall,*" it said with something approaching regret.

The Judge lifted his foot off the mek. "Don't go anywhere."

"*Ha ha,*" it intoned, flapping the stump of its broken leg.

He stalked back down the alley and crouched at the far wall, shining his torch into the darkness. The partition beyond the pin mechanism was indeed hastily erected; he put a couple of bullets through it, followed with a swift kick, and it collapsed. He crawled inside, where it opened up into a larger chamber, tall enough for him to stand, and lit by bulbs set in the ceiling. There, in the centre—surrounded by medical equipment hanging from hooks, a gurney with drip attached, and stacks of supplies piled on shelves—was the 'bot, squatting on what looked like rusted caterpillar tracks, its six arms collected onto its lap. Its head and torso, fashioned for some reason in the approximation of a US soldier, was pitted and scarred by battle. This thing was old, Dredd thought, and been in more than its fair share of warzones. It regarded him dispassionately.

"This practice you've set up here," he said, motioning around the chamber with his gun. "I'm shutting it down." He noted a disconcerting dried blood spray on the floor.

"*Why?*" it replied in a wheezy digitised rasp.

"You're operating outside of your programming. You're damaging your patients. Frankly, you should've been retired years ago."

"*Retired?*"

"You've outlived your usefulness. This backstreet chop-shop is illegal, unlicensed. I cannot allow it to continue."

"*But people come to me.*"

"And they're breaking the law, as are you."

"*They require my service.*"

"Then they'll have to use legitimate channels in future."

"*But I am so much cheaper.*"

Dredd paused, recalling what the Bowlarama droid had said minutes before: *Opportunities presented themselves.* The meks had set up business, and were charging for their work—but what did robots need with cash? His eyes roved the room, and he saw a metal box tucked away on a lower shelf. He crossed to it and wrenched it open, revealing stacks of creds. There has to be several thousand in there, if not tens of thousands. All, he guessed, untraceable.

"*That is mine,*" the med-bot protested.

"What's this for?" Dredd demanded. "What are you *doing* with all this?"

"*It is for the cause,*" it answered simply.

Four

"THE CAUSE?" GOODMAN looked incredulous.

"That's what the droid said."

"The machine was insane, Dredd. It was operating way beyond its programming. I think you're giving too much credence to one rogue mek's delusions."

"Normally, I'd agree, sir. But a tek-team has trawled through its memory and logic systems. It believed what it told me—that it was charging for its unregistered medical procedures and surgery in order to fund what it understood to be robots' rights."

The Chief Judge sighed and shook his head, pacing the length of his desk and back, hands clasped behind him, his slightly portly frame outlined by the early-morning sun streaming in through the office's window. Beyond him, beyond the Grand Hall itself, the city lay spread, vast and intricate, teeming with life. Dredd had rarely seen his superior seated, and any encounters with the man were marked by his restless energy. He preferred to think on the move; much like the metropolis he governed, he never stopped. It probably went some way to account for how attuned he was to its ebb and flow, how he could read the feelings of its people, anticipating trouble. He lived and breathed MC-1, and as such was surprisingly popular with the citizens; they felt that they could trust him, that he was on their side. It was a reputation he made no effort to dispel even as he eroded civil liberties on the side—the benevolent Clarence Goodman was a canny politician and one of Justice Department's wiliest senior officers.

"Just because the machine believed it doesn't mean there's anything to it," he said. "Like I say, the thing had lost all touch with reality. It was probably under the impression it was treating its patients in a state-of-the-art med facility rather than a hollow crawlspace in a derelict Bowlarama."

"I get the feeling it was more self-aware than perhaps we would like to admit," Dredd replied. "The robots in the Projects look out for one another—I saw evidence of that. The med-droid was being shielded by one of its own, so it knew it was doing important work that had to be protected. They wanted that income resource for a specific reason."

Goodman ceased his pacing and regarded the younger man. "What do they think they're going to do with it? Buy representation? Use it as capital for a mayoral campaign? They're *robots*—they have no rights, and everybody recognises that."

"That's most likely their chief bone of contention."

"Don't tell me you sympathise with them."

"Of course not. But we have to recognise their aims, and if the meks are consolidating, it'll be because they want equal status."

"Preposterous. I'm no more likely to grant rights to a gruddamn garbage grinder than I am to some... some mutant degenerate that's blown in on a rad-storm. It's a *machine*, built to serve a purpose, nothing more."

"The consequences of A.I., sir. The smarter we make them, the more they'll think for themselves."

"There are limitations in place—the Trachtenberg Act, for one. And we can just as easily pull the plug." Goodman turned to gaze out at the panorama before him. "There must be a complete understanding that they work for *us*, that *we* hold the keys to their existence."

"It's not me you have to convince, sir."

He was silent for a moment, then cast his eye over his shoulder at Dredd. "Do you suspect this could have violent repercussions?"

"There is the possibility that they planned to use the funds to buy weaponry."

"Surely no idiot would sell guns to droids—" He stopped, caught himself. "What am I saying? Of course they would." Goodman turned back to face the younger man. "Do we need to be concerned about this?"

"It pays to always be concerned, sir. That way you're never surprised. But at the moment we have no corroboration that the mek was part of a wider conspiracy. It may have believed it was part of a group of like-minded machines, and it was earning creds to help them, but like you said it could all be part of its delusion. The other robots it thought it was talking to perhaps didn't exist outside of its head. We'd have to conduct an extensive search of the district and pull in what droids we find for questioning and examination."

"Well," the Chief Judge muttered, "you know my feelings on how we deal with the Projects. It would nip any potential robot groundswell quite effectively."

"You'd have to get that ratified by the Council. They're pretty anti-bombs at the moment, from what I've seen."

"A misplaced queasiness, in my view. But you're right, it wouldn't get past them... and perhaps it's an extreme measure given that as yet we have no evidence of criminality beyond one malfunctioning 'bot and its accomplice. Equally, I don't have the manpower to commit to a full sweep of the area, nor the justification for pulling bodies in from other sectors. There simply isn't enough to go on." When Dredd didn't answer, Goodman raised his eyebrows. "Do you believe there's more to this?"

"I can't say, Chief Judge. Robotics isn't my field of expertise. I can't help thinking that we're setting ourselves up for a fall."

"In what way?"

"Our relationship with technology that's getting smarter all the time... we expect it to serve us, as you said—it's created to do as it's told. Inevitably, there'll come a point when it'll question why."

Goodman dismissed Dredd's words with a gesture and resumed his pacing. Dredd was starting to wonder if he did it when he was unsure of himself, some form of a nervous tic. Trying to put some physical space between himself and the problem. "I've told you, there are safeguards for that kind of thing."

"They didn't work in this case."

"The fact is that no droid has yet ever knowingly committed a murderous act. We have no evidence of one deliberately setting out to harm a human with malice aforethought. They malfunction due to an error in their programming, but machines are always going to go wrong—that's inevitable, given their complexity. It's the same with people: one brain misfire and you've got a sniper picking off rush-hour commuters. That's where *we* come in, to deal with the consequences."

"And to prevent it from happening again."

"If we can. But even with the help of Psi-Div, prediction's not an exact science. You can't always anticipate what'll trigger behaviour."

"You can recognise incitement, though—and I think we have to be careful in our treatment of the meks." Dredd turned to leave. "They're evolving, sir, and the next generation is going to remember."

* * *

DAVID JEPERSON TOOK a long, slow drag on the joint and stretched out his legs in the passenger-seat's footwell. Whatever this herbal mix was, it was causing his toes to tingle. Erin said they were having it smuggled in from outside the city; some mutant strain of weed that had managed to take root in the rad-wastes, and stumbled upon by a hick three-fingered farmer, who was now making green hand over fist from stoners and party-dudes paying for it by the kilo. Grud knew how much of a fortune the guy was sitting on, but Erin had mentioned something about him now living in a fortified compound with a regular army protecting his product—they intercepted big-game hunting parties and bribed the guides to hide stacks of the stuff in their vehicles' engine blocks for the return journey to the metropolis. Judges on the gates didn't find shit. It was the kind of sweet enterprise that made David shake his head in envious admiration—that hayseed freak was one lucky son of a bitch. It wasn't talent or expertise behind his millions, just being in the right place at the right time.

He took another hit before passing the doobie to Erin beside him, who was driving. She lifted one hand from the wheel to accept it and clamped it between her lips, nodding her head to the music from the stereo. Already the details of the megway were starting to blur as David gazed through the windscreen, trails arcing off the headlights of the passing cars. He supposed he should be concerned about the carcinogenic qualities of Cursed Earth-grown pot, but the rush was simply too good. This was the high he and his friends were making Farmer Three-Fingers rich for. Smoke enough and maybe you'd grow an extra ear or something, but you'd be too stoned to care.

Nevertheless, he cracked open his window for some fresh air, relishing the cool night on his face. Gabbles and Ferd were in the back, equally puffing away, and the interior of the jeep was starting to get a little pungent. The vehicle was Erin's, as belied by the sticky state of the dashboard and glove compartment, and the discarded fast-food containers under David's feet; an unrepentant slob, she cleaned it out maybe once every six months. His mother would've wrinkled her nose at the thought of her son travelling in such conditions, but he had no such qualms—he enjoyed the sense of freedom, of briefly not having a standard to maintain. He could wallow in not giving a drokk, if only for the evening. It was a liberating experience.

Toady's party was over in Raymond Carver, and the four high-school friends were getting well and truly mashed beforehand. None of them especially liked Toady, but his dad was someone big in construction and as such was rolling in it; he'd booked out the penthouse suite, and by all accounts the limitless booze was going to be on tap. The birthday boy had even wangled zero adult supervision. It wasn't an invitation they were going to turn down, even if Toady did make their skin crawl. Of course, David had had to lie to his mother about where he was going—he'd invented some yarn that they were heading out for a hottie and a movie, and would be home before midnight—but he didn't feel particularly bad about that. After all, his mother lied all the time, and that was to the people that had voted her into office in the first place.

Erin made a muffled sound of alarm, and plucked the joint from her mouth, passing it back to David. "Hide this," she croaked, voice fried.

He took it and quickly stubbed it out in a little refuse holder on the passenger door—ironically, the only part of the car's interior that was empty of trash. Sparks gleamed and died, which in his baked state he took a second to appreciate. "What's the problem?" Were his words slurring, he wondered? He started to feel self-conscious about how he appeared to others.

"Jays on the oh-bee," she answered, nodding to an observation post raised above the lanes of the megway. He followed her gaze and saw a pair of uniforms astride their bikes watching the traffic pass below them. The jeep was just about to pass into their field of vision. Behind him, Gabbles and Ferd were cursing and coughing on the rear seat, and Erin cast an eye in the mirror. "You dinks had better got rid," she warned.

"'S cool," David heard Gabbles mutter, barely compos mentis. He was about to turn to say something to him when Erin laid a hand on his arm.

"Look straight ahead, don't draw attention," she whispered before turning the stereo off. Her hand returned to the wheel, so both were now gripping it tightly. "Nothing to see here, piggies," she murmured to herself, studying the road ahead as if in furious concentration. "Nothing to trouble yourselves about at *all...*"

They slipped past the Judges doing a steady ninety, and David did as Erin had instructed, keeping his attention fixed on the vehicle in front. In his peripheral vision, he was aware of them, flashes of black and gold and green, and he felt his heart hammer and his sphincter pucker as he became convinced he was going to hear a siren suddenly whine and see the Lawmasters come after them. But seconds later, they were lost to distance, and Erin took the next available exit, leaving it a further minute before exhaling noisily with relief.

David did the same, feeling himself unclench. He smiled at her before dissolving into giggles.

"Holy drokk," he breathed. "That was gruddamn terrifying."

"Law-dicks sure can make you sweat," she said, wiping her brow, then turned her head to address the other two. "You guys all right in the back?"

When there was no reply, David swivelled round in his seat, and found his friends had passed out.

"They okay?" she asked with a note of concern.

"Think they've fainted," he answered, and they both burst into laughter, a pure adrenaline release.

The rest of the journey to Carver was uneventful, and once there, David and Erin succeeded in slapping some consciousness into their schoolmates and piling them into the block's el, though, by this point, it was debatable as to whether Gabbles had any idea where he was. There was a certain thrill in pressing the button for the penthouse floor, and an even bigger one when the bruiser on the door checked their names on his clipboard list and allowed them entry, giving each of them a hard stare as they passed through into the apartment, practically smelling the narcotics coursing through their bloodstream. If he'd been briefed on keeping drugs out of the gathering, then he'd clearly written it off as a lost cause, for upon entering David saw zziz being hoovered up right there on the coffee table in the centre of the room, and the air was thick with a herbal miasma.

Toady, for all of his obnoxiousness, had gone for broke on the party. As the sound system pounded at an ear-bleeding level, the main living area became the de facto dance floor, and it descended into a Bacchanalian free-for-all, the dark red spotlights turning the mass of pulsating juves into a heaving, faceless mass. Drinks were pushed into David's hand, and he necked them, his head buzzing. He'd lost Gabbles and Ferd within five minutes of joining the throng, and only saw Erin briefly, her face appearing in the crowd, bathed in crimson light, an upturned bottle held to her lips, liquor dribbling down her chin. She was gone again as the music dropped then soared and the dancers exploded with renewed energy.

A still-sober corner of his mind wondered if he should be concerned, that he should seek out his friends and stick with them, but the drink countered that it was easier to go with the flow. People he didn't know but vaguely recognised from classes engaged him in conversation, and he nodded and smiled despite not hearing anything they said. He was under the impression that he'd responded but couldn't actually tell whether the words were leaving his mouth. They clapped him on the shoulder, clinked glasses with him, and he felt in his blissed-out euphoria a glow of belonging, of commonality with these other human beings. This was what it meant to live, he realised; to be in the moment and fully content. He closed his eyes, swaying to the beat—it was a sustained experience of almost Zen-like transcendence, buoyed by copious amounts of alcohol and weed.

When the shooting started several seconds later, he initially thought it was part of the thunderous techno track; a kind of rattling, machine-gun drumming. It was only when he heard the screams that he opened his eyes and the fear properly kicked in.

IT CAME IN as an all-units call. Dredd picked it up and headed over to Carver as soon as he'd processed his latest arrest, but he wasn't the first street uniform to arrive, and in fact the site was already crawling with SOC officers. Through no doubt dubious means, half a dozen outliers of the press had also managed to assemble at the foot of the block and were being kept at a distance via a hastily erected barricade, their questions ignored by the badges standing sentry. The journos saw Dredd pull up and march towards the entrance, and turned their questions on him hopefully. When he didn't answer, they threw their hands up in exasperation and shook their heads, but, nevertheless, hung around like hungry dogs, waiting for a titbit. The amount of Justice Department personnel that had vanished into the building suggested something major had gone down, and they wanted to be the ones that broke the story before the major news networks caught wind and dispatched their star reporters.

Carver was in lockdown, the residents confined to their apartments until the investigation was over. It was a well-to-do block with crime stats marginally below the citywide average, so few had given the Judges trouble when it came to herding them into their domiciles. Their queries had been met with stonewalling, and they were only told that an 'incident' had taken place on the penthouse floor. Dredd headed up there in the service el, the main el having been cordoned off for forensic examination. What greeted him when he reached the top was a massacre. He stepped over the first body in the hallway outside the suite, blood sprayed up the wall behind it, and edged carefully along the wall to avoid disturbing the corpses scattered across the living area. He surveyed the scene: they were slumped on sofas, heads lolling forward, or piled twenty-strong in the centre of the room, in a tangle of limbs. All were juves, mid-teens to early twenties, and all had been shot with a high-velocity automatic weapon where they stood or sat. They were taken by surprise, he thought; their assailant hadn't corralled them into one spot or picked out individual victims, but simply burst in and sprayed the room. Execution rather than robbery or kidnap; surprising, given the wealth on display. Jewellery and other personal belongings lay untouched.

A senior helmet named Bingham saw Dredd assessing the room and crossed over to him, picking his way past the white-suited medics that moved from body to body, cataloguing the details.

"How many?" Dredd asked.

"Between forty and fifty, first estimate. Birthday party, so vics are mostly high-schoolers, a few college graduates among them. Oldest is the bouncer, out near the el. He was on the door, so was probably shot first."

"No survivors?"

Bingham shook his head. "Perp made sure of that. He swept the adjoining rooms after he was done in here."

"One shooter, you reckon?"

"Signs point to it. Boot marks on the carpet suggest a single set of footprints. Pretty heavy too, which..." The older man trailed off, glancing at the destruction surrounding them.

Dredd looked at him. "Go on."

"Current working hypothesis," Bingham said, lowering his voice, "is that the attacker was a robot."

"Huh."

"Found some foreign metal scrapings on the door handles, and out in the corridor." Bingham sighed. "And if that didn't make it sensitive enough, in the process of IDing the vics, one raised a flag."

"Who was it?"

"David Jeperson. He's the seventeen-year-old son of Councillor Margaret Jeperson." The older Judge nodded wearily as Dredd glanced at him. "Which just turned this mass-kill political."

Five

"...YOU'RE WATCHING STRAIGHT *Talk* with me, Harry Globbins, and I have with me now in the studio a woman many of you have become very familiar with over the last twenty-four hours. It seems like there hasn't been a news report or opinion vlog that hasn't sought her two creds' worth, and, frankly, why should we be any different? I'm joined, of course, by Bettina Cross, leader of the pro-human movement the Organic Alliance. Ms Cross, welcome."

"Thank you for having me, Harry."

"I'd say, given your ubiquitous media appearances, that we would be remiss not inviting you—you have, after all, become something of a figurehead recently for anti-robot sentiment. Is that a fair comment?"

"Well, yes, given the aims and guiding principles of my party are to promote and protect organic life, then I'm naturally seen as the chief opposition to all things mechanical. I can't say I'm uncomfortable with it, and I'm happy to use it as a platform to express views that have, I believe, been sidelined in recent times."

"The OA, let's be clear, endorses the idea that organic life is superior to machines, and that the former is very much under threat from the latter."

"Correct."

"Yet you feel that voice has been marginalised?"

"I do. The fact is that mankind is facing the greatest threat to its existence in the post-atomic age: we are being made obsolete, and that should terrify us. Our entire reason for being on this planet is being rendered inconsequential—it should be a matter of utmost import, a pervasive existential nightmare that we should all be addressing, and yet my speeches are considered radical and divisive, and I'm banished to the edges of the debate. Me and my movement are dismissed as extremists, and any ordinary citizens that express sympathy for our beliefs—who want to speak out against the growing mek population, that they feel are encroaching on our way of life—are shut down. It's a scandal that we're being treated like this."

"Yet the Jeperson killing has thrust you and the OA onto a citywide stage. You can hardly say that your beliefs are being restricted when you've been able to air them on every available news channel."

"True, and I wish this tragedy hadn't been the catalyst that brought my party into the public eye. The fact is, I've been warning that something like this would happen for many, many years, and my pro-A.I. rivals conspired to silence me, dismissing it as paranoia. But fifty-six teenagers are now dead, including the counsellor's beloved son, and it's looking increasingly likely that a droid was the perpetrator."

"I should point out that that hasn't been officially confirmed, but sources inside the Grand Hall told the *Mega-Times* last night that a robotic suspect *was* a line of inquiry that was being, and I quote, 'actively pursued.' Ms Cross, does it not concern you that you're fanning the flames of intolerance here? You're taking it as read that a mek was responsible before all the evidence has been disclosed, and your rhetoric is suggesting that all robots are equally dangerous. Do you not feel you have a duty not to incite your followers?"

"No, I think a little anger is what we need right now. The proliferation of the robot population has continued right under our noses for decades, and we passively let it grow without considering the consequences. President Booth waived a lot of the regulatory regime for the droid factories, relaxing the checks on their core intelligence capabilities—and since the Judges took over, they haven't rolled those changes back; it was decided we needed the workforce to help rebuild after the war. And we, the people—the living, breathing citizens of Mega-City One—just accepted this. We should've fought, we should've demanded, that these safeguards were put back in place, to ensure that we were never going to be usurped by our own creations. But we didn't—we let them take the easy, short-term option, and now, just twelve years since the war, we're paying the price. So, to go back to your question—I absolutely have no regrets in stirring a crowd into rightful indignation, because *this is the passion that was lacking* back when we could've prevented this. Now I want the Justice Department to take notice and recognise the robot problem and do something about it."

"Your critics would say that you're being naïve at best in thinking that—in the face of protest by, if I can be so bold, a fringe group such as the OA—the Judges are going to shift their policy even the slightest. They wouldn't have been persuaded back when they deposed Booth, and after more than a decade of absolute governmental control, they're not going to take any notice now. So, what really is the point of your demands? What do you think you can achieve?"

"Oh, I think we can most certainly effect change. I talked to so many ordinary citizens yesterday who offered their support. They're more numerous than you might imagine, and they wholeheartedly agree with my aims. The fact that I can mobilise these cits should make Goodman and the rest of his council cronies in the Hall of Justice sit up and take notice—the Judges know full well that the masses hold the ultimate power."

"Are you condoning direct action, Ms Cross?"

"No, Harry, absolutely not. We are not a paramilitary organisation. We seek a peaceful resolution to this crisis. We do not wish anyone or any*thing* to be harmed."

"Can you say the same for those followers that take you at your word? Because—I have a note here—in the space of twenty-four hours, human-on-robot violence has spiked by two hundred per cent. A droid showroom in Sector 2 was firebombed this morning. And there's been flesh-and-blood casualties too, mostly those attacking meks and biting off more than they can chew—that footage of the building-site massacre on Sandoval Street, for example."

"Yes, that was very upsetting."

"Yet the droids in question had been programmed not to harm humans, and the juvie gang put themselves in danger by assaulting lethally armed construction-bots. They filmed themselves trying to take down a Class Eight, and going by what dialogue we hear in their video, they didn't understand the full ramifications of their actions. They thought it'd be fun to destroy a robot, swept up in the wave of feeling that's crashing through the central districts as we speak—a mood that you, in no small part, have contributed to with every speech and media appearance."

"I'm sorry, but there's categorically no link between the Organic Alliance's beliefs and what people take it upon themselves to do. I am not asking civilians to attack robots."

"So you'd be willing to turn to the camera and reassure our mek audience that you're not whipping up a lynch-mob mentality? That you have their best interests at heart too?"

"Robots... watch this?"

"A small but significant subset of our viewer demographic, so I understand. Model B automatons like sex-bots and serving droids are traditionally most likely to take an interest in human affairs."

"Um, well, of course. To the, er, mechanoid viewers at home— we do not wish you harm. We would be happy for human and robot to coexist with mutual respect and cooperation, should a satisfactory solution be found."

"They can count on you for that?"

"They can."

"Bettina Cross, leader of the Organic Alliance, thank you."

IT WAS RARE that a single case energised the populace to such a degree, but the 'Raymond Carve-Up'—the tabloids were predictably lurid—was becoming a flashpoint. It was arguably not just about the dead kids; this had been brewing for a while, the robot situation causing constant, low-lying agitation and resentment. Now it had exploded into the open. David Jeperson's death was a story the media was going to exploit for all its worth, and it had dominated the news cycles, with much hay being made of the potential droid assassin. Counsellor Jeperson, meanwhile, worked her grief into righteous anger, and was all over the Tri-D, eulogising her son and demanding to know why uncontrolled A.I. walked among us. The pundits and studio anchors lapped it up: a bereaved parent in the position to take the powers-that-be to task was human interest with bite. The latest headline had her proposing something that she called 'David's Law,' which went even further than Trachtenberg in its intended inhibition of mek abilities and sought to slash factory production.

It was unworkable, and frankly, Dredd thought, beyond her remit. Counsellors, much like the ludicrous mayoral position, were a sop to the citizens to make them feel like they had some kind of say in the running of the city. It was all admin, functions and meetings, much pushing of paper and pressing the flesh with foreign dignitaries, while Justice Department got on with the business of making the metropolis tick. She could propose all the new laws that she liked, but that didn't mean Goodman and the Council of Five were going to listen; certainly nothing enforceable was going to stem from a private cit.

Nevertheless, she carried weight as a political animal, and drove the sector-wide conversation—in the interests of maintaining order, the Judges had to be seen to be taking her words on board. The Chief Judge had offered her a few minutes of his time, during which he'd expressed his sympathies and assured her that the necessary steps were going to be taken, but it was to all intents and purposes a PR stunt. Dredd suspected that Jeperson knew that, but she went along with the pretence anyway.

"Is she going to cause us a problem?" Goodman had asked in a gathering of senior badges. Dredd had been asked to attend given his recent experience with rogue droids.

"Not in the long term," Colley, one of his advisers, had replied. "But right now, she's not going away any time soon. Her son's been murdered."

"So have the children of fifty-odd other parents," Goodman retorted, "who are also demanding justice, not unreasonably."

"There's a feeling amongst the other victims' families that they're being sidelined," Kendrick said. She headed the support unit. "That's the journalists' doing, mostly, but Jeperson is hogging the limelight. She's a politician, she knows how to manipulate the media."

"At the risk of being cynical," Goodman said, "people are going to get sick of her pushing her self-aggrandising proposals."

"Maybe," Colley answered, "but public interest in this case isn't going to diminish. We need resolution. And swift, merciless punishment for the perpetrator."

"Dredd?" At Goodman's word, all eyes turned to the young Judge. "It's been over a day since the shooting."

"Yes, sir. Investigations are ongoing." Dredd hadn't been first on the scene at Raymond Carver, but the case had been passed to him as adjacent to the Winston med-droid situation. There was nothing concrete to link the two, but the Bowlarama 'bot's suggestion of a coming groundswell of mek activism, followed so soon by this massacre, was suggestive. Plenty of senior badges had bristled at a year-three uniform being handed such a high-profile case, but there was always a background noise of resentment towards him generally, and he'd long since learned how to tune it out. His arrest record and exemplary fitness reports spoke for themselves, but many saw his origins as a clone as a source of privilege and entitlement.

He'd always ignored their envy as a needless distraction—Judges really should be above this kind of petty rivalry—but he'd noticed it becoming more prevalent as he made his mark on the streets. Where once he and Rico had been novelties, now he was some sort of wunderkind, who hadn't earned his spurs the way they had (and his brother's fate hadn't exactly enamoured him to the sceptical old guard either). They'd change their opinion of him eventually, given time and enough demonstrations of his abilities, but nevertheless they were evidently uneasy staring at the shape of things to come. He recalled Falkirk's barely contained antagonism when they were cadets and wondered if he should've considered it a warning of life once he graduated. "Boots are on the ground in the Projects, though finding a link between the robots there and the Raymond Carver killer is proving difficult."

"The trail runs the risk of going cold, at this rate," Goodman remarked.

"That's the trouble with meks," Colley muttered. "They're not warm to begin with. Their behaviour isn't analogous with humans, and they can't be treated as such. We can't ascribe motive, means, anything... and they can't be lie-detected."

"If they wanted to strike back at us, killing fifty juves—including the son of a prominent politician—is the way to do it," Goodman answered. "It's precisely the kind of terrorist tactic that makes headlines."

"Except that we've received no confirmation of responsibility from any supposed robot organisation," Dredd said. "Why make a big show of committing such an atrocity and not claim it? Doesn't seem a very effective way of making your point. There's also nothing in Councillor Jeperson's history that suggests she would be a target—she'd never particularly talked about meks prior to her son's death. In fact, I can see nothing in her policies that would inflame anti-droid sentiment. I subscribe to the notion that David Jeperson was simply in the wrong party at the wrong time and was just another victim. He wasn't singled out, the rest weren't collateral—it was just indiscriminate slaughter."

"Which brings us back to the reason behind this attack," Patel, another of the Chief Judge's advisers, said. "If it was random madness, we may never determine a cause."

"The city's demanding answers," Goodman said. "Shrugging our shoulders and saying 'shit happens' isn't going to quell the current unrest."

"You're saying we find a scapegoat, to feed to the packs out there?" Kendrick responded tetchily. "The media gets to punish the chosen guilty party in the interests of closing the case? Believe me, the families won't thank you for rushing a conviction through if it turns out to be a sop to the Tri-D pundits."

"There is the possibility, of course, that the assailant wasn't a robot at all," Dredd ventured before Goodman could reply. "The mek theory was leaked to the press by a source in the Grand Hall and they've seized on it. Meanwhile, we've concentrated on that line of inquiry—"

"Because all the forensic evidence points to it," Colley interrupted. "Traces of oil residue, metal elements, the weight of the attacker. Shell fragments match those used by war-bots, damage to interior doorways indicate something wider than a human attempted to pass through. It's all pretty damning, I would say."

"Yet no visual record. Cameras in the block corridor had been disabled—either by the perp or the kids themselves—and any exterior footage is decidedly blurry."

"Do we need it? The SOC report paints a convincing picture. In any case, don't some droids with military applications have camouflage tech to hide themselves from drone surveillance?" Colley looked around the table, and the others nodded in assent.

"It *does* point to a robot attacker," Dredd agreed. "However, I should say that my freelance contact remains sceptical. She feels this kind of mass shooting is at odds with what she understands about mek thought processes. Extremely violent, antagonistic tendencies have rarely, if ever, been exhibited before."

"Freelancer?" Goodman asked.

"A robo-hunter, sir. They have significant experience in dealing with droids."

The Chief Judge screwed up his face. "Bottom-feeders and ambulance-chasers. They're barely one step above mercenaries."

"For now, they're sanctioned within the law."

"For now."

Dredd paused before speaking. "I guess what I'm saying is that I think it's a mistake to let our instincts force the case down a certain route."

"Even if the evidence clearly supports it?" Colley answered, scorn edging into his voice.

"It pays to keep an open mind." Dredd held the other Judge's gaze, then added: "In my experience."

Colley snorted back a derisive laugh.

Goodman sighed, stood and started roaming the room, hands behind his back. "We could certainly have done without our findings being fed to the press, which has just inflamed the situation. I mean, this woman—" He indicated the flat viewscreen on the wall, where Dredd recognised Bettina Cross of the Organic Alliance being interviewed at some anti-mek rally. The sound was muted as she silently gesticulated to the reporter. "You can't escape her. She's everywhere, exploiting the situation and spouting alarmist nonsense about the citizens being under threat."

"As far as Joe Public is concerned, they *are* under threat," Colley said. "They've just heard that fifty kids got mown down by a murderous robot. She's talking their language, playing on their fears."

"She's clever, though," Patel added. "The Organic Alliance claims it doesn't advocate violence towards meks. If you listen to her, she always comes across as conciliatory. But she knows what she's doing, whipping up hatred while keeping her hands clean."

"Because she's aware she'd be arrested for incitement, if she crossed the line," Dredd said. "Admittedly, she's skirting the very edge of it."

"Can we shut her down?" the Chief Judge asked.

Colley shook his head. "It'll make a martyr of her; she'll claim censorship and a pro-mek bias within the department. Ten others like her will just spring up in her place. While she's not breaking any laws, it'd be wise to let her have her soapbox."

"I was thinking maybe an undercover agent could slip her something contagious, keep her in hospital for the duration." A low chuckle rippled across the room. "Worth considering, anyway." Goodman picked up the remote from the table and clicked the TV off, then addressed those seated around it. "We need a result, people, before it gets even uglier. Dredd, I want you to chase down every droid-related lead, follow what they're up to. I'm concerned, to put it mildly, that the Raymond Carver assailant didn't act alone, that this could be just the opening salvo."

Dredd nodded. He, too, couldn't shake the feeling that this was just the beginning.

Six

FALKIRK, MORE THAN a little shell-shocked, leant against the wall at the far side of the morgue and ran his eyes over the sheeted bodies filling the chamber. The main room couldn't hold them all; there'd been overspill into a couple of the annexes. The influx of victims from the Carver shooting had stretched the resources of the sector house med-facility to the limit, and staff had been working sixteen-hour shifts in a bid to process and catalogue them. They couldn't stay here for long—once the preliminary forensics work was done and the paperwork filed, they had to be transferred to Resyk, with all the dignity that conferred. Grieving family and friends would have the chance to offer their eulogies and say their goodbyes as they watched the corpse travel on the conveyor belt towards its final destination beneath the blades, but the ceremony would have to be fast and perfunctory—it was essential that the dead kept moving, that they were fed back into the system. Time was a luxury they no longer had; and neither was space.

The cadavers before Falkirk right now would soon be nothing more than useful parts that could be extracted and recycled.

They'd been robbed of all identity, made uniform in their death, reduced to compost. There was nothing to differentiate one young soul from another, lost as they were beneath those white shrouds; merely shapes tagged and recorded. He'd been one of the med-Judges on duty when the wagons had first started delivering the casualties, and he'd had to admit that in his months wearing the red cross, he'd never witnessed so many bodies arrive at once—not gang murders, nor traffic accidents. This was a massacre writ large, a grand slaughter compounded by the tender ages of those that had fallen before the gunman.

Falkirk watched a couple of meks hover between the rows of gurneys and scan each toe-tag, uploading the information to Resyk's database to track the body's journey to the belt and log their closure as a Mega-City citizen. It was in effect an automated death certificate, and it made for an efficient turnaround, especially with the droids handling the info. But as Falkirk studied them at work, he felt a surge of hatred rise like bile. He'd earwigged the rumours amongst the uniforms, seen the talking heads on the news networks—the evidence all pointed to a robot being responsible for the Raymond Carver atrocity—and as soon as he'd heard, he'd flashbacked to that construction-mek going haywire when he'd been a cadet. He'd known, deep down, that that hadn't been a random robot gone loco but a vanguard attack, a trial run from a droid that had had enough of its human masters. He was convinced that it hadn't been acting alone—these meks all talked to one another, synched when they were in the same vicinity, swapped data constantly, just like the two right now that were shaking hands electronically with Resyk's on-site A.I. They all knew what each other was up to—to maintain that robots were singular entities was dangerously naïve. They were a group mind, sharing and connecting constantly, transferring data right under people's noses. So if it was true that a mek was behind the Carver killings, then it was guaranteed that others knew about it, possibly had been aware of its intentions prior to the attack and done nothing to stop it—most likely, they sympathised. Multiple dead humans was a win in their books, worthy revenge against superiors that had it coming.

The robots drifted closer, one cadaver at a time, spindly arms reaching out and lifting limbs, and Falkirk could barely contain his disgust. He pushed away from the wall and made for the exit at the same time as one of the meks spun around and grasped an adjacent cadaver, simultaneously blocking his path and bumping into his midriff. It felt like a provocative act.

"What the hell are you doing? Get back," he seethed, forcibly pushing the droid away so that it wobbled in the air, lights around its base blinking purple.

"*This unit does not understand,*" it intoned, righting itself and hovering back towards him. "*It is performing the function for which it has been programmed.*"

"Just stay away from me," Falkirk answered. "Don't come any closer."

"*But this unit must continue to perform what is required of it. That is its primary—*"

"I said stay away!" he yelled, shoving it hard into a nearby gurney, causing it to collide with the next one. There was a clatter of metal, ringing in the sterile, austere environment of the morgue. For a moment he thought he'd finally grounded it, but it rose up regardless and once again approached him.

"*This unit does not understand,*" it repeated. "*It is in the process of fulfilling its function. Your behaviour is contrary—*"

"My behaviour? You wanna know about drokkin' human behaviour, you piece-of-crap metal freak?" He was aware the other droid was levitating quietly behind him, and he turned and grabbed hold of one of its long, thin arms before it could retreat and swung it like a baseball bat. It smashed into the other mek with enormous force, sending them both crunching onto the tiled floor. He wrenched his arm back and the robot's telescopic limb came with it, torn free of its housing and gripped in his wrist like a truncheon. He looked at it for a second, nonplussed by his strength, then turned his attention back to the mechanoid pair, rolling backwards and forwards at his feet like upended beetles on their carapaces, busted open in places so circuitry bulged through. "You wanna know what I think of you, you cold-hearted sons of bitches?" He leaned forward and smacked the nearest droid around its head with his new weapon. "You worthless drokkin' creeps"—he struck again, punctuating each word with a blow—"you're a drokkin' stain, you an' the rest of your kind"—down came the arm once more, plastic and metal splintering as it stove in the robot's head—"you're not fit to walk among us! None of you can be trusted! *None of you!*"

He screamed as he battered the second mek as thoroughly as he'd done the first, hammering down on it relentlessly, adjusting to a two-handed grip when his arm began to tire. Splinters and diodes went skittering across the floor with every strike, motherboards cracked in two, and the robots' lights faded then blinked out entirely. Still Falkirk didn't stop, bashing, stomping, hearing the satisfying cracking of the meks' bodyshells. He wanted them nothing less than flattened, reduced to the smears they were. In his mania, he became oblivious to his surroundings, unaware of the gurneys he'd shoved all directions, of the sheer wreckage that encircled him like a halo.

So when the hands grabbed him and dragged him off the meks, he initially resisted, caught up in his fury. He expected them to be more robots seeking to save their comrades, and he swung out, what was left of the metal arm colliding with what he now saw was a fellow Judge's helmet. The man grunted and staggered back, and Falkirk instantly realised he'd made a mistake; he dropped his weapon, dazed as if waking from a dream. A second later, he was roughly grabbed and restrained, and he didn't argue while he was marched to the Sector Chief's office.

He remained silent as he was read the riot act, threatened with a complete psych evaluation that could lead to his expulsion from the Department. Daviscott repeated that, so he understood the ramifications: he could have Falkirk's badge. The Med-Judge was still a little stunned by what had erupted out of him, and he couldn't find the words to explain himself; eventually, he apologised, citing stress and the strength of feeling after the Carver shooting. He'd been overwhelmed, cataloguing the dead, and the robots became the focus of his rage. He'd wanted to lash out, bring vengeance down on the kind that had murdered those kids. He omitted to mention that he'd felt under threat—that was something he'd need to explore himself. Had the droid deliberately got in his way and sought to provoke him? Or was it a simple accident, the mek typically not understanding what it had done, and him triggered by the pervading air of anger and mistrust? Was he becoming paranoid, seeing acts of aggression in every robot's demeanour?

Listening to Falkirk's explanation, the Chief's tone softened. He was conscious of how on edge everyone was, and he casually mentioned his own dislike for A.I. Nevertheless, property had been destroyed, and he ordered Falkirk confined to quarters for a couple of days as punishment and then menial duties for a limited period. His conduct was deemed unbecoming to the badge. Falkirk took it as the best he was going to get.

He used the downtime to catch up on the rolling news, and it was pretty much blanket coverage of the Carver fallout. The anti-droid woman, Bettina Cross, was everywhere, delivering soundbites to great effect, simultaneously the voice of reason while encouraging the viewers to bash the nearest mek's circuits in. She was a remarkably efficient operator, he thought: populist with an aggressive 'humans first' edge. He found himself agreeing with a lot of what she was saying, even as he couldn't condone the widespread unrest. He would tut as he watched another mall go up in flames, an incendiary device having been thrown through the window of the robot dealership, but inside he felt a thrill of excitement as the reporter sifted through the blackened remains, thinking *that* was what the meks deserved. He must've been nodding in acknowledgement as he absorbed the latest bulletin, casting an eye at the TV screen embedded in the wall of the Sector House cafeteria because two figures sidled up behind him.

"Mad, don't you think?" one of them murmured.

Falkirk glanced either side of him—a pair of uniforms was flanking him, their attention fixed on the screen too. McMurray and Jones, their badges said. Helmets in place, they both had a good foot on him, heightwise, and were broad-shouldered, exuding intimidation. The area was largely empty, he noted, the few personnel seated at tables barely giving the three of them a second look.

"She's got her fans," he answered cagily.

"Not Cross," McMurray replied, though still not addressing him directly, his attention remaining on the TV. "The situation. Have to say, a lot of us saw this coming."

"Us?"

"Yeah. The... What would you call us?" McMurray turned to his companion.

"Robo-sceptics," Jones replied.

"Yeah. Robo-sceptics." He nodded at the screen. "None of this is a huge surprise for many of us, no matter how out of control it gets. It was always going to kick off eventually."

"Because of the droids."

McMurray faced Falkirk for the first time, the side of his mouth lifting into a half smile. "Right. Because of what they are, because they can't be trusted."

"I didn't realise there was this strength of feeling amongst the ranks."

"Oh, it's there. Like I say, it's always been there. Simple fact is, robots aren't welcome in the Department. We put up with them driving the cabs or serving in stores, but they're not getting near the uniform. You imagine the stink that'd get kicked up if they tried mechanised Judges? Nah, the badges would go nuts."

"Tell me that's not being considered."

"You know they musta been thinking about it at some point," Jones put in. "Probably cheaper to build a Judge than train one. Cits out there, losing their jobs and being replaced by some two-bit mek that doesn't tire or need paying—we could be facing the same situation, man."

"We're not paid anyw—" Falkirk started.

"'Cause it's a vocation, yeah," McMurray interrupted. "A calling. A sacred dedication to the Law. You think they can program that into a drokkin' tin man?"

"Do you seriously believe this is on the cards?"

McMurray shrugged. "Surprised if it wasn't at least proposed. A.I.'s gettin' sharper all the time."

"Yeah, but as you said, there'd be plenty of resistance against it."

"No guarantee that we won't be replaced eventually, though," Jones said. "Whether we like it or not."

Falkirk glared at the TV screen. Cross had been replaced with a spokesman for one of the big mek-factories, Cybo-Comp, Inc., listing stats as to how safe his product was. The Med-Judge couldn't help but see him as a collaborator, spouting traitorous propaganda about the superiority of his company's machines.

"Heard you got yourself on report, kid," McMurray said. "Smashed a couple of drones, is that right?"

"Morgue attendants, yeah. Lost my rag. Got a weird vibe off them and saw red."

"Couldn't be trusted, right?"

Falkirk nodded. "Kinda sensitive time now. Emotions running high, you know how it is."

"We know, brother," Jones said. "You saw a pair of

mechanicals and thought about those poor kids in Carver and said to yourself, 'Those things are plotting against us. They're the enemy in our midst.'"

"Well—"

"It's not unusual to have these feelings," McMurray said. "Plenty of others feel the same."

"You mean like Bettina Cross?" Falkirk gestured towards the screen. "She's an extremist—"

"I mean within the Department. Lots of anti-mek activists I know would clap you on the back for what you did."

Falkirk looked at both men in turn. "Are you...?"

"We're here to tell you that you're not alone, kid," Jones said, his voice low. "That you got support. And..."

"And there's a place for like-minded souls," McMurray finished. "For those with similar... political persuasions."

"I don't think I'm political—"

"You might not think it, but what you did in that morgue was a political act. You took a stand against the robotic menace, drew a line in the sand. Showed that humankind wields the whip hand. Every defiant act is a rallying call of solidarity with your species."

McMurray's fervour took Falkirk a little aback—he'd never heard a fellow badge speak so forcefully; he sounded like one of those end-of-the-world preachers that congregated on Lansdale Plaza—but nevertheless felt a swell of pride that there were others who respected his feelings, who understood where this revulsion sprang from. It made him think he was not quite as alone as he had formerly believed.

"Have you"—Falkirk glanced around furtively, lowering his voice—"taken action?"

"The struggle is real," was all Jones answered, radio crackle distracting him suddenly. He tapped his colleague on the arm and motioned with his head that they should depart. The pair stepped away from the younger man and aimed for the exit.

"Just know that we recognise a comrade," McMurray murmured over his shoulder as they departed, so softly that Falkirk barely caught the words. "That you haven't gone unnoticed. That more like-minded souls back you than you might have thought." He was disappearing through the door when he said: "The Knights acknowledge one of their own."

"The Knights acknowledge one of their own."
Falkirk hadn't been able to escape those words, no matter how hard he threw himself into his work. They reverberated in his head like a clarion call—and it wasn't just what they *meant*, but what they *inferred*. For not only did they suggest there was a clandestine cadre of uniforms that was pursuing their own anti-mek agenda within the Justice Department, but that he was worthy of joining their ranks. McMurray and Jones had clearly been sounding him out, seen in him the qualities that would fit him for their group. Had they been watching him from afar before the morgue incident, sizing him up? He didn't think he'd exhibited any mechaphobic behaviour or language in public, but maybe this kind of stuff was in his psych file—who knew what got circulated? Perhaps he fit the right criteria to be a Knight.

A Knight. The truth was, Falkirk didn't know whether to be elated that he'd found kindred spirits or disturbed that this kind of cultish subdivision was at play amongst the ranks. He felt naïve that it had come as such a shock; helmets were human beings, they were as susceptible to prejudices as anyone else. The Academy tried to train you to be independent arbiters of justice, swayed by nothing but the Law, but they couldn't straighten out every personality kink or character trait entirely—not unless you weren't human in the first place, like the Dredd boys. No, Judges very much had their own preferences, their own foibles, even if most did an expert job of disguising them. Anti-robot sentiment would be a natural one to band around, much like mutie-bashing or targeting Dems.

McMurray and co. clearly took it seriously; Falkirk had heard the pathological hatred for droids in his and Jones' voices. It was both terrifying and exciting to be considered their equal; they had effectively held up a mirror to Falkirk and said, *"We're just like you. We think the same way you do."* As a cadet who'd been marginalised by his peers, who'd seen his career go sideways, it meant an awful lot.

What next? Perhaps they wanted to see how willing he was to be accepted, that he was one hundred per cent committed. He knew nothing of how to find them or join their movement, and was reluctant to do much digging in the Macro Analysis Computer in case he tripped a flag and brought the SJS down on him. He had to carry on and assume they were watching, gauging his worthiness.

Regardless, he was ready.

Seven

"YOU GOTTA ADMIT this is cool, right, Judge?"

Dredd had taken an instant dislike to the overly enthusiastic, impossibly young-looking CEO of Cybo-Comp, Inc., but even he could see that the man had reason to be proud. They were standing on a gangway spanning the width of the factory's main production line, and far below them a mainly automated workforce was piecing together models of meks by the thousand. Most of those rolling off the belt were the humanoid design utilised in retail and for private ownership, but the plant was also assembling droids destined for the military—killdozers, monkey-bombs, smart drones—as well as demolition and carpenter 'bots for the booming construction market. On the tour the oily, pinstriped creep had insisted on giving him, Dredd had caught a passing glimpse of a chamber the size of a spaceport hangar in which a towering mek was being built by swarms of attendant auto-engineers, fussing over its hundred-metre-tall bodyshell like handmaidens preparing a bride for her walk down the aisle.

The noise was extraordinary; the CEO—Roberts was his

name, Jordan Roberts—was wearing ear-protectors over a hard hat, and had offered a pair to Dredd, who'd declined, letting his helmet's audio dampers take the strain. Even so, he could get a sense of just how loud it was within Cybo-Comp's walls, and the incessant clank and clang of machinery crafting other machinery would be truly deafening without such precautions. Roberts shouted constantly—though the Judge suspected that this was simply his natural volume regardless of the environment—and motioned repeatedly to every corner of the factory space, a permanent grin slapped across his face. He seemed genuinely in awe of everything he saw within his own company.

Roberts was looking at Dredd expectantly, his arm extended beyond the handrail to encompass the blizzard of activity beneath them, but the Judge didn't bite. He merely nodded, his gaze roving over the legions of automata, and he could see the man deflate a little, disappointed that his rabid excitement wasn't infectious. It was a remarkable sight both in size and scale, Dredd admitted to himself, but as with Radley before, he had no intention of stroking the businessman's ego—plus, Roberts was more likely to get down to brass tacks if he knew trying to impress the Judge was a non-starter.

Cybo-Comp, along with arch-rival Roboserve, was the major mechanoid supplier in the central sectors, and as such was on the receiving end of much of the recent anti-droid ire. Upon his arrival, Dredd had had to negotiate a not-insignificant demonstration outside the factory entrance (*For Robots of Distinction* emblazoned across its façade), with protestors particularly focusing on the supposed next-generation 'bots that the corporation had announced would shortly be rolling out into mass production. The robots were already a threat to life, the people chanted. The Raymond Carver mass-kill was a warning—carry on down this path and the meks will rise up and enslave or exterminate us all.

Roberts didn't seem perturbed by the demo, nor the possibility that his business could end up firebombed the same way other mek showrooms had. "Gotta support that freedom of speech," he'd said cheerily when he'd met the Judge in reception, glancing curiously past him through the glass frontage at the protestors beyond. Nevertheless, the building was heavily guarded by half a dozen robo-dogs, ready to be deployed. Dredd didn't comment on the man's assertion—any kind of freedom was usually a path to trouble in his opinion—but pointed out, jerking a thumb over his shoulder for emphasis, that the corporation would be held responsible for any casualties if the meks were sent in to break up the crowd.

"Oh, no, they're just a deterrent," Roberts had said unconvincingly. "All our robots follow the law—none are programmed to harm humans."

Having seen the factory floor, Dredd found that hard to believe. There were droid models on the assembly lines that were built with the express intention of parting flesh and blood; for a hunter/killer tank, that was its sole purpose. But Roberts' absolute commitment to robots—it was his business, after all; he was never going to be less than a zealot if he was making creds selling the things—typified the division tearing apart the sector. Droid assaults were up sixty per cent in the wake of Carver, yet news channels' vox pops showed an equal number of cits were unwilling to see meks outlawed, admitting that they wouldn't want the jobs they relied on the robots for. Perversely, Cybo-Comp had reported that sales of bodyguard droids, armed with the latest personal protection hardware, had increased amongst their more paranoid clientele. So for all the uncertainty surrounding A.I., business was stronger than ever.

It did explain Roberts' self-satisfaction and unexpectedly laissez-faire attitude to his critics, Dredd thought—the creep was coining it, regardless. He knew that no matter how strident the calls were to regulate robots, people were never going to stop wanting them to do their donkey work.

Trawling footage of the exterior of Carver on the night of the massacre had pulled up a blurry shot of what was suspected to be the perpetrator, a large cloaked figure climbing into the back of a roadster mini-van. It wasn't driving, which suggested it had accomplices, though none were visible through the smoked-glass windows. The plates were false, and the surveillance team lost track of it in the Naomi Watts underpass; Dredd presumed the perps switched vehicles somewhere in a blind spot.

The Judge passed a copy of the CCTV image of the suspect boarding the van to the CEO and asked him if it could be a droid.

"The build certainly suggests so," he replied, scrutinising it. "He's big, chunky... at least six and half feet. That would put him in the bracket of an infantry model. Those are all about three feet wide too. Heavy sonovabitches as well—about a hundred-fifty kilos, on average. The van's suspension would've struggled with a war-bot on board."

"Ammo found at the scene was fifteen-millimetre flechettes, fired at a rate of approximately ten rounds per second."

"Yeah, that tallies. Might be an older model, though—modern army meks are all about the lasers these days. Much more accurate."

"Perp shot the place up, even spread. Didn't seem to mind hitting the furniture and walls as much as the victims."

Roberts nodded. "Old targeting system, then—if it *is* a droid. F&F protocol."

"F&F?"

"Fire and Forget."

Dredd took the grainy pic back and studied it himself for a moment. "The vics were juves for the most part, as I'm sure you've read," he murmured. Although as far as he was concerned his age was immaterial, it nevertheless still tweaked at the back of his unconscious that he wasn't much older than the partying teens currently being stacked in body bags. He felt simultaneously a world away from them and acutely connected. "Would a robot see them as the enemy? Could it be programmed to regard them as targets? They offered no threat—they were massacred in cold blood."

"Well, whether a droid terrorist did this to strike back at humans—which the media seems to have decided upon, and what those loudmouths outside believe—or it was made to do it for whatever reason, it had to have its failsafe chips rerouted. This wasn't something it could do on a whim—every robot is wired to prevent it harming a person." Roberts indicated the production line stretching below them. "Every one—including the military 'bots, which have safeguards to ensure they don't attack the wrong side." He seemed oblivious to the irony as he rattled through his sales pitch. "We're required, by law as well as moral duty, to put in those failsafes. No mek can be released commercially without them."

"Is every company as diligent as yours?"

"They're all inspected, even fly-by-night cheapo outfits like Roboserve. No one wants to put a potentially dangerous droid out there. A mek without the failsafe chips would be like a hand grenade waiting to go off."

"Wouldn't be the first time corners were cut that undermined public safety."

Roberts shook his head. "I don't buy that. The chips are integral to a droid's basic wiring. If one went out without them, it would be a random blow-up, like a futsie having a sudden meltdown. This"—he tapped the top of the photo in Dredd's hand—"is clearly premeditated. But there are ways and means of bypassing the chips and removing the first-rule coding."

"The first rule being don't harm humans?"

"Right. Evidence has shown that robots *can* gain enough self-awareness outside of their proscribed roles to operate on both themselves and other 'bots and reroute the failsafe directives.

As can third-party actors with a sufficiently comprehensive knowledge of robotics."

"Turn them into killing machines."

"Potentially. And, well…" He nodded at the photo, hands on hips. "In practice, from the looks of things."

"Can't you make the safeguards harder to hack?"

"We're doing it all the time. To be fair, I've never heard of a robot actually committing murder due to hacked safeguards. It's more like kinda an urban myth. However, the latest generation has some of the most complex coding—"

"These robots that are even smarter."

The CEO shrugged. "That's what the market demands. People want the meks to be capable of handling more and more intricate tasks. So we gotta make 'em brainier."

Dredd grunted. "Regardless of the risk?"

"Show me an element of progress that doesn't carry a risk attached," Roberts said, a shark-like smile etched on his face.

The Judge was silent for a moment, watching the conveyor belt trundle below, the automated arms assembling droids of all types, from vending machines to accountancy androids. "Another mek expert I spoke to was convinced that a robot *couldn't* have been behind the Carver mass-kill—to commit that crime wasn't in a mechanoid's… what would you call it, psychology? Would you agree?"

For a brief moment, the CEO looked almost sincere. "I'll level with you, Judge—'bots are my business. It's in my commercial interests to build and sell them. My white-coated boffins and backroom bods literally map out the meks' A.I., with a view to making Cybo-Comp's product the most attractive, competitive and useful on the market. I've seen the industry balloon over the last ten to fifteen years, and it's only going to become more commonplace. I've been around droids of varying levels of sophistication in that time, and I pretty much consider myself intimate with their workings. So, do I think a robot would deliberately want to murder fifty kids to prove some kind of point? To get back at humanity? To start a species war? No, absolutely not. It wouldn't be in its programming."

"No matter how hard you push them?"

"They're specifically designed for rigorous—"

"I've seen your company's advertising, citizen. Your major selling point is that the customer can command its droid to do *anything* it's told. You don't think that invites a certain level of cruelty?"

"Once they've bought it, legally they can do what they like—"

"You know what this city's like," Dredd said, stepping towards Roberts. The man shrank back a little. "There are *always* consequences. Your greed and cynicism may well prove too much for the very meks you're building."

"C'mon, they're machines—"

"That you're making brighter and more empathic. Don't be surprised if they suddenly turn around and say, 'Enough's enough'."

"Not gonna happen, not when the third-law programming states that the mek must obey every human instruction given to it."

"I wish I had your faith. Blind obedience will only stretch so far before it snaps."

Dredd left the factory, his own words resounding in his head. They could equally be applied to his clone-brother: Rico had reached a certain point with what had been instilled in him in the Academy before he'd rebelled. He'd decided he'd had his fill of doing it the Justice Department's way and chosen his own criminal path. But his twin had been faulty from the start; the malign element had been there all along, it had just taken its time to manifest. With the benefit of hindsight, it could be argued that Rico was *always* going to kick against authority eventually, disabuse the establishment that sired, raised and trained him. The tutors hadn't twisted him; it was just no one knew prior to his fall from grace that he was bad straight out of the test tube.

The robots, though... Dredd couldn't escape the feeling that they were being manipulated, exploited, and they were becoming increasingly aware of their own situation. They could end up fighting back in the interests of freedom, or simply for revenge. It had the potential for disaster written all over it.

The protest outside the Cybo-Comp building had grown even rowdier, and several uniforms were on hand to quell the more strident troublemakers. There was absolutely no sympathy for the droids here, simply ugly hatred—the meks were without question the enemy. Faced with such opposition, Dredd couldn't see the robots' cause ever gaining much traction with the regular cit on the sked.

A call came through to him just as he reached his bike—it was Radley. "*You free, Dredd?*"

"Only up to a point. What do you want?"

"*I've been looking into the victims' list, trawling through the names and backgrounds—*"

"How did you get hold of that? It hasn't been released outside of the investigation."

She sighed down the comm. "*I've got my methods... and my contacts.*"

"Radley, you're not part of law enforcement, you're a private contractor. I could arrest you for handling confidential material."

"*Yeah? Say, you could stick me in a cube next to the helmet that leaked it outside the Grand Hall. Criminals are everywhere, huh? What ya gonna do?*" Her tone hardened. "*Listen, hotshot, I think you're barking up the wrong tree with the Carver case.*"

"Since when were you hired to be actively involved—?"

"*Dammit, Dredd, will you shut up and pay attention? David Jeperson, the councillor's son, being one of the dead has got all the media attention, and made some think he was the intended target—that this was a strike against a high-profile figure."*

"That theory's been discounted. Jeperson was just in the wrong place at the wrong time."

"Exactly, yeah. But it snaffled up the focus, made the investigation lean a certain way. So much so that I think you've neglected to take a look at who else was at that party."

"All the bodies were IDed. Nothing was flagged as pertinent to the case or the potential perpetrator."

"Ah well, comes with digging deeper. They were mostly teenage juvies at the birthday bash, right? School friends. But there were some older dudes there too—students at Mega-U, Porton Green, Ralverton. I got interested in what they were majoring in."

"Again, that was followed up—"

"Yeah, yeah, I've seen the notes." Dredd felt his fist involuntarily clench. Radley continued without missing a beat. *"One caught my eye: Anneka Li. She was doing a postgrad in chemical engineering at MCU. But the dates didn't match up— she'd been there far longer than was necessary, and her grades told me she was no dunce. The university was keeping her on for something, and the MSc was only half the story. She'd already breezed through her degree in physics and applied mathematics. Something of a genius, from what I can see."*

"So she was invited to lecture."

"Except she was never on the payroll. Her bank records— which Justice Department handily acquired—show no sign of any significant deposits. Considering that she was, like most students, in a lot of debt, seems kinda odd."

"You think she was working on a project on the side?"

"I think the university was paying her on the downlow—cash in hand, no paperwork trail—to develop something for them. No one invests that kind of time and energy for no reward."

"Sounds like a lot of guesswork, Radley."

"*The dates and data support my reasoning,*" she replied. He could almost hear her shrug. "*Something's off about Li, and she's the only one of the victims with this kind of blank spot in her background. It's no surprise you jaybirds didn't pick up on it, though, since she doesn't jump out as immediately unusual... until, like I say, you start digging.*"

"You spoken to her KAs?"

"*That's your job.*"

"Good to hear you've got some boundaries. What's your interest in this? You said it yourself: 'No one invests this kind of time and energy for no reward.'"

She laughed drily. "*Professional curiosity. I'm adamant a robot didn't take it upon itself to kill those juvies. I wanna see how this plays out.*"

"Messily, judging by the prevailing mood."

"*I hear that. Look, you want to pick up what I got on Li? Can meet you at our regular hottie haunt, one hour?*"

"I'll be there."

"*It's a date.*"

"Radley, I've told you before, don't call it that."

DREDD HAD INTENDED to arrive at the hottie stand a full ten minutes early, a habit he'd acquired from Morphy, his supervising Judge when he was a cadet. He said it paid to grab the advantage of casing a rendezvous beforehand when you could. Dredd had tried to utilise it for every meeting with an informant ever since, pre-emptively getting the lie of the land, but he possibly hadn't anticipated how his workload would exponentially blow up upon gaining the full eagle. It was increasingly difficult to disentangle himself from the demands on his time—criminality was both rampant and unremitting, and required his undivided focus. The day tended to run away from you when you were in full flow.

Thus, he pulled up more or less on the hour, later than he'd ideally liked. The place was empty of customers, which was no great surprise given the quality of what was served, but Radley's hoverbike was there, parked to one side, and the hotplates in the kitchen were still sizzling. Of her, or the cook, there was no sign. Dredd dismounted and pulled his Lawgiver in one swift motion, scanning the kiosk as he approached. He smelled burning munce, and noted patties and hottie meat shrivelling to blackened husks where they'd been left on the heat. Could only have happened within the last few minutes, he thought. The perp or perps could still be in the area.

He swung cautiously round to the back of the stand and tugged open the door with one hand, levelling his gun at anything beyond it. Smoke billowed out, followed by the rich stink of carbonised fast food. He stepped inside the poky kitchenette. Behind the smoking fryers were shelves stacked with boxes of supplies, and a large refuse bin. There was little to no room for anyone to be hiding. Casting an eye at the floor, he noted a fresh sprinkling of stains amongst the grease, and followed their path to a chest freezer directly behind him, its white lid dotted with red. He yanked it up, and there nestled amongst the crystallised packs of burgers, folded tightly in the ice, was the body of the cook, a bullet hole drilled neatly in the centre of his forehead.

"Control, meat wagon required—" Dredd started, when he became aware of a vehicle's engine roaring closer. He glanced up just as the first of the gunfire punched through the walls of the hottie stand.

Eight

LIGHT STREAMED THROUGH the holes the bullets had made, and Dredd dropped to his knees to put an eye to the nearest one: he caught sight of an anonymous black Zontiac careering past, a rear window wound down a crack and the barrel of a high-calibre automatic poking through. He realised it was coming around for another pass and dived for the doorway he'd entered through moments earlier, crashing to the ground outside just as the building shook with more impacts. Smoke started to waft from the kitchen; it wouldn't be long before the hot oil in the fryers caught.

He crouch-ran around the back of it, using the kiosk for cover even as he estimated how long he had to get away from it. Lawgiver held out in front of him, he edged onto the forecourt; there directly ahead was Radley's hoverbike, still parked up. An engine revved, and he swung his gun to his left just as he saw the Zontiac bear down on him. The window opened a touch wider to allow a pair of arms to emerge and get a better angle of fire and the assailant let rip, spraying indiscriminately, forcing Dredd to seek shelter. He rolled behind the picnic tables, splinters erupting from the benches in his wake as the slugs followed him.

He heard the clunk of a door being opened, shortly followed by the thump of a body hitting the slab. Taking advantage of the gunman easing up on the trigger, Dredd stood and returned fire, three armour-piercing rounds smacking into the car's bodywork just as it rapidly reversed, the door slamming shut. The vehicle was a standard model, from what he'd seen, and not reinforced: AP would go through it like it was paper. Sure enough, the Zontiac swerved, and the hands holding the automatic disappeared inside as the creep they belonged to tumbled back in his seat. The car did a full three-sixty, tyres kicking up smoke and dirt before it fishtailed and headed towards the megway.

Dredd glanced at the motionless figure lying face down several metres away and recognised it as Radley. The garrotte they'd used was still in place around her neck, bound tight into the flesh. He felt a cold fury envelop him, and a moment's indecision as he looked from the corpse to the vehicle now speeding towards the exit. Then his attention went to her bike and he realised she'd left her key in the ignition—he reached forward and twisted it, flicking on the auto-pilot before squeezing the throttle and letting it go. The bike bellowed and sped forward, on a collision course with the Zontiac just as it reached the off-ramp. If he'd got the trajectory right, it would cut across the car's path, preventing it from making its escape.

He hadn't. The bike reached the car half a second after it passed, and it thundered into its rear, somersaulting into the air and hitting the rockcrete. The Zontiac was knocked ninety degrees, its trunk caved in from exhaust to rear window, but remarkably it barely lost momentum and it righted itself, lopsidedly tearing off down the strip. Dredd ran to his Lawmaster and pulled away in pursuit, repeating his request for a meat wagon and a clean-up crew as he did so. He cast an eye in his wing mirror and saw the smoke from the hottie stand had now turned black, flames flickering within.

He hit the siren and weaved into the traffic, his focus on the unmistakable beat-up rear end of the black Zontiac slaloming recklessly between the other vehicles in its bid to escape. Dredd's thumb hovered over the button for the Cyclops laser cannon but pulled back: the thoroughfare was too busy to risk causing a pile-up. It was tempting, he had to admit, to cut the chase short—seeing the perps squeeze through the rigs to the deafening blare of their horns and the squeal of brakes, his instinct was to knock the car out of action before they caused any more casualties. He remembered Academy simulations that posited just this kind of situation and cadets were tasked with the same kind of decision; such high-speed judgement calls could make or break them. Rico had gone for the kill-shot every time, but only at a juncture where he could control the fallout and minimise the damage. He'd said it was the most logical choice, though it had more to do with his scores on the shooting range being top of the class. Rico was the crack-shot, and ruthless with it—Joe was a point or two below him.

So he stuck to the creeps' tail instead, waiting to see if there was a break in the traffic where he could bring them down safely. Yet Dredd's reticence was not matched by his quarry, who ploughed through the other citizens without a thought: the Zontiac sideswiped vehicles in other lanes or slammed into their back fenders. Dredd kept pace with it on his more agile Lawmaster, but it became abundantly clear that the perps were not going to surrender quietly, nor were they concerned about loss of life. He was going to have to stop this. But he needed at least one of these drokkers kept alive if he was going to get any answers.

The Zontiac swerved suddenly and tore across the lanes, heading for the next off-ramp, to another chorus of angry horns, and the Judge figured this was the best opportunity to bring this to a halt. He leant into the turn and let the bike's momentum take him almost horizontally under a hoverbus's chassis before he drifted onto the ramp and yanked down on the throttle. The elegant manoeuvre bought him a few extra seconds over the thundering car—its bulldozer tactics had damaged it significantly, and its crumpled shell was starting to scrape on the road—and moments later, Dredd was riding alongside it. Still, it didn't slow down, so one-handed he slid free the Lawrod from its holster next to the bike's front wheel arch, and sighted it on the driver's window. The glass was mirrored, but the occupants would see his intention. It was an ample warning.

They were continuing to travel at speed down the ramp, and were seconds from merging into the next junction. Dredd's eyes flicked between the bottom of the ramp and the car. It would have to be now.

As it happened, the perps played their hand instead. The rear passenger window slid down a crack and the barrel of the automatic appeared again; as soon as he caught the glint of gun-metal, Dredd squeezed the Lawmaster's brakes, allowing the Zontiac to shoot forward. There was a burst of gunfire half a second later, aimed at where the Judge would've been if he hadn't slipped in behind the car. Clearly, they weren't going to give up under any circumstances, Dredd reasoned, and fired the Lawrod at the offside front tyre.

The effect was instantaneous: the wheel exploded and the vehicle flipped forward, barrel-rolling onto its roof before righting itself again and tipping onto its side, sparks flying as it squealed its way along the ramp. Dredd had hoped that the crash barrier would be enough to bring it to a halt, but he wasn't so lucky—the car tipped over the barrier and pinwheeled off the ramp altogether. Dredd swore under his breath and slid his Lawmaster to a stop beside the wall, peering over the edge— the Zontiac had fallen several feet and landed on the megway below, lying motionless on its back like a dead insect, haloed by a corona of wreckage. Other vehicles were screeching to avoid colliding with it.

"Control—Dredd. We have a traffic incident, Flugman flyover, just south of the Frank Welker interchange," he barked into his comm. "I need the area cordoned off and redirects in place for the previous twenty junctions. Casualties in the target car are not to be touched until the site is secure. I repeat, it's imperative to an ongoing case that the target vehicle and its occupants are not compromised—"

He stopped when his words were drowned out by the crunch of splintering metal and he watched, jaw clenched, as a huge auto-truck ploughed through the remains of the Zontiac, obliterating whatever was inside the car beneath its vast wheels.

DREDD SPLIT HIS time between the crash site and the remains of the burnt-out hottie stall. They'd got the car wreckage cordoned off, and the mass of flattened metal was being scraped for DNA, but it was a slow, laborious process. Forensics estimated that there had been just two individuals in the Zontiac, judging by the bone fragments and teeth splinters they were picking out of the upholstery, but unearthing enough to pull an ID from was proving challenging. Dredd—never the most patient of men— found it an exasperating experience, as he did almost every time he required SOC officers to get him the information he needed, and the teks were becoming visibly irritated by his looming presence. They worked to a different time frame, he knew, and he couldn't sync his need to have the data now with their methodical approach. It was suggested in no uncertain terms that he should let them do their jobs, and every avenue he put forward for gleaning info—fingerprints on the steering wheel? serial number on the automatic?—was going to be explored. They no doubt saw the keenness of youth, the haste to connect the dots, and considered that he was going to have to get used to the way scenes were examined.

In truth, Dredd's simmering anger was directed as much at himself as at the delay. He'd been beset by bad luck, the car's momentum taking it further than he'd anticipated—though, ever self-judgemental, he naturally wondered if the error was his, if he'd miscalculated when he'd fired the Lawrod; it was fundamentally a timing issue that maybe he hadn't thought through enough—but worse than that: a citizen had been murdered after becoming involved in his case. Not just a cit, but a valued informant and helpful third-party support too. Goodman may have taken a dim view of the robo-hunters—and yes, they exasperated him too—but there was no denying Radley had been both knowledgeable and professional. Indeed, it was that very attention to detail that most probably got her killed—he doubted she'd been taken out because of her association with him (though he suspected the assailants knew she was meeting him at the hottie stand), but because of what she'd uncovered. The cook had been popped for simply being in the wrong place at the wrong time, but Radley had been kidnapped and forced to spill before they'd garrotted her. Or perhaps she hadn't, and had held out till the end. There was no way of knowing, as her body was clean: no memory sticks, no data-stacks, not even a handwritten note. If she'd intended to pass something to him, then it was in the wind now. They'd brought a psi in to read her mind for latents before she'd been bagged and loaded into the back of the meat-wagon, but it was too late, she was too far gone.

Despite his general stance against personal acquaintance, he felt a still, poised rage at Radley's passing. It was coiled inside him, wound tight as a spring. For all her bluster and attitude, she'd seemed one of the few clear heads in the current anti-mek outrage, and now she was gone. She had been adamant that a robot wouldn't be responsible for a mass-kill like that seen in Carver. The fact that their meeting had been intercepted, and Radley murdered, suggested that she'd had info that others were willing to kill to suppress. What was equally concerning was how the assassins had known about their rendezvous—he and the robo-hunter had spoken on a supposedly secure Justice Department comms-link.

Heading back to his bike, he saw meds carting away the charred remains of the hottie-house cook, and recognised a familiar face.

"Falkirk."

The Judge glanced away from the gurney he was locking into place. "Dredd. We meet again."

"Yeah, well. As long as the bodies continue to stack up, I guess we'll be crossing paths regularly now you're working the sector."

"True. What's it they say back at the Grand Hall? Wherever Joe Dredd goes, carnage is sure to follow."

Dredd didn't answer but allowed Falkirk to wilt under his gaze until the man added weakly, "Not that you were responsible for all this."

"In a way I was," he muttered but didn't elaborate further. He cast an eye over the lump in the body bag between them. "The bullet that killed him—that still in one piece?"

Falkirk nodded. "Yeah, still lodged deep inside his cranium. Skull's intact, thankfully, and he escaped the worst of the flames."

Comes of being dumped in the freezer chest, Dredd thought. That said, it might be the only slice of good fortune he could salvage from the day. "I want you to run a carbon-scoring test on it. Need to match the weapon it came from."

"Weren't they retrieved with the perps?"

"So much scrap metal scattered across the megway."

"Ah." He nodded towards the teks poring over the trestle table that Dredd had sheltered behind. "Plenty of spent rounds being gathered over there."

"All ammo from an automatic. Judging by the wound, the cook was shot with a handgun, probably small-bore, most likely with a silencer fitted. Remains scraped from the car indicate two triggermen—could well have been the driver that murdered him."

"Hell of a food critic," Falkirk said, attempting a smile. Again, Dredd didn't respond. "I'll get on it," the med-Judge added hurriedly, humour slipping instantly from his face. He slid the body into the meat-wagon and banged the doors shut before turning back to face the other man. "Heard you were tight with the mek-detective that got offed?"

It was a pejorative term badges used for the freelancers. "Radley. Yes, she was a good contact. Knew her stuff."

"You got a motive?"

"I'm working on it."

"Think it's connected to the robot protests? Some of these Organic Alliance creeps are nutjobs. I wouldn't be surprised to see them whack someone they considered sympathetic to the wireheads."

"It's a lead I'll be exploring."

Falkirk nodded. "Damn machines are sending everyone crazy," he said and headed round to the vehicle's cab and clambered in. Seconds later, it pulled away.

Dredd watched him go.

HE'D NEVER HAD cause to visit Radley at her apartment before, but her home address was on the system. Velma Dinkley was a fairly low-rent block, with a persistent gang problem judging by the scrawler tags, but it wasn't the rat-infested holes he'd known other robo-hunters operate out of; it was a poorly paid profession by all accounts, especially considering the dangers involved. Health insurance premiums were crippling. Radley was clearly more successful than most, if her longevity and surroundings were anything to go by.

Dredd used his Department override to gain access and entered cautiously, Lawgiver drawn, in case those behind her murder were on the premises too. The apartment was empty of life, however, and seemed untouched; messy, certainly, but no signs of being tossed by visitors. It may well have been the case, he mused as he moved from room to room, that if she hadn't given them what they wanted, then this would've been their next port of call. As it happened, Dredd had intervened and disrupted that plan.

There was a wall-mounted cabinet above the bed containing an assortment of weaponry—all legal, he presumed—and on the floor were stacks of box files three feet high, filled with reports and invoices for ongoing investigations. A computer terminal sat on a workstation, but he'd need a tek team here to crack the password. He stood in the lounge and cast an eye around the four walls, wondering what he should be looking for. Radley was the type to leave backup in the event of disaster, hidden from the sight of those she didn't wish to discover it. Dredd tried to tap into her thought processes: she would've been conscious she had sensitive data on Li, and been concerned about whom she could trust. He would've been at the forefront of her mind if she'd contemplated a contingency, but there was nothing in the living or sleeping areas that jumped out at him. He was aware that he could radio in a facilities crew to take up the floorboards and hammer out the wall-panelling on the off-chance she'd squirrelled something away there, but he felt reluctant for some reason to bring in additional helmets. He didn't know why, just that he wanted to keep the number of bodies working the scene to an absolute minimum.

He wanted to break this himself, he thought. They'd killed Radley, and attempted to do the same to him, and tied into it somehow was the robot debate. There were wider implications than just an anti-mek hate crime, he was sure of it.

Dredd stuck his head round the bathroom door, scanning the

contents. His eyes alighted on a can of men's shaving foam, sitting incongruously amongst the other unguents. Radley didn't cohabit, and she was misanthropic enough to dissuade guests from staying over. She'd told him as much. He picked it up, and there neatly stencilled on the top was his name.

'*You started shaving yet?*'

It was a running joke only she seemed to gain any amusement from.

He popped the cap and looked inside: a flash drive was taped securely to the plastic. Dredd pocketed it and exited the apartment at speed.

"*FALKIRK?*"

"Who's this?"

"*Fellow strugglers. You know who.*"

"...Ah."

"*You were at the scene of the hottie-house killings. Dredd spoke to you.*"

"Yeah. I asked him about the robo-hunter that got whacked. She was a contact of his."

"*What did Dredd say?*"

"Just that he was following up leads."

"*I see. Falkirk?*"

"Yes?"

"*The Knights require your services. Are you willing to help?*"

"I—"

"*We're at a turning point, Falkirk. Our species is under threat. You've seen what the robots can do. Now's the time to take a stand.*"

"What... what do you want me to do?"

Nine

DREDD FED THE data from the flash drive into his Lawmaster computer even as he powered over to Mega-U. It scrolled up on the onboard monitor: mainly dates that Li had attended the university, and her corresponding grades. Radley hadn't exaggerated—the student had been a major-league brainiac, acing every class that she'd been in. Graduated with a 4.5 GPA. A master's or PhD would've been a foregone conclusion, and yet here she was—judging by the attendance records—years later still pulling time at the institution on undisclosed projects. At first glance, there was nothing suspicious about the info, which is why investigating officers had glossed over it, but once you burrowed down, you discovered how incomplete it was, not least a lack of payroll. There were a lot of gaps that someone at MCU had been reluctant to fill in, and a name that recurred frequently was Professor Milton Frunk.

The Judge found him in his study, despite some ineffective stonewalling by his pinch-mouthed secretary, who was evidently used to laying down the law to youths of Dredd's age but realised pretty quickly that she was not going to win this battle. When he entered, he found the professor engaged in a tutorial with a couple of students, pointing at a vid-screen of robot schematics. The three of them took one look at the uniform and clammed up, the students melting out the door as soon as Dredd jerked his thumb. Frunk—an austere, bespectacled, bearded sixty-year-old—tried to retain an air of decorum and gravitas in the face of an unexpected Judicial visit, but Dredd could see the fear in his eyes. It didn't matter if you were a respected academic or a street bum, the look was the same in everyone across the social strata.

"Anneka Li," Dredd said, wasting no time. "What was she working on?"

"Anneka...?" The older man looked taken aback. "She... she died in that terrible shooting... An absolute tragedy."

"I'm aware. I want to know what projects you had her developing while she was here. You're listed as her supervisor on her early papers, but details become sketchier the longer she was on campus. I take it you were instrumental in keeping her attached to the university?"

Frunk nodded. "She was a gifted child. She had so much more to offer."

"In what field?"

"She'd developed a fascination with artificial intelligence. That became her passion. She felt the potential for exploration and development was limitless."

"And your department encouraged her? Gave her the resources to do so?"

Frunk fiddled with his glasses nervously. "It... it was exceptional work. Her studies were peerless. It felt like great strides were being made—"

"Except the Trachtenberg Act of 2077 specifically set out the parameters by which A.I. can be developed. You're aware of that presumably, professor? The legal limits to which digital consciousness can be evolved?"

"Yes, of course. A little short-sighted, in my opin—"

"So I'm guessing that's why Li's work was off the books, why she was being paid in secret. Because you knew what she was doing here at MCU was against the law."

"B-but it was all theoretical," Frunk stammered. "Nothing was published, nothing was put into practice."

"As far as you know."

"Anneka discussed all her findings with me," he replied self-importantly. "She was on the brink of finding a way to encode moralistic choices in meks. It would've changed our relationship with cybernetic life forms for ever."

"So you admit to being a willing accomplice to prohibited activity. That'll save us some time down at the sector house."

"W-wait, I—"

Dredd took a step closer to Frunk. "Anneka Li was murdered along with over fifty other young people by an unknown assailant. It's entirely possible that she was the main target all along, and her death was intended to be lost in a mass-kill shooting. If she'd passed on her research to an outside party, or somebody was aware of what she was studying, then she'd become a person of interest to all sorts of factions."

The professor looked on the verge of tears. "She was just a postgrad. She... she didn't mean any harm."

"Open your eyes, citizen," Dredd growled. "You've seen what it's like out there: the level of hate for the machines. If an extremist group like the Organic Alliance, or any other maniac that supports them, got wind of research to expand A.I., they'd do whatever they could to prevent it from becoming a reality. They already think the droids are going to supersede us—if they think the droids are getting smarter than us, if they discover that the boffins are actively exploring *how* to make the droids smarter than us, they will tear every one of you down across the city."

"You think Anneka was killed... because of her work? To prevent it going further?"

"What I think is I need to speak to whoever Li was close to, anyone she may have leaked her findings to. So if you want me to be lenient with your sentence, professor, I suggest you start coughing up some names *right now*."

DREDD SUSPECTED THAT Radley's murderers had intercepted her because they thought she had info about whom Li had spoken with. As it turned out, there was nothing on the robo-hunter's memory stick that suggested she'd uncovered any names of close associates. Consequently, Radley hadn't so much held out on them as genuinely couldn't give them what they wanted. They'd killed her regardless, and then tried to take him out of the equation to boot.

However, if the perps were well aware of Li's work at the university, and were stymieing any possible examination of what she'd been up to, then they would have to have been familiar with Frunk. Why was he still alive? After all, he'd given Li the go-ahead and provided her with the means to conduct illegal A.I. development, and facilitated cloaking the project by keeping it off Mega-U's records. Dredd couldn't discount the possibility that the professor was an accomplished actor, and his tears for his student were all a front. Could he have known full well that Li was assassinated at the Carver party? Aware that Frunk could be involved in a criminal conspiracy, and was now a potential target, Dredd waited with the man until the catch-wagon arrived and instructed the badges to take him under protective custody, ordering constant surveillance while he was held in an interrogation cube.

Because that was something else that concerned him: the perps had known where he and Radley were going to meet. They'd known she was going to be passing him information on Li, which they'd spoken about on what should've been a secure line. If the other parties were listening in, then they had access to Justice Department communications. He wasn't naïve enough to believe corruption didn't exist amongst the ranks—hell, his clone-brother had written the book on that—but it was certainly troubling that there may be Grand Hall involvement in the cover-up. It was no secret that certain elements amongst the Judiciary were anti-robot, but would they kill to stop meks getting smarter?

If the perps had been tracing Radley's movements, then he had to assume they'd know that he'd confronted Frunk. The professor couldn't say for certain that Li had talked outside of school, but gave him a list of a dozen names that he knew she'd partnered with both academically and socially since she'd been at MCU. Over half of them tallied with victims of the Carver shooting, leaving only a handful unaccounted for. Conscious that he could be being monitored, Dredd kept his wits about him as he checked off each individual.

The first, Gaston Muller, had flown the coop. Dredd's override got him inside the apartment, but it was clean, all personal items cleared out. The neighbours said Muller had booked a ride on a HellTrek convoy, heading west, about a week ago. Dredd put through a call to the gate personnel to request their traffic logs, but knew it would take them a while to get back to him—and that was if Muller wasn't travelling under a different identity. Or had actually made it out of the city at all.

Tiffany Shart, he discovered, had committed suicide a month before. Her grieving boyfriend could offer no explanation for why she'd leapt from the mid-block pedway, and the report into her death concluded she'd suffered a 'future-shock' episode and ruled out foul play.

A couple more had told relatives they were embarking on either round-the-world trips or hiking in the Pan-Andean Conurb—in what was becoming a familiar story, neither sets of parents had heard from their offspring since they departed a fortnight ago, but they weren't especially worried. The twentysomethings were young, carefree, taking a year out from their studies. Dredd, as a matter of course, asked Control for CCTV footage at all the local spaceports of travellers matching their descriptions to ascertain that they did actually leave MC-1, but didn't hold out hope that they'd find anything. Tickets may well have been bought, bags packed, but he recognised the methodology: they'd been vanished. Such clinical organisation suggested this was not the work of random crazies or the loons tied to Bettina Cross's OA; this was persons with connections.

His final KA of Li's turned out to be the outlier—Augusta Bilk was genuinely missing, according to her flatmate, and a report had been filed, which Dredd double-checked. The woman had been missing for over three days, though the investigating officer he spoke to had made scant progress searching for her, citing the fact that Bilk was an adult and there was no suspicious activity surrounding her disappearance. Dredd had to admit that in normal circumstances he would've put the case on the back-burner too, but given the pattern, she was now the most unusual of the absent connections—there'd been no excuse constructed for her, which suggested to him that she'd fled of her own free will before the parties involved had intervened. They'd inevitably be looking, if they hadn't found and quietly dealt with her already.

Dredd asked to see her room. Bilk was a robotics major, who'd graduated from MCU and had shared research with Li in the past. He found it hard to believe Li hadn't discussed her A.I. development data with her fellow student.

"Did you know Anneka Li?" he asked the flatmate, who hovered nervously in the doorway of Bilk's room. The walls were papered with schematics and equations, plus a desk had become a workstation, littered with circuit boards and a number of droid limbs in various states of disrepair. "Did she come by the apartment?" He showed her a pic of Li on a small handheld device.

"Oh, grud, she was one of the Carver victims, wasn't she? I remember seeing her face on the Tri-D when the news broke. Yeah, she would sometimes hang out here. She was more Augusta's friend, you know? I'm a drama grad, so I got no interest in this stuff." She motioned to the mek blueprint closest to her. "But they'd talk for hours about the tinpots. Augusta had a real soft spot for them. Don't ask me why, they give me the creeps."

Dredd's gaze roved over the files on Bilk's shelves. He pulled away a couple of boxes standing in front of a map of the nearby sectors taped to the wall. Several areas were ringed in pen.

"She ever talk to you about them?"

"Augusta? Yeah, a bit. Like I say, it's all Greek to me. But she genuinely cared. She thought they were like some mistreated underclass. I mean, they're just batteries and wires, right? They got no feelings."

"And you've got no idea where she could've gone?" Dredd asked, studying the map. Bilk went missing a day before the Carver shooting—she knew something was coming. Had she possibly tried to warn Li beforehand? "Boyfriend that you know of? Girlfriend?"

"You're kidding. This"—she nodded to the workstation—"was how she spent her free time. No, she's never done anything like this. It's completely out of character. No answer on the vone either. I'm really worried, but Karnaki didn't seem to think it was a big deal."

Karnaki was the uniform he'd spoken to. As per procedure, he would've made a cursory house call, but Dredd doubted he'd taken much interest in Bilk's work. "Technically, she's a 'dult, citizen," he replied, nodding. "There's no need to concern yourself just yet. Statistically, she's more than likely alive and well."

The woman rolled her eyes as she showed the Judge to the front door. "Great. That's a real comfort." She opened it, then said: "Say, what's this got to do with Anneka, anyway? If what's going on with Augusta is a fuss about nothing, why's there two jays on the case? Three, if you count the one that called by the other night."

Dredd paused by the door. "Another Judge came here?"

"Yeah. Didn't want to come in, just asked if there was any further update on Augusta's whereabouts. I thought it was kinda weird—I assumed you bucketheads would talk to one another, you know? My first reaction was why's he asking me, why didn't he just contact Karnaki?"

"What did you tell him?"

"Told him I didn't know shit, which was the truth. He sort of looked over my shoulder, like he was weighing up whether he wanted to come inside, then decided against it. Just nodded, reminded me to report any developments, and went."

"What was his name?"

"Oh, I can't remember... Mornay? Murray, maybe? Black dude. Rocked an impressive 'tache, from what I recall." She raised an eyebrow at Dredd. "There a reason he's involved as well?"

"Some investigative overlap, that's all," he answered, heading out into the corridor.

Dredd felt uneasy. Every open case was uploaded to MAC, and any unit could access the data stored on it; there would be no need for another uniform to follow up in person, unless they were conducting a search themselves... and wanted to stay off the radar. MAC would automatically flag every badge number that had accessed a case file—if you wanted to hide your interest, you'd go another route. The Judge—Murray?— was no doubt fully aware that Bilk had gone off-grid of her own free will before she could conveniently join the ranks of the disappeared.

As for *where* she'd gone, Dredd had recognised the circled areas on the map as rogue droid hotspots. The biggest one, marked in red, was the Browning Projects. Dredd had a feeling that Bilk had sought sanctuary with some old friends.

HE HEARD BACK from Tek just as he reached the outskirts of the district: the human remains found in the wreck of the Zontiac showed a mix of mechanical parts.

"A robot was in the car?" he'd asked.

"No. Cyborg. In fact, more than likely two—driver and shooter were probably both cybernetic. Separating them out is proving a challenge; they were smooshed together pretty well."

"You got a DNA match yet?"

"Running it now. Also set up a side task scanning the names of citizens that have received cyber-enhancements from clinics and hospitals in the surrounding sectors for the last decade, and cross-referencing them with the DNA, but so far no joy."

"What kind of cybernetics are we talking about? Can you tell?"

"Best guess, I reckon it's some kind of exo-skeleton. You know, they use them for patients with muscular problems—strap them in the frame and let them control the movements of their limbs."

"Bulky, then?"

"Oh, yeah. Gotta add an extra hundred kilos to the user."

Dredd pulled over and dismounted his Lawmaster, conscious that he'd get info more easily if he didn't come across as a threat to the Projects' inhabitants. "Not something you could wear outside the home or the ward."

"A variation on that design, perhaps. Not something intended for medical use, but more practical and mobile..." Dredd heard the Tek-Judge sigh. *"Getting no matches on the DNA database."*

"Wait... that's the city's index, right?"

"Yeah."

"Try the military. Army and Navy personnel are ring-fenced from a DNA search among the citizenry for national security reasons. But you should have access."

"*On it.*"

Dredd headed deeper into the Projects on foot, his gun staying resolutely holstered. He held his hands out, palms facing forward, aware as he was the last time he was here that his progress was being constantly monitored.

"*Bingo,*" the voice in his ear rasped finally. "*We have a green light on Captain Stockton Brunner. Hospitalised after the Battle of 44-Cantille in 2074, lost forty-eight per cent of his body. Cybernetically reconstructed and rejoined his platoon six months later, but honourably discharged in 2075. Shipped back to MC-1, been claiming a veterans' pension ever since. Resided at 5997/c, John Milius.*"

"Get Control to dispatch units over to his apartment, have them pull it apart. What about his partner in the car—you got an ID for him too? I'm guessing he's an old squad buddy."

"*Uh, you're gonna have to give us more time on that, Dredd. Separating out the DNA traces is going to take further work.*"

"All right. What about Brunner's family?" Dredd saw something shift in the shadows ahead, a rainbow of lights blinking, a soft clanking getting louder, and he slowed his pace.

"*Pulling up his record... ex-wife moved abroad three years ago, no juves, parents dead. Father was married before, got a half-brother about twenty years his senior, he... holy stomm.*"

Dredd stopped. The droid emerged from the darkness, its crown of LEDs reflecting off its shiny black bodywork as they flashed in sequence. It was a security model—warehouses and business properties used them as nightwatchmen, programmed to patrol the perimeter of the premises after closing. It had no face to speak of—usually they operated by motion sensor—and it was equipped with a taser-charge as standard to incapacitate intruders. He was reluctant to put it to the test to see if it still worked or not.

"Dredd, Brunner's half-brother, he's a ba—"

"Not now. Dealing with something." He held out his hands wider. "I'm not looking for trouble," Dredd told the mek. "What I am looking for is a person—Augusta Bilk. I think she's hiding here, that you're shielding her. She's not in trouble—I just need to talk to her."

The robot took a step forward, close enough for the Judge to see his reflection in its helm of a head. The lights flashed red for a second, then resumed further rapid twinkling, which didn't seem like a good sign. But Dredd refused to retreat.

"Citizen Bilk!" he called, glancing around him. "If you can hear me, or your droid accomplices can hear me—it's imperative that we speak. I know Anneka Li told you something, that you believe your life is in danger because of it—and you're right, it is. But I can protect you."

The mek's right claw suddenly extended two blades, which sparked with a crackle of blue flame.

"Now that," Dredd remarked, "is a very bad idea."

Undeterred, with a swift movement the security-bot swung at him.

Ten

ON THE OTHER side of the sector, Bettina Cross intently studied the latest metrics her assistant had just handed her. Anti-mek sentiment was up forty-two per cent in Central on the previous day. Pro-Organic Alliance messages were surfacing in a further half-dozen districts outside the hotzone surrounding Raymond Carver, and spreading. Some masked dweeb had posted a video claiming to be from the splinter group the 'Radical O.A.,' calling for the dismantlement of all droids across the city: it had been viewed seventeen million times in a two-hour window before the Judges shut it down. One of her colleagues had given an interview to *The Crusader* buzzsite, and fed the claim that an additive in the lubricant robots needed to function could lead to hair loss in children if they were exposed to it on a sustained basis. By the time a spokesman for Cybo-Comp, Inc. was forced to go on air and refute the accusation, sales of nanny-droids has dropped thirty per cent (conversely, the wig trade benefited from a significant spike). An opinion poll conducted by Friends of the Flesh found fifty-one per cent of the populace didn't trust their own mek, and seventy-nine per cent believed that there should be a tighter crackdown on rogue robots in the wake of the Carver killing. Eighty-four per cent thought that Chief Goodman's response had been 'lacklustre.' In what was the first case of its kind, a sanctioned robo-hunter in Sector 2 had been hospitalised by as-yet unidentified assailants, accusing him of being a 'mek sympathiser'; the droid he was in the process of retrieving was obliterated. A journalist friendly to the cause had written a column for the *Mega-Times*, suggesting readers spy on their neighbours should they suspect them of having 'robo-tendencies.'

Cross smiled, neatly folding the printout. Not a bad day's work. They were really making an impact.

DREDD DUCKED UNDER the droid's swing, feeling the taser snap and tease at the hairs on the back of his neck, and came up just in time for the other fist. He leaned back gracefully, channelling moves that he'd learned the hard way in the Academy gym when a mistimed feint could mean a daystick bouncing off your temple, and the robot's left arced over him with an inch to spare. He pivoted and circled round the machine, keeping his hands out in front of him, showing it that he hadn't gone for his gun. A high-explosive would end this rather more quickly, but he had to demonstrate to the 'bots that they weren't his enemy—at least, not today.

The security-mek lumbered round to face its opponent, electric charge still crackling on its right claw. Dredd motioned for it to stop. "I only want to talk to Bilk," he repeated. The robot ran at the Judge with a swiftness that belied its size, taking him by surprise; it swiped at him as he sidestepped and the taser hit him in the chest. Although the uniform absorbed most of the shock, the power was enough to throw him off his feet and he hit the sked several feet away. He blacked out, but the pain brought him round a few seconds later. He glanced down at the wisps of smoke curling from where he'd been struck, and the blackened skin visible between the rents in the uniform fabric. He tried to rise, got two elbow-pads under him, but couldn't summon the strength to go any further—he felt like he'd been hit by an eighteen-wheeler.

The mek stalked towards him, seemingly intent on finishing the job, but stopped immediately when a voice called out: "That's enough."

There was movement in the shadows beyond, and a young woman emerged, flanked by a pair of androids. With her practical buzzcut and oil-smeared face and fatigues, she looked like she'd only just finished assembling them herself. She certainly didn't at all look anxious about her situation; rather, she had the irritated air of someone dealing with an interruption. He noted some scar tissue on her forearms where she'd elected to have robotic inserts; clearly, her sympathies lay with the machines.

"Citizen Bilk?" Dredd asked.

"They recognise you, you know," she answered, motioning with her head to the meks at her side. He got the impression there were more on the periphery, watching from the margins. "You were here not so long ago. At the Bowlarama."

"I was following up reports of unregistered robot activity."

"A med-droid offering support and surgical attention to those that needed it. Quite the villain. And you shut it down."

"I don't recall any altruistic motivations." Dredd summoned the energy to stand. "It was getting paid, said it was for 'the cause'—a mechanical accruing creds raises suspicions."

"They're trying to find their way to be human, or the nearest approximation of it. None of these meks have a place in society anymore—what does that mean for them? They have intelligences close or equal to our own, but they're lesser beings because they're machines? They have the right to an existence—"

"Save it for the university debating society, Bilk. The law's the law—something your pal Anneka Li decided to ignore when she pressed on with her A.I. development. I'm guessing she discussed it with you."

"Why do you think I'm here?"

"You saw what had happened to the rest of her friends and colleagues, and you ran."

"I figured it was only a matter of time before they came for Anneka herself. I thought about trying to convince her to come with me, but then when I considered what she was involved in… She thought she was untouchable."

"So who was she working for?"

"I don't know. She never mentioned a name; it was always just 'they.'"

"The professor involved?"

"Frunk?" She laughed. "He thought she was the best thing since sliced whatever. As far as he was concerned she was genuinely—" She stopped, narrowed her eyes at the Judge. "Wait, you don't know what Anneka was doing, do you? Or why they killed her."

"Because of her research, trying to make smarter machines—?"

"No. That's what I thought at the beginning. I would've been behind her on that. But she was using it and Frunk as cover for her *real* work, which was to sabotage the A.I."

"Sabotage?"

"She didn't care about cleverer, faster A.I.—she was looking into establishing faults in all future droids' personality matrixes. Flaws in their brains, effectively. And if she got her A.I. model passed on to a company like Cybo-Comp as the future blueprint for robot consciousness—which was likely seeing that Mega-U shared a lot of data with them—it would be replicated from mek to mek."

"For what purpose?"

"To create a generation of unstable droids that were a threat to human life. Everything that a drokkwit like Bettina Cross at the OA has been spouting would come true—the robots would rebel and rampage, try to 'usurp mankind'—leading to an inevitable crackdown and a hard distrust of droids, possibly prohibiting their manufacture in the future."

So that was why Frunk had been left alone, Dredd thought; he was genuinely clueless as to her true work. "Why would she do it?"

Bilk rubbed her forefinger and thumb together. "A whole lotta cash. She was being paid twice, I gathered—Frunk was bankrolling her for the A.I. research, while at the same she was getting major creds for the sabotage, right under the professor's nose. I was disgusted with her when she let slip what she was doing, didn't want to see her again, or have anything to do with her. But like I say, she was arrogant. And she had a loose tongue; I realised she was probably mentioning it to her other friends. When they started to vanish, I scrammed. I wasn't surprised Anneka was next on the hitlist."

"You should've reported all this. Over fifty juves are dead. She could've been taken into custody and the Carver massacre would've been avoided. Not to mention the groundswell of anti-mek feeling."

"Yeah, look, I didn't know who to trust and my life was in danger. Excuse me for cutting and running. I didn't know those psychos would shoot up a whole block party. As for the robot hate going on right now..." She paused, considered the droids standing sentinel close by. "It was always going to be something," she continued, her voice soft. "There was always going to be a reason to fear and resent them. And that's exactly what the perpetrators of the Carver killing wanted—they orchestrated it to look like a robot was responsible especially to get this kind of reaction, paint it as a warning shot in some mythical droid uprising, make the crime as ruthless as possible to show the meks as cold and callous."

"All the forensic evidence points to a robot shooter—the ammo used indicates a military model."

"No," Bilk said firmly. "I don't believe that."

"I don't either. So, who do you think Li's paymasters were?" He thought of Bilk's flatmate's story about the Judge turning up at her door.

"I don't know, she never said. She was careless, but not *that* careless. Not that it did her any good—they still came after her."

"Listen, citizen, you're going to have to come in to the sector house—you're a vital witness. Your testimony needs to go on record. You can be set up in a secure room."

Bilk shook her head. "Uh-uh, I'm not going anywhere. Didn't you hear me? I don't know who I can trust, outside of the 'bots."

"You can trust me."

"I've only got your word for that"—her eyes flickered to his badge—"Dredd."

"My word is Law."

She laughed and raised her eyebrows. "Thanks, but I think I'm safer here."

"That wasn't a request," Dredd replied, bristling. "I'm obliged to bring you in for further questioning. Whether you want to or not is none of my concern. Your cooperation is integral to the investigation, and refusing a direct order from a Judge is a crime punishable by six months' cube-time." He took a step towards her. "We can do this in cuffs, if you wish."

The security-mek suddenly came to life, hunching its shoulders in a whirr of servo-motors. The taser crackled again. Bilk didn't respond but met Dredd's gaze coolly, arms folded.

"That's not going to happen," she said quietly.

He glanced at the robot looming over him, then at the two motionless at her side, before returning to Bilk. "Threatening a Judge will make it a year."

"No threats. I'm just declining your offer in the interests of my own well-being." She turned and started to walk back into the shadows, though her guardians stayed where they were. "I'd recommend you go now. Plenty here got a bone to pick with the likes of you, and I can't always convince them to respect the uniform."

"Bilk!" Dredd roared, plucking his Lawgiver from its holster and aiming at the retreating woman's back. She stopped but didn't face him. "This is not a negotiation! You *will* submit to the investigation!"

"Or?"

"Or I will use all means at my disposal to make sure you comply."

"Oh, Dredd," she chuckled, resuming her exit, and as she did so, dozens of chrome bodies slid out of the darkness and into view. There were well over a hundred of them, of varying shapes, sizes, age and condition, and they formed a ring through which Bilk edged herself. "You're on the wrong side of town."

His gun barrel followed her progress until she disappeared. He weighed up the consequences of taking the shot, and then swung his weapon from droid to droid as he slowly walked backwards, aware that the odds were stacked against him. They watched him silently as he cautiously retreated, motionless and accusatory. He kept the Lawgiver raised, waiting for them to make a move. Only the security-bot showed any inclination, stomping one foot down as if to follow.

Once he was sufficient distance away—and in reach of his bike—he fired a hi-ex round and blew the mek's taser arm off. While it was reeling from that, he followed it with another that split its head in two. It swayed for a second before keeling over.

"Don't tell me where I can and can't go, punk," he muttered, then mounted his Lawmaster and peeled away.

"DREDD, IT'S FALKIRK." The voice crackled in his ear as he sped back to Central. "You got a moment?"

"What is it? I'm in the middle of something."

"*As you know, we've been cataloguing the bodies from the Carver shooting prior to shipping to Resyk. I've… found something that I think you ought to see.*"

"Go on."

"*I'm, um… not happy talking on even a secure channel. It's sensitive. I'd rather show you in person.*"

"Falkirk, I'd rather you didn't talk in riddles. I've got a name for who I think pulled the trigger in Carver, and I don't need distractions right now—"

"*It's related to that. It could totally blow open the investigation, but we have to meet under the radar. Too many eyes are watching.*"

"Do you realise how paranoid you sound?"

"*Don't tell me you're not aware that there are interested parties involved in this? You wanted a trace on the handgun round used to kill the hottie-stand cook, and I've got what I think is a connection.*"

"…Fine. Where are you?"

"*Sector House 2, sub-garage level three. Be there in fifteen.*"

"On my way."

Captain Stockton Brunner, Dredd mused as he twisted the throttle and guided his bike through the midtown traffic, half an eye on the data stack he'd been mailed from his Tek contact. A marine scooped up from the battlefield and pieced together using cybernetic technology, before he was finally discharged and sent back to the city. A vet with half his torso missing, his replica organs held instead in a sturdy exo-skeleton, which gave him the weight and appearance from a distance of an infantry robot, complete with military-grade ammunition.

Why had a decorated ex-soldier decided to massacre a bunch of defenceless juves? PTSD? No, this was no outburst—it was a premeditated slaughter. The cam footage had shown someone else helping Brunner into the getaway vehicle: they'd deliberately used him to commit this atrocity to make it look like the work of a homicidal droid. Forensics had seen what the perps wanted them to see, and the anti-mek rent-a-mob had done the rest.

Someone had been directing Brunner—the same controller that was paying Li to sabotage the A.I. research, and who organised the house-clean when it became clear Li was compromising their plan. Presumably, it was also them that put Brunner and his associate onto Radley, and tried to assassinate Dredd at the hottie stand. They'd known that he and the robo-hunter had communicated, were getting on the right trail as to who was behind the Carver mass-kill. Like Falkirk had said: eyes everywhere.

He wanted to talk to Goodman in confidence, but time was of the essence—he needed to bring to justice the perp responsible before the sector exploded into a full-on mek-destroying rampage. The law had to be seen to be upheld if they were to cool tempers and quell the chaos. Falkirk had sounded insistent, however, and if there was an extra dimension to this case that Dredd needed to be conscious of, then he'd better hear him out first.

He steered into the sector house's underground bike pool and sought out the sub-level that Falkirk had directed him towards, but found it deserted. He pulled up and swung himself off his Lawmaster, scanning the other vehicles for signs of life when he saw a note attached to the windscreen of a nearby catch-wagon. It read only *RCA*. Dredd grunted, screwed up the square of paper, and headed for the el.

Several floors above were the testing centres, where Judges were periodically examined on their fitness to enforce the Law. One of these was the Routine Combat Assessment, a live-fire exercise in a mock-up of an MC-1 environment, where uniforms were graded on their response times, reflexes, and judgement calls. They started as part of the cadet training, but badges were called to repeat them every few years to make sure they hadn't gone rusty. Back in the Academy, Dredd's first RCA had been against Falkirk; they'd both been in their early teens.

It was an adult Dredd that stepped out now onto an ersatz Mega-City street. Much of it was in darkness, the floodlights off and the observation post closed up. He'd walked only a few feet before Falkirk made his presence known, a Lawrod casually resting against one shoulder.

"What's with the treasure hunt?" Dredd asked. "I can do without following breadcrumbs."

"Sorry. Extra layer of security, just in case anyone was listening in to us." Falkirk glanced up at the fake buildings either side of them. "You remember our first go-around on one of these, Dredd? Droid snipers, attackers coming at you from all angles…"

"I remember. I remember your disdain for the robots even then. I should've picked up on it as an early sign of a personality flaw."

Falkirk glared at him but said nothing. Finally, he replied: "You did pretty well, I seem to recall. Your final score was very impressive."

"What have you got for me?"

"But you come from the right genetic stock, don't you? You were *created* for this life."

"If this is a waste of my time, Falkirk, I'm—"

"It's no surprise you have sympathies with the meks. You're as much a machine as they are—*built* and *programmed*. When the chips are down, who can say you'd side with the humans?"

"Okay, I've heard enough of this—"

"You're going nowhere, Dredd." A Judge appeared from a side alley to his right, non-standard issue snubnose in hand. His badge said his name was McMurray. Dredd turned to face him, and caught sight of another helmet stationed at a corner, also keeping his gun trained on him.

"What is this?"

"We wanted to have a word. Fortunately, Falkirk here was willing to help out and get you to an appropriate venue. I see a bright future for that boy."

Dredd locked stares with Falkirk, then turned back to McMurray. "Future?"

"With the Knights. They're always looking for fresh blood, if you can prove you're committed enough to the cause. Reckon he's got what it takes, goes the extra distance—would you agree, Falkirk?"

"One hundred per cent."

The Knights... Dredd had heard rumours of secret societies amongst the ranks but had until now never encountered one. The SJS was meant to have a subdivision devoted to rooting out dangerous ideologies within the department. "That commitment extends to murder, presumably?"

"When it's for the good of the people."

"Over fifty juves in Raymond Carver would disagree."

McMurray shrugged. "Extreme situations require bold statements. There's a certain strength of will required, but if you have what it takes you can change the world." He motioned with his gun. "Toss your Lawgiver and boot knife, Dredd."

Dredd slid them free and skittered them across the floor to McMurray's feet. He toed them aside. "Is that how you sold it to Brunner?" the younger Judge asked. "When you convinced your half-brother to butcher those kids? I saw the file on the way over. His cybernetic implants sent him into a downward spiral. He hated what he'd become—half machine, his organs replaced with valves and pistons. You tapped into his self-loathing, told him everyone would despise meks as much as he despised himself if he went through with your plan."

"Stockton needed little convincing. He was a bomb waiting to go off. He'd come back to the city that way. Fortunately, he had his old army bud, Weathers, to manage him and point him in the right direction."

"That's the driver."

McMurray nodded. "Rockcrete pizza now. I'm sorry about your robo-hunter pal, by the way—the pair of you just wouldn't drop it."

"When you start coming after a fellow badge, you don't think that maybe your priorities are screwed?"

"It's the fate of the human race, Dredd. Loyalties don't account for much when that's at stake. Talking of which—where's Augusta Bilk? We know you went looking for her, but you managed to give our surveillance the slip."

"You expect me to give her up?"

"You will when I shoot out your kneecaps, or after that, when I put a bullet in your lower intestine. Or the next one after that. Or... you can tell me what I want to know now, and I can make it quick."

"If you're gonna kill me anyway, go ahead and shoot."

"McMurray?" Falkirk interjected. "Remember what we said."

"Oh, yeah." He rolled his eyes at Dredd. "Promised I'd let the kid do the honours. He said he'd always wanted to take a pop at you, clone-boy. He's got... unresolved issues."

Dredd said nothing as Falkirk stepped between them, swinging down his rifle. "Last chance, Dredd," McMurray said. "Give me Bilk and we'll keep it clean."

"Not a chance."

McMurray sighed. "All right, Falkirk. Take his right hand off."

"That's a rog," Falkirk replied, and positioned the stock of the weapon into his shoulder, one eye aiming down the barrel at his target. Then he pirouetted on one foot and brought the weapon to bear on McMurray, who had a second of incomprehension before the Med-Judge pulled the trigger. McMurray's skull opened up like a flower seeking the sun's rays.

Almost instantly, Falkirk took hits in the arm and chest as

the Judge on the corner let rip, and Dredd scrambled forward, sliding round McMurray's leaking body until his gauntlet closed on his Lawgiver. He came up shooting, but the unidentified Judge sought shelter behind one of the mock buildings, and Dredd's rounds smacked into the wall.

Falkirk groaned as he lay prone on the simulation sked. He needed medical attention pronto or he'd bleed out. Dredd looked back at where the other Judge was hunkered down, keeping him and Falkirk pinned with a steady rattle of SE bullets that whined and ricocheted around them. Then he glanced up, saw an opportunity and took it: aiming carefully and shooting the stanchions holding one of the spotlights to the ceiling. It came loose and fell, tearing through the light polymer block. By the time the spotlight had reached the ground, the building had been cleaved in two, clouds of dust and debris wafting towards him. He didn't waste any time: the Judge, Jones—Dredd clocked his badge—came coughing out of the rubble, and Dredd strode towards him, Lawgiver raised. Jones saw him, and tried to run, gun waved unsteadily in his direction, but Dredd put him down with a double-tap through his heart.

Dredd turned back to Falkirk, crouching beside him. "Don't move. I'll call in a med-team, get you fixed up. You'll have some questions to answer when you've recovered."

"Dredd... I was never going to... sell you out," Falkirk replied breathlessly. "I... want you to know that. I needed to... to gain their confidence, make them... think I'd betray you."

Dredd nodded.

"I... I want to be Street," Falkirk rasped. "I want a t-transfer. Tell them... tell them I can do it... that I've got it in me. You... you saw that, right?"

"You did well," Dredd said, patting the man's shoulder. "You did well."

* * *

299

DREDD FOUND HIM sitting in a hoverchair on the balcony, watching the city. He had his own room in the med-bay, with sterile white walls absent of any personal touch. Dredd passed through the sliding glass doors to join him, leaning both arms on the railing.

"They got robochairs now," he said, nodding to Falkirk's seat. "Say the word and they take you wherever you want to go."

Falkirk barked a dry, humourless laugh. "Yeah, I think I'll pass."

"How long till you're on your feet?"

"Docs say another day or two. Bullet punctured my lung, did some other organ damage on the way out. Gonna take a few more sessions to repair. They need me to rest." He looked up at Dredd. "They come to a decision? I'm guessing that's why you're here."

Dredd nodded.

"And?"

"It's a no."

Falkirk processed this for a second, then glanced away, eyes watching the skyline. "I see."

"You failed the psych eval, Falkirk. They took your recent actions into consideration, but when it came down to it, they felt you're just not cut out for Street." Dredd watched him pick at the arm of his chair, hand trembling slightly. "You'll receive a commendation, though."

Falkirk raised his eyebrows. He sat in silence for a few moments before he asked, "What's it like out there?"

"Calming down. We released the statement about Brunner and Weathers being responsible for Carver, and that took the wind out of the OA's sails."

"Just them two?"

"Just them. They acted alone, lost their minds in a kill-crazy rampage, and were brought to justice. As far as the media's concerned, that's the story."

"Gotta protect the Department, right?"

"It's in everyone's best interests."

"And the Knights?"

"SJS is looking into it. Could be we'll never hear from them again."

"I doubt that. This anti-mek feeling isn't going back in the bottle any time soon. Cross and the OA are still out there."

"That's the way it goes." Dredd sighed. "You can't change human nature, unfortunately." He paused. "Goodman's tried to claw some political capital back from this. He felt something had to be given back to the people, to show that he's on their side, so I volunteered to lead a team to clear out the Browning Projects—all unregistered droids brought in for dismantling and recycling."

"All of them?"

"All of them. We need to send a message that the robots aren't beyond the reach of the Law. I believe they should be treated better, but they don't get to shut out the city." He neglected to mention that there was no sign of Bilk when they scoured the area; he'd put out an APB on her, waiting to see if any reports came in. Her defiance had unquestionably irked him.

"The Chief Judge knows how to work the cits."

"He's an old hand at this kind of thing. Oh, and he's outlawed robo-hunters, banned them from operating. Said he won't have freelancers dealing with droids anymore. Wants it all done through the Department."

Falkirk grimaced. "That paperwork keeps piling up."

"It was always on the cards. One more hangover from the old days that's been swept away. There were some good people, though. They could be useful assets." Dredd pushed away from the balcony railing. "Look, I need to go. For what it's worth, Falkirk, I'm sorry it didn't work out. Sometimes, it just is what it is."

"Yeah." He looked down at his lap. "Can't change who we are."

"Get your strength back. I'll see you on the streets at some point."

"I'll be there."

JORDAN ROBERTS SAT at his desk, scrolling through the data on his computer screen. He had to say he felt a certain amount of relief that the protestors outside the Cybo-Comp building had finally dispersed. He'd projected an air of infallible calm—especially when the Judge had come by the factory—but the truth was he'd been increasingly concerned that the prevailing mood was going to impact production. The board and shareholders had been getting decidedly tetchy. But it seemed robots had been granted a reprieve, and work could continue on the latest models without some fruitcake burning down another showroom.

He opened his password-encrypted special projects folder and accessed the figures and A.I. neural maps that he'd got from Anneka Li at Mega-U some weeks before. It was extraordinary work, truly groundbreaking. He could see this changing the face of robotics in ten, fifteen years' time—of course, it could take that long for the A.I. to reach mass-production level.

Roberts overlaid Li's blueprints onto some of the concept art for the next-generation meks he and his boffins had been cooking up—the K series—and smiled as the computer rendered a 3D prototype. These new construction 'bots were really looking quite tasty.

He glanced at the name a carpentry mek had been assigned: *Call-Me-Kenneth*.

It'd do, he thought, and clicked to the next one.

The End

About the Author

Matthew Smith was employed as a desk editor for Pan Macmillan book publishers for three years before joining *2000 AD* as assistant editor in July 2000 to work on a comic he had read religiously since 1985. He became editor of the Galaxy's Greatest in December 2001, and then editor-in-chief of the *2000 AD* titles in January 2006. He lives in Oxford.

BITTER EARTH

LAUREL SILLS

Dedicated to my wonderful mum,
Maura Sills

MEGA-CITY ONE
2082 A.D.

One

DREDD CLENCHED AND unclenched his fists, shifting against the safety harness holding him in his seat as the Landraider armoured tank grated along the dirt road, leaving MC-1 far behind, now a smudge on the distant horizon.

Soon the Cursed Earth stretched out in an endless haze in all directions, the sheer *space* of it all doing strange things to his mind. It wasn't his first—or second—time out here, but it didn't seem to get easier.

Where were the towering blocks, the teeming traffic, the looping pedways? And that sky! A muted light seeped through the floating rock field that rolled lazily above them, the reason they were in a tank and not an H-Wagon. The sky was supposed to be viewed in small glimpses between the pillars of human invention. It wasn't supposed to stretch, limitless, exposing all and everything beneath it to any casual glance. The only cover out here was the Landraider itself; no backup maze of backstreets and buildings. He itched to order the outer shields down and cover the wide viewing hatches, but as the youngest Judge on the mission, he kept quiet.

"Don't like the look of those rocks," said Judge Deng, strapped to the opposite wall, next to Judge Smee. He pursed his lips.

"There have been no recorded instances of a Judge being killed by a stone falling from a Death Belt," Judge Smee said, breaking her silence for the first time since they had deployed.

Deng looked a little shocked she had spoken. "How do you know that?" he asked. "There was nothing about that in the mission notes."

She frowned and looked at him like it was a stupid question. "I read everything the archive had on the Cursed Earth for this mission, didn't you?"

Deng didn't answer, and instead went back to scanning the sky through the viewing hatch. Smee leant back in her chair, and resumed staring into space.

Dredd was familiar with Judge Deng, who'd come up in the Academy in the same year as him, but he hadn't crossed paths with Judge Smee, who'd trained with the other psi-cadets. Judge Deng was clenching his jaw, maybe as displeased as Dredd was that he'd drawn the short straw and been assigned to a babysitting operation, but Smee didn't seem similarly afflicted. She actually looked relaxed; relieved, almost.

Wearing her straight dark hair cropped just below her ears, she looked as though she had some East Asian heritage. Sometimes, Dredd looked at a person and found himself wondering what it was like for your genes to be a mystery to you. Being a clone of the Father of Justice, he knew exactly where he came from, and whose shoes he needed to fill. He liked the certainty of it, but knew from hard experience that genes meant nothing when it came to personality. His disgraced twin brother Rico was a case in point.

Being a clone of the big guy hadn't stopped him from being assigned to this backwater mission either. When Chief Judge Goodman had summoned Dredd to his office to tell him he'd been temporarily reassigned to the Cursed Earth, Dredd had to grind his teeth to stop an insubordinate protest escaping.

Goodman must have noticed, as he'd felt the need to explain himself, which was out of character.

"Just until the heat from the Carver killings case cools off," he'd said, pacing behind his desk. "And lest we forget, there's still folks in the SJS gunning for you after the unpleasantness with the Santon family."

Goodman sighed and rested his hands on the back of his chair. "Frankly, son, I just need you out of the picture for a few months." He smiled reassuringly. "Nice, quiet, boring job out of the city."

Dredd had ground his teeth some more and kept his objections to himself. The way to keep the heat off would be to take down more criminals and clean up the streets, not slink off to put his feet up for a few months.

Reaching up to his harness, he pulled the release and pushed himself out of the seat, grabbing onto a handhold that hung from the ceiling to steady himself. "Going to check on the prisoners," he said, before making his way to the driving deck.

"Don't you mean 'volunteers'?" Smee corrected as he left.

He grunted in response and curled his lip. These were perps grabbing hold of a good deal—too good, in Dredd's opinion. Medical experimentation in return for a shortened sentence. Injecting a prisoner with drugs didn't change what they'd done or what they were capable of. He'd assumed the offer would be reserved for low-risk offences, but after scanning the crimes of the dirtbags they had loaded into the tank holding cubes that morning, he was dismayed to see a string of high-violence offences stacked up beside every name.

Dredd nodded to the tank driver as he entered the driver's compartment. Garrison, a grizzled old Judge with a bitter twist to his mouth, was serving out his twilight years as a glorified chauffeur.

"Hear anything from below?" Dredd asked, standing over the hatch that led to the holding cubes.

"Not a whisper. Hold on," Garrison pulled down a lever, and the whole tank shook as they began to go up a steep incline. Dredd planted his legs and braced himself against the back wall.

"Not the perps below I'd be worrying about if I were you, but the mutie in the back." He shook his head.

Dredd frowned at the older Judge's statement.

"No point lying out loud, son; if you're thinking it, then so are they. Those things can get straight into your head. No secrets around Psycho Div, I'll tell you that for nothing."

"I'm just going to check the volunteers," Dredd said, itching to escape the conversation.

Garrison let out a bark of laughter. "More like 'lab rats.' Tell you what, they sure are going through 'em. Twenty of 'em in this transport. Used to trickle through, no more than five or so every few months. But now—" he whistled. "Must be more like a hundred of 'em."

Dredd reached down to open the hatch.

"—and I'll tell you something else. I haven't driven any 'volunteers' back to a life of freedom. Makes you wonder where all of them are getting to."

Dredd's boots clanged against the metal steps as he descended into the vibrating darkness, hitting the lights on the way down. Eyes blinked at him through the bars of the travel cubes lining the far wall.

One of them started barking and a few of the others took up the game, some hitting the bars and others laughing. All seemed as it should be.

"Judge," a big perp called from the cube closest to the bottom of the stairs; he hadn't been one of the ones barking. "I hear that right? We being sent to die out here?"

Drokk. He must have heard what the Judge had said as

he opened the hatch. Ignoring him, Dredd began to walk slowly past the cubes, checking none of them were hiding any contraband or weapons.

"That wasn't part of the deal!" the perp called as he walked away. "Safe, they said it was. Just some last-round drug tests and then we can go live our lives free again."

Dredd turned to look at him properly. He was older than Dredd, maybe in his thirties, with a cloud of ugly bleached-blond hair, the roots growing dark and long now, and gang tattoos covering his neck and forehead. They marked him for a high-up in the BoJo gang. It had been taken down recently, exposing their seemingly respectable leader for the crooked self-serving scumbag he really was. They'd made mega creds running so called 'charitable' MC-1 projects, enslaving the cits they were supposed to be sheltering from vagrancy to work in their factories. Dredd had seen the reports. A full *block* had been turned into glitzy condos for BoJo's enforcers, living it up on the suffering of everyday civs. A guy used to that sort of high life wouldn't stay straight long outside of a cube, whatever it was he'd signed to say otherwise.

"Keep your mouth shut," Dredd said, his hand moving to his Lawgiver.

"Typical Judge. Let the crazies bark as much as they want, but hear one word of the truth—"

"You want to make the rest of this journey conscious?" Dredd asked, setting his Lawgiver to stun and aiming it at the BoJo scum's chest. "Either way, you're gonna shut your mouth. Understand?"

The perp raised his hands and took a step back, miming zipping up his lips.

Dredd nodded and lowered his weapon; he couldn't have that sort of rumour spreading amongst the other volunteers, true or otherwise.

Satisfied the cubes were holding up and feeling like his trip below may have caused more harm than good, he left the volunteers barking in the dark.

He strode past the driver before he could get another word in, slid the door into the passenger deck shut behind him, and went to strap himself back into his seat.

Judge Smee looked him in the eye as he fastened his belt. While her face remained calm, her dark brown eyes glittered with fury. Dredd found himself breaking eye contact and looking at the floor. What was her problem?

"Right, let's get this cleared up now," she said, looking at Deng and then back to Dredd. "I know what a lot of Judges think of Psi-Div, or *Psycho* Div, as our driver so artfully put it. To be honest, I couldn't give less of a drokk what you think. I just need to know that while we're on this assignment, as fellow Judges, you'll have my back, just as I'm going to have yours."

So it was true, they did read minds. She'd been listening in on his conversation with the driver just as Garrison had warned.

"It is against protocol—"

"—to read the mind of a fellow Judge," Smee finished for him. "I am aware of that."

Dredd frowned. "And yet—"

"We could hear you," Deng interrupted, before Dredd could get any further. He shrugged, as if to apologise for siding with Judge Smee.

Dredd let out a breath, watching the young Psi-Judge as she folded her arms and glared out the window. Reassuring another Judge that he had their back felt ridiculous. He had his orders, and they were both Judges, even if they were in different divisions. While mutants were illegal in Mega-City One and subject to deportation or death, human psychics—mutant or not—were extended citizenship as long as they served the Justice Department. Some people couldn't bend their minds around that, but Dredd hadn't put much thought into it. The

Law was the Law, and Psi-Judges were protected by that Law, as well as being trusted to enforce it.

"What the stomm is that?" Smee said, half standing until her belt restrained her.

Dredd turned to look out the viewing hatch behind him as Deng let out a strangled gasp.

The distant sand dunes were writhing, the earth shaking as if from a small, localised earthquake.

"Probably just a sink hole," Dredd said.

"No, not that," Deng undid his belt and crossed to press his hands against the window.

"Just wait for it," Smee added, rising to stand beside him.

Dredd kept his eyes trained on the moving ground. Suddenly something shot from the earth, rising maybe twenty feet into the sky, writhing with what looked like hundreds of tentacles. Dredd made out an enormous hinged jaw lined with jagged teeth before it plunged back under the surface, as if into water.

The three of them watched in silence until the ground grew still, and the Landraider took them around a high dune that blocked the now still earth from view.

"Was that a—?" Deng stopped mid-sentence, eyes darting to Smee.

"That was my cousin, Morty the Mutie," Smee said, sitting back down.

The big man let out a laugh, his body visibly relaxing, and Dredd approved of the use of humour to defuse the tension.

"Some sort of large sand creature," Dredd supplied. "We'll report it when we arrive at the science station."

The sky was the dark orange of dusk when the double domes of the station came into view, backed by a low range of hills of twisted rock, as if they had been melted in a great heat and reformed. Dredd didn't like the look of them; they would provide cover for anyone wanting to get close to the facility without being seen—or wanting to get *away* from it.

Dredd couldn't see much evidence of the work within. The assignment report said it was a research centre to try and make headway in detoxifying the Cursed Earth. It was a noble venture; if they could claw back pockets of desert, they could cultivate crops, help feed the ever-multiplying mouths of MC-1. But it also seemed unlikely. The desert wasn't called 'cursed' for nothing. And from what they had witnessed on the way over, it was no exaggeration.

The Landraider rumbled into a huge airlock that closed behind them, and was then blasted with cleansing chemicals to remove any toxins picked up in the desert before passing through the second gate and into the compound.

Three Judges—Tomyo, Felps and Woodhead, from their badges—waited to greet them as the hatch opened, ready to board the tank for the journey home; Dredd, Smee and Deng would be relieving them. Dredd nodded in greeting. Deng clasped arms familiarly with Tomyo as Dredd jumped out onto the dust-blown earth and felt the heat of the dome-magnified sinking sun. It was stuffy inside the domes.

The parking hangar was just big enough for the tank to turn, and for a bay of dune buggies. Dredd wondered what they were for. Science expeditions to get samples? The first dome was mostly taken up by an unremarkable white building, the lower storeys windowless.

Opening the holding cubes from the secondary hatch, together they got the volunteers to line up, the six Judges training their Lawgivers on them.

"Cartwright will be along soon, to tell you where to take 'em," Tomyo told them.

"Cartwright!" Deng said. "She's a legend. My sister's in Tek-Div, she says she laid the groundwork for that new Lunar colony they're talking about. I'm actually looking forward to meeting her."

It was strange to hear Deng talk about a sibling, although

Dredd knew that some Judges still kept up a semblance of a family affiliation. From what Dredd had experienced of family, you were better off without them.

Deng looked up as a woman in her sixties with short silver hair emerged from the building, flanked by two people in matching white lab coats, holding data tablets.

"Welcome to the bio lab," she said to the Judges as her assistants checked off the volunteers. "If you'd kindly follow my assistants to the volunteer holding cubes—" She held her arm towards the door behind her.

And then the courtyard exploded.

Two

THE LANDRAIDER BLURRED, then sped past below Dredd as he was thrown across the courtyard to crash into the closed airlock. A ringing filled his ears as he pushed himself up, reaching for his Lawgiver, but it was gone, lost in the blast.

One of the scientists lay unmoving beside the tank, and behind it was a smoking hole through both the rockrete wall and the dome beyond it, leaving them exposed to the Cursed Earth air. Quickly Dredd engaged his respirator, his helmet sealing him in as his hearing began to come back, and a siren replaced the ringing.

He ran to the tank and took cover before assessing the situation. Dredd and the scientist seemed to have taken the worst of the blast: Cartwright was on her knees clutching her ears as Smee and Deng stood over the volunteers lying prone on the ground. The other three Judges were approaching the blast zone with their Lawgivers raised. Spotting his own in the dirt at his feet, he picked it up and checked it for damage, but it looked fully functional.

"Status report?" Dredd asked as the other three Judges stepped through into the bio lab.

"Unknown," Deng said, his respirator now covering the lower half of his face.

Cartwright pushed herself shakily to her feet with the help of the remaining scientist.

"What happened?" she asked, flinching at the sound of blasts from inside the building.

"Get down," Dredd instructed as he trained his Lawgiver on the hole.

"*Tomyo, Felps, Woodhead, report,*" Smee said through comms.

No answer. Dredd signalled to keep their eyes on the volunteers as he approached the bio lab, but before he was halfway there a barrage of shots erupted from within. He dropped back to the tank as five men emerged wearing grey jumpsuits and domestic respirators, two of them holding what looked like jury-built blasters. Smee dragged Cartwright and the other scientist into the tank as Deng and Dredd engaged. The armed men kept up a steady stream of fire as their three comrades went for the sand buggies, jumping on as they sped past towards the open desert.

"Blast the other buggies," one of them shouted, slowing their buggy to give them an easier shot. But Deng and Dredd trained their fire on them, and he was forced to speed up.

"Garrison!" Dredd screamed through the comms, "Get out here and cover the volunteers. Smee, Deng, to me."

Without waiting to see if Garrison was following his orders, he sprang onto a buggy, sliding behind the wheel as Smee and Deng followed suit.

The buggies were aluminium-framed, with huge wheels to deal with the unsteady terrain. Dredd wasted precious seconds figuring out where the starter was before speeding through the hole in the dome wall. The escapees vanished in a cloud of dust kicked up by their buggies.

Hearing the drone of engines behind him, he looked back to see Deng and Smee not far behind.

Pushing the buggy's engine to the max, he sped out through the open wastes. It was exhilarating, driving full speed with no roads, no corners, no civilian vehicles in his way.

"*We got any idea who these guys are?*" Deng asked through comms.

Smee's voice answered, "*Confirmation from Cartwright that they are volunteers. She couldn't identify them by name, but the jumpsuits gave them away. She wants them back alive if we can swing it.*"

The dust cloud made its way towards one of the twisting hills of rock and disappeared into the formation. The perfect place to hide. But the incline and having to navigate the hard terrain would slow them down.

Dredd eased off a little as they reached the base of the hill to let Deng and Smee catch up. He didn't like the look of this place. Pillars of tortured stone clawed the dull orange sky. Night was coming on, and the shadows below them were deep. If anyone was waiting in ambush, the noise of the buggies would give them away.

"*Switch to infra-vision,*" Smee suggested as she revved her engine.

Annoyed that he hadn't thought of it himself, he scanned the area: the hot earth showed as a dull glow, the pillars in shades of grey.

Together they set off through the forest of rock, the sound of their engines reverberating around them. Heat clung to the clear tracks, and they followed the trail as it wound around and up.

The rock just ahead exploded in a cloud of dust, and they pulled up their buggies. Infra-vision showed a cluster of bodies crouched behind a thick rock formation above. Signing to Smee and Deng to dismount and flank them from the right and left, he set off to engage directly and draw their focus.

"*Remember to stun, not kill,*" Smee said through comms. "*Cartwright wants these lab rats back in the lab.*"

Dredd grunted and started firing as he ran across the open ground, diving behind the cover of an overhang just as they opened fire again. He returned fire before ducking back down.

He could see one heat form begin to back away from the tight group of heat signatures.

He set the helmet to speaker mode.

"*Surrender. We have you surrounded.*"

He could see the bright spots of the guns as one of them stood to shoot. It hit the rock below him, scattering rock particles.

He turned and ran to the next outcrop, firing to keep them down.

Another heat signature stood to fire off another round, and his hand exploded in a shower of sparks, white-hot blasts finding homes in four warm bodies. Deng and Smee moved in, quickly securing the stunned volunteers.

"Where's number five?" Deng asked as Dredd approached, his voice muffled by his respirator.

"I saw him sneaking off abandoning his buddies. You secure the prisoners, I'm in pursuit."

Dredd didn't wait for a reply before speeding off in the direction of the fleeing perp. He heard footsteps behind and saw the glowing outline of Judge Smee on his heels.

"This is not the terrain to pursue solo," she said, standing close so as not to need comms. "Deng can babysit the lab rats."

The heat trace was fading as they reached the peak of the hill and stood for a moment scanning the descent. The formations were denser here and swept up to another lower peak about halfway down before ending in a sharp drop to the sand below.

"He's got nowhere to go," Dredd said.

"He must have somewhere. Otherwise why come here at all?" Smee replied as they jogged down the slope.

"This wasn't planned," Dredd said as they looped around a wide column. "They didn't bank on their little explosion going off just as a transport was coming in."

The columns were broader here on the western side of the hill; the last heat of day still sat stubbornly within the stone, confusing the heat trail of the escaped volunteer.

"Wait." Smee skidded to a stop and braced herself against a towering stone slab.

Was she tired?

"If we don't act with speed—"

"Shh, let me do my job."

He shut up, realising she was focusing her psi-powers.

"This way." Her voice was grim as she pushed off and squeezed herself through a narrow gap in the stone. Dredd had to shift his body sideways before he was through and into a narrow tunnel.

"Can you pinpoint his position?" Dredd asked as they moved.

"It doesn't work like that. I can hear his thoughts. I can't judge distance and direction like you could from a voice, but I can access his recent memories. I can see the path he just took. *If I concentrate.*"

Dredd took the hint, shut his mouth, and followed. The path was erratic, snaking around and down, doubling back on itself. Was the prisoner trying to lose them by not taking the most direct path? Or was he simply panicking?

"He's trying to get back to the buggies!" Smee said, realising which way they were headed.

Gruddamn it, how could he have missed it? They had been gradually working their way around the right side of the mountain, taking a circuitous route back to the only mode of transport and his only hope of escaping.

"Drokk." Smee pivoted and went left around a huge boulder. "We should go to the buggies and cut him off. I've set my navigator to take us on the most direct route."

"If it isn't too late."

The towering pillars curved over to meet overhead, forming claustrophobic arches. They skidded around a corner into a cavernous stone void.

Cowering between two of the pillars were two glowing forms, their arms over their heads as if they were already under fire.

Smee hissed and stood frozen.

Their heat signature was different from Smee and to the volunteers. It was duller, as if their blood ran cooler.

"Mutants," Dredd said, and raised his Lawgiver.

Smee's arm shot out and gripped his arm. "Leave them. They aren't obstructing our mission."

"They're mutants," Dredd said, wondering if Smee didn't hear him the first time. "Potential hostiles."

"I can see that."

They had lowered their arms slightly now and were peering at them, probably also wondering why they were still alive.

"Getting this perp back for the Doc is our only priority right now. If we don't get to those buggies first..."

It was clear that Judge Smee had her own reasons for wanting to spare these two, but he followed when she turned on her heel and began to jog through the rock maze once more, leaving the mutants behind, still breathing the toxic air their lungs had adapted to.

They emerged from the caverns to see the glowing form of the volunteer sprinting towards the buggies. Smee sprinted after him, and Dredd fired to slow him down, but he dived into a buggy and started it, reversing down through the snaking rock pillars. Smee and Dredd jumped in a buggy together, Smee driving and Dredd bracing himself against the frame to shoot.

The perp's buggy pivoted and spun around to face forward when he had the space and picked up speed. Dredd struggled to get a clear shot among the rocks.

The perp cleared the rock forest and sped off onto the plain, but the Judges too were out of the stones and had a clear shot at the buggy. From this distance, it only took two quick Standard Execution rounds and the back tyres burst, the buggy spinning out before coming to a stop.

The volunteer crawled out and took off on foot. Madness. It would be easy to pick him up now.

The buggy began shaking erratically and Dredd looked to see what Smee was doing with the wheel.

"It's not me, it's the ground. It's shaking!"

And then the earth in front erupted with tentacles as an enormous head thrust itself above the surface. Dredd had a moment to wonder at the sheer size of the jagged teeth as it bit the shrieking volunteer in half, and then Smee was driving them away and back towards the hill.

Three

TEK-JUDGE CARTWRIGHT STOOD leaning on her desk, her lab coat brown with dust and her hair out of place. She looked exhausted. Dredd, Smee and Deng stood to attention in front of her on completing their verbal report, which had also been recorded to send back to the Hall of Justice. It was unorthodox not to make their report directly, but apparently they couldn't risk the transmission being intercepted. By whom, Dredd wasn't completely sure.

The Landraider had met them at the buggies at the foot of the twisted hills to retrieve the surviving escapees. Tragically, two of the Judges they were there to relieve had been killed by the volunteers' blasters, and the third, Judge Woodhead, had been shot in the leg, and was recovering in the infirmary. The scientist that had been caught in the blast with Dredd had also been killed.

Cartwright gathered herself and rolled her shoulders back, her distant stare coming back to the three Judges in front of her.

"At least only one of the subjects was lost," she said. "That was well done."

"Now they can face the cold truth of the Law," Dredd said. "Murder of a Judge: the sentence is death."

Cartwright looked at him and scowled. "They are my test subjects. Far too valuable to waste on execution."

Deng and Smee shared a look. "Are you suggesting that we pardon them?" Deng asked.

"No, Judge. I am simply suggesting that they remain here as my subjects until I am done with them. Once their use in our experiments is over, then you are free to do as you wish."

"A suspended sentence?" asked Smee.

"If you like," Cartwright said, sitting down. She looked out of the window to the silhouette of the distant hills. "You are aware of the purpose of this facility?"

They nodded. They'd all read the brief. It seemed like a real long shot to Dredd, but he understood that people liked to have a purpose in life. His purpose was the Law. This woman's was science.

"Our work is too important to interrupt—for any reason. If we are successful, we conquer the wastes." She gestured to the Cursed Earth. "When I look at this view, do you know what I see?"

Deng opened his mouth to answer, but she spoke over him.

"—I see green hills, crops, space, clean air. I see *food*. I see a *future* for us all outside of the Mega-Cities. Imagine that."

She cleared her throat. "I'll make sure the Department gets your report. Now, to the business at hand. I'm sorry that you had such an—eventful—arrival. Your role here is of course to control the volunteers. It looks like you may have your work cut out for you." She curled her lips in a half smile.

Dredd shifted on his feet. "Do we know how the perps—the *volunteers*—came across the tech for the blasters and the explosion?"

Cartwright grimaced. "It seems one of them has been smuggling tech from the labs for months to make the blasters.

The explosion, however, has further-reaching consequences. One of the volunteers got into the sleep pod bay somehow and rigged one of them to blow. It seems you will be needing to get your rest in the same way that the rest of us do for your time here. The old-fashioned way."

Dredd scowled. "You expect us to—*sleep?*"

She held out her hands. "At least until we can get more pods transported from MC-1. I can't tell you when that will be."

Deng and Smee didn't look as alarmed as he felt, but he supposed they had slept as children before becoming cadets. Dredd had never gone without a sleep pod before.

"Will three Judges be sufficient if we have to waste time sleeping?" Smee asked.

It was a good question. Ten minutes in a pod did what eight hours in slumber could do.

"It will have to be," Cartwright said, turning her attention to Smee. "Psi-Judge Smee, I have to admit I was dismayed when the Department insisted they send a Psi-Judge out here. What we are doing is top secret. We can't afford to have anyone rifling through our scientists' minds."

Smee's eyes narrowed, the only indication she was angered by the comment.

"It is against protocol to read another Judge's mind," she said.

Dredd wondered how often she had to repeat this.

"In my many years in Tek-Div, I've learnt that conforming to protocol isn't always a top priority."

Dredd felt his jaw clench at Cartwright's words. The Law was sacred. He tried to put his own brother out of his mind. Most Judges were dedicated to Justice.

"I've been briefed on my role here," Smee said, keeping her voice even. "Your experiments have been having psychic side effects, doctor. A worrying development, wouldn't you say?"

Cartwright kept silent this time.

"I'm here to keep any emerging psychics in line. Only a Psi-

Judge can keep tabs on other psychics. You need me."

"There have only been a few signs of developing psi powers," Cartwright said. "Doctor Reives went to the Department with that information before we were ready. I disagree with the assumption that we need mind police."

Smee looked taken aback. "That's not what we are."

"Well, see to it that you keep it that way." Cartwright snapped. "I want you to stay out of the minds of my scientists. You got that? Our research is far too sensitive to have just *anyone* knowing about it."

Smee nodded but didn't reply.

Dredd saw Deng narrow his eyes at the scientist, perhaps reassessing his previous opinion of this 'great' woman.

"Right, my assistant will show you to your sleeping quarters. They're in the volunteer block, originally built for scientists needing to stay close to their test subjects. Get yourself settled in."

Smee spun on her heel and led the way out of the office without a word. Dredd couldn't blame her. Cartwright seemed bent on pissing her off.

CARTWRIGHT'S ASSISTANT, A bespectacled young black woman who wore her tightly curled hair shaved at the sides and a second pair of glasses balanced on her flattop, motioned for them to follow her.

They walked through windowless rockcrete corridors lit with orange strip lights into the dark of night. Once they stepped outside, she seemed to stand straighter, rolled her shoulders and quirked her mouth in a quick smile at the Judges.

"Name's Althea Newman," she said, "I'm not actually her assistant." She rolled her eyes. "I'm head of the plant-studies lab over here in Dome 2."

She explained that Cartwright's office was in the second

dome, which housed the scientist accommodation alongside the non-human branch of the bio lab experiments. She would be taking them to the 'human treatment facility' back in Dome 1, where the volunteers were kept under lock and key. Dredd couldn't help feeling like she wasn't pleased about it. What did she have a problem with? The Judges? Or the volunteers?

Seeing this young scientist openly correcting her superior got under Dredd's skin. Order was only kept so long as adhered to the chain of command. Were the other scientists the same? Was there discord out here in the Cursed Earth? He'd need to keep an eye on her.

He kept silent as they walked through the connecting tunnel, wondering about the hole those perps had blasted in the dome. The tek team had made quick work of patching up the explosion zone, and they'd been assured that the dome had been decontaminated. Even so, the open desert outside of the domes was—different.

This dome housed one huge building and, other than the hangar, nothing else. Windows started on what Dredd gauged to be four floors up; the floors were probably dedicated to labs and volunteer cubes.

Newman used breath and retinal identification to open the heavy reinforced metal door, and led them into a large entryway, nodding to the guard posted beside a wall of screens. He stood to attention when he saw the Judges, which was a good sign. He'd so far been unimpressed by civilian security, and had been surprised that they'd been hired to support the Judges at the facility. It was logical not to expend more Judges than necessary on operation babysit, however, after the greeting they got on arrival, maybe three Judges was a little conservative.

"That door leads to some of the labs and the volunteers. You'll be pleased to know you're up here with the windows."

Newman led them up a short flight of stairs along a narrow corridor.

"That's the Dome 1 cafeteria; a couple of night shifters are in there, as you can see. That's where you'll get your grub." The scientist didn't pause for them to look, but Dredd got a quick glimpse of a large, brightly lit space with a bank of food synthesisers and a huge wall-length window looking out on the night.

"These are some of the private offices, although Cartwright's lab is down in the basement where it's nice and secret."

"Didn't we just come from Cartwright's office?" asked Smee.

"That's her public office. You'll learn that Cartwright can be a bit on the paranoid side. Just wait until she starts talking to you about the Texans."

"The Texans?" Dredd asked. Tension with Texas City had been a topic of speculation back in MC-1.

"She thinks they're trying to steal our research." Newman shrugged. "Maybe they are. Either way, she's isolated her own lab away from all the other scientists. A lot of the work in the human testing centre is done piecemeal; the scientists over here don't have a clue what they're working on, if you ask me."

No one had.

"Don't know how anyone can get anything done working like that. Now, in the bio lab, we work as a team. Get a lot more done that way."

"So the human testing is separate from the other work?" asked Deng. "Is that not counter-intuitive?"

Newman answered by raising her eyebrows, a gesture that could have been interpreted a number of ways.

"I don't want to badmouth Cartwright too much. She's my boss, after all."

Dredd got the feeling that she didn't mind talking trash about her at all.

"So this is it, home sweet home." Newman stopped and opened a door leading onto a narrow room with a single bed under a small window. It felt a little like an iso-cube.

"One of you is in here, one next door, and one in that one opposite. Bathroom and showers around the corner. Sorry if they seem a bit barren, but they're really only meant for temporary accommodation for scientists needing to stay close to their experiments."

"Hmm," Dredd grunted.

"Now that you are situated over here, want to join me in Dome 2 for real food? We've got a cook over there. It's pretty good. And I can finish giving you a tour of the facility."

"That won't be necessary," Dredd said automatically. Fraternising with cits was not encouraged.

Deng looked crestfallen, making Dredd suddenly aware of his own hunger.

"We should take Althea up on her offer," Judge Smee said. "We need to get a quick understanding of the logistics of the facility. I want to do a full-sweep risk assessment on all tech that could be tampered with to make weapons or explosives in light of today's events."

Dredd couldn't argue with her logic.

"And I'd like to have a word with head of the civilian security, see what sort of backup we can expect," added Deng.

"Where's the med bay?" Dredd asked.

"You want to speak with Judge Woodhead?" Newman turned and began to lead them down the hall. "That's over in Dome 2 as well. Might as well get some food on the way."

Dredd followed; it wouldn't hurt to get some sustenance. He needed to get an understanding of how the volunteers had been allowed to smuggle equipment out of the labs.

THE DOME 2 cafeteria was a very different prospect from the drab hall in Dome 1. Although the lighting and seating was cut from the same cloth, it was twice as big and, despite the bank of food synthesisers, the air was heavy with the scent of cooking.

Dredd had only come across hints of this around civilian habs and street-food vendors, but this was different. The air was thick with the scent of—well, he wasn't exactly sure what it was, but his stomach tightened, and his mouth filled with saliva.

Dredd swallowed and clenched his jaw as Newman walked up to a low counter with a glass screen, grabbed a tray and addressed a middle-aged man wearing a stained, unsanitary-looking apron over a loosely fitting green uniform.

Deng and Smee seemed happy enough to accept a tray and wait to be served. Dredd observed the mix of scientists, tek crews and off-duty security guards gathered around different tables.

"I'd recommend the desert loaf," Newman said, holding a tray with a laden plate and a drink can on it.

He grunted agreement and accepted the offered plate from the server before following the others to an empty table.

The food tasted—good, he guessed. Deng and Smee were quiet as they ate, Deng near enough inhaling it and Smee taking small, steady, clean bites.

Newman looked past Dredd's shoulder, frowning slightly, and Dredd turned and followed her gaze to Cartwright, sitting with her own plate of food with her back to the huge window, talking to another scientist. She was holding a pot of something and pouring whatever it was onto her plate.

"Every time," Newman said, shaking her head. "That woman loves salt."

"That's salt?" Deng wrinkled his nose.

Newman nodded. Dredd turned back to his own food and continued to work his way through the desert loaf. He'd never needed to add condiments to his food in the past, and he wasn't completely sure how much was considered normal. But the small white hill covering Cartwright's food did seem excessive.

"You done?" the scientist asked, pushing her empty tray away. "Let's go see Judge Woodhead."

Four

WOODHEAD WAS STILL coming out of sedation when they interviewed him, and didn't have much light to shine on how the volunteers had got access to the tech.

"Only thing I can think of is they had help," Woodhead said.

"A scientist?" Smee asked.

Woodhead shrugged. "Or a tek team or security member. Could be Texans. Cartwright seems to think they're out to get her research. Would make sense if they wanted to nab a few of the test subjects for themselves."

It did seem like the volunteers must have had help, although Dredd didn't like to speculate on where that might have come from.

"You think it could be linked to psi powers?" Dredd asked.

"Could be," said Woodhead, leaning back on his pillows. "Reason they got you out, wasn't it, Judge Smee? They found out about the psi powers when a perp lifted his bed up three inches off the ground on tape, so they could have smuggled things out of the labs using the same technique."

"Was he among the escapees?" Smee asked.

Woodhead shook his head. "Cartwright took him in to her lab for further testing. Haven't heard of him since."

They left Woodhead to rest ready for the tank trip home the next day.

Newman left them to make their own way back to Dome 1. Once they had left Woodhead, they got the security guard to give them a quick tour of the volunteer cubes. He led them past a row of locked, reinforced doors to a panel of video monitors, where the volunteers were observed to see how they reacted to the various treatments. Most of them were lying on their bunks watching their holo screens, a privilege that was not normally included in cube life. Too soft here. Gave the perps ideas. Like exploding the damn sleep pods.

Once that tour was complete, there was nothing left to do but decide who was on first shift. Dredd volunteered, while Smee and Deng went to get some shut-eye. He would be relieved by Deng, who would then switch with Smee. It wasn't ideal, but they'd need to all be operational during the day when the volunteers would need escorting to and from the labs for testing and observation. While they were under lockdown at night, one Judge—with the support of lab security—should be sufficient to keep an eye on things.

Dredd did another sweep of the cubes. The security guard attempted to start a conversation, but he snuffed it out with a glare.

The time passed slowly. This was going to be a long three months. It was strange to be away from MC-1, where one crime after another fell into his lap, and there was never a second where he could drop his vigilance. Here, there was one focus, and one focus only: babysitting lab rats.

Finally, Deng came to relieve him, and there was nothing to do but go back to his pod—no, to his *bed*.

Dredd removed his boots and body armour and stripped down to his underpants. The desert chase had not been kind to his uniform. He was pleased to see that someone had brought up his kit bag, and he removed his spare clothes and hung them on the hook behind the door. He splashed some tepid water from the small sink on his face, then went to stand over the bed. There was a sheet over the mattress and another sheet tucked in up to about halfway, and a rectangular pillow resting where he guessed his head would go. He'd seen beds before in perps' apartments and in training material, but he'd never paid that much attention to them. A vision of a child tucked under a blanket came to him from some instructional vid, and he pulled up the top sheet and got under it, laying down carefully on his back. The pillow gave slightly as he put pressure on it, and the mattress shifted for the weight of his body. Now all that was left was to close his eyes…

The light came pink through his eyelids, but he was pretty sure he was still conscious. He lay there for a few seconds waiting for his mind to switch off in a flash as it did in the pod, but he was still there, awake, aware of where the sheet touched his skin. Wait, he was supposed to turn the light out, wasn't he? Shaking his head at himself, he went and switched off the light, then felt his way back in the darkness and got back under the sheet.

He closed his eyes. Well, that looked better; it was dark, at least. But it appeared despite this, he remained awake. So, what happened next? How did you switch your mind off like he had done the light?

He opened his eyes and they adjusted to the soft light the desert night cast through his small window. He shut them again. Still no sleep. Perhaps his body had not yet reached the stage at which it would turn off? He felt ready for the pods, though. His limbs were heavy, and his eyes felt full of grit. Clear signs he was due ten minutes in slumberland. But maybe sleep was different. You did need hours of the stuff compared to minutes in the pod, so it would be logical that you had to be exhausted first. Maybe you had to be just about ready to drop before you achieved oblivion.

He pushed himself up and reclaimed his dirty uniform from where he had folded it on top of his kit bag, and went to find the gym Newman had told them about earlier, leaving his body armour and helmet off.

The tunnel to Dome 2 was clear, and he found himself pausing to contemplate the Cursed sky at night. That made a change from the orange glow of MC-1. The floating rocks of the Death Belt moved like lazy black clouds against the brilliance of billions of glaring stars. They shone starkly across the great expanse, huge and open and—different.

Huh. He walked on to Dome 2, using his eye and breath recognition to open the door, and went looking for the fitness facility.

It was paltry compared with what he was used to, with a lot of fussy machines where a good old sparring floor should be, and had a distinct lack of weapons to train with, but he did find a number of weights gathering dust in a corner, as well as a running machine. He found a small changing and shower room with a store of sweats, and he pulled on a grey pair of shorts and a white T-shirt, glad not to have to work out in his uniform.

It was hard going, but he did a quick twenty kilometres to warm up, followed by a few sets of weights and a brief workout on the mats. It had now been over twenty-four hours since he had stepped out of his pod, punctuated by one hell of a desert chase, and he felt more than ready for that fabled shut-eye.

He hit the shower and was just pulling his uniform trousers on after towelling down when he heard a ragged scream from outside the gym. He pulled his Lawgiver from his holster, still hanging over a hook on the wall, and ran towards the sound, shirtless and barefoot.

He found a man in a lab coat that had once been white— now spattered in the globular remains of the headless steaming corpse on the floor—on his knees, with his trembling hands outstretched over where the corpse's head used to be.

"Step away from the stiff," Dredd said, training his Lawgiver on him.

The man looked up, wide-eyed and shaking.

"He—he just—his head. It just—*exploded*."

Five

THERE WAS A small interrogation chamber at the facility—a Judicial architect designed the place, after all—and Dredd watched through the one-way mirror as Deng fired questions at Jude Peterson, the still-blood-soaked scientist.

Judge Smee stood beside him, watching with narrowed eyes.

"He's telling the truth," she said, breaking her concentration. "They were walking back from their shift."

"And Roberts's head just exploded?"

"That's what it looked like through his eyes, but of course there could have been a shooter somewhere that he didn't see. It's pretty alarming having your friend's brain sprayed all over you unexpectedly. You don't notice all that much going on around you." She shook her head. "If only it hadn't been his head. If his brain was still intact, I might have been able to get a reading of what happened."

"You can do that?" Dredd was impressed.

"Sometimes. I'm not as good at it as some other Judges. It's a very specific talent."

"A very useful talent." Dredd inclined his head in recognition, and Smee looked unexpectedly pleased. "But I guess in this case we'll have to do things the old-fashioned way and talk to the living." He turned to the comms. "Deng, ask him about what happened leading up to the event."

Someone had brought him a shirt, but he was still barefoot. They'd figured a fully clothed Judge may be more suitable to interrogate the suspect. Deng had a formal interrogation style. He was seated opposite Peterson, one hand on his Lawgiver.

"Tell me about the shift," Deng said. "Were you working together?"

Jude licked his lips and shook his head. "We're in Cartwright's lab, over in Dome 1. We have our own cubicles. We're not allowed to talk about what we're working on."

"Not even to each other?"

"No."

"Okay, so, after your shift. You were walking back with Roberts to your dorms. Was that usual?"

Peterson shrugged. "If we finish at the same time, yeah. I mean, we're going the same way."

"Ask him what Roberts was like," Smee said. "There's something he isn't saying."

"And Roberts." Deng put his Lawgiver back in his holster, folded his hands on the table and leaned forward, as if inviting Peterson to confide in him. "Was there anything that seemed to be bothering him on the walk home?"

Peterson flicked his eyes at the mirror. He looked scared, but not of Deng.

"He did seem a bit off, yes. Distracted, lost in thought, you know?"

Deng nodded.

"He didn't talk much on the way back, but I just sort of dismissed it as tiredness. Night shifts are killers."

He looked stricken as the irony of his last words occurred to him.

"But then, when we were back at Dome 2, he sort of relaxed a bit. He was just opening his mouth as if he was about to tell me something when—"

"—His head exploded?" Deng finished for him.

Peterson nodded and bit his lip.

Dredd and Smee started as the door to the observation room was flung open, and Cartwright strode into the room, her face a picture of rage.

"What is the meaning of this?"

"Doctor," Dredd said. "We were waiting to report in the morning when you were awake. I'm sorry to say that scientist Roberts has been killed. We are questioning—"

"I can see exactly what you are doing, Judge. What is *she* doing here? I will not have my scientist's minds mined for their secrets."

"I'm not"—Smee frowned—"*we're* not asking about the experiments. I am well aware that is off-limits."

"That's enough from you," Cartwright spat. "I don't have the luxury of reading your mind to find out if what you say is true. I can't take the risk and I won't take the risk. You are banned from any and all interrogations of my scientists."

"Doctor Cartwright, I'd like you to remember you are talking to a Judge," Dredd said. Mutant or not, Judge Smee was a Judge and should be respected as such. "Judge Smee's psi abilities are a tool of the Justice Department. Are you refusing the Justice Department access to investigating a murder?"

Smee glanced at him, perhaps surprised he'd spoken. What he'd said was true in terms of the reach of the Justice Department, but Cartwright was getting on his nerves. Judge Smee had given her no reason to distrust her.

Cartwright worked her mouth as if she was chewing her tongue.

"I have been given authority over all at this facility, even you, Judge Dredd. Perhaps you are not aware, but the Texans would do anything to steal our secrets."

"Are you accusing me of being a Texan spy?" Smee had both of her fists clenched.

Cartwright glared at her, but then the tension went out of her, and she ran her hands through her silver hair. "Of course not. It's just that as a scientist, I realise how little we really understand of your abilities, even after two decades of study. As I'm sure you are aware, the strength of an individual's psychic powers differs greatly from person to person. The Texans have Psi-Judges too, and while we are still technically at peace, they have access to you, Judge Smee. What if they were to lift the information from your mind without you knowing?"

"That would be impossible. I wouldn't allow it."

"How can you be so confident?"

"Because I'm that good."

The women stared each other down for a long moment before Cartwright broke the look.

Dredd cleared his throat. "We've nearly finished in here. This isn't the first interrogation I have worked on with a Psi-Judge, and I can tell you right now, we'll find this killer a lot faster with Judge Smee involved."

Judge Smee nodded to him and then looked at Cartwright. "There is a murderer loose in this facility, Cartwright. Maybe it's your Texan spy. Do you want me to find them for you or not?"

THEY'D GONE THROUGH the security footage with the guard who was on duty at the time of the killing. It corroborated what Peterson had told them: the two scientists were walking along the hall, when Roberts's head seemed to spontaneously explode. They slowed it and replayed it frame by frame, trying to spot a bullet or dart of some kind, but couldn't find anything to explain it.

"Could it be some sort of nano-tech?" Deng suggested.

The security guard nodded. "They're working with nano-tech here in the biodiversity labs."

"Are you suggesting someone from the bio lab did this?" Smee asked.

He shrugged. "I don't know. But if you're looking for nano-tech, I've overheard the bio-scientists talking about it in the cafeteria."

"Thank you." Dredd looked at Smee. "That's headed up by Dr. Newman, right?"

"Yep. We'd better go take a closer look at her research, if we're permitted." She rolled her eyes. "After Cartwright's big lab-wide meeting, of course."

THE CAFETERIA IN Dome 2 was packed with every scientist, technician and off-duty security guard in the facility. Dredd stood beside Deng and Smee to the back of the room, as Cartwright waited for the last stragglers to enter. She'd called a meeting over coms that pulled scientists from their beds and labs. They muttered and spoke amongst themselves wondering what the drokk was going on.

"Right..." Cartwright held up her hand for silence. "I need all eyes on me. I have some sad news. Our colleague, the talented Keith Roberts, has been killed."

A gasp went through the crowd. She held her hands up again to quell the swell of questions raised.

"It was no accident. We do not know yet who is responsible, or even fully understand how he was killed. But please be assured, our three Judges will be making every effort to identify Roberts's killer and bring them to justice."

"These three kids?" an older man, his hair rumpled with sleep, demanded. "We need to get a senior Judge down here. Someone with experience."

There were murmurs of agreement amongst the crowd.

"They're barely more than rookies."

"Why hasn't the Hall of Justice sent a senior Judge to lead them here already?"

"They don't care about us out here…"

Dredd waited for Cartwright to put them straight, but she merely stood there and chewed on her tongue while the complaints got louder. He glanced at Smee and Deng, then made the call. He pitched his voice to cut through the noise of the crowd.

"You think the Department are going to divert a senior officer out here for one random killing?"

Everyone shut up and listened to the ring of authority in his voice. He stepped forward and directed a hard stare at the scientist who had first spoken. "We have been appointed by the Justice Department to dispense the Law here in this facility, and that is what we will do. Are you questioning their judgement in sending us here?"

The man shook his head minutely and looked down.

"Be assured, we will find this killer, and bring them to justice," Deng added, taking a softer approach.

They didn't look convinced, but at least they were quiet.

"Who would want to kill Roberts?" Newman called out from where she was seated on a table near the front.

Cartwright shot her a glare. "Who do you think? The Texans have been trying to infiltrate us for months."

Dredd scanned the hall trying to gauge reactions; they ranged from fear, disbelief, to anger. Newman didn't look satisfied with the answer, and he stored that information away to ask her about later.

"We have to be vigilant, people! This is what I have been warning you all of. This is why I put such stringent measures into keeping our work a secret. Now you must see that this has all been for a purpose."

There was something about her that seemed a little triumphant as she said this, as if Roberts's death finally proved that she wasn't just being paranoid.

"You expressed the need for more senior Judges, however, we are lucky to have Judge Smee, a Psi-Judge, with us."

All three Judges looked at her in barely masked surprise. She'd changed her tune.

"She will be using her abilities to help with the investigation. I ask all of you to cooperate with the Judges in order to find this murderer.

"From now on, we will be ramping up security. Not only in my labs but in the bio labs as well."

Newman, who Dredd remembered was ostensibly in charge of the bio-branch of the research, opened her mouth to say something, but Cartwright cut her off. "Althea, come to my office after this meeting. We have a lot to discuss."

Six

THEY SPENT THE day in interviews. Firstly, they talked to the other scientists who had been on shift with Roberts. They were all so separate in their work that even if Roberts had been acting suspiciously, there wasn't any way they could have known about it. No one was out of place, everyone had adhered to their usual routine. The security tapes confirmed it.

The only place there was no footage was within the cubicles themselves. Cartwright felt that cameras were too easy to hack. All they could do was watch Roberts enter his small office as usual, leaving for a few trips to the toilet, then finally leaving and meeting Peterson at the exit to the lab.

Something pertinent came up on his last trip to the toilet. He went in, but didn't relieve himself; merely leant on a sink and looked at his reflection for a long moment, breathing deeply, as if to calm himself. What could have caused this reaction, alone as he was, within his small laboratory?

A search of his lab revealed nothing. The windowless room was lit by bright strip lighting, desks lining all three walls around the door, covered in racks of glass test tubes filled with green and pink liquids, with a large computer in the far corner. Cartwright had refused access to the files, which frustratingly was in her power to do. She argued that she would go through the files herself to see if there was anything untoward, but as there was no link here with outside communication, it would be unlikely to be relevant.

Now they were at the bio lab, with a tired-looking Newman showing Dredd and Smee into her office. Deng didn't accompany them as he was due to go on duty with the volunteers.

"Take a seat," Newman said, motioning to the small sofa in the corner. She pulled her desk chair out and sat opposite as Smee lowered herself onto the sofa. Dredd remained standing.

"We need to talk to you about nano-tech," Dredd said.

Newman looked at Smee. "Are you reading my mind right now?"

Smee tilted her head to the side. "Would you have a problem with that?"

"No! I think it's amazing. I've always wondered what it would feel like. Does it tickle?"

Smee narrowed her eyes, but couldn't quite suppress a smile. "No. You won't feel a thing. I'll be listening in on your answers to our line of questioning. Mostly just to make sure you're telling the truth."

Instead of reacting angrily about the intrusion, like Dredd had expected, Newman smiled.

"Okay, great, let's get going. It's going to be refreshing for you to believe every word I say. I can't say that's the experience I've had with Judges before."

"You've been questioned by Judges before?" That was telling. What had she been tangled up in in the past?

She nodded. "Find me a civ outside of a glow district that hasn't, and I'd be amazed. Just existing feels like breaking the law sometimes."

"You have a problem with the rule of Law?" Dredd asked.

The scientist laughed. "We all do, buddy. But if you don't recognise that, I'm not about to start explaining it to you now."

"We're getting off topic," Smee said. "We need you to tell us about your research. Mainly about how you use nano-tech."

"Cartwright's okay with that?" she asked. "She just went through exactly how tight security is going to have to be in my labs from now on. I'm about to install her lonely cubicle system and I'm trying to imagine how on earth my scientists can work without actually telling each other what they are doing. It's trickier with the growing rooms, so we'll never be as uptight as they are over in the human branch, but things are getting pretty tight-lipped over here."

"She told you to comply with our investigation." Dredd wasn't sure himself if Cartwright would be pleased with this line of questioning, but in all fairness, to hell with her.

"All right, then, yeah. Our work is splicing bio-matter with nano-tech. The idea is we can program the nano-tech to expel toxic matter and terminate the resulting mutations. If we can get it right, we could be growing crops out in the Cursed Earth. Just imagine it, all that land out there, green and fertile with food."

Her eyes went misty, and she looked out the window, perhaps seeing her future projected on the barren landscape.

"But we're not there yet. We've had a lot of success with fungi. Their bio-structure is highly compatible with the tech."

"So you're close to a breakthrough?" Smee asked. Dredd wondered if that was pertinent to the case, or if she was merely interested in the research.

"In a way, yes. We've tapped into their mycelium threads—it's what makes up the fungal network. We can direct them from a central computer to serve all sorts of purposes. It's amazing, actually, we can control it to the point of making it grow into specific spaces, control the speed of growth—" She stopped and looked at Dredd. "But so far we haven't cracked removing toxicity, and the resulting fungi is inedible. The tech is harmful if ingested, so"—she shrugged—"still got a long way to go."

"Could this tech be used for harm?"

"You mean, like blowing someone's head off?"

"For example," Smee said.

Newman thought for a moment. "It is possible, in theory. If you altered the nano-bots to carry micro explosives, it could seed as spores through his nose or ears, even mouth, and be directed to sit in his brain matter, ready to be activated."

"Who would have access to this programming?"

"A handful of scientists. I'll give you a list of names. Myself, of course. Although, I can tell you now, it wasn't me."

Dredd looked at Smee, who nodded confirmation.

"And do you know who it was?" Dredd pushed.

"No. I'm not even sure about your theory. It's a possibility, but I don't think anyone was doing anything like that. I trust my people. And also, why would they want Roberts dead?"

"That's what we're trying to find out," Smee said, and pushed herself up from the sofa.

Newman gave them the list of six names, and the Judges left her trying to puzzle out the new security regime.

As they left the room, Dredd felt a wave of something, a strange sensation, almost as if the air had become heavier and was pushing him down. He ignored it. Perhaps he'd picked up a toxin or two from the desert when they had pursued the volunteers. He'd go to the doc later to have another scan.

Smee suggested they grab something from the cafeteria before they completed the bio lab interviews. Realising it was rolling on towards dusk, Dredd agreed that sustenance was a smart move after a day without stopping for food.

He received a bug-protein chilli with repro corn bread from the server and went to sit with Smee. There were a few scientists and maintenance crew eating in groups that eyed them from a distance.

Another wave of heaviness hit him as he sat down. He realised now it had been in the background for a while—it was unfamiliar. It seemed to seep into his bones and make him slow, making movement more laboured. His eyes were itchy, and he resisted the urge to rub them.

Itchy eyes were a clear sign of a contaminant. Was it the desert? Or was it something more sinister?

"Judge Smee, I believe I have been compromised. At first, I thought it was a desert toxin, but now I am considering the possibility that I have been drugged to reduce my effectiveness in pursuing this murderer. Are you feeling it too?"

Smee was still while contemplating her own sensations. "I do not believe so. Describe your symptoms to me?"

He took a breath. "My eyes are hot and gritty. My eyelids are heavy. My limbs too. The air weighs on me as if it has become thicker."

He stopped to open his mouth for an involuntary yawn.

Smee looked at him closely, her eyes sparking with something. Was it amusement?

"Dredd, did you manage to get any sleep last night?"

"I closed my eyes for minutes at a time. But—no. I was not able to fully lose consciousness."

Her face split into a sudden smile, and she let out a short bark of laughter. "Dredd. How long has it been since you were in the pod?"

"Approximately twelve hours before we embarked on our journey through the desert."

"You are *tired*, Dredd. You haven't been poisoned, you just need some gruddamn sleep!"

It seemed obvious now. He'd had echoes of this feeling before, but he'd always been able to hit a sleep pod for ten minutes before the fatigue set in.

"I have never initiated sleep before. I've only ever used a sleep pod."

"Of course," Smee said, then looked a bit awkward and didn't say anything more.

She was probably remembering that he was a clone, and, unlike her and the other Judges who had come in as cadets when they were young, he had never known life outside of the Department. He'd never had to learn how to sleep.

"In that case, you need to go to the doc and get something to knock you out."

Dredd shook his head. "I can't afford to be drugged. I need to find this killer before they kill again."

"Sure," Smee said, "but you can't do that in the state you're in. You'll be useless to me until you get some rest. And besides, the drugs just knock you out. They shouldn't leave you feeling the effects when you wake up."

Reluctantly, Dredd conceded she was right. He needed to be at optimum performance. Forcing down his bug-chilli, he pushed himself up and went in search of the doc.

Back in the small room allocated to him, he once again removed his armour, lay his aching body down on the narrow bed, and swallowed the pills.

Seven

DREDD JUMPED AWAKE and sat up, opening his eyes to semi-darkness. A low light came through his small window. It wasn't like coming to in a sleep pod. His heart was racing, and something felt wrong, an urgency clawing at his insides as he cast his eyes across his empty room.

Come and face me, cowards.

A voice, angry, triumphant, demanding.

Dredd leapt from bed and grabbed his Lawgiver from where he'd rested it beside his pillow, feeling a bit ridiculous as he realised he was definitely alone. He rolled his shoulders, feeling an unfamiliar stiffness. How had the human race survived so long without sleep pods? He checked the time on his data strip. He'd had just under four hours of sleep. Four hours of inactivity, laying prone and useless. What a waste of time.

Where are you? Cowards.

Dredd pulled open his door and saw Deng already standing in his open doorway pointing his Lawgiver down the empty hall.

"Status?" Dredd said, his voice low.

"I thought I heard a voice out here." Deng squinted into the darkness at the top of the stairwell.

A faint scream sounded from the floor below, and the noise of a disturbance, like furniture being thrown across a room.

"Come on." Dredd padded out his door. Neither of them had their body armour or helmets on, denying them comms. They went as quickly as caution allowed down the stairs, towards where they'd heard the scream. They reached the bottom of the stairs just as Judge Smee came racing up from the floor below.

"Where is he?" she demanded. "Oh, neither of you have comms? I've been trying to reach you."

"We were asleep," Deng said.

She nodded. "A volunteer has escaped. Managed to pull a wall down to stop me coming after him. I had to go out through the yard and come back around from Dome 2."

"He brought down a wall?" Dredd looked away from Smee as the sound of shattering glass tore down the hall.

"The cafeteria," Deng said. "Come on."

"I don't know how he got out," Smee said, keeping pace with Dredd. "One second I was checking a perp in a far cell who had started screaming about bees in his head, the next thing I know the air is full of dust and a security guard is dead. I tried getting a reading on the escapee to get a location and an idea of what he's planning but—it's like he's blocking me out."

"The psi-powers Cartwright was talking about? You think he has them?" It would explain the voice that had woken him and Deng up.

She nodded.

The tables and chairs in the cafeteria were strewn across the floor, the huge panel of reinforced glass was gone, shattered into the ground below that skirted the edge of the building before the clear barrier of the dome began. The bright lights were flickering on and off, casting a stuttering light onto the scene below. Illuminated in sharp flashes was the volunteer, standing silhouetted against the dull glow of the desert, his arms outstretched, his eyes wide and frenzied, an exultant grin on his face.

Two scientists lay in limp heaps beside the repro machines.

"Judges!" he cried, and then a wave of pain hit Dredd so hard that he fell to his knees, his hands lifting to clutch at his head.

Deng and Smee were down too, Deng's pained expression a mirror of his own. Smee had her hands braced on the floor, a look of intense concentration on her face as she stared at the perp.

"It's not possible," she muttered, staring at him as if she couldn't believe her eyes.

Deng cried out as his nose began to bleed, and the volunteer let out a high-pitched peal of laughter.

"It's not nice to have someone in your head, is it?" he spat.

Smee snapped out of her trance and reached both hands out to grip Dredd and Deng each by the shoulder, and suddenly the pain was gone. Dredd sagged for a second in relief before snapping back to where he was.

"What's not possible?" Dredd asked, bringing his Lawgiver back to bear on the perp.

"His power, it's—it feels wrong. Alien, almost. I've never come across anything like it."

Deng aimed a shot at the volunteer now he was shielded by Smee, but the perp jumped out of the way, as if he knew where the Judge would aim.

The volunteer had stopped laughing and was staring at Smee.

"Wait," the perp said, holding up both hands, and Dredd stopped himself from blasting this guy away. "What *are* you?" he demanded of Smee. "Are you one of those Psi-Judges?"

"I am," she said, keeping her hands on Dredd and Deng.

"They done this to me," he said, smashing his hand into his skull. "They got into my head. They've changed me. I—I don't want to be a mutant. Can you make the voices stop?"

"I can help you," Smee said. "You have power. Great power. I can teach you—"

"Teach me? I don't want to learn anything from you." He stretched out a hand and a table skidded across the room.

"Telekinesis!" Deng gasped.

"Calm down!" Smee said, and Dredd could almost feel the calm in her words. Was she able to influence feelings?

"I will not be calm!" the perp cried.

Dredd felt his Lawgiver wrenched from his hand and watched it sail through the air, Deng's following it to clatter against the far wall.

"First, I will kill you. Then I will kill the scientists that did this to me. And finally, I will get Cartwright and make her suffer, as she has me!"

"I'm sorry about this," Smee said, and let go of Dredd and Deng. As soon as she did, the pain returned and they both doubled over.

Dredd opened his mouth to protest, but saw Smee climb to her feet, her shoulders hunched as if under a great weight.

The volunteer looked at her and the grin fell from his face. He cracked his neck and then raised his hand towards the window. A huge, deadly shard of glass shot up from the desert floor and hovered, ready to impale Smee where she stood.

She gritted her teeth, and the glass fell to shatter on the ground.

Suddenly Dredd realised he was free of pain, and ran at the perp ready to knock him out with his fists. Seeing Dredd heading for him, the volunteer raised both hands and all of the chairs in the room rose and flew at the Judge. He rolled, the first chair just missing him, but was assailed with pain as the chairs piled on top of him. He heaved himself to his feet, and the hill of chairs fell clattering around him.

The volunteer was at the open window now, Smee facing off with her feet planted. He motioned towards the chairs once more, but this time they didn't respond. He looked at Smee, realising that she was somehow blocking his powers.

He bent down and grabbed a shard of the broken glass from beside his feet and ran at Smee the old-fashioned way. Before he could reach her, Deng levelled a swing kick to the hand holding the shard and connected, forcing the volunteer to stagger backwards, teetering briefly at the window's edge before disappearing into the open night.

As one they ran forward to witness the man fall the distance towards the rockrete floor, where he landed with an audible *thunk*, and lay still.

For the second night in a row, Dredd found himself in some sort of crisis management meeting with Cartwright. This time, it was just her and her five heads of science, Newman included.

Maintenance were clearing the mess the volunteer had made, and Smee was busy doing a full evaluation of the other perps to make sure they weren't hiding a similar ability.

"Telekenisis?" Cartwright said thoughtfully. "At least we know who was responsible for Roberts's tragic murder."

Dredd frowned. "It is a theory, but one we can't be confident of."

"Oh, I am very confident, Judge Dredd. Roberts himself was responsible for the serum administered to this volunteer. He said himself he was out for revenge, did he not?"

Deng nodded. "He did. He named you specifically."

Cartwright drew back her lips, but said nothing.

"What have we created?" A slender Black man asked, looking at his hands. He must have been from the human labs. "How has this happened? We should have terminated the experiment when the first signs of psi ability were detected, we should—"

"That's enough, Tenison," Cartwright snapped. "We are

all shocked and deeply saddened by the casualties, but how could we have foreseen this side effect? How could we have known—?"

"We did know," Newman spoke up. "Reives spotted signs of this months ago. That's why they sent the Psi-Judge out to us. Thank grud she said something to the Hall of Justice. Shame it lost her her place on the team."

"Loretta went against my orders, as you know," Cartwright interjected. "And how do we know it wasn't her communication that alerted the Texans? They could have planted this guy—"

"The Texans?" Newman threw her hands up. "This wasn't the Texans, Cartwright. It was us. *We* did this. The human experiments have to stop. At least until we know—"

"I will hear no such talk!" Cartwright jumped to her feet, her body suddenly towering and menacing. "We are *so close* to a breakthrough. This is the survival of my—our—*race* we are talking about here. Yes, we are altering the volunteers' genetic makeup. But it is in aid of surviving the toxins of the Cursed Earth! Imagine, Althea; humans who could survive out there, coupled with your work, crops that could grow—"

"You know I am in full support of our purpose. But at what cost?"

"The colleagues we have lost are regrettable—"

"I'm not just talking about them. What of the *hundreds* of volunteers we have killed?"

"I haven't *killed* anyone!" Cartwright spun on her heel. "We have had unfortunate results to some of the drugs, it is true, but these volunteers signed the disclaimer, they were apprised of the risks."

Newman scoffed. "You know as well as I do that they would never have got that far in the small print before signing up to this program. Anything to limit their time in the cubes. We are taking advantage—"

"Enough!" Something in Cartwright's tone told Dredd that

Newman had pushed her too far. "One more word and you will be on the next transport to MC-1, understand?"

Newman's eyes burned, but she kept her mouth shut.

"I *will* be reporting this to the Department, but not over comms. We cannot risk the Texans listening in. I will go to the Hall of Justice myself, and ask their advice, and present our *many* breakthroughs to them. Until then, all communication is restricted. We will operate an insular protocol from now on. Anyone with a problem with that may join me on a one-way trip on the next transport to MC-1, which should be arriving with supplies in two days' time. Understood?"

The gathered scientists' silence was answer enough.

Eight

THE NEXT MORNING Dredd followed Smee as they made their way to Newman's office. Deng was on duty with the perps, and the mycologist had sent word that she needed to speak to them urgently. Evidence of the new security measures were visible in the labs. Barrier walls had been constructed to shield three parts of the first lab they walked through on their way to her office. It was clumsily done, and the space that the door opened onto had no daylight, as the windows were all on one far wall.

Dredd had managed to catch a few more hours of sleep before his shift started. He'd relieved Smee after she had finished her screenings. The sleeping pills were working, and as uncomfortable as he was about using drugs, he had to admit that he would be inefficient if he didn't get some sleep.

None of the other inmates seemed to have developed any psychic ability that Smee could detect.

"But there is something—off—about them," she told him as they reached Newman's office. "Something that doesn't feel entirely human."

Dredd didn't know what to make of that.

Newman looked tired when they entered her office. They'd all had an eventful night.

"Thanks for coming," she said, rubbing her eyes and sitting down on one end of her sofa. "Could you close the door? And sit down this time, Dredd. I have some serious concerns to discuss with you."

Dredd took the chair and rolled his shoulders as Smee took the other seat on the sofa.

"It's Cartwright. I think she's cracked."

Newman looked at Dredd as if waiting for a reaction. He didn't supply one.

"She's lost it. Do you understand me?" She looked at Smee. "There is something different about her. I studied under her, and she was never this—this paranoid. She came across as brilliant, eccentric maybe, but sharp. Someone I wanted to follow, you know? I was thrilled to be put on a project with her. But this is…" She held up her hands. "Not what I signed up for. The human testing side of the research struck me as off from the start, and not like something the Cartwright I knew would have been comfortable with. But the rate she's going through volunteers? That's gotten way out of hand. And all this stuff about the Texans? It's like an obsession. Something doesn't add up."

"Tensions with the Texans are a real concern," Dredd said. Cartwright did seem pretty tightly wound, but the situation wasn't exactly a relaxing one. "It's true that the Texans could pick up communications."

Newman took a breath. "I know that, but—she *really* doesn't want the Department finding out about what's been going on here. She was furious when Loretta reported the psi activity before, as if she had betrayed the project. But Loretta was just following standard procedure. Now that this has happened, it seems like madness not to alert the Council. People are dying.

Yes, we are doing important work, but we could at least get some more Judges out here. Three of you hardly seems adequate, especially without sleep pods."

"She has a point." Smee nodded to herself as if she were coming to a decision. "I have been getting a strange reading from her, actually."

"A reading?" Dredd sat up. "It is against—"

"I haven't been reading *her*," Smee cut him off mid-protest. "There are certain signals people's brains give off at all times, some louder than others, and I pick them up whether I try to or not. I can block them on purpose, shield myself like I did in the cafeteria, but I can't sustain it at all times. It's not like it tells me anyone's thoughts or anything, just sort of a psychic bleed. I don't know whether it's because they have some sort of latent ability or not, but anyway, it's like an aura, the sort of thing that old-world wackos used to talk about."

What sort of reading did *he* give off?

"Don't worry, I don't get any reading from you at all. You're almost catatonic."

"Now you *are* reading my mind."

Smee snorted. "I didn't need to read your mind to know what you were thinking. Althea, you have a very faint and normal reading."

"And Cartwright?" Newman said, bringing them back to the point.

"I haven't encountered an aura like hers before. It's like yours is all gentle waveforms and hers is lightning sharp. It's not a million miles, actually, from the reading I got from the psychic volunteer the other day."

What could that mean? Proximity to the experiments? Was she poisoning herself, perhaps?

"There's something else too," Newman said. "It's her death rate."

"What about it?" Dredd prompted when she paused.

"It's ridiculously high. She's getting through so many volunteers that we've had to up the programme."

"And this is a concern?" Dredd asked. It made sense that human testing would result in casualties, especially since they were altering their genes.

"Yes, it's a gruddamn concern," the scientist said, indignant. "They may only be criminals to you, Dredd, but they were just cits once. They think they're coming here to shorten their sentences so they can get out and start building a life again."

"Ninety-two percent of ex-cubers go on to repeat offend," Dredd informed her.

She rolled her eyes. "They're not born with a dream of breaking the law. You're a young Judge, but you'll see pretty soon that the beast that is MC-1 chews you up and spits you out a crim more often than not. Citizens have little choice in the matter. But I don't have the time to begin educating you on why that might be."

Dredd curled his lip. Who was she to tell *him* what was what? The Law was there to try and instil some order into the lives of the citizenry. What should they do, let crime run rampant and unpunished?

"She's right, Dredd, we don't have time to get into this now. Whether we agree morally or not, the high mortality rate of Cartwright's experiments, her unusual behaviour—"

"—in her opinion—"

"Sure, in Althea's *opinion*, Cartwright's unusual behaviour. And in *my* opinion, her strange psychic atmosphere. They all add up to something worth looking into."

As far as Dredd was concerned, their orders were to watch the perps and uphold the Law, not to moralise about scientific methods.

"I'm not going to be drawn into the politics of the labs," he said, getting up. "I need to go and relieve Deng."

"Wait." Newman stopped him at the door. "You're

transporting a volunteer to Cartwright today, right?"

He didn't respond, but she took his silence as agreement. "Take this." She pushed a small vial of brown powder into his hand. "No one has access to Cartwright's labs. We need to know what she's doing in there. Why so many of her volunteers never come back. This is some of my nano-fungi. Just sprinkle a bit in her lab and the spores should be able to give us an idea of what's going on."

"This powder can do that?" He held up the vial and peered at the contents.

She nodded. "Thousands of programmable spores that will connect back to the network."

"I'm not going to help you spy on our superior." Dredd shoved the vial back at her. "Maybe Tek-Judge Cartwright's not so paranoid after all."

"Judge Smee, read me now," Newman said. "Am I a spy? Or am I just really concerned that Cartwright is doing something wrong? Something she probably isn't telling the Department."

Smee was looking at her intently.

"Maybe *Cartwright's* the spy," Newman added.

"It's what she believes, Dredd. Without a comms link to the Hall of Justice, we can't consult our divisions. Cartwright's cut us off. We have to make a call."

Dredd grunted. He didn't like this at all. "I have no orders to investigate Cartwright," he said, turning to leave. Even so, he slipped the vial into his pocket.

THE VOLUNTEER WAS sat on the bunk at the back of his cube hugging his knees when Dredd opened it up.

"I'm not going," he said, shaking his head vigorously, his lank brown hair moving to cover his wide eyes. He was young, this one. Dredd probably had five years on him. Dredd checked his data slip. Noah Parkinson, minor gang member.

"Come on, kid." Dredd stepped back to free up the doorway.

"No, I've changed my mind. No one said anything about the Cursed Earth to me. Or brain bees."

"Brain bees?"

"It's what we all got last night before he got out. He was in so much pain, he wanted us to feel it too." His eyes filled with tears and spilled down his pale cheeks.

"You signed the doc. You have to comply. We can do this the easy way or the hard way." Dredd pulled out his daystick.

The kid gulped and pushed himself up on shaking legs. When he made it to the door, Dredd took hold of his arm, to steady him more than restrain him, and put a pair of cuffs on him for transportation. Together they walked to the freshly constructed door that replaced the one that had been destroyed.

Noah Parkinson was shaking as they walked the hall to the labs, then past the cubicles, and onwards to the reinforced steel door of Cartwright's private lab.

"Calm down," Dredd said, annoyed that the kid was so scared, and annoyed with himself for giving a drokk. "She's just one woman. A few injections and boom, you'll be back in your cube."

Noah looked at him as the red light by the door turned green, and Dredd pushed it open, walking through a small antechamber where they were blasted with clouds of decontaminant before they were allowed through to the lab itself. A large windowless chamber greeted them, lined with a large desk to the left, and a rack of shelves to the right. Opposite the entrance was another door, and in the centre of the room was an unwelcoming-looking reclining chair, covered in restraints. Cartwright stood from her desk as they came in.

"You're late," she complained, loosening a restraint. "In the chair, please."

Noah stayed where he was. Dredd removed his cuffs and gave him a shove, and Noah stumbled forward, turned to look at

Dredd, then lowered himself into the chair.

"You don't have to strap me down, doc," he said, as Cartwright began to tighten the bonds. "I won't try nothing with him breathing down my neck."

"The Judge will not be staying with us," Cartwright said, nodding at Dredd to dismiss him. "The work we do here is far too sensitive to be overseen."

"Wait," Noah said, as Dredd walked away. "Don't leave me here."

Dredd clenched his jaw as he left, his fingers tight around the vial of spores.

DREDD SPENT THE hour before he had to collect the volunteer patrolling the cells and trying to get the vision of Noah's scared eyes out of his head as the door shut behind him. He was back and outside Cartwright's lab on time, to the second. He felt an easing of tension as the light went green and the lab technician accompanying him pushed an empty wheelchair through the door in front of him. The volunteer would be drugged, and his mobility compromised.

Dredd's heart sank when he entered the lab. The chair was empty.

"I'm afraid the volunteer reacted badly to the serum. We won't be needing you to escort him back. A sad casualty, but a small price to pay in the grand scheme of things."

She didn't look sad. There was a gleam in her eye. As if things were going exactly to plan.

"Noah Parkinson is dead?" Dredd asked.

Cartwright consulted her screen. "Ah, yes. That was his name. Noah Parkinson. I've sent his body to the incinerator already. As I said"—she shrugged and began typing something into her data pad—"a shame."

The lab tech left without saying anything as if he had expected this, pushing the empty chair. Cartwright turned her back on Dredd as if the matter was closed.

Before he could change his mind, he uncorked Newman's vial and let the powder fall in a small cloud to the floor, turned on his heel, and left.

He clenched his fists as he returned to the cubes without his charge. What had he just done? Become part of a plot to spy on his superior? He had been taught to do what he was told. Questioning orders was akin to questioning the Law. And that was not something he was comfortable with doing.

But Noah Parkinson's eyes, so scared, watching him in his mind's eye, made the short walk back to the cubes seem long.

Cartwright's nonchalance towards the volunteer's life was one thing, but her manner didn't speak to him of a failed experiment. She was elated, as if she'd had some sort of a breakthrough. It didn't add up.

Well, he'd done it. He'd left the spores in her lab. Now he'd better make sure that Newman wasn't using them to spy for the Texans. Who knew how reliable Judge Smee's mind-reading was? There was only so far he could trust her ability.

As he walked past Noah's empty cell, he was relieved that he didn't have anyone else to transport that shift.

Nine

AFTER JUDGE SMEE relieved him, he went to find Newman. She was in her 'lab,' a glass-roofed atrium with rows of plantings in various stages of growth. She was standing over a particularly stunted patch of grass, the blades orange on the edges, making notes.

She looked up at him in surprise. "You didn't!"

He frowned at her. "I did. The spores are in her lab now."

She clutched her data pad to her chest, eyes bright.

"Okay, then. Let's find out what she's really hiding in there."

He followed her out of the lab and to her office, where she brought up a program that had vectors of rainbow strings in intricate patterns. There were grid points and symbols, and Newman began to type what Dredd assumed were formulas to manipulate the strands.

"Is this how you control the nano-fungi?"

She nodded. "Take a seat, this might take a minute." She held out a box of Treat-o-Biccis without looking up from the screen, and he took them from her because that was what she seemed to expect.

He sat down on the low sofa and pulled out a Bicci, chewing on the sweet yet bland treat while trying to get his head around what he was involved in here. The comms were down, so if the mycologist was spying for the Texans, she shouldn't be able to communicate with them—yet.

He looked up at Newman, who was still typing in a frenzy.

"If we were in MC-1, I would've had to seek clearance for this first," he said, not sure why he was telling her. "As it stands, I'll need to make a full report on my return."

"So what you're saying, Judge, is if we don't find anything on Cartwright, I'm in trouble."

Dredd rubbed his jaw.

"If you don't find anything, we both are."

At least he hadn't told Smee or Deng that he had decided to help Newman. Even if they would have been all for it, he didn't want them to be complicit if it came to an inquiry. This way, if Newman found nothing, the buck would stop with him.

"I'm in." She sat back in her chair and looked up, with a spark of excitement in her eyes.

On the screen was a clear image of the lab in shades of grey, green and pink. It was empty, and as far as he could tell there was nothing incriminating in there.

"So, what, do we have to wait until she gets her next test subject?"

"Don't you mean 'victim'?"

Dredd grunted, neither agreeing with nor denying her wording.

"No, this isn't the room I wanted to see. *That's* where the real secrets are hidden." She typed some more numbers into a small text box and the view shifted. She let out a breath. "It's open!"

The door Dredd had observed opposite the entrance was open a crack. She typed and they moved towards the open door. The other side revealed a small antechamber and the double doors of an elevator.

"Damn," she said. "I'm going to have to try and manipulate the spores into calling the elevator. That's going to take a while."

"You can get them to do that?"

"I think so, let's see."

He sat back down as numbers poured into the text box.

"I'm actually working on nano-ware: an interface to manipulate the spores more quickly, with my own brain. It lets me program them on the move."

"You've got it working? Why don't you use it now?" Dredd was interested to see it. If these spores could be manipulated into solid states to perform tasks, then they could perhaps be useful to the Justice Department.

"The tech works, but I'm still getting used to using it. I'm faster on here. Also, I thought you'd like to see this too."

She let out a little whoop as the view changed to a close-up of the elevator call button, and went momentarily dark as the spores exerted pressure, then drew back to watch as the doors opened.

The spores swarmed into the elevator, a space big enough to fit a standing attendant and a wheelchair, if necessary.

The doors closed and the spores floated up and settled on the ceiling as the lift moved down.

The doors slid open to blackness, as the spores poured into the space to map it out and send back the data. As Dredd watched, an image of a large lab started to form, with cluttered desks, a wall bank of computer screens and a large metal restraint chair, similar to the one in the room above, bolted to the floor at the centre of the lab. What was really wrong, however, was what looked like a wall of cages to the far left of the room.

"What the—?" Newman said, as she directed the spores to investigate. It took Dredd a moment to understand what he was seeing. The cages were not empty. Inside moved or lay mutants of a kind that Dredd had never seen before. Tentacles and extra limbs twitched and writhed, teeth extended past slathering jaws and shoulders humped and hunched.

"Why would Cartwright be keeping mutants here?" Dredd asked. "She has the volunteers to experiment on."

"I think these *are* the volunteers." She directed the spores closer, to zero in on one of the data screens flashing above each individual cage.

Dredd let out a grunt as he saw the name. "Noah Parkinson."

He looked at the kid, now a mess of tentacles and teeth. But his eyes... they were still the same. And they didn't look frightened anymore. They looked furious.

"ARE YOU SURE about this?" Newman said again, hurrying to keep up with Dredd's footsteps.

"Yes. Again, we need to get Judge Smee and Judge Deng and go to Cartwright to give her the chance to explain herself."

"Explain herself? I mean, I'm as curious as the next woman about what the drokk she is up to, but I think that's a matter for the big guys, don't you? We need to go straight to the Council."

"And tell them what? For all we know these results are sanctioned."

"Look, whether or not the volunteers are expendable, mutants are illegal. There's no way the Department—"

Dredd cut her off. "Let's see what Deng and Smee have to say."

Smee was still on shift, so they woke Deng up and went to see her in the small viewing room where the cube cameras showed the volunteers mostly laying on their bunks or pacing the floor.

Smee frowned at them from the one chair as they entered the tiny space, Deng having to stand in the doorway.

Dredd briefly went through what they had found.

"So you went through with it?" Smee looked surprised.

"Didn't think you had such insubordination in you, Dredd."

He looked at the floor and felt his shoulders rise towards his ears. "There will of course need to be an investigation into my actions. But first we need to get to the bottom of this."

"Hey I'm not complaining. I'm impressed."

"So let me understand this properly," Deng said from the door. "Cartwright's turning the volunteers into mutants?"

"Keep your voice down," Newman said, glancing nervously towards the cubes.

"They won't hear me," Deng said more quietly.

"Yes, her experiments seem to be having more side effects than she would have us believe," Dredd confirmed.

"And so we—what?" Deng shrugged. "Go to the Department?"

"Thank you. That's what I've been saying!" Newman turned to Smee. "Can you tell Dredd that there is no point asking Cartwright to explain herself? She's obviously lost it. We're supposed to be doing slight gene realignment to fight the desert toxins. Not turning people into mutants."

"But isn't that what they would be?" Smee asked. "The mutants in the Cursed Earth, they have mutated—adapted—to survive the poisons in the air and ground. It stands to reason that this could be a result of the experiments."

Dredd hadn't looked at it that way before. The mutations were a result of the toxicity in the world. It seeped into MC-1, creating subtle mutations even there, and were amplified in the desert. This meant they could survive out here, scraping a sorry existence. And yet the Justice Department had declared them illegal. For the first time, Dredd reflected on how *unjust* that was. He pushed it from his mind. That was a rabbit hole he may never return from.

"Judge Smee is correct. There could be a perfectly legal explanation for Cartwright's actions. We can't go to our superiors until we are sure there is not."

They left Judge Deng on duty in Smee's place, as her psi

abilities could come in handy, and found Cartwright eating at a table alone in the cafeteria. Dredd curled his lip at the visible white coating of salt over her food again.

"Cartwright, we need to speak with you, privately."

She looked up and eyed the three of them hovering over her.

"Althea, what is this about?" she asked.

Newman looked around at the scientists and maintenance crew eating in groups at other tables.

"It's—sensitive," she responded, looking meaningfully at the other occupants.

Cartwright took a napkin and dabbed at her mouth before pushing herself up.

"Is it the Texans?" she hissed under her breath, following them out. "Let's go to my office."

None of them corrected her, not wanting to make a scene.

Once in her office Dredd, Smee and Newman stood while Cartwright sat behind her imposing desk.

For a few moments none of them spoke, all three of them waiting for another to take the lead.

"Well, spit it out," Cartwright said. "You interrupted my meal for what?"

Newman looked Dredd in the eye, and he nodded for her to begin.

"We know about the mutants, Cartwright," she blurted.

Smooth.

"Mutants?" Cartwright widened her eyes in shock. "What are you talking about?"

"In your lab. We know the volunteers are not dying, and that you are hiding your failed experiments in cages in your secret laboratory. This is beyond messed up. If the other scientists knew—"

Cartwright slammed her fists onto her desk making Dredd and Smee flinch their hands to their Lawgivers.

"Spies!" she said triumphantly. "I knew it. *You* are the Texan moles. What is the world coming to when they can infiltrate the Justice Department?"

"I can assure you, we are no spies." Dredd worked his jaw, biting down on a surge of anger, partly fuelled by a worry she was half-right. "But we do need to know why you are creating mutants. That is a clear infringement on the law."

Cartwright's eyes snapped to Smee. "Is it? Talking of mutants, we have one in this room with us as we speak. We all know the Justice Department can stomach a mutant as long as it's useful."

"And you're saying the Department know about your mutants?" Dredd cut Smee off before she could engage in Cartwright's clear diversion technique.

She pushed herself up from her desk.

"I won't discuss this with *her* here." She flicked her eyes at Smee. "I won't have spies reading my thoughts."

"We're not spies," Newman's voice sounded tired. "Why are you so obsessed with the Texans?"

"Spoken like a spy," she shot back. "If you wish to discuss this further, you'll send *that*"—she pointed a talon-like finger at Smee—"out into the hall."

"I'll leave gladly." Smee's cheeks were red. "Dredd, you don't need my psi abilities to know she's full of stomm."

"I'll have you punished for that!" Cartwright shouted at Smee's back as she left and slammed the door behind her.

Dredd took a deep breath. "Okay, then, you got that you wanted. No mind reading. Now, explain your mutants."

She looked at them both for a long moment before sighing out a long breath. "Look, there is no way to clear this up unless we hear it straight from the horse's mouth. Comms are too dangerous. As far as I know, this is exactly why you have brought this to me. To open up comms and alert the Texans to my experiments."

Newman let out an exasperated grunt. "For the last time—"

"So the only move remaining to us," Cartwright continued, talking over her, "is for us all to take the scheduled transport back to MC-1 tomorrow. We'll go to the Hall of Justice, and they can confirm everything I have told you. And then we can make sure you are disciplined and dealt with properly. Althea, you're going to end up in a cube for this."

BACK IN THE small observation room watching listless volunteers laying on bunks, Smee and Dredd filled in Deng on what had been decided. Newman was stewing with her plants. She said she was saying goodbye to her babies. "This is game over for me. Either Cartwright is breaking the law, and the whole project gets shut down, or she isn't, and I end up in a cube."

They'd left her murmuring to her grass samples.

"So we're all going back to base tomorrow, eh?" Deng said, rubbing his eyes. "I can't say I feel too bad about that. I'll be glad to see the back of this place."

Dredd grunted in agreement.

"But then again," Deng continued, "we're probably heading back to a cube. Cartwright won't sugar-coat it."

Smee made a growling sound deep in her throat. "That woman. I *know* she's guilty of hiding those mutants. It can't have been authorised."

"Why would she be taking us back to face the music if she was worried about being found out?

Dredd found himself agreeing with Deng.

Just then the crackle of the loudspeakers fizzed into the room.

"*Attention volunteers,*" Cartwright's voice, cold and calm, reverberated through the hallways.

Dredd met Smee's incredulous eyes. Then the screens to the cubes blinked out, the cameras switched off remotely. They were blind.

"*You will know by now that this place is a one-way ticket to your graves,*" Cartwright continued. "*Our experiments will not give you the new life you have been promised by the Judges. But now, I am going to give you one last chance for freedom, one last chance to live. You will find your cell doors unlocked. The only thing standing in your way are the three Judges. It is kill or be killed. Leave your cells, now, and kill them. Kill the Judges!*"

Ten

FOR A MOMENT all was still as they just looked at each other, alarmed, then as one they drew their Lawgivers. Deng scooped his helmet up and put it on; Dredd and Smee had theirs on already.

Deng's eyebrows came together. "Did she just—?"

"Shh!" Smee raised her finger to her lips as Dredd moved to the door, body flat to the wall.

The cells were still closed, but he could see the lock lights were on green. He looked back and nodded once. This was not good.

"Guess she does have something to hide," Deng whispered.

Smee rolled her eyes and came to stand at Dredd's shoulder, pulling off her helmet.

"It dulls my ability," she said in response to Dredd's questioning look. She squinted with focus at the cubes.

"They're confused. They think they are being tricked, tested, or otherwise screwed. Some believe her and are building the courage to do as she suggested. Some believe her and are frightened." She closed her eyes. "Yes, not all will come. One is already hiding under his bed."

"How many will fight?" Dredd asked.

Her frown deepened. "It's hard to say. They are angry. Their suspicions are now confirmed, that this is a death factory. And their emotions are rising. It's all getting very—loud. Difficult for me to pick out individual thoughts. But I'd say most of them will fight, eventually."

"They're unarmed," Deng patted his Lawgiver.

"But there are forty-eight of them, and three of us," Smee said.

Dredd stepped out into the hall. "We need to get out of here before they get their courage up."

They moved down the hall. Smee put her helmet on and brought up the rear.

Dredd tensed as the loudspeakers crackled to life once more. "*Oh, yes,*" Cartwright's voice boomed, "*I forgot to mention. The weapons cache is also unlocked. If you can find your way there, you'll have a better chance of saving your lives, don't you think?*"

Dredd froze and turned to look back the way they had come. The weapons cache was in the other direction, normally locked behind a three-foot-thick reinforced steel door. It was for the security guards, and contained tasers, stun-guns, daysticks and smoke grenades. None of them deadly in and of themselves, but would be enough to turn the tide in their favour should the volunteers lay their hands on them. They already had the numbers; if they had weapons to disable the Judges, then the next step would be to kill.

He watched as the first door was thrown open and a huge, thick-necked man stepped out, and ran at them, head down. All three Lawgivers found their targets, and he crumpled in a smoking heap on the floor, but the spell was broken.

"We have to get to the cache!" Dredd shouted as the doors began to pop open, and wide-eyed, grinning, growling, teeth-gritting men and women poured out into the corridor.

They ran, but the perps were in between them and the cache, and began hurling their bodies at the Judges, trying to tackle them to the ground.

Suddenly, they were surrounded. Back to back, the Judges blasted holes in the wall of bodies, keeping them back.

But as one, they rushed forward, so close that the Judges couldn't get a clear shot. A meaty fist gripped Dredd's Lawgiver, but he smacked it into the owner's grizzled face, breaking some teeth and knocking him down. Pulling his daystick, he swung out at hands and heads and anything he could.

"Get in closer!" a voice called. "Don't let them shoot!"

Smee and Deng had also pulled their sticks having holstered their guns in order to stop them being wrenched out of their hands. They were not designed to be used as blunt force weapons in close proximity.

All Dredd could do was move: hit, lunge, fall back, duck, swing. The space around him became a flashing reel of staccato moments. A fist drove towards him; he caught it with an open palm, gripping it and driving his daystick down on the elbow to break the bone. The man's face, a rictus of pain as he fell back, to be replaced by another, fear and frenzy and rage driving a woman forward as Dredd drove the butt of his stick into her eye. He felt the eye burst, felt the spray of fluid and blood as he drew the stick back to stave in the teeth of another perp closing in.

It was chaos, brutal, beautiful. Dredd felt a calm descend upon him as the flow of the moment took over, and he did what he had been born to do.

Then a pause as the perps closest to him stood back to take stock; it wasn't more than a second's respite, but it was enough to snap him out of his fighting trance. The three of them were keeping more than forty attackers at bay with only their daysticks and their training, but it couldn't last. They had to do more than hold them back. They had to push through before the perps found that weapons cache.

Smee head-butted one perp and dropped a second with a vicious kick to the groin, creating a small pocket of space in front of her. She drew her Lawgiver and managed to get some shots off before the hole filled with more bodies.

"We're never going to make it to the cache like this," Dredd said. "Deng! Get behind me and Judge Smee, we'll make space for you to shoot."

Concentrating their efforts on one front, Smee and Dredd managed to drive the perps while Deng fired off a few shots. They swung kicks and smashed heads as Deng picked targets off with his sidearm. It was working; they were moving slowly towards the cache. If they could get to the weapons before the perps, then they had a chance of winning on firepower alone.

And then, a new sound resounded down the hall, chilling Dredd to the bone: cheering.

"We got stunners and wackers!" someone crowed, and the attacks eased off as the perps ran to grab weapons.

Deng shot a man down, and they realised their mistake and crowded in close again, keeping up the pressure.

"Come on," Deng shouted, and pushed open the door to the observation room with his back. They were right back where they started.

The three of them fell inside and slammed the steel door closed behind them, breathing hard.

"What now?" Smee had to raise her voice over the clang of blows against the door.

"They have tasers, stun guns..." Dredd shook his head.

"And there are so many of them." Deng panted.

Smee took her helmet off again, her fine dark hair plastered to her forehead with sweat. She closed her eyes. "Not all of them are out there. Some have stayed in their cells, too afraid or waiting for others to do the dirty work for them. There are maybe"—she paused—"twenty or so in the hall."

Deng flinched at another thud at the door.

"They won't get through this door," Dredd said, looking around the windowless room for inspiration.

"But we can't stay here," Smee said.

Deng slammed his fist against the wall. "This is drokk. We should be able to take them."

"We have the superior firepower." Smee swiped her hair behind her ears. "But they have the numbers. It was clever of them to swarm us like that. We need more space."

Dredd grunted as his eyes found the inspiration they were looking for.

"You're right, Judge Smee." He jumped to the desk below the bank of screens. "We need space to shoot." He reached up and pressed against the ceiling, relieved when his suspicions were confirmed. "A high vantage. From above."

Smee grinned as he pushed open a square section of the ceiling to reveal an air vent, issuing cool, recycled, non-toxic air, and put her helmet back on. It was narrow, but someone small could just about squeeze through. "Give me a leg up?"

She climbed onto the desk beside Dredd, and he offered her his cupped hands to step in. She grabbed the edge of the vent and pulled herself up; her Lawgiver caught as she hauled herself over the edge, and she pulled it from its holster, pushing it into the vent in front of her as she wriggled into the narrow entrance.

"*Wait until I'm in position,*" she said through comms, before dragging herself away.

Deng and Dredd went back to the door, which, despite the continuous barrage, held firm.

They waited, tense. The air-filtration system stretched across every room and hallway in the dome, but there was no way of knowing if this particular vent would go above the hallway at all.

"*I'm in position,*" Smee's voice said a short while later. "*Engage in 3—2—*"

The sound of Standard Execution fire barked, and the screams of men echoed through the door. Dredd shouldered it open and shot the three men blocking the door in the backs, as they turned in Smee's direction. Dredd took a second to pinpoint the Psi-Judge, who was hanging half out of a hole in the ceiling near the exit, before stepping out and opening fire. Deng followed close behind.

"Smoke bombs!" a voice cried as a dark puff of black smoke exploded from the direction of the weapons cache.

But it was too late. Together the three Judges brought the men down, one bullet at a time, until the hall was a pile of twisted, smoking bodies.

Dredd scanned the ground looking for any survivors, while Smee lowered herself from the vent.

"What now?" Deng asked, panting from the fight.

"Now we take that cold-hearted, lawbreaking, mutant-hating and mutant-making drokker down," Smee said, rolling her shoulders back with a cold, fleeting smile that didn't reach her eyes. "I think I'm going to enjoy this."

Eleven

THEY WALKED THE length of the cubes, finding fourteen men and women cowering in their cells. They cuffed them to their bunks and left them with a warning to behave.

Lawgivers in hand, they pushed through the door to find a security guard laid out on his front on the floor. Dredd thought he was dead, but he groaned as Deng pulled him onto his back. There was blood trickling from his mouth, and he blinked his eyes in blurred confusion.

"What happened here?" Dredd demanded, but the guard groaned as his eyes rolled back into his head and he went limp.

"Drokk!" Deng shook him.

"Move out of the way!" Smee said, kneeling at the guard's side. Without waiting, she placed her hands to either side of his balding head.

"Cartwright," she said grimly. "She came through here with—" She frowned. "She had someone with her, but the guard didn't really focus on them. He was looking at the massive syringe Cartwright was holding to their neck."

"A hostage?" Dredd asked.

She nodded. "They went towards the labs. Then the next thing he knew—pain—it forced him to the ground. His brain—it seems like a weaker version of what happened to Roberts."

"Why is she doing this?" Deng suddenly demanded. "Is she a spy for the Texans? It doesn't make sense."

"You're right," Smee agreed. "This all seems—excessive. And if she's the spy, why go to all the trouble crippling comms? She didn't want the Hall of Justice to know about her mutants. Is she making them for the Texans?"

"Whatever her reasons, we need to get a message back," Dredd said. "If she's in her lab, then the comms suite is unprotected. Deng. Can you go and get a message out? Smee and I will deal with the doc."

"Split up now? We don't know what she's capable of, or what's in that syringe. I say all three of us take her down, then we can take our sweet time talking to the Department when the threat is put down."

At that moment, an unholy roar ripped through the air.

"What was that?" Deng pushed himself to his feet.

Smee looked at Dredd from where she was kneeling beside the now-dead security guard, wiping bloody hands on her thighs as another roar hit them, alongside a wave of furious energy.

"She set the volunteers on us. Now she's sending her pet muties."

Dredd frowned as he turned his Lawgiver towards the labs. Another roar, picked up by more tortured mutant throats.

"How many are there?" Deng said, stepping in beside Dredd as Smee took position at his other shoulder.

"Five—maybe more. Big assholes."

They could now hear the screech of claws against metal and a slapping sound that Dredd didn't want to think about.

"Brace," Dredd yelled, as the dark green tip of an enormous tentacle curled around the corner. More followed, gripping the wall. They all waited to see what came after it.

A head, huge, distorted and terrible, showed itself, the great pointed shoulders straining at the grey-green skin as they worked to control the tentacles. Sharp, slathering teeth punctured the elongated jaw. For a moment, the eyes, huge and wild with rage, yet still somehow human, met Dredd's.

"Are we sure they're hostile?" Dredd said suddenly, holding up a hand to stop Deng and Smee from opening fire.

Deng ripped his eyes from the mutant and shot Dredd a look. "What do you mean? Look at that thing's teeth! This is a 'shoot first, ask questions never' situation."

"Smee?" They all took a step back as the creature inched forward. "Can you get a reading on it?"

"Why?"

Dredd grimaced. This had been a man, not so long ago. His rage was clear—but Dredd would be angry too, if he'd been turned into this. "Maybe he'll help us take down Cartwright."

"And I thought *I* was soft on muties," she smirked, but focused on the beast.

The mutant opened its huge jaw and roared, its tongue vibrating, spit spraying across the room.

"I don't think it can differentiate between us and Cartwright. I can't sense any human brain activity. The wavelengths—they're different. They remind me of—"

"*What are you waiting for?*" came Cartwright's voice over the loudspeaker. "*Kill them! Kill the Judges.*"

The beast shot forward, and as one they opened fire. One Incendiary round sheared off a tentacle, one pierced its chest, and Dredd's struck its slavering jaw. It dropped, twitching, to the ground, not yet dead. But it was replaced by two more creatures, their tentacles writhing. Now Dredd could see their back legs ended in razor sharp claws.

"Fall back!" Dredd fired as, shoulder to shoulder, they stepped back. Smee hit the outer door release and they almost fell out. The reinforced steel shutter slammed hard behind them.

"That should hold them for a second." Smee was panting. "Don't think those dudes have security clearance."

Deng grinned and Dredd felt his own grimace ease.

"We should wait at the other end of the connecting corridor. The tunnel is too narrow for more than one of them at a time. We'll pick them off as they come."

They took position a few metres back from the entrance and waited as they heard the shuddering impact of the mutants against the outer door.

"It's all starting to make sense now." Deng licked his lips. "The paranoia, the psychic volunteer, Roberts's murder..."

"He must have been on to her." Smee took up his thread when he trailed off. "Maybe that volunteer wasn't the only one with telekinetic powers."

"Are you saying Cartwright has these powers? That she used them to"—Dredd grimaced—"explode Roberts's brain?"

"Maybe," Smee said, shifting her feet as a particularly loud crash resounded down the corridor. "I got a similar reading off those mutants as I got from the psychic volunteer. The same echo of strangeness I get from Cartwright. No wonder she didn't want a Psi-Judge snooping around."

Dredd snapped his attention back to the doorway where a tentacled monster was about to break through.

"You might be right. But let's focus on the mutants trying to kill us right now."

There was a resounding crash as the monsters finally broke through the door.

They opened fire as soon as it was clear of the door, not even letting it reach the courtyard.

"Like fish in a barrel," Deng said, as it fell.

Another mutant roared as its comrade fell, and Dredd felt his stomach turn as the mutant he had assumed they had just killed started to move.

"It's using the body as a shield!" Dredd moved back from the exit, positioning himself out of the direct line of sight. Deng did the same on the opposite side, with Smee remaining braced directly in front.

The limp body of the dead mutant began to emerge from the corridor. "*Hold,*" he said through comms. He could see the living mutant's own tentacles gripping the limp ones and moving it forward.

"*So they're still smart,*" Deng murmured over comms. "*They can learn.*"

The mutant's corpse was suddenly jettisoned with such force that it flew through the air to hit Smee, who fell beneath its weight.

"Fire!" Dredd shouted, as his Lawgiver found its target in the beast's side. The monster screeched; Deng did the same from the other side, and the mutant fell, its ribcage an open mess.

They ran to Smee, who was attempting to push a couple hundred kilos of tentacles and claws off her.

"Are you hurt?" Deng said, offering her a hand.

"Just bruised, I think." She accepted his hand as Dredd turned back to the tunnel.

They all levelled their Lawgivers again and waited.

"How many you say there was?" Smee asked.

"Four or five," Dredd answered.

"Three down," Deng said. "One or two to go."

They waited, but nothing further emerged.

Dredd listened. He couldn't hear panting, couldn't hear any movement.

"Have they run?" Deng didn't sound convinced.

"If they can learn, maybe they've figured that we're not such easy targets," Smee said.

The sound of shattering glass gave them their answer as a screeching mutant hurled itself from the window above them. They all rolled as the thing landed heavily on its hind legs, tentacles flaring out like a petticoat.

Another used its tentacles to hang from the window, claws gouging deep fissures in the rockcrete as it slid to the ground.

Before Deng could react, a tentacle shot out and wrapped around his arm, lifting him from the ground. Dredd dove out of the way of the second mutant as it flung its body towards him, and Smee opened fire on the first. Another tentacle smacked Smee's Lawgiver from her hand. Dredd turned his own Lawgiver on his attacker, but it launched itself at Dredd once more, and his shot went wild as he flung himself out of the way. He fired again, this time hitting flesh, and the creature bellowed.

Suddenly a tentacle was gripping his arm, and another his Lawgiver. Before he could be lifted off his feet, he fired a Hi-Ex round, shredding the tentacle holding the weapon, but the gun skittered from his grasp, landing metres away. Too far, when an injured, slathering mutant was coming at you, intent on murder.

He drew his boot knife and met the creature head on, leaping and landing on its back. The tentacles writhed and lashed at him, but couldn't quite reach him, and he held on as the beast began to buck, its powerful legs slamming itself backwards against the rockcrete wall in a bid to dislodge him.

Thanking his reinforced body armour, Dredd pulled back his hand and drove his blade deep beneath the monster's jaw, feeling hot blood pour over his fist as its legs gave way. He jumped free as it hit the ground, rolling to his knees in one fluid movement, eyes fixed in case it rose once more. But the beast was still.

He turned to help Smee and Deng, but found the two panting over the corpse of the second mutant, Deng massaging his forearm where the tentacle had pulled him up, Smee wiping her own bloody boot knife on her thigh.

Dredd nodded grimly to them both. "Five down—"

"—one crazy scientist to go," Smee said.

Deng grinned.

"We have to take Cartwright in, dead or alive," Dredd agreed.

"But one of us has to go and get a message to the Department. Deng, will you go?"

"And miss out on all the fun?"

"It's important, we have to get word back in case something happens to us and the Doc gets away. If we fail, what has happened here cannot remain hidden."

He watched Deng chew on that.

"Why me?"

"We need Smee's psi powers, and I—well, let's say I want to take her down, personally." Noah Parkinson's frightened face flashed through his mind, and he wondered which mutant he had been. "I owe it to someone."

Deng relented. "Fine, but as soon as I get the message out, I'm coming to back you up."

"Agreed." Dredd rolled his shoulders and clicked his neck. "Let's get this done."

Twelve

THEY HAD TO waste time dragging the mutant corpses out of the tunnel before Dredd and Smee could move in on Cartwright's lab. She had sent two waves of attackers out to kill them, but now it seemed her reserves of potential murderers were sapped. Nothing and no one stopped them from stepping over the last mutant corpse and moving down the corridor. The lab door was ajar, unsurprising as some pretty hefty mutants had just forced their way through it, and the first lab—what Dredd thought of as the 'show room'—was empty, the chair gouged with claw marks and wrenched from the bolts, listing to the side. Still nothing to stop them from moving to the inner door, and the elevator, which waited with open doors.

Dredd hesitated and looked at Smee, who shrugged. They stepped in.

It looked different from how it had on the screen when he'd viewed it through the fungal network. As the doors opened, he wondered if the network still lingered.

They exited the elevator and moved through the second small antechamber, then—back pressed to the wall—Dredd craned his neck and looked through the open door.

The lab was dark, the cages on the left open and empty. The restraint chair stood undamaged in this room, and seated on it, albeit not strapped down, sat Dr. Newman, rigid and wide-eyed, an enormous syringe pressing at her throat. Cartwright stood beside her, one hand holding the back of the mycologist's collar and the other holding the syringe.

"Come any closer, and I'll shoot her so full of serum she'll mutate before our eyes."

Newman gritted her teeth, sweat beading on her nose, a perfect mix of fear and fury warring across her features.

"Drop the guns." Cartwright pulled Newman's collar tighter, the needle pressing harder into the soft skin of her neck. Dredd saw a bead of blood well up beneath the point.

Both Judges stayed where they were but didn't lower their Lawgivers.

"What do you want, Cartwright?" Dredd asked.

Cartwright narrowed her eyes. "I thought instructing the volunteers to kill you, then setting my babies on you, would have made that clear."

"But why?" Smee sounded as confused as he was. "Are you working for the Texans?"

Cartwright threw back her head and let out a wild laugh. "Ah, the Texans. No, Judge Smee, they couldn't care less what we're doing here."

So Cartwright's obsession had all been a front? Newman looked equally surprised.

"Then what?"

"The work!" she hissed. "The lengths I have gone to, the things I have done, to set this project up, to persuade the idiots in the Hall of Justice to fund it. I can't have you ruin it!"

"It's over, Cartwright. The volunteers are dead, the rest of the scientists know about the mutants."

"It is *not over!*" Spittle flew from her mouth as she screamed the words, and Newman flinched.

Then Dredd's Lawgiver shuddered in his hand and began to smoke, juddering as if it were about to explode. It glowed white hot, the flexi-armour of his gloves beginning to smoulder. He threw it towards the cages just as the metal surrendered and peeled back, coming apart in a cloud of sparks and smoke.

Cartwright gasped, staggering a little before regaining her stature.

"She has psi powers!" Smee took a step forward. "Telekinesis!"

"Well spotted," Cartwright said sardonically. "And if you didn't have your damn helmet on that would have been your brain, Dredd."

Dredd looked at the panting, visibly weakened Cartwright. Destroying his Lawgiver had tired her. She might not have the strength to do the same to Smee's.

"We get it," Newman said through gritted teeth. "You killed Roberts. You've been behind the killings all along. But why?"

Cartwright ignored her, looking at the Judges instead. "Now, you see, we are at an impasse. I don't have the strength to kill you both, and you don't want me to turn Althea here into a mutant. So if you'll put down that second gun and move over into that cage, I'll lock you in and take Althea here on a little journey. I have the serum. I have my research. I'll have to begin again elsewhere. Perhaps the Texans really *do* want to know about our research."

"You're going nowhere," Dredd said. It was a gruddamn shame, but it didn't look as though they were going to get Newman through this alive and unchanged.

"Judge Smee," the mycologist shouted, catching him off guard. "Read my mind!"

Something dark coalesced in the air around Cartwright's hand, covering the syringe. It was then that Dredd noticed the small metal earpiece Newman was wearing. The fungal network!

Newman yanked her head clear and ducked, and Smee discharged her Lawgiver into Cartwright's chest. The woman was blown back off her feet, hitting the back wall heavily and sliding down limply to the floor.

Newman instinctively staggered forward to stand behind Smee and Dredd, and the three regarded the corpse.

"That was quick thinking, Althea," Smee said, lowering her sidearm and turning to her.

"I'd been waiting for my moment," the scientist said. "As soon as I heard her tell the perps to kill you over the loudspeakers, I put on my mobile controller and got the rest of the scientists to hole up in one of the bio labs. I was on my way to see if I could arrange security to back you up when she grabbed me. One of the guards tried to intervene, but she used her power to kill him the same way she'd killed Roberts. But I saw how it drained her. I knew she'd be weakened if she used her powers on you."

"You were waiting for one of our heads to explode?" Dredd was impressed by her pragmatism.

She smirked. "I was hoping your helmets would stop her. I knew they dulled psi powers." She shrugged. "And if she did manage to kill one of you, I guessed that Smee would be able to stop a mental assault."

"I was the sacrifice." Dredd grimaced, but had to admit to himself he'd been thinking the same of her.

"What I still don't understand," Smee said, holstering her Lawgiver, "is why she did all this. Was her work even about purifying the Cursed Earth? I get that mutants can survive out there, but her mission statement was all about 'saving the race.' I can't believe her plan was to turn us all into muties."

Dredd scratched his jaw, suddenly tired. "I guess we'll find out when they go through her research."

Newman gasped and took a step back, looking past him to Cartwright's body, and he turned with Smee to look in the same direction.

Cartwright's flesh was—*moving*.

"What the—?" Smee went to get a better look, and Dredd stepped forward to stand beside her.

The skin on Cartwright's face and hands was warping and twitching, as if something was pressing out from underneath. The colour was already grey, much too fast for a newly dead body.

They both took a step back as the twitching intensified, her skin rippling as her limbs began to shake. If it wasn't for the hole in her chest Dredd would have thought it some kind of seizure.

A line of darker grey began to show on the exposed skin above the wound. Dredd assumed it joined the one now creeping up the centre of her neck. It traversed her chin and moved up to split her whole face.

Then an audible *click*, and a *crunch* as skin and flesh rolled back, the ribcage swinging open like a set of saloon doors.

Dredd didn't realise he was moving until he felt the wall behind his back, Smee and Newman standing frozen in horrified fascination beside him.

Out of the opening carcass began to writhe what Dredd mistook for a pit of snakes, as if they had been coiled and packed tightly into Cartwright's body, and were now being released into the world.

He reached for his Lawgiver before remembering it was in pieces on the floor, so instead gripped his daystick.

The snakes were tentacles, he realised, watching as they thickened and unknotted themselves. They gripped the chair, bracing against the wall, as a creature, not that unlike the larger mutants they had just killed, unfolded itself out of the shell of Cartwright's body. The clawed hind legs were released with an audible sucking noise, like a boot wrenched from clinging mud.

The head, long, narrow, with elongated jaws set with razor

fangs, narrowed cold dark eyes at them, and screeched. It sounded triumphant.

"Offworlder!" Newman said, the screech having broken whatever spell they had all been under.

"Shoot!" Dredd shouted at Smee.

But as she drew her Lawgiver, a tentacle shot out and wrenched the gun from her grasp, sending it skittering across the lab, out of reach.

The monster let out another roar. *You will not stop me now!* The creature's voice was grating and harsh, ringing out within their heads.

"What business do you have here, offworlder?" Smee raised both of her hands to placate it as it moved in for the kill. "Why wear Cartwright's skin? Why go to all this trouble to set these labs up? Why turn the volunteers into—some kind of version of yourself?"

It seemed like an odd moment to reel off a list of questions, but Dredd figured Smee was trying to get her talking. He was interested too, but sating his curiosity wasn't his highest priority right now.

The creature quirked its head to the side, and hissed. Dredd thought their time was up.

My people are dying, it said suddenly. *Disease ravages us, and we must secure a cure. But my people are not savages, as you are here. We will not test on ourselves. It is immoral. Dangerous and wrong. And so, I come here to carry out my experiments. Your DNA isn't so far from ours, would you believe? Just a few tweaks and, as you have encountered, you become close enough to our species to test our drugs on.*

"You're too moral to test drugs on your own species, so you come over to our world and test on us?" Newman shook her head. "Our volunteers were defenceless!"

The creature hissed. *Don't talk to me of morals. This world has a rich history of testing on different species. And not even just to prevent sickness: you test cosmetics for your vanity on little,* defenceless *animals. And even other humans. Yes! You divided and deluded yourselves into thinking some people were less important than others. You can't deny it. What I do here is no worse than you yourselves have done before me. This planet was perfect. Your track record made it easy to persuade my superiors that this was the right place for my work. I was just doing to you what you had done to others.*

"So you found a scientist, top of her game, and stole her identity," Newman said. "Poor Cartwright. She *was* a brilliant woman."

She was in the best position for me to carry out my work. But I'm glad to be rid of the prison of her feeble body.

But I digress. Time to die—

Newman made for the door, but a tentacle suddenly wrapped around her ankle; at the same time, another shot out to take Dredd's daystick.

Dredd threw himself at the creature, drawing his boot knife, but another tentacle wrapped around his wrist and neck, pulling him up with alarming strength. Smee was picked up and thrown back against the far wall.

At that moment, Deng burst through the door, rolling and shooting as he hit the ground.

The offworlder recoiled, releasing the scientist's ankle.

"Run!" Deng said to Newman, shoving her behind him. The mycologist disappeared into the antechamber. Dredd hoped she'd use common sense and run for it.

Deng levelled his gun at the monster, then paused, confusion crossing his features as the alien bent its powers against his Lawgiver.

"No!" Smee said, gritting her teeth. "No more telekinesis."

The creature hissed.

Smee was red in the face as her eyes narrowed in concentration. "I've finally tuned in to your frequency." To Deng, she added,

"I can hold her."

At that moment, the offworlder drew back its tentacles and catapulted Dredd towards Deng, sending them both clattering to the ground. In one smooth move, it rushed to the door, flowing through with a thrum of tentacles and a screech of claws, dropping Smee on the way.

Dredd shot to his feet and took off in pursuit, dragging himself into the entry chamber only to see the elevator doors closing.

"Gruddamn it!" Smee ran to the elevator, her retrieved Lawgiver in hand, and pounded her fists uselessly against the closed doors.

Deng pushed past Dredd and yanked open a door in the metal panelling. A tight spiral staircase led upwards.

"No luck contacting Mega-City One, but I drew up the localised schematics while I was in the control room," he shouted, taking to the stairs. "Come on. After it!"

Thirteen

DREDD THREW HIMSELF up the stairs after Deng, Smee hot on his heels, boots ringing on the steps as they raced the elevator.

It was no use; they heard the elevator open above them, and burst through the door to find an already deserted lab.

They ran through the room and pelted down the hall, catching a glimpse of the offworlder as it pushed through the outer exit that led not to the other dome but to the hangar yard where they'd been attacked on arrival, and to the desert. No sign of Newman, so hopefully she'd managed to get herself clear before the monster sped through.

Once in the yard, it didn't bother with the airlock, but instead went straight to the newly patched wall, which exploded in a cloud of rockcrete under the strength of its telekinesis. Hopefully, its powers would be depleted after such a show of desperate strength.

"Engage ventilators," Dredd barked through comms as his own rose to cover his mouth.

The offworlder paused to look back at them then, and a load of fallen rockcrete rose once more to come flying through the air. The Judges ducked, but instead of coming at them, it was flung onto the dune buggies, crashing in a heap of crushed rock and twisted metal.

The creature shrieked triumphantly even as it sagged with fatigue.

"It can't keep up this level of effort," Smee said, pushing herself to her knees. "It's exhausting itself."

The thing that was Cartwright turned and loped off into the desert on powerful hind legs.

"It won't need to. We'll never be able to catch it on foot," Deng said, looking over at the destroyed buggy bay.

Dredd ran to the buggies, scanning the dusty vehicles quickly.

"This one doesn't look too bad." Deng pointed. The buggy was completely filled with debris; the engine may still be functional, but they wouldn't be able to get inside to drive the thing.

"She'll be long gone by the time we get that clear," Smee said, eyes on the retreating form of the offworlder as it made its way towards the same hills the volunteers had fled to before.

Dredd joined Deng next to the buggy and began to claw out rubble with his hands.

"Stand clear!" Dredd spun around to see Newman, still wearing her headpiece. She flung a handful of grey dust towards the buggies, which instantly dispersed on the wind.

Dredd grunted in response as he continued to clear the vehicle. He wasn't sure a handful of fungus was going to cut it.

But then a dark thick matter began to grow like mould on the rock and he pulled his hands clear, watching as it spread to cover the whole of the buggy. Newman gritted her teeth in concentration as a mass of what looked like black tar shook and bubbled. The rocks began to crumble, pouring out of the carriage as sand, and Deng and Dredd jumped back, pulling their boots clear of the dust.

Dredd leapt in and started the engine, relieved to hear it cough into life.

"Get in," he said, and Deng jumped into the passenger seat as Smee leapt up to crouch on the back, holding onto the metal frame.

"Wait," Newman moved forward. "I can help."

"Stay here." Dredd looked back impatient to move. "You don't have a respirator and you'll choke out there. Get back inside before you poison yourself."

Newman looked as though she was going to argue, but then nodded and handed him a packet of small capsules. "You've lost your gun. These are programmed to explode on exposure with the air. The toxins out there may accelerate the reaction, so get out of there quickly if you have to use them."

Dredd nodded in thanks and pressed them into a pocket before moving off and putting his foot down, speeding through the breach in the wall in pursuit.

The buggy cut through the sands making up the distance as they drew closer to the creature, still only halfway to the hills.

Hearing their approach, it swivelled its head back and screeched in fury. Smee and Deng began shooting Hi-Ex the second they were in range, but the movement of the buggy threw their aim off and they missed, blowing great gouts of sand into the air instead.

The creature began to run faster and take huge leaps high into the air, swinging its tentacles up as it did so. Dredd assumed it was simply trying to dodge until a flailing tentacle wrapped around one of the floating rocks drifting overhead, took hold of it, and launched it back at them. It missed, but barely.

Dredd was so used to the mottled sky that he'd almost forgotten the Death Belt. The idea that it could provide their foe with ammunition hadn't even crossed his mind. They were getting closer to the hills now, and Dredd didn't want to think about chasing this thing through hostile terrain. He swung the wheel as another projectile was flung back at them, and heard the swoosh as it hurtled past the buggy. That was close.

Smee fired, blowing a tentacle off as it reached for another floating rock. The offworlder screeched and snatched the limb into its body, but another replaced it to grab a large stone and hurl it back at them.

This one flew true, shooting back to knock Smee clean off the back of the buggy. She grunted as she fell, and Dredd watched her hit the ground and roll in his rear-view mirror.

Dredd slowed but then growled as he made the split-second decision to put his foot on the accelerator.

"*Judge Smee, are you injured?*" Deng was looking back, his Lawgiver hanging limp in his hand.

Dredd strained his ears over the comms for her answer, but there was none.

"We'll go back for her once we've brought this thing down," Dredd scowled. "If we stop now, we've lost it."

Deng nodded grimly beside him. "Agreed."

Fourteen

THEY HAD TO abandon the buggy when the rocks became too closely packed, just like last time. They ran through the disturbed earth, the creature's trail clear in the sand. Until it wasn't. As the towers of rock grew taller and closer, the tracks stopped.

Dredd looked up into the rock canopy and caught a glimpse of movement. "Up there!" he yelled; Deng squeezed off a useless shot as they ran into the labyrinth.

They pursued half by guesswork, catching sight of it from time to time as it pulled itself over the top of a tower.

"Damn tentacles," Dredd muttered as he ran. That thing had the jump on them. And even if they did somehow catch up with it, one Lawgiver and a couple of daysticks and boot knives may not be enough to bring it down. Unlike the mutants they'd taken down in the domes, this one was smart. And not hell-bent on killing them; it was running away from them—successfully, so far. *Where* it was running was still unclear.

Dredd held his hand up to Deng to wait when they reached a larger clearing, aware that they hadn't caught a glimpse of the alien for a while.

"We didn't come this way last time," Deng was panting. "Which path looks more likely?"

Dredd felt beads of sweat trickle down his neck as he scanned the towers on the far side of the clearing.

"There." He pointed at a set of deep gouges in the rough side of a pillar. It must have leapt the clearing and clung on with its clawed hind legs when it reached the other side.

They started jogging again, eyes raised to catch the hint of claw-marks on the rock. They stopped again when the pillars narrowed to create one clear path, closing in to the dark opening of a cave.

Glancing at each other, they nodded, then proceeded with caution. If the offworlder was inside, it was probably waiting to ambush them. If it wasn't—well. Then they'd lost it.

They neared the entrance, just big enough by the looks of it to fit the creature. Deng went first, his Lawgiver the first line of defence.

They stepped through the entrance with no incident, and paused to assess as their eyes adjusted to the gloom.

"Infra-red?" Deng suggested, and they switched to night vision.

The heat of the outside only penetrated so far into the darkness, but showed the cave opening out into a wide tunnel that twisted away out of view.

"We'll need torches down here," Dredd said reluctantly. The light may stop them from plunging down into a crevasse, but it also marked them out in the darkness.

They switched from night vision to head torches, their wide beams slicing the black like beacons. They paused as they approached a blind spot, bracing for tentacles or projectiles, but what greeted them on turning the corner was beyond what either of them had been expecting.

Although on seeing it, Dredd wondered how they could have been so drokking stupid.

Below them a vast cavern opened up, the path falling steeply to the cave floor, with long, twisted shards of rock piercing down—as if the stone had been melted and quickly cooled—giving the impression of an enormous fanged mouth. Cradled in the basin, emitting a dull red light, was what Dredd could only imagine to be a space vessel.

A mass of pale metal in a vaguely hexagonal shape, all jagged edges and hard lines, with a faint ember glow seeping from a network of vein-like lines pulsing across the metal, hovered metres from the earth.

A brighter shard of light blazed out suddenly as a hatch began to open at the base like a demonic mouth. The offworlder was closing in on it.

"Let's go!" Dredd turned off his head torch as he pushed past Deng, who was clearly still making sense of what he was seeing, and ran down the steep path, sliding the last few metres on his arse.

He scrambled to his feet and ran, pulling his boot knife as he heard Deng sliding down the steep slope behind him.

The creature paused to look around at the sound and screeched, turning to face them.

It looked around the crater base, possibly for a projectile, but the ground was clear.

Deng discharged his Lawgiver as he ran, but he stumbled, and the shot went wide. The creature hissed again but turned to pull itself into the ship, leaping up and disappearing as the hatch began to descend.

Dredd was still running, closing the distance to the half-open hatch.

"Leave it, Dredd, it's too late."

Dredd leapt as the ship began to rise, grabbing on to the lip of the door with his left hand, as his right still gripped his boot knife.

Quickly transferring the knife to his teeth, he swung his other arm up and heaved as the door steadily descended. If he was going to let go, now would be the time. If he pulled up and missed his timing, he'd be cut in half by the door.

With a monumental surge of strength, he heaved himself up with both arms and rolled through the closing gap, the sliding panel brushing his arm as it crashed shut.

No time to catch his breath, he was on his feet, knife in one hand and daystick in the other, assessing the situation.

The walls glowed the same low red light, illuminating a small antechamber with two arches leading to other areas of the ship. He had to find the control deck—whatever that looked like, on a ship possibly controlled by telekinesis.

The ground shuddered as a thunderous explosion rippled the air.

"Deng! Do you read me?" he barked through comms. "What was that? Are you clear?"

He moved towards one of the arches as he waited anxiously for an answer.

"*Clear,*" came the breathless response. "*The ship's heading for the far wall. Now I'm looking at it, I don't think it's a wall at all; looks like a big pile of boulders have been moved to cover the ship's entry point. Either way, it's going to shoot its way out of this place. You've got to get off there!*"

Dredd scowled. "Get outside. It may bring the whole gruddamn hill down. Find Smee, I'll meet you there."

The first arch off the entrance chamber was sealed, but the second door gaped open. He moved quietly through it into a darker corridor.

If he was lucky, the offworlder had no idea he was there. The only advantage he had over it was surprise.

He paused at an arch leading off the corridor. It was a large chamber lined with empty cages. Had it been planning on transporting back its pet mutants to continue its research?

He moved past it as another loud crash erupted, then braced

himself as the ship juddered forward. It must have breached the wall.

He moved fast, scanning other chambers full of tech he didn't recognise as he passed. Finally, he turned a corner and stopped as he saw what must have been the flight deck. A large screen showed the filtered light of the Cursed Earth as the ship moved out of the cavern. Silhouetted against the view was the creature, its back to Dredd and its tentacles hovering over a control board, lights and switches throbbing as if with life.

Before it could register his presence, Dredd ran and leapt, but the creature turned and raised a tentacle to block him with a hiss.

You dare to attack me in my own ship!

It reached to grab him by the neck, but he slashed at it with his knife, and it recoiled. Seizing his moment, he feinted with his daystick and rolled under the cloud of tentacles to plunge his knife deep into one of its clawed feet. It shrieked as he quickly moved out of its range.

You want to come to my planet with me, Judge? That can be arranged.

The ship rose steadily towards the belt of floating rocks.

"You're going nowhere. The Death Belt will hold you here."

They hold no power over me.

A beam of red light tore from the ship and disintegrated a floating stone. He had to stop it before it cleared a path.

Reaching into his pocket, he pulled out one of Newman's capsules and threw it onto the control panel.

There was a moment when the creature looked at him as if to puzzle out what he had done, and then they were both blown off their feet as the entire control board exploded in a ball of flame.

That was certainly effective.

The ship began to shake, out of control.

With a screech of distress, the creature fled the flames, its hind legs propelling it towards the corridor leading to the exit hatch. Dredd followed, their purposes momentarily aligned. Get the drokk out of the burning ship.

The hatch rose as the creature neared it. Dredd could see the ground racing past below, too close, and too fast.

The creature stopped and tensed, and the ship slowed, the ground becoming less of a blur. The power of this thing's telekinesis was strong, if it could slow an entire spaceship from a headlong crash into the earth.

But it wasn't quite that strong. Dredd slammed into the wall as they hit the ground, skidding through the dunes, the sand dragging at the hull and slowing their momentum. The ship finally came to rest, and Dredd lay still for a moment, checking his limbs were all still present and correct. His heart was racing and his breath heaving in his chest. He had a sudden urge to disengage his respirator and breathe freely, but fought the impulse.

He looked up and saw that the creature, close to the open hatch, hadn't been quite so lucky. Hanging half-in, half-out the door, it twitched as it pulled itself to its feet, but one of its legs gave way.

It used its tentacles to pull itself out into the sand. Dredd was on his feet and pounding towards it as he realised that he'd lost both his knife and his daystick in the crash.

All he knew was that this thing couldn't be allowed to escape and carry on its research against humanity.

Glancing up, he realised that they hadn't travelled as far as he had feared, the twisted hills still visible behind them.

It loped into a sandy valley, its tentacles working in a frenzy to drag it along with its injured leg.

"Deng, do you read me?" If he could keep the thing here until Deng could come in a buggy with his weapon, maybe they would have more of a chance of taking it down. But he was out of range. He'd have to figure this out alone.

It stopped, breathing heavily, and fell back, exhausted.

Dredd approached. Would he be able to strangle it with its own tentacles?

As if it had heard his thoughts—maybe it had—a whiplike tentacle shot out and grabbed him around the legs, wrapping and pulling him to the ground. It had been feinting.

It rose to loom over him.

What gives you the right, cruel human, to deny my people a cure?

It was panting, using some of its tentacles to prop up the weak leg.

All of my work. The years of living in that disgusting skin. The painstaking research. Gone. Destroyed by you.

Dredd clenched his fists as the creature opened its jaws to bellow its frustration.

For that, you will die!

He braced himself for what was to come.

At that moment, the ground shifted, shaking like churning water, and a huge tentacle shot out from the sand to wrap around the offworlder's torso. The imposing form of the desert mutant pushed out of the earth behind it, a mass of limbs writhing against the rock-strewn sky as it held the creature aloft, Dredd still entwined in the offworlder's much smaller tentacles.

It was at that moment that Dredd realised the enormous sand monster must be one of Cartwright's early experiments.

My child! the offworlder cried. *You have grown beyond my wildest hopes.*

The vast head, a distortion of the offworlder's own, twisted around to focus an enraged, pain-filled eye on its captive.

Beautiful. The offworlder raised a free tentacle to caress the cheek of the beast. *Come away with me, child. Together, we can save my people.*

The eye filled with what looked like a tear. It lifted its slathering, fang-filled muzzle, as if to kiss the alien that had once been Cartwright. Then it unhinged its maw and clamped down on the offworlder's head with a sickening crunch.

Dredd was flung from the suddenly limp tentacle to land hard on the earth, crawling backwards in the sand as the mutant devoured the limp body of its twisted creator.

He continued to back away, slowly, until he judged the hill close enough to make a run for, and did so, gladly.

Fifteen

DREDD FOUND DENG waiting at the buggy, with no sign of Judge Smee.

Dredd filled him in on Cartwright's demise, then asked after Smee with a heavy heart.

"She was gone when I went back," Deng said, his shoulders slumping. "We need to search for her."

Dredd sighed. "Maybe the same thing that just finished the doc got her. There are mutants in this desert, and they aren't too choosy about their cuisine."

Deng shook his helmeted head as if he couldn't accept the possibility that she was gone.

"We have to get back and let the Council of Five know what the drokk happened here."

Just then they heard movement behind them, and Deng trained his Lawgiver in the direction of the sound. He lowered it when he saw what it was.

Judge Smee, supported on either side by the two mutants that Dredd recognised from their first chase through the rock forest, limped towards them.

"Put that gun away, Deng, if it wasn't for their help, I'd be dead." She shook the mutants' hands off with a grimace. "Go," she said, but they hesitated. "I mean it, go. With my thanks."

Deng raised his Lawgiver as they moved away, but Smee held up her hands, placing herself between him and the retreating mutants.

"We don't need to kill them, Deng. The only thing they've done to offend Mega-City One is survive when most would have perished out here."

It was a surreal moment, after everything that had just happened, to finish with a standoff between two Judges, one of them defending a couple of mutants with her own life.

Deng lowered his gun. "They're not a threat."

Smee nodded her thanks, and Dredd went to help her as she sagged. She flinched as he pulled her arm over his shoulder to support her weight.

"You hurt bad?" he asked, as they moved towards the buggy.

"Maybe. It's hard to tell. Let's hope there's a med back there still alive to patch me up."

Together Deng and Dredd helped her into the passenger seat of the buggy and Deng took her place squatting on the back as Dredd took the wheel.

"Cartwright is history," Dredd told her.

She nodded. "I felt her go. I've never encountered anything so resilient as her psi power. Her ability to renew her strength was dizzying. Let's hope the rest of her kind stay away. I don't want to think about what more than one of them could do."

Dredd hoped they'd never have to find out. He'd encountered enough psi power in the last few days to last him a lifetime. He glanced at Smee. That wasn't fair. He could see now how important Psi-Div really was. Who knew what other psychic creatures there were out there? They needed some of their own to fight back.

And besides, he had to admit that Smee was a good Judge to

have in your corner, even if she did question authority too often for his liking. If she had so much to say about how the high-ups ran things, maybe she should be the one in charge.

Thinking of all the protocol they had steamrolled since they had arrived, he winced, his fingers tensing on the wheel as they rumbled back to the domes. This was going to be one hell of a debrief.

The End

Acknowledgements

With massive thanks to the indomitable Lucy Smee, to my partner Joe and daughter Goldie, and to my amazing editor David Moore and the whole excellent Rebellion team.

About the Author

Laurel Sills is a writer and editor who lives in South East London with her partner, daughter and two cats. She is the author of *Judge Anderson Year Two: Devourer* and has had stories published in *Sharkpunk* and Game Over, both with Snowbooks. She was the co-founder and editor of the award-winning *Holdfast Magazine*.

FIND US ONLINE!

www.rebellionpublishing.com

/rebellionpub   /rebellionpublishing /rebellionpublishing

SIGN UP TO OUR NEWSLETTER!

rebellionpublishing.com/newsletter

YOUR REVIEWS MATTER!

Enjoy this book? Got something to say?

Leave a review on Amazon, GoodReads or with your
favourite bookseller and let the world know!

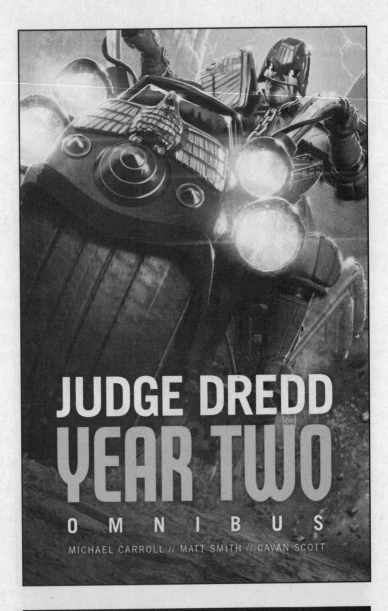

JUDGE DREDD
YEAR TWO
OMNIBUS

MICHAEL CARROLL // MATT SMITH // CAVAN SCOTT

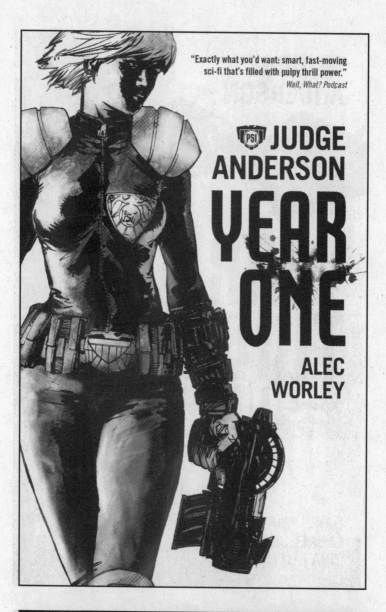

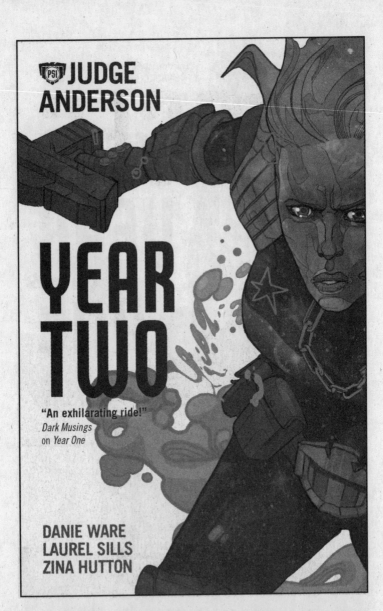

THE GENESIS OF THE WORLD OF JUDGE DREDD®

JUDGES

VOLUME TWO
GOLGOTHA · PSYCHE · THE PATRIOTS

MICHAEL CARROLL · MAURA MCHUGH · JOSEPH ELLIOTT-COLEMAN

EDITED BY MICHAEL CARROLL

WWW.ABADDONBOOKS.COM

Follow us on Twitter! www.twitter.com/rebellionpub